The Seventh Circle

L. P. Brooks

L. P. Brooks

First edition

E-book ISBN: 979-8-9995658-2-2
Paperback ISBN: 979-8-9995658-0-8
Hardback ISBN: 979-8-9995658-1-5

Editing by Meg at Clarity Copy Co.

Cover art by Matisse

To those who have been met with words that tried to reduce their worth:
It's time to unleash your power.

***

To my E's—everything I do is for you.
I love you.

Trigger Warnings

As an author, I have tried my best to take note of themes that might be sensitive to some readers, but I recognize there may be additional topics I missed. Please take note of the following to see if this fictional work is right for you:

Death, loss of parents (off page), wartime violence, gore, decapitation, murder, depression, substance abuse, suicidal ideations, open-door romance with moderately detailed scenes.

Craighton

Hasûtleri

Wild Country
Uelthis

Daylor

Redbough

Areon

Mournefrve

Lukas

Killing Bones
Islands

Mercyth

Almer

Teakin

Cybric's Hall

Northern Woods

Sistern Keep

Zennagberg

Fyom's Point

Balnan Forrest

Dokvalon

Deep of Aorr

The Moon Pony

Gria

Doloch River

Orovec

Canal Manor

Venfar Hall

Shimmering
Mountains

Falling Wilds

Fnadesia Pass

Rising Hook
Tangle

Grailmoor

Dead Downs

Arch of
Aegir Islands

Wieldera

Pronunciation Guide

People of Gria

Ophelia "Phe" Endromeon
(oh-feel-ia 'fee' in-dro-me-on)

Aurora "Ora" Endromeon
(ah-roar-ah 'or-ah' in-dro-me-on)

Sury Anmathios
(sir-ee an-math-ee-os)

Cendio Vovias
(sin-dee-oh voe-vie-us)

Ariadne Terrigan
(air-e-ad-knee ter-ee-gan)

Imily & Kykan Endromeon (deceased)
(em-e-ly & kigh-can in-dro-me-on)

Peiro Brozneil
(peer-oh brahz-kneel)

Fyom Tresdore
(figh-ohm tres-door)

***

Words of Wieldera

Gria: 'gree-ah'

Grianmore: 'gree-an-more'

Veik(s): 'veek(s)'

Ruron: 'roo-ron'

Bratrian: 'bray-tree-an'

Giants of Wieldera

Ednos, giant of earth
Guean, giantess of air
Aorr, giant of water
Khilmira, giantess of fire
Iasis, giant of healing
Aksyn (sun) & Nyska (moon), celestial twins
Ythos, giantess of life
Thuvina, giantess of death

***

Minor Giants
Domesis, giant of fortune
Cisoi, giant of death's door
Ruheia, giantess of the hunt

CHAPTER 1

"You know what this means, right?" I asked as I looked over to my younger sister, who donned the same dark green dress as me. Hers was threaded in gold versus the silver in mine. "This means you will now be queen."

Aurora shed a solitary tear as we stood on the constructed dais overlooking the city streets of Grianmore and watched the funeral procession pass by. The sun's setting rays beamed down on us.

"I don't want to be queen," Aurora whispered sternly.

Her lips quivered as the small band of percussion instruments, horns, and lutes strolled by, all playing a solemn tune for the ceremonial march that wound through the streets. The never-ending turns carried them from the palace to the burning burial grounds beyond the city gates.

"You're older, Ophelia," Aurora hissed. "Why can't this go to *you* instead? Other kingdoms have done it—gone by order of age, not strength in power. You handle court politics better than me."

It was true. Aurora was the spitfire to my natural reserve.

I took in the city streets made of gray and tan stones. Citizens and merchants alike respectfully paused as the royal court began to file past, clad in their ceremonial attire of greens and golds—every face held high but completely expressionless, trying to mask their emotions.

"Because I can't take the throne. Not like you, Ora. You know that." I sucked in a quick breath. I rarely called her by her full name, mostly sticking to the nickname I'd coined for her when we were children. We reserved our full names for when we needed one another's immediate attention or if one of us was highly peeved with the other.

"My magic isn't powerful enough to succeed, and you know the succession will skip those with limited power and go to those who Wield the strongest in our bloodline. It's been this way since the people were blessed with Wielding." I couldn't help but give a small eye roll. She knew this was the way, whether we liked it or not.

Wielding was a gift from the giants, we were told. The godlike creatures were said to have blessed only a small number of humans with the power to control specific elements of the world, shaping the magic that defined our kingdom of Gria.

But their gift could also be very cruel.

The giants seemed to have blessed humans with their gifts and simply vanished with no instruction on what Wielding was supposed to be used for. There had been centuries of debate on whether Wielding was meant to be used to foster unity or sow division. The world had finally settled on the latter through years of bloody politics and war. These highly powered Wielders were to control the continent and its citizens—both other, lesser-powered Wielders and those who were not blessed with magic, the Veiks.

Ora shed another tear as she tightened her jaw in defiance. The act made her look more regal than she intended. "I know," she said as she clutched her fist tightly over a simple white stone set in a golden-chained necklace—the same heirloom necklace our mother gifted her on her eighteenth birthday five years ago. The day when Aurora was officially announced as heir to the throne. Growing up, we had giggled in awe at the golden veins that wove delicately through the stone. Ora had always sworn that the stone felt warm in her hand, but I only ever felt it as the cool, hard rock that it was.

It is full of more power than one could bear and provides wisdom through all things, Mother would tell us as we sat in her lap and took turns holding it as it hung around her neck. She never told us where she got it, and we never asked.

I eyed the stone as it caught the sun's rays and sparkled against Ora's dress. A fine craft set by the finest jewelers in Grianmore, with thin strands of gold interlocking and webbing over one another to hold the stone in place.

Side by side, we stood watching the bannermen holding the Royal Crest—a golden sun—and the court passed by, knowing the most painful moment was about to come. I took my sister's hand and gave it a tight squeeze as both of our hearts began to break. The pallbearers, in sets of two, began to make their way down the street, carrying the glass-cased coffins side by side. Each coffin was made of pure gold and precious metals, bejeweled with rubies, sapphires, and amethysts. White gypsophila was carefully positioned around the two bodies, as if they were resting on a bed of flowers. A dark metal that mimicked branches rested on our father's head, and the white crown, with a heavy emerald adorned in the middle, lay on top of our mother's.

I didn't know if it was Ora's body that began to shake or my own as we looked at the faces of our mother and father, the Queen and King of Gria, the twin black bands upon their middle fingers symbolizing their union and Faded Hearts. We were always taught that the beauty of Fading was two-sided. One was the impossible beauty of finding someone to whom your life is linked in every way and whose destiny is intertwined with yours forever. The other side is the mythical chance that you and the one you're connected to would die together. Hand in hand, crossing over into the ethereal land of the giants.

Our mother and father just proved that part of the myth was indeed real.

Mother's golden-brown hair was styled in her usual long braids, which cascaded over her shoulders. I remembered practicing endlessly to match her elegance, though I always fell short. Her lightly tanned skin had only a few worn lines of age around her eyes and mouth, from where she always smiled like the sun. Our father's alabaster skin was even more ashen against the thick black beard and the raven hair that was only touched by small strands of gray at his temples.

It was strange seeing him so still. Memories flooded of him chasing me through the gardens, letting me ride his shoulders through the castle, or holding me in his strong arms as he read me endless stories of mythical magical beasts and ancient entities that haunted the lands.

"Life is cruel," Ora whispered as she took the sleeve of her dress and caught a tear from her eye.

"We knew they would Fade together." I pushed the words out in a slow breath. "That this time would eventually come." Even though it felt like their time was too soon, I couldn't allow myself to feel in this moment as I watched the coffins draw nearer. I had been repeating those same words to myself since they passed, clinging to the painful truth just to keep myself together.

I didn't mean to sound cruel, but I knew my sister would face a court that held little to no empathy for one another or the lands they individually ruled, with each one regarding themselves more elevated than the previous. She wouldn't be able to avoid the endless debates on the next steps for her ascension. The court had already expressed their uncertainty about my sister before our mother's death, stating she was too young and inexperienced to lead. Mother didn't have a chance to argue against their apprehension before her time to ascend back to the giants.

"That's the miracle of finding someone your destiny is intertwined with, right? You live and Fade together," I said with a softer touch.

Their sudden and simultaneous deaths left double the wounds for closure. We could feel these wounds festering in us as we watched.

"They look like they have so much more life to live," Ora managed to say before she finally broke down in tears and crumpled to her knees in heartache.

I fell with her and scooped her into my arms. We held one another tightly as my little sister wept. Normally, any member of the royal family or court was expected to hide emotions until in private, but I always knew my sister was different. From birth, Ora had radiated in sunshine and golden rays, bringing happiness and smiles to a seemingly harsh and cold court—so similar to our mother.

The Grian kingdom had become prosperous in many ways since it intertwined with the ruler's magic, and I suspected that Ora would bring more prosperity to an already growing kingdom.

My magic was little more than a vibration compared to my younger sister's Wielding power. Hers was a celestial power that harnessed the forces of the sun and its rays. This power defined our family line—the Endromeon line.

I held Ora tightly as she shook with tears and began to wail. Though any sign of emotion was a weakness in their eyes—something to be exploited by enemies or the humans who could not Wield—I didn't care about the court's thoughts and held onto my sister tighter. She cried into my shoulder as the pallbearers marched on, my own eyes welling with tears. Once the end of the procession had passed, I helped Ora rise and tucked a few strands of her misplaced golden hair behind her ear.

It was uncanny how much we resembled our parents, like warped mirrors of another time. Ora was like our mother with her golden hair and bright gold eyes. I was more like our father, the stark contrast of pale skin with dark hair. The only difference was that I had inherited bright teal eyes and not his deep, glowing amber. This set me apart from the family since I did not inherit their golden hues, and even more so from the late queen.

A trait of Wielders was their bright, glowing eyes. The power that coursed through a Wielder would illuminate their eyes to have an ethereal glow compared to the duller colors of browns, blues, and greens the Veiks shared.

Gingerly, I wiped away the last remaining tears from Ora's face before kissing her on the forehead. "Aurora, Mother and Father loved you, us both, very much. They left you in good hands, and I know they will be proud of the ruler you become. Not only will you bring this kingdom more sunshine, but the energy you've brought in your mere twenty-three years is enough to light the dark cloud that hovers over our court."

Ora took my hand and gave it a brief squeeze. "You think so? Even Snotty Old Vovias?"

Cendio Vovias was our mother's top advisor and the strongest Wielder in fire, established in place even when her own father ruled. Our mother never challenged him for reasons unknown.

"Even Snotty Old Vovias." I chuckled and gave a small smile.

Ora responded, "I hate that bastard." She giggled and took a deep breath. "How Mother even tolerated the sourpuss is beyond me. He is so *hateful*!"

"She and Father had the patience of a saint." I looked at Ora wearily. "Something I guess you'll need to learn soon."

Ora rolled her eyes. "Phe, you're ever the diplomat." I could tell she was peeved by the way she emphasized my name, but I only smiled.

We stayed hand in hand as we made our way to the pyre beyond the Grianmore gates to complete the ceremony. A slight breeze chilled the warm air, the regular song and dance between spring fighting off the remnants of winter. The rows of trees, bright contrast against the gray buildings around us, shook their vivid green leaves and tiny flower buds as if waving off the cold.

I welcomed the swirling breeze and the fresh air as we walked through the plazas of brick and stone, following the procession before us. The smell of freshly baked goods brought forth a small memory of when we all gathered for a meal around a small table set in the royal gardens. My smile disappeared as quickly as it appeared when I looked around at the citizens and the pity that clung to their faces. The pity for our realm. The pity for our loss.

But I also saw the pity they had for me—which I hated. The pity of the *poor sister who holds the weakest power in all the Endromeon line.* It was the same pity I was used to seeing through the years. I'd taught myself not to show how much it bothered me, until I finally became numb and cold to it. The perfect mask.

Those who grieved waved small silk ribbons toward Aurora. Others threw dried, deep red rose petals at her feet, a Grian symbol for the next heir. For them to walk in the blood of those who served before them, who shed from their own veins in times of war and peace.

The path of their loyalty to the kingdom and its people.

CHAPTER 2

The sun began to set across the mountains, making the sliver of the coming moon appear brighter as it ascended. The air was cool but was not to blame for the shivers that ran down my spine.

The funeral pyres were built high and were made of the strongest trees from the kingdom. In the field where we stood, the Royal Court and citizens made their way to stand by to honor the Faded and formed a crescent moon shape, giving distance to us, the princesses, who stood front and center of the pyres.

"I can't do this, Phe," Ora whispered low enough that no one could hear.

"Mother and Father are looking down on us, giving us the strength to do this," I whispered back. I couldn't admit that I didn't know if I could do it either. My heart was in pain, but

I forced myself together to support my sister like I always did. Never once had I regretted it.

The High Priestess of the High Seven, the temple that taught the beliefs of the giants to the masses but the power of Wielding only to the select few, strode quietly across the field to where we stood. Her golden robes billowed in the faint breeze, and her long, red curls whispered behind her. Gold necklaces and bracelets lightly clinked with each step before she stopped and turned to face us and those who gathered behind.

Dull lines of copper danced around her fingers and wrists and vined their way up her arms, which were hidden beneath her robes. She looked only a handful of years older than our mother but showed little signs of aging. *A blessing to the devout*, she would say. As she neared, I noted how her ivory skin was pale against the fierceness of her jade-colored eyes.

High Priestess Ariadne held her hand out, the jade of her nails a perfect match to the intensity in her eyes, as if asking for permission while reaching for Ora's hand. Ora faintly nodded and let the Priestess take her hand in a tight clasp.

"My Princess," the woman purred, "my heart is deeply sorry for your loss. Your parents, Queen Imily and King Kykan, were exceptional rulers, and I know you will follow them and make them most proud."

She gave Ora's hand another tight squeeze before letting it go and turned to me.

She held out her hand as she motioned for me next. A small smile crept over Ariadne's mouth as her hand hovered over mine and looked into my eyes, transfixed. It seemed she was about to say something but stopped herself.

Quickly she grabbed my hand and held tight, looking into my eyes as her nails dug deep into my skin. I refused to hiss at the pain, though I knew small, crescent-shaped arches would be indented into my flesh. I'd had numerous run-ins with Ariadne throughout the years when I'd studied magic at the High Seven Temple. She would always find a way to ridicule me in front of others or in private lessons on how faint my magic was—not only in comparison to the other students but also to my *own* sister.

"Regardless of the gifts you may bring to this kingdom," the Priestess finally said, "you will be a great support for the future queen." Ariadne leaned in closer to whisper, "It's a pity that this part of the ceremony requires so much...*fire.*"

Fire traditionally ended the burial ceremony and represented the old and new chapters of the turning reign. It had been well documented that the Endromeons all successfully completed the ceremony by lighting the funeral pyres and setting it ablaze. No one took the time to figure out how to rewrite the ceremony because no one had ever heard of an Endromeon who was unable to Wield fire.

Until now. Until me, Ophelia Endromeon.

Ariadne squeezed my hand tighter, finally forcing a small gasp of pain from my mouth. I shot the Priestess a warning glare before she turned to walk toward the crowd. I might not have magic strong enough to take her on, but I'd be willing to rip the golden hoops from her ears if I needed to.

I doubted I truly would if it came down to it. And I hated that I wouldn't.

I watched Ariadne hold her hands up high as she began to sing in the Olden Language about the giants who gifted the people their Wielding. About their fight for the prospering land against the old warring kingdoms. When she was done, she turned back to us and pointed to the pyres to cue our turn in the ceremony.

Ora took light steps to the pyre that held our mother. One queen to the next. One ruler to the next, one to end a chapter and one to begin anew. I watched her kneel beside the pile of wood and whisper a prayer that no one could hear.

I watched as she stood next to where our mother lay. As Ora held her arms out, a ribbon of glittery, gold energy flowed from her fingertips and wove through the air and around the dried logs before her, setting the wood ablaze. The crowd behind her chanted in the Olden Language, sending the final farewell to their deceased queen.

Nervously, I stepped to the piled-high wood that held our father, the king. Memories began to play in my mind of my father laughing and chasing me down the castle corridors. Helping me feed the royal dogs my meal scraps under the table. Making silly faces at me during the boring court meetings I was allowed to attend as a small child.

A single tear formed at one of my favorite memories. I was close to turning seven, and by then, the whole kingdom knew my magic was practically unusable. My mother tried comforting me in her own way, but Father knew me the best.

"You know, we're both kind of misfits in our own right," he said as he scooped me into his arms. "Your mother chose to marry me, someone from a faraway land, with little to Wield myself."

"But you're the king, Daddy. Everyone still listens to you," I said as I gripped his shirt, trying my hardest to be a big girl and not cry.

"You're right. I am a king but with very little magic. Your mother's bloodline is some of the oldest and most powerful magic in our realm. But us misfits, you and me, have the power to change the world in much different ways. I help guide and advise your mother as she needs, and you will be the best royal advisor to Aurora when she comes to rule. Never feel like you're powerless, regardless of your magical abilities." He kissed me on the forehead and wiped away the tears that escaped my eyes.

"Daddy?"

"Yes, my darling?"

"Can we make a court for misfits like us?"

The king's laugh rang like a song in my little ears. "Of course we can! And you'll lead!"

I started to smile as my eyes began to sparkle. "What should we name our court?"

The king's face turned quizzical in thought. "What about the Powerful Powerless People?"

I chuckled. "But can we add the dog? I don't think he's very powerful either."

"Of course we can add the dog! That'll be our second order of business!"

"The second? Then what's the first?"

"Why this, of course!" He shifted me away from him as he stood to walk over to the bits of fabric I had played with earlier that the tailor had left from making new dresses. The king turned around and showed me a braided ring of cloth that he then set on my head. "Every ruler needs their own crown."

I smiled wide as I gave my father a tight hug. "I'm glad we can rule together."

The memory faded away as I took a deep breath and concentrated on the energy building inside my abdomen and the tingling through my fingers. The same way all Wielders were taught to access the magic that ran inside their veins. Small bits of static bounced on my fingertips as I kept my eyes closed, concentrating on the building sensation. I could hear the faint whispers behind me. The same whispers that had haunted me for years and refused to relent, even on this day when we laid our parents to rest. I shouldn't be surprised by the court's ceaseless cruelty.

I thought royalty was supposed to have more Wielding power than the commoners? Someone said.

It was true. The Endromeon line was powerful and had produced heirs that Wielded strong magic for centuries. Power that turned the tides on battlefields. Power that spread peace amongst quarrels. Power that demanded respect.

But I was an anomaly. A thing ridiculed, like I was a poison or a disease.

"Please don't let me disappoint," I whispered to myself as I pushed more energy through my gut to my fingers and placed my tingling hand on the wood, trying fiercely to set it ablaze. I was already considered a pariah of sorts and didn't want to break the traditions of the Endromeon line. Didn't want that added to my growing list of failures.

You know very well you cannot summon fire. Why are you trying? What are you trying to prove?

That voice of my doubt was ever-present. Ever strong. Like it was sentient itself.

My fingers began to tremble as I tried to pull any kernel of power that would make my family proud. Hoping everything up to this point was a mistake. I tried again, building the energy again within me, urging it to flow faster from my fingertips. Earthen was the only Circle of Wielding I had successfully summoned, and barely even mastered at that. Anything pushed further and my Wielding would simply resist as if it were hit against some unknown wall.

I dug my fingertips into the soft grass by the pile of wood, hoping to find any spark I could. Instead, the green stalks under my palm turned into a dulling brown. I'd practiced on a plant in the garden days ago, but I only made the bright stems wither.

The murmurs from the crowd pushed the doubt deeper into my mind. "*Nerves.* You poor soul," I heard the priestess say loud enough for the crowd to hear. The sneer behind the words made my anger rise and the doubt settle in faster.

You know what she's doing. She knew you couldn't Wield fire and yet she still persuaded the court to follow this custom. You're such a mockery to your family, and everyone knows it.

I caught sight of Ora walking away from the adjacent pyre that was ablaze for our mother. Ever so gently, she placed her hand on top of mine for both comfort and guidance. She leaned in close enough to whisper so only I could hear. "Regardless of abilities, I know Mother and Father loved you, loved us so much, and are proud of *you*."

"You shouldn't be the one helping me, sister. I should be the one guiding you." Frustration and anger spewed between my teeth.

"That's a worry for another day," Ora said calmly as she continued. "I'll help amplify before everyone's whispers grow louder. Even now, as our mother turns to ash, the court still sneers. I'm sure Mother is glad to be rid of them as she walks with the giants." Ora briefly looked over her shoulder with a cold glare before turning her attention back to my hand. "When you're ready to release, I'll add my own."

I drew in a tight breath, battling the balance of my grief for our parents and anger for Ariadne. On a steady exhale, I let my magic flow once again to my fingertips and gave the cue to Ora, who in turn warmed my hand with amplifying energy. Sparks and ribbons of twinkling silvers and grays flowed through my hands and onto the wood, setting fire to the pyre that held our father.

I gasped at the strangeness of Ora's magic compared to my own. Sunbursts and energy ricocheted against every nerve that was dark and dulled. And yet it felt like a magnetic pull—like it called to something deep within me. A tingling sensation prickled my fingers as the force slowly ebbed and flowed away like a river that narrowed into a brook.

We stayed there, kneeling with our heads low to pray to the giants while the crowd slowly sang the last verses of their chant before leaving. It was customary for the royal family to leave first, to walk away from the blazing embers to symbolize the dawn of a new era, leaving the past behind.

But we refused to move. We sat there, the heat of the pyre against our skin forcing the chill of the night away. We sat there until this chapter of our lives burned to ash.

CHAPTER
3

A few days had passed, but the smell of smoke still lingered across the city. Banners of black or forest green hung in windows, in shops and homes alike, paying respects to the mourning kingdom.

I found Ora sitting alone in her room, already changed from her mourning clothes and back into her favorite violet-colored gown. Ora's bright golden waves rippled down over her shoulders instead of being pinned up in the style meant for mourning. I tapped lightly on the door to signal my arrival, but Ora waved me in without looking, sensing me.

She stared out her bedroom window overlooking the city and fields outside the Grianmore Castle gates. I followed her gaze to the striking spires of the High Seven Temple a few miles beyond and to the deep woods of Bainas Forest to the west and the north. Grianmore was the heart of the realm of Gria. I had never traveled far outside of our city walls to see how our prideful city compared to others in the realm. Instead, I'd relished the stories our father would tell us when he paid visits to the territories that answered to Gria.

I stepped in, my dark hair loosely bound as I wore my mourning blacks. "You've already changed?" A gentle spring breeze coursed through the room. Faint smells of lilacs coated the air, near the castle's walls that held the private royal gardens.

"Seriously, Phe, do you do everything that you're told?" She emphasized my name again, hinting at annoyance.

I rolled my eyes and mumbled remarks about tradition as I walked toward the window where Ora stood. Her room was directly beside mine, and matched in terms of size, but hers was adorned in hues of warm pinks and golds, beautifully capturing the colors of the sun's rays during a sunset.

"Easy to say when you're the future queen." I gave my sister a playful elbow nudge.

"Black is a dreadful color, and I know Mother would hate to see us grieving like this." Ora gestured to her brightly colored dress. "I want to put this behind me as quickly as possible so I can move on."

I knew what she meant—wanting to bury it deep inside until it became numb and turned your heart cold. Just like we saw in the court and even in our own parents at times for diplomatic matters. But I knew my sister better than that. I gingerly took Ora's hand into my own, noting how faintly cold it was despite her radiating warmth.

"I know you want to move on. And you will. We will. In time. Together," I said as I tried to give Ora a small smile. "You don't need to rush this. Matter of fact, you can change the way of things, including needing more time before 'moving on.'"

Ora nodded faintly, taking in my words. "Well, since I'm to be queen and can begin to change things," she started as she turned her body to mine, "you shall now be my official royal advisor. Then no one can tell *you* what to do either. Oh! The mischief we could cause!" A wide smile beamed across her face.

I smiled softly and turned my gaze to the north, staring at the tree line ahead. I could sense Ora pushing her humor through. To anyone else, it would be an image of a young woman smiling through a tough moment in her life. But I knew she was trying to rush through her grief.

"Oh, how funny *you* are." I smiled, still looking at the trees. "You know well that I can't officially advise...but," I turned my gaze toward hers, "I can certainly help however I can behind closed doors." I wished I could share in my sister's ideas, but I knew that these rules were in place for a reason. "You'll change rooms soon, you know? Instead of being next to me, you'll be facing the heart of the city."

"And let the sun wake me up as it rises? I believe the second order of business will be to order thicker curtains. I don't see how Mother and Father ever did without." Ora lightly chuckled.

I nudged her shoulder as we both continued to stare out the window. "Are you ready for The Rising?"

Ora's forced smile dropped as she sucked in her breath. "Will it hurt? Do you know if it'll hurt?"

"From what I could find and read, there are no accounts of it hurting."

Ora stepped away from the window and turned her back to think. I caught her pensive look in the window's reflection as she began to slowly pace around the room.

"Remind me, please, of what you read? I need to know what the Secondary Viziers are talking about when we discuss these next steps, and you explain these things so much better than what I read." She waved her hand in the air. "So they'll take me more seriously despite being young. Which is quite ridiculous, since Mother started her rule not too much older than me!"

I finally withdrew from the window and sat on Ora's soft bed as we began to recount we knew about The Rising. The ceremony itself was only known to the upcoming ruler with their high priest or priestess during their reign, before passing the details to the next ruler in line. Mother should be sitting here teaching Ora, not me.

"The Rising began a few centuries ago, at the dawn of our line, as the official coronation. The people wanted their rulers to be dedicated and held accountable so the power wouldn't corrupt their minds like it did the Scholars. So, each ruler has followed King Clorithian Endromeon, the first ruler to unite Gria after the Original War, to vow and imbue their power into the land, Mother's included. Each ruler dresses in charred mud—"

"They dress in mud? Are they mad? Mud! How could I have forgotten about the mud?"

I rolled my eyes as I continued to explain my findings. "Yes, mud. Don't be such a prude! The mud signifies all the elements bound into one before imbuing their essence into the land, sealing their promise to be a great and just ruler."

"And the imbuing part doesn't hurt?"

I shook my head. "Not from what I read. In all the records, it seems to be quick. Although it's preferable to be completed during the Blood Moon to signify that you're dedicating your blood to the people, and then your vow is sealed into the Rising Rock."

No one was allowed to see the Rising Rock unless they were completing the coronation ritual. Only a select few from the High Seven Temple were even allowed access to the Rising Rock in fear that someone's ill intent would taint the rock itself. All our mother had shared in stories from when we were younger was that it was a monument of sorts that was linked to the giants, where you promised yourself to your land and to your reign.

"The fact that we have a Blood Moon already on its way is a miracle. Many rulers had to wait months before their coronation." I playfully rolled my eyes at Ora. "But lucky that you would be granted a Blood Moon so quickly af-ter...everything." I heard my voice drop to a whisper.

Ora nodded her head in understanding and slowed down her pacing, but her face was still scrunched in deep thought. "It just all seems to be moving so fast."

I moved from the bed to where Ora stood and took her by the shoulders. "It's okay to be nervous, but nothing bad will happen. It's all a bit symbolic really, and you're more than ready to lead. I believe in you, just like Mother and Father did from the moment you were born."

Ora leaned into my arms and surprised me with a tight embrace. "Thank you," she whispered into my shoulder. "You've always had such confidence in me, and I wish you would save some for yourself."

I could only stand there in silence, holding my sister as we waited for her to draw in strength before letting go. "Come now, ole Snotty Vovias will be highly annoyed if we show up late to your first court meeting as the *queen-to-be*!"

"Oh, but Phe! That makes it even more fun to be queen! Let's pass through the kitchens first before we make our way to the meeting halls. I sure do hope the kitchen has made plenty of soft cheese pastries!"

I couldn't hold in my smile as I silently agreed and followed.

***

I fiddled with my hands as we walked the castle halls to officially meet the court with Ora as the queen-to-be, and not the princess they watched grow up before their very eyes. Every one of them was a powerful Wielder in their own element, just like every Endromeon recorded.

"Will they all be there?" Ora whispered toward me as we neared the doors. I could practically feel her nerves rolling off in waves, though she held her head high.

"All but one, from what I was told," I whispered back as I smiled at a passing servant. "Don't let them unnerve you. You know them. They might hold their seat and act like pompous pricks but you've proven just how strong our line can be."

Each Endromeon ruler had the power to harness the celestials. That's what made our line so unique and powerful. It seemed the giants favored us to Wield the skies in the form of the sun or, on rare occasion, the moon. All but me. The one who could barely sputter magic from her fingertips.

"But why can't someone just hurry the hell up and challenge Vovias's seat? I'm sure there's someone out there. Maybe we just haven't heard of them yet?"

"If we haven't heard of a stronger Fire Wielder by now then you probably have to wait for his seat to be released once he dies."

"Although, I do like Lady Samolson. She's been rather nice to us over the years after she joined court when we were little. Mother was rather impressed in how strong Lady Samolson was with her power. I remember her turning bits of my water into ice to cool down my drink during the summer solstice parade a few years back."

"As long as no one challenges her with their Water Wielding, and wins, then I suspect she'll be here to stay."

We stopped right in front of the closed doors where two guards stood at attention. Ora stepped in front and quickly fixed a pleat of her dress before straightening her back and rolling her shoulders.

"Shine like the sun," I whispered over her shoulder just as I nodded to one of the guards to signal him to open the doors.

Ora turned her head slightly over her shoulder and gave me a mischievous smile and a wink before stepping through the threshold of her favorite meeting room. It held a natural glow against the light brown walls. Each of the windows pictured a bright sun that beamed jeweled light to the ground below. In the room's center sat a long, dark wooden table. The six men and women of different ages sat up straight and shared inquisitive looks—all except Lord Cendio Vovias.

My eyes narrowed on him as he alone slouched in his chair on the left side of the table, a seat away from the head where the crown sat, with boredom painted on his face. He lazily held his head up with his fist and rested his elbow on the arm of his chair. The picture of indifference.

He had been one of the advisors during the time of our grandfather, King Patrek Endromeon. Vovias had shown strong power in fire and was placed inside the court as a young man and now, he was in his elder years. His dark brown hair was flecked with grays and receded at his temples. His soft chin was hidden by a gray and white beard that was a stark contrast to the tanned skin from his mixed heritage. The Iron Hand, he was called, since he advised the former queen with a stern and precise push on Wielding policies. Policies he urged would benefit the Wielding in powerful ways, regardless of who was crushed in their wake.

Many strong Fire Wielders came from the Shadow-craig Mountain region in the northwest, home to Gria's most powerful forges—including The Melted Forge, an armory-turned-manor that supplied much of the kingdom's weapons.

The thought of having him at our mother's table always baffled me. Not because he was ill-tempered and approached every decision as if it were a crumb under his nails, but because of his proposed policies against the Veiks. He strongly believed that the Veiks should be subservient to the Wielders—or completely abolished. It was the opposite of what our grandfather stood for. What our mother stood for.

Why did she establish him as the lead advisor chair? Why keep him so close to her ear?

Across from Vovias, in the traditional seat for the High Priest or Priestess Established, sat Ariadne Terrigan. Aside from the royal line, she was the highest-ranking Wielder in Gria. It was known to select few that she had achieved the Seventh Circle, the seventh and final test, amongst those who tested and practiced at the High Seven Temple. The first in many generations.

By old Wielding Law, those who held the power of the *illicitus* were put to death, but Ariadne had somehow been able to save her neck by telling others her death would invoke the wrath from the giants. And those who were devout would never risk the giants' attention on them.

Which was why our grandfather never dared to execute her.

She vowed to not showcase her source in fear of hurting those around her, but made it well known that the giants had blessed her in other valuable ways. Ways that elevated her to be the High Priestess. She claimed she could talk to the giants, and since they blessed her with this knowledge, she alone could lead the believers. That power made her one of the highest-ranking members of the court.

When asked by skeptics about her power, she always went out of her way to humble herself in front of royalty and the court by stating that she never wanted to put those around her in danger due to the uncontrollable nature *illicitus* provokes.

"Oh, my high queen. Your Majesty. Your Graciousness. The giants continue to teach me about this blessing, this curse, every day. I would never want to jeopardize your safety or your daughter's safety for mere parlor tricks. Let's take this seed of doubt and cultivate this into a way to fortify our faith in what the giants teach us."

I huffed at the memory of her practically groveling until my father's annoyance was so tangible that Ariadne took one look in his direction and instantly began walking backward toward the doors as she continued to *humble* herself.

On this day, her wild red hair was shaped in a mass of braids and curls, the latter meticulously styled to shape her pale face, illuminating the faint coppery lines that peaked up from her rich brown dress. Her eyes twinkled in a strange excitement, and each finger, adorned with golden rings and jewels, danced on the table. Deep golden earrings matched the brooch on her chest that seemed to hum and pulse like a heart.

All stood quickly as my sister, the queen-to-be, walked in. I took note and nodded to each attendee as Ora focused on the last bite of her pastry and silently licked the crumbs from her fingers. She took her chair at the head of the table while I sat at the opposite end. The chair was typically reserved for anyone in the royal line attending court meetings with little to add. Each member took their seats and faced Ora. I winked at her with a slight smile and a look that said *you can do this.*

Ora scrunched her face and shook her head as she rose to stand. The others looked at one another in confusion before slowly following rising to their feet.

"No, no. You all stay seated," Ora said as she shook her hand to signal them to stop. She rounded the table and walked toward where I sat before stopping beside my chair.

"*What are you doing?*" I hissed between my teeth.

Ora motioned me to move. "Up."

I looked around the table, seeing all eyes on me. I felt the blood rush up my neck and over my cheeks as I gently pushed my chair back and stood. Once I turned and clasped my hands together in front of me, I caught a gleam in my sister's eyes. The look I knew all too well and told me she was up to something. *Oh no.*

"Yes? Your Highness?" I asked gingerly, really hoping she hadn't planned something *too* stupid. I knew she was set to make her own mark, but I had hoped she would wait until after the coronation. I had the strong feeling that I was very wrong.

"Come," was all Ora cheerfully said. I looked at her in confusion, slightly shaking my head to stop her from whatever madness she was concocting. Her reply came with the standard eye roll as she grabbed the back of the large wooden chair and dragged it away from me and down toward the opposite end of the table.

I prayed to the giants that the noise wasn't as loud as it seemed. I watched in horror as the court's eyes all looked at me in shock and swiveled their heads to watch their queen-to-be drag an enormous chair and settle it close to hers...*at the head of the table*. I gulped as I watched her sit back down in her chair and quietly tap the chair next to her, ordering me to sit.

All the heads swiveled back to me and watched with large eyes.

Oh, Ora would soon pay for this embarrassment. If she would have told me her plan, we could have made a better statement. But then again, I would have more than likely told her *no*. And she knew that.

I sighed and faked confidence as I settled down next to her. Not one eye looked away from me. I turned my head down and locked my gaze on my white knuckles gripping the fabric of my skirts.

"Welcome to our first call to council. I know things will not be ceremonially official until The Rising, but nonetheless, thank you for your continued support through this period of grief and transition." Ora donned a bright face as she acknowledged the others, emitting the well-cultivated voice from years of lessons and practice.

The court looked at one another and nodded their heads. "I don't believe things will look too different from my mother's rule," Ora continued, "but I would like to propose a small change to the advisory roles and add my sister to the official advisory."

I instantly turned to her in shock as the other court members shared their surprise.

This had never been done before. Ever. Before I could speak against the notion, a ratty voice spoke up.

"This cannot be done! The advisory council is full. Other than Lord Beralt's absence, all *seven* seats are taken, and all represent each circle of Wielding as necessary. Might I remind you that it's also completely uncustomary for the reign to have bloodline in a council seat? This can prove problematic and imbalanced in decision-making!"

It wasn't lost on me, or on Ora based on her furrowed brow, that Vovias had blatantly disregarded one of the court seats that *was* present.

I looked coldly at Vovias who in turn looked coldly at Ora. The rest of the *eight*-seated court sat in stunned silence from the outburst—all but a deep, creamy voice who spoke up from the furthest end of the table. A young man, not too much older than I, looked at Ora. He had bronze-brown skin and dark hair that was cropped closely to his head. Strands of longer hair draped over his forehead, and his dark brown eyes bounced from the us to the old man.

"It seems you forgot one chair of representation in your rant, but on the contrary, Lord Vovias, the rule is loosely interpreted. There is evidence that cousins sat at the same table as the reigning power and provided excellent service for their people in the years past. The rule leans more into the vote of removing power *if and only if* unjust decision-making does occur. Given the representation of both princesses, it should go without debate that they are both levelheaded decision-makers in their own right. Hence, they would be excellent upholders of our laws and provide due services to their people across the realm of Gria and the continent of Wieldera."

Ora beamed at the young man. I saw the intense gaze held between the two and nudged my sister's foot under the table. "You can daydream later!" I whispered.

"Regardless of bloodline, the *other princess* shows very little reliability in her Wielding power!" Vovias shot a cold look at me before he continued. "She can barely hold enough Earthen Wielding as it is, and Lady Simret already has that seat here." He gestured to the woman who sat between Ariadne and the younger man. "Not to mention that she is a much more powerful Earthen Wielder than *that princess*. There's no point in having two Earthen Wielders here."

My back straightened as I felt the insult hurl toward me just as my knuckles tightened around the loose fabric of my dress.

Do not let them see you angry, I repeated to myself as I took a steadying breath. *His words mean nothing*. A similar mantra I told myself through the years to choke down the words that wanted to batter against me. Prove me worthless. Even if I did feel the truth behind them.

The severe-looking woman with umber skin and high cheekbones raised a sharp eyebrow in Vovias's direction. Her crystal-blue eyes looked as if they were made of glass and were much sharper than the soft curves of her mouth. "Leave my name out of your mouth, Vovias," she sneered.

Vovias continued without acknowledging the woman. "What official use will the *other princess* be to this court other than a mockery to the great powers that Wielded before her?" He turned his cold glare to the man who had spoken up before he continued, "Mighty that you, *Lord Sury*, should have such high opinions, being the newest member of this court. Let us hope you bring the same *gusto* that your father brought before you. I don't understand why your kind even has a seat here, given that your family are Veiks." He shot Lord Sury a final glare.

Some of the older civilians still held prejudice against one another, but that thinking grew smaller and smaller every year—even despite those who tried to incite violence in the name of *change*. Still, some wanted the Wielders to rule over the Veiks like cattle. The vision of the early Endromeon rulers was to create a system of trust. That vision was finally achieved when Arjun Anmathios was offered a seat at the council table when he was not much older than me, under Patrek Endrome-on's rule.

A symbol of unity while also ensuring there was a system of checks and balances within the kingdom.

Now his son held that seat.

Lord Sury Anmathios turned his bright gaze back to Ora at the high seat and *winked*.

"Lord Vovias," Ora grated through her teeth, "should you have anything to say about *Princess Ophelia's* abilities, then we should discuss the matter in private. She has fully completed the first test of the Seven Circles of Wielding, which is enough power to sit here at the table, *officially*. As for Lord Sury's non-Wielding family, my mother's ancestors had a vision to unite us all—not continue to divide the continent based on Wielding abilities. Grandpapa, King Patrek, finally put the vision to work by inviting the Veik representation to this table. You will respect the laws laid before you, or I can excuse anyone here who does not believe in equal representation!" Each word grew louder and more clipped than before. "Do not make me remind you of the repercussions for breaking the peace treaty our ancestors signed after the Original War." The other members of the court murmured and nodded in agreement.

The corners of my mouth turned up ever so slightly as I felt pride in my sister beam within my chest. She always knew how to shine.

"The only *mockery* I see today is this outburst you have caused, *Lord* Vovias. You will do well to ensure you're aligned with this court." Ora huffed with a heated breath as a faint, golden glow silhouetted around her frame. Slowly, she blinked twice before smoothing the lines of her dress, noticeably taking large breaths. The glow receded until it disappeared.

I followed her gaze as it found Lord Sury's with a smile. "Thank you, Lord Sury, for your words of encouragement. Since it looks like the majority of the court agrees that *Princess Ophelia* can hold a seat at the table, then let us discuss our upcoming travels and the coronation preparations," Ora concluded, and the court dove into the logistics for the ceremony.

While I was content with being my sister's shadow, it would seem that she clearly had other plans for me. Wanted me to shine with her.

I would much rather stick to the shadows that I've grown so fond of.

Lady Samolson, next to Vovias, who controlled the seas to the east, spoke through the part she would uphold through our travels. Healer Nesco, sat to her other side, and echoed his role in the preparations, all the while Lady Simret continued to throw daggering glares at Vovias. I was secretly glad Beralt didn't make it to this court session, despite his strength as an Air Wielder. He was almost as much of a pompous ass as Vovias.

I watched Ora, intently listening and occasionally glancing at the young man who had spoken in my favor, while I continued to sit there in utter silence and prayed silently that everything went to plan.

CHAPTER 4

I changed out of my mourning blacks. The act felt like I was forgetting my father too quickly, as if the moment I wore another color, his memories would fade away.

I knew in my heart that wasn't true, but I needed to focus on the present. My sister needed me more than ever.

It had been a few days since the court meeting, which had ended disastrously with Lady Simret threatening to Wield vines around Vovias's mouth. It took all my strength not to snicker, but Ora outright laughed, which infuriated Vovias even more before he stomped out of the room.

The air was crisp as I checked my horse's straps for the third time to ensure everything was secure. I hoped Ora would take note of the difficult terrain and would choose riding boots over ornate slippers. My fingers clutched my royal green coat tightly over my shoulders as a gust of wind ripped through the courtyard. The material was threaded and lined in gold. It bore the royal insignia stitched to the chest and felt like the heavy embrace of my father.

Strands of my bound hair came loose in the wind, and I quickly tucked them behind my ears to keep them out of the way on the journey through the southern edge of Bainas Forest and toward the Rising Rock Temple in the west. The open-air journey was another symbol for the up-coming reign-to-be. A journey marked by challenges and high points, where one might take in the landscape and observe how the land shaped its people. A place surrounded by threats. What it meant to rule, and of what the rulers went through at the Rising Rock.

Mother's journals described the journey as mostly sym-bolic, and spoke of how imbuing her magic at The Rising was a beautiful feeling. The travel itself was usually unevent-ful, even with rumors of urthens. Many Wielders said that the beasts were a hoax and that the reported attacks were merely Veiks who sought revenge on those with magic.

I believed these vile creatures to be a fairy tale until sleep evaded me one night when I was eight, causing me to wander through the castle like a tiny beetle, skittering across the carpets. I stumbled upon a guard in the servants' quarters, half mauled and screaming about a large beast of the dark. A frantic servant who caught me spying told me it was a mountain lion. After that, I wasn't sure what to believe.

I took a deep breath as I buried the memory. Regardless of the truth around that night, I rarely ever left the castle and made sure to carry a Healer's dagger for cutting herbs within my skirts.

It's just a half-day's ride, I told myself. *You have guards with swords who can Wield strong shields. Nothing lives within those trees but birds and vermin.*

As the few guards and members of court checked and rechecked their things, I turned my back and hid my hands inside my cloak as I tried to feel for my Wielding. A slight tickle brushed my fingertips as sparks of electric blue and silver flared at the tips, dancing from finger to finger and down into my palm. The sensation intensified, spreading through my hand then up my arm and neck. It slowly snaked along my veins and sent tiny pulses to my nerve endings until the same sparks danced down my other arm and into the opposite palm.

"Is that a smile I detect, my dear sister? I see you've been practicing!" Ora's warmth radiated from her smile as she stepped around the horse's muzzle. To my surprise, she not only wore the suggested riding boots but had also donned riding leathers with her dark green cloak.

I stuffed my hands deep into my pockets, immediately extinguishing the tingles, and tried to hide my embarrassment at being caught practicing. "Good morning, Ora. How are you feeling about today?" I asked quickly. "Better than yesterday since we talked through more of the ceremony?"

"Oh, come now, why must you hide your Wielding? You're as good as anyone else who Wields it. Believe in yourself. *I* believe in you," Ora said as she took my hands out of my pockets. "I don't understand why you shy away from it like you do. This is a gift! No matter what *circle of power* you are."

The last part stung.

I knew she didn't mean for it to sound cruel, but it was all I had heard my entire life. Images swirled in my head of Priestess Ariadne and other tutors scolding me when I was younger and didn't Wield my magic in the right manner, or when I couldn't accurately recall the correct ingredients for salves or incantations for charms.

"Stupid, silly girl. Waste of talents to a strong name," Ariadne would spit each time.

I remember coming home from lessons in tears from the shame. The whispers and voices from the High Seven Temple continued to spin inside my mind with words like *humiliation, embarrassment, undeserving.* Mother would come into my bedroom, prying my hands away from my tear-streaked face, trying to mend the damage.

Her words were often too heavy to understand and felt too bold for my young heart.

No matter what kind of smile my mother wore, I could always see there was a tinge of sadness in her eyes, even in the moments when she tried to encourage me. But her eyes would always brighten any moment Aurora displayed her magic. Aurora was so like Mother in that way. Her Wielding seemed effortless. Mother would practically laugh with glee, praising Aurora any moment she could.

My bright sun, the queen would say. *You will shine so radiantly!*

No one had to verbally confirm what I'd known for a long time: that my younger sister would take the throne and be praised as the new queen.

I never felt mad or held any ill feelings for my sister. It was the way of things and had been driven inside my brain since I began learning my letters—the strongest power held the royal position.

Secretly, I grew to be glad that I wasn't responsible for the next reign.

It was also why I had a closer relationship with my father. His magic wasn't among the strongest either, but it never seemed to bother the queen. Mother seemed to hold a special heart for all, regardless of their Wielding abilities. But behind closed doors, when it came to me, it felt different. Her eyes were always so full of pity—not to mention she would always avoid any Wielding talk in my presence.

"You have such unfounded confidence in your subjects and council, my dear sister," I said, burying the rising humiliation as I held my head high, mocking the regal court around us in jest and shaking off the unwarranted stares thrown our way. "Is the future Royal Majesty ready to take the next stage of her journey?"

Ora extended her arm for me to walk her back to her horse. "I shall say, my dearest pupil," she said with a smile, returning my jest. "I think this kingdom is nowhere near ready for the ruckus such a young queen will bring to her people!" The last bit was said loudly as we passed Lord Vovias's horse and young stable hand, who trembled terribly as he checked the saddle of the lord's horse and the carriage a few mounts back.

"*Princess* Aurora." Annoyance radiated from the lord and fell heavy upon us. "Your carriage has been arranged for the journey." A glint in his eye sent small goosebumps along my arms.

"*Lord* Vovias," Ora returned in equal sarcasm, "I think I shall enjoy the fresh air and view the *strenuous journey* as a series of life lessons through the perils and triumphs of one's rule. Plus, I think I shall enjoy the outdoors with my subjects and sister. Care to disagree?" Ora cocked her head a little to the left and raised her eyebrows.

I hid my chuckle with my free hand as Vovias gritted his teeth while resisting an impending eye roll—though the twitch in his eye said far more. "My, *Future Queen* Aurora, I shall say that you have silenced Lord Vovias for once in his career," I said. "It seems he must be learning his place."

Vovias's face twisted into a tight, forced smile that didn't reach his eyes. He slightly dipped his head in a bow. "My deepest apologies, *Princess*." He turned to the trembling boy and scolded him about something to do with buckles and clasps.

"Is the Future Majesty ready for her journey?" The smooth voice belonging to Sury came from our left. He casually leaned against one of the stable walls as he took a bite out of an apple.

He wore typical brown leather pants and boots. His gray tunic was slightly undone at the top, and his navy-blue jacket was fully open. Something flashed across his eyes that would have been missed by most, but I instantly noticed how Ora's cheeks held a light tinge of pink at their peaks.

Ora slightly bowed her head and smiled brightly—practically a beam. "Thank you for your inquisitiveness, Lord Sury. I'd like to think of myself as ready as ever."

In one motion, Sury took another bite of his apple and chucked the rest into a trough for the horses to find. He swiped his bottom lip with his thumb before licking the remnants off the pad. In just a few swift steps, he walked toward Ora to close the gap and bowed, never unlocking his eyes from hers. Ora's gasp was audible as Sury said, "It'll be a pleasure to serve you, my queen." I could have sworn I saw the deep veins in Ora's neck throb.

I rolled my eyes as I let out a loud cough, acting as if dust had caught inside my lungs before anyone else could see their exchange.

Sury rose, standing just an inch or two taller than Ora, and glanced at me as he dipped his head. "Princess Ophelia. I hope you are having a merry day," he said with a smirk before locking eyes with Ora once more. With a small wink to my sister, he walked back to his horse, which was conveniently close to hers.

I'd noticed their flirtatious behavior growing over the years, but these last few weeks, it seemed to grow tenfold. I worried for my sister's heart. Her hand would more than likely be given away to some royal or dignitary from elsewhere, urged by the court.

A royal marrying a Veik would be out of the question if the court had their say—no matter the peace that was so carefully built between us.

"Could you two be any more *obvious*?" I asked. The amount of eye rolling I did while I was around my sister might cause them to roll right out of my head.

"I have no idea what you're referring to," Ora said as she tugged me along to where her horse stood in front of the royal company. In a smooth motion, she grabbed the reins of her straw-colored mare and pulled herself up into the saddle, disregarding any help from the stable hand. I snickered at the poor boy, whose jaw seemed to drop to his knees. Ora always did have a way of radiating confidence.

"Ora, are you sure you're ready?" I grabbed her hand as she adjusted herself again.

Ora leaned down close and smiled. "I'm ready because you helped me be ready. You're the force behind me that I can trust. Mother and Father would be proud of not just me, but you too." She steered her horse around to see that everyone was mounted and ready.

I fumbled over my own saddle as my riding skirts caught between my legs, earning me a few questionable glances from the stable hands and a small snort from the gray steed I bravely tolerated. I waved them off, feeling the heat of blood rushing to my face, as I stamped down the rolling embarrassment. Once I was finally adjusted and my cloak was draped comfortably by my back, I steered the horse toward where Ora's stood.

She gleamed as she turned her attention to the small crowd in the courtyard.

"For the goodness of our kingdom, I promise to rule with a golden heart for all the subjects of our realm and beyond. Let us reflect on this journey as we prepare for the start of a new reign that will leave everyone in awe!"

And with all in tow, she nudged her horse to walk out of the castle gates, through the streets that led across the field and into the forest beyond.

CHAPTER 5

I followed closely behind Ora as most of the party rode in silence, finally crossing over the roaring Dolock River that partially divided the land. I internally chuckled at Healer Nescoe and Lady Samolson, who rode not too far behind me, and their failed attempt at *whispering* about their ongoing affair. At their volume, I guessed that even the birds at the tops of the trees could hear all their dirty secrets.

Lord Vovias rode closely behind Ora, flanked to my right, with a bored look plastered on his face. The carriage at the rear clinked slowly forward as we trekked across the flat dirt road snaking through the forest to the temple.

Lord Sury followed closely behind Vovias but kept his gaze fixed on Aurora.

I could practically see his pulse quickening as he gazed in her direction, acting as discreet as he thought possible. His face flushed every time he looked, his eyes drawn like a magnet.

As children, anytime Sury visited court with his father, Lord Arjun Anmathios, he would relentlessly pick on the two of us, chasing us around the palace until our lungs felt on the verge of bursting.

Now it would seem that things are very different.

It wasn't until last summer that Sury and Ora, who used to pull each other's hair, finally *noticed* one another and tried to hide their feelings from everyone. I would never tell them, but one night that summer, I caught the unchaperoned and dreamy-eyed pair in one of the castle gardens before he came to lordship.

I snickered at the thought. They did a very terrible job at hiding it. At least to me.

Some Wielders were stronger than others, and those who showed great power usually married or bred with those of equal or stronger power to keep their Wielding lines strong and pure. It would be a beautiful thing if Ora could marry Sury for love—if she wanted that.

I had read stories from various lands on how marriage was different there compared to Gria, how it wasn't only viewed as a duty or a peace treaty, but for love. I would never wish a loveless union upon my sister. Hell, I doubt she would go down lightly if the court ever tried to force her hand to some ugly, crooked-nosed asshat from a realm across the sea. Or even from Mercyth to the north. I shivered at the thought.

A few Royal Guards led the party, flanking us from the sides and behind, their faces plastered in neutrality. I could hear the ones directly behind me, their voices echoing against the trees as we trekked forward.

"Yer know, it was rumored once that urthens of all kinds crawled through the forests. Creatures of the night," one guard said to another.

Seems like the guard has heard the same rumors as I had.

"Now wait just a minute. When have *you* seen an urthen?"

"That's just it, innit? Nor'one has laid sight of 'em in decades." The guard craned his neck over his shoulder and up to the trees. "Some say it was only tales to scare the chil'ren to stay in their beds, but tales nonetheless that should be heeded in warning."

The second guard scoffed. "Get that nonsense out of your head. They're exactly what you just said—stories. My own ma read about them to me from those penny booklets from the market."

"You don' believe 'em? But wha' about that poor bloke who was attacked?"

"Band of..." the guard whispered the next part much more quietly, but it wasn't hard to tell he was referring to the same rumor we'd all heard—that a band of Veiks went on a revenge killing spree. "He was also a known user. Nothing more of it."

"But wha' about the missing guards?"

"Hush it. You'll piss your trousers from scaring yourself before night falls. Keep a lookout for any movement. Sword up, shield ready."

I watched as they created their ethereal shields. To the normal eye it looked like hardly anything was there to protect them, but pulling from your source to create a barrier was one of the first defense lessons Wielders underwent. I could see the details of the blues and greens within their shields, faintly bouncing against the sun's rays.

A light breeze passed and the warm sun shone through the leaves above and spread its beams to the floor below. The path itself was smooth and not as strenuous as we had imagined. Thankfully, the earth was soft and carried a faint sweetness from blooming flowers, mingled with the tang of fallen leaves from the previous season.

A slow ache began to rise in my lower back and my ass was going numb from sitting so long.

I looked over my shoulder and found that everyone wore the same indifferent look as they had before, but this time with sleep in their eyes. All but Sury, who continued to keep his eyes glued to my sister.

I sat in silence with my thoughts as the time passed. Soon it would be dusk, and we would reach the Rising Temple for camp.

My eyes traveled over the guards' faces and up to the small banners two of them carried. One was Gria's flag that boasted the large, golden sun on a deep green canvas. The other bore the golden symbol that's been seared into the minds of every Wielder—the seven circles of power. The four interlocking rings in its center symbolized traditional magic of the elements, all linked together with a fifth circle: the Healer's circle.

I was always in awe watching a Healer work, seeing their ability to tap into the elements—even if it was ever so faintly, just enough to produce their needed elixir or to soothe someone's pain. Healers were few and far between and coveted amongst those who could afford to keep them in their purse. Other Healers would work in the free clinics within Grianmore and surrounding townships. Only a few would travel from place to place to minister care to those in need before moving to the next village.

But the sixth circle that encircled the first five on the banner, tracing the edges of the elemental circles, boasted the brightest circle of them all. The power that represented my sister so beautifully and how she could not only muster the strength to control them all, but how she shone so beautifully when she did. The celestial circle of power that our ancestors claimed, giving them control from the sun.

I was saddened when I learned that the knowledge of anyone harnessing the moon had faded with history. I could empathize with the moon giantess, Nyska, and how she was pushed to the shadows, remaining unassuming only because she didn't shine like the stars around her. But what then when she eclipses the sun? Is she still unassuming then?

The thought of the dark shadows made my eyes linger on the last circle on the flag—the one that encompassed them all. Its stitching was much thicker than the rest, symbolizing the magnitude of this forbidden power. It was said that the *illicitus* was not only powerful but deadly to anyone who had the ability to Wield it and dare touch its source. Theories of why the giants even blessed us with something so tempting had been argued over the known history and deemed it the most dangerous magic of them all.

I read that the known Wielders of *illicitus* were either put to death by the High Seven Temple or ran to hide—not that I can truly blame them. Even with it being an illegal magic, Ariadne vowed she would never touch the source or she would forfeit her own life.

We were taught at such a young age that the Wielder who touched the *illicitus* would go mad, claiming awful things about magic and those around them, and about how unnatural it was to extend someone's life or bring them back from the grave. The thought instantly made a shiver travel down my spine.

As beautiful as it was to have power, it caused the Great Divide centuries ago, pushing Veiks to be subservient to Wielders. Even amongst those who had power, there was always a vicious debate of which power was more important and who held a higher station in society. I chuckled at the irony that Earthen Wielders were considered the lowest in power and yet here I was, a woman with royal blood. The highest of highs while also being the lowest of Wielding lows.

Regardless, I practiced my Wielding all the same. I wanted to prove to myself—and, selfishly, to others—that I was more than merely the sister of a future queen.

That I could contribute to my kingdom in my own way.

With that thought, I pulled my cloak around my shoulders tightly to cover most of my hands. I focused on the inner song of my own magic and watched the dim, ethereal blue glow lazily dance to my fingertips.

Ever so slowly, the light bounced and dipped toward the creases in my palms and formed tiny, pebble-like orbs. It was dim compared to most Wielders, but seeing it practically pulse in my hands brought a small, sad smile to my face.

Hello, you, I said within my thoughts, greeting my power as if it could hear me.

I turned my attention to a flower in the distance that was in the middle of a budding bloom, and felt my magic roll deep within my gut before a tiny silver spark danced on top of my palm. It joined the lazy blue orbs, all burning dimly in my hand. Aiming my fingers toward the flower, I recalled old lessons and visualized slowly, delicately peeling back each white petal to reveal the bright yellow center within.

The flower in the distance began to twitch, as if a phantom wind had flown by, and a single petal began to uncurl. Ora's head snapped up to attention, like she had sensed my magic, and turned to face me, smiling brightly.

I quickly dropped my hand and stuffed it back under my cloak, feeling the same embarrassment I always felt when people watched me practice—especially her. Ora's magic was a thing of beauty and power. Not frail like mine. She gave a small shake of her head, as if knowing exactly what was on my mind, before turning again to face forward.

The trees became thicker and the road narrowed. The sun began to dip low behind the clouds, casting dark shadows on the forest floor. Ahead, I could make out the decrepit stone pillars jutting up from the earth, all wrapped in vines and moss.

Beyond them sat the Rising Temple. The beautiful white marble was crafted into pristine steps and pillars that gleamed in the setting sunlight. The temple looked completely out of place surrounded by the greenery of the forest.

Reliefs of images and words were carved into the stones, depicting parts of the ritual itself and other messages the realm had long forgotten. Although it was ancient, deep care was taken to protect the structure, what it housed, and the ritual performed within.

Only a select few were allowed to step into the temple during the sacred ceremony—just the one coming to reign and the priest or priestess, for fear that too many visitors would evoke anger from the giants. The rest of the court would wait until the High Priestess completed the ceremony within the temple before concluding with the coronation.

I would watch the coronation from a distance, careful not to disturb the process.

Ora gave the order to stop the horses and the sweet, welcomed relief from riding greeted my body as I finally set my feet on solid ground. The horse huffed in agreement and nudged me in the side as a gesture of thanks.

The handful of servants quickly went to work grabbing supplies and tents from the carts, setting up camp, and preparing fires.

"Well, we *have* told each other before that we would like to camp outside in the garden one day, right?" Ora spoke as she rounded a few horses and stood before me, looking at the temple in awe. "This can be close enough."

Nodding, I wandered over to the crumbling structures set to the side, Ora in tow. Years of dirt and grime made home to the once magnificent temples that now lay ruined at my feet. I had read stories about more temples, smaller in structure, that had been built through the years to house various rituals.

"I wonder what these were used for," Ora asked. "I just remember bits of what Mother shared, but not much."

I placed my hand on a fallen pillar and felt a slight hum vibrating through the stone. I gasped lightly at the touch and let a small stream of my magic rise to the surface, intertwining with the greeting from the broken pillar.

"I'm not entirely sure. But I would love to check the library to see if anything is mentioned about the carvings."

Ora nodded in agreement and looked off to the Rising Temple and the brilliance it exuded amongst the vegetation that encased it.

The stark white marble reminded me of a grove of birch trees I once saw in a book. Each angle was delicately crafted and smoothed down to a fine touch. The stairs leading to the open floor behind a set of pillars were cradled in jasmine vines that burst their scent into the air. Copper lanterns stood on the smooth white marble floor, all perfectly distanced apart, leading into an inner chamber far behind a white stone wall.

Ora's gaze was fixed on the temple ahead. "It's a bit ominous, don't you think? To do something so great in secret and so deep in the forest?"

Before I could reply, we both saw a shadowy figure move between the stark, white pillars. Instinct drove me to reach for the small Healer's dagger that hung at my belt, no bigger than the palm of my hand, and step in front of Ora.

"Welcome, Princess Aurora, to the Rising Temple." The sultry voice of Ariadne echoed as she emerged from the front of the temple and to the top step. She wore bright, golden robes stitched with fine black thread that shimmered with each step she took. Her deep red hair flowed in a phantom wind behind her and her eyes were smudged with kohl, intensifying her jade irises and alabaster skin.

She looked like she had been carved from the marble itself.

The court and servants immediately stopped what they were doing to place their fists over their hearts in a unified greeting. I followed Ora as she did the same. Both of us tilted our heads in acknowledgement to the High Priestess.

"I see you made it safely, High Priestess Ariadne." Ora gingerly made her way to the temple, careful not to trip over any roots in her path. "I hope your journey was not treacherous or too taxing."

Ariadne slowly stepped down to the forest floor, her feet bare. She gently bowed her head. "Not at all, Princess. I came as soon as the council meeting was over to have a moment of reflection in the forest and to prepare for this mighty moment."

I watched her closely as she clasped Ora's hands between her pale ones. The sleeves of her robes allowed the coppery ink to shine in the beams of sunlight, snaking up her arms. Each finger wore a golden ring, some in intricate designs, and others held precious stones. Around her eyes was a soft mask of delicately painted white dots, starting from the innermost part of her fierce eyes and gingerly following a pattern around to her brow, ending with three solid lines down the bridge of her nose.

"Now is the time to rest and reflect as well. I will summon you when the Blood Moon is at its highest, and then we shall begin." She bowed her head again before striding away and backing into the temple. Around the pillars and just outside of the inner chamber, I saw the shadows of a few acolytes, all dressed in gold chiffon dresses. Their faces were partially hidden by painted-on white designs, each with a slightly different pattern.

I turned, with Ora in tow, and retreated to our tent.

***

The sun set deep behind the forest and cast dark shadows amongst the trees. Oil lamps had been lit around and within each tent. Campfires nearby had been set for cooking and song amongst the resting servants and court members.

We turned to our shared tent that had been set around a great oak tree, with two cots lined with furs on either side. Ora's trunk held various bits of clothing, trinkets, and herbs, while mine was neatly organized with a couple of simple dresses and all the books from the royal library that I could fit for a couple of days in the wilderness.

Books on the sciences, magics, and legends of the north. They were my safe space and where I found comfort. As we waited, I stuck my nose into a book about curious magics that had been practiced in ancient times within ancient realms.

Ora had already shed her riding clothes and donned the simple white cotton dress for the ritual. The dress wrapped loosely around her soft waist and clung to her curves. I peeked over my book as I watched her tuck some loose hair into the braid I had helped with many times before, showing her delicate shoulders and clavicle.

I noticed her grip on her white stone necklace was firm as she paced back and forth. Her bare feet scraped across the thick rug on the tent's floor.

"How are you so calm?" She rubbed her arms as a slight shiver of nerves ran down them.

"Someone has to be," I replied with boredom plastered on my face. "Since you easily show your emotions, I might as well remain dull to keep the balance in this tent." I shook my head and continued reading.

Ora huffed and crossed her arms. She plopped down next to me on my cot and rested her elbow on my shoulder. "What are you reading about?"

"I wanted to read about different Wielding theories to see if there's anything different I could do to enhance my own, but I saw this book misplaced on a shelf in the Elementis section. The title is worn on the cover, but it looks like something about old Wielding stories that seems to be forgotten."

Ora gave me a pointed look as if telling me she wasn't following along.

I shook my head. "Just poems about old incantations Wielders might have practiced, it seems." I flipped back and forth between the pages before I continued, "But some of the words and symbols are faded or in the Olden Language. I can't make some of it out."

Ora studied the book over my shoulder, taking in the faint illustrations and symbols on the pages, and pointed to a page that looked like a poem had been scribbled upon it. "Looks like old fables."

"From what I've read so far, it doesn't seem important."

"I wonder if Ariadne knows if there are old incantations. Interesting that there are aspects that we might've lost or forgotten about, if this book is true."

"Not sure, but maybe," I said with a shrug.

Ora tapped her chin in contemplation. "Between us, I question her. I mean, as a teacher, she helped me greatly with my magic and helped me to enhance, but I don't want her as an advisor. Something about her just seems *off*. I can't put my finger on it, but I can feel it.

I need you to be there regardless of what she or Vovias thinks of your power. That shouldn't matter. I mean honestly, look at Vovias. He might have achieved the fourth circle and is the most powerful Fire Wielder in Gria, but he's a self-fulfilling ass. There are far better people out there who might be weaker in fire that would serve this kingdom better, and yet we have him in his *lordship* seat."

"Ora, if our mother trusted them and kept them close, I think it would be wise to consider why." The annoyance wasn't hidden in my reply. "Not to mention, no one can take his seat until the next strongest Fire Wielder comes of age—whenever that may be. By the time anyone challenged him, he'd be dead from old age with all the political ribbon you'd have to cut through."

"We could kick him in the balls, then kick him out of his seat," Ora said with a high-pitched giggle.

I cut her a glance.

"Oh, Phe! Live a little! Break out of those rigid lines of yours." Ora playfully shook my shoulders.

"Not everyone has the luxury to live as freely as you, *Your Highness*. You've always had freedom to do what you want. You could Wield as soon as you left the womb; hell, you probably *did* Wield inside the womb! Some of us have to stay within the lines to survive. Practice day in and day out just to get a wisp of magic to leave their fingers. Stay status quo. Stay out of sight and not draw attention when we don't want it."

That inner voice spoke a whisper deep inside my thoughts: *Not that anyone would notice you anyway. You have little to offer.*

Ora huffed again and rested her back against the tent's wall. "One day, I hope you see yourself the way I do. You were destined for greatness. You're an *Endromeon,* for giants' sake, but you let everyone rule over *you*. You're royalty, too." She crossed her arms. "You could tell them to eat horse shit if you really wanted to. The power has always been ours. The question is: will you claim it?"

I said nothing as I turned the page of my book to a text with an illustration of a dark shadow beneath it.

"Oh, what is that?" Ora inched closer.

Something about the image forced my heart to flutter and a sensation to roll deep within me. My eyes felt glued to the page—a moth to a flame. Quickly, I brought the text closer to my face to read the tiny print, almost smudging the faded ink on my nose.

The shadowy figure had no visible mouth or nose, but the whites meant for eyes shone bright. Wisps of black clouds, like a vortex, encircled the figure, making it appear as if it were leaning out of the page.

"All it says is...the *Ancient One*?"

"You mean the fable Father teased us with to make sure we ate our peas or went to bed at the proper time? *That* Ancient One?" Ora asked.

"Maybe this is another version? I don't remember the stories being this frightening."

"Well, go on, then. What does it say?"

"My translation is a little rusty. It seems like it doesn't have a name but that in this version...it Wields *raw* magic? Maybe black magic from...?" I wrinkled my nose as I tried to decipher the Olden runes and interpret their meaning. "I can't make out what it says, but that looks like a symbol for urthen or *death*? Or it could be a symbol about something else. Is it an apple? An apple wouldn't make sense."

"You of all people don't recall our lessons on Wielding runes? Madam Fligan would have an absolute episode that her star pupil doesn't recall a rune."

"Shut up." I sighed. "Not like you can recall any Olden runes. Not everyone could have their schoolwork done for them simply *because*."

Ora faked her shock. "Excuse me! I did not. Okay, maybe just a handful of times. Besides, like anyone would purposely tap into the black Wielding of an *illicitus,* unless they were absolutely insane. Not to mention the death sentence that comes with even trying to Wield it if you could. But what's the purpose of this version of the Ancient One? Other than looking like an ominous entity on the page."

I wrinkled my nose again as I skimmed the pages. I couldn't look away from where the creature's eyes were meant to be. I felt as if I were glued to my cot, slowly being pulled into the worn pages. Ora's muffled voice called out to me. I blinked my eyes and rubbed them tightly.

"Sorry," I quickly said. "All the text says is something about a *weapon*. I've never heard of this before. It seems different from the tales Father told us." I flipped back to the cover of the book, trying once again to make out the title faintly etched on the leather and failing.

"Are you sure you didn't pick up one of those grim books written to scare the reader with stories of those mythical creatures everyone yaps about? Those are just dreadful stories yet everyone pretends as if they're real. If strong, fae males were real, then by all means, please whisk me away." Ora chuckled into her hand. "Could you imagine?" She asked as she giggled harder.

"But there was that..." I stopped myself. "Yes, you're right. If this *was* real, it would be helpful on any warfront."

"Yes—just think of what you could do with a thing like that if you could command it." Ora huffed in boredom and shifted herself into a comfortable spot next to me and closed her eyes. "Well, I guess we need some baleful ancient thing to help us get this show on the road. I'm growing tired. How do we call on this Ancient One to do our bidding and hurry all of this the hell up?" She twirled her hands in the air in an exaggerated fashion.

I continued to look at the page, feeling a draw of sorts to the words scribbled in faded ink. "Looks like there's some kind of poem next to it...but I can't tell what logographic language this is."

"Enough ghost stories, Phe. It's just a myth, like you said. *These* are the kinds of stories people fret about for no reason. Let's focus on the present at hand. Both of our lives are about to change."

She was right. We needed to focus on the here and now.

I sighed as I put the book down and drew Ora into a loose embrace.

"How are you feeling?" I whispered as I, too, rested my eyes.

"If I'm honest," Ora whispered back, "I'm scared."

"I think that's normal. But you were made for this," I said as I planted a small peck on her hair.

Exhaustion took over, forcing us to rest before our lives—and the kingdom—would change forever.

CHAPTER 6

Screams pierced the night and forced me awake. I wasn't entirely sure when I had fallen asleep, but the light outside the tent was completely gone and the oil lamp had dimmed too low to see clearly inside.

Ora had already sprung from my cot and withdrawn a tiny dagger she had placed underneath her cot's pillow—ready to strike at anything that came inside the tent. Her other hand filled with the bright golden glow of her Wielding.

"Put that out before anyone sees!" I whispered as more screams bellowed from outside. I carefully opened the flap of the tent just enough to see the commotion taking place. Figures of soldiers on horses, clad in black armor and helmets with silver insignia on their shields, tore through the camp as they swiped with their broadswords.

I couldn't make out the faces that lay scattered on the ground, covered in dirt and blood. Their lifeless bodies had been trampled by those trying to escape. Soldiers of the Royal Guard fought on horseback to push against the assault.

A whizzing noise in the distance drew nearer and I watched in horror as two arrows struck through a Royal Guard's neck, blood splattering the trees. The poor soul reached up, trying to tug at the arrows before sliding off his horse with a sickening *thud*.

Tents were being torn down and set ablaze as a tall figure in black armor carried a torch, lighting each tent on fire as he passed. He moved at an unnatural pace, jagged in the joints. The sight reminded me of the time I witnessed a fawn being born, trying to find its balance.

A growl echoed through the trees.

I felt my heart thump hard against my chest, trying its hardest to escape from its bony cage as I witnessed all before me. Another large figure in black armor, one I could have sworn was half the size of a tree, slowly walked through the camp holding the thickest chain I had ever witnessed.

I understood quickly why the chain was so thick. It dragged through the dirt, blood, and gore, pulling along a creature I had never seen before. A creature that was connected to the chain through a thick collar.

At first glance, it looked like a large dog. A huge, tortured-looking animal that bordered on the size of a small horse. It stalked on four legs with movements that mimicked a barn cat that chased mice away. Its skin was tight and ashen-black, and its head was square in shape with pointed ears like a mongrel ready to attack.

Three large claws were set at the base of each leg. They looked like their length could fit in my outstretched hand from the tip of my middle finger to the base of my palm.

But the teeth drew my breath short.

Its lips pulled back into a snarl under its pointed nose, revealing jagged teeth that could easily slice and chew anything that was caught in its jaws. Long strands of saliva leaked through its mouth and dropped on the ground.

Not saliva, I realized—but blood from its latest victim.

I finally found a faint sense of courage and turned to grab Ora's hand. I pulled her to the back of the tent, then grabbed another small dagger from my trunk and began cutting a ragged hole in the canvas for us to escape through.

Ora grabbed hard onto my arm. "Who's out there? What's happening?"

"Black Raiders. We have to get you out of here. NOW!"

"But *how?* They haven't left their realm in ages!"

Black Raiders were the cavalry and spies of Dokvalon. Our enemy from the west. A treaty was made well before we were born that forced them to stay on their side of the Shadowcraig Mountains. The Grian Army stationed at the mountain's base usually kept them at bay before they trekked further into Gria. Until tonight.

"I don't know! But it looks like one of them has an urthen."

Ora gasped. "How in the fuck did they get an *urthen*? I thought they were just stories, Phe!"

"I forgot to ask—I'll make sure to do that right before it decides to sink its teeth in us!"

I cut as fast as I could with the stupid, tiny dagger. A shadowy figure paused at the front of our tent and entered, torch in hand. The large man dragged the chain as it clanked against the forest floor, pulling the dog-like urthen into the tent.

The smell was atrocious. Like something died, came back alive, then died some more. Bile crept up my throat as the smell filled the tent. Empty sockets I assumed were meant for eyes were instead filled with putrid tissue, which explained at least part of the fetid smell.

The man made slow but wide steps in our direction, pulling the urthen creature with him. I heard Ora grunt as a bright glow illuminated the tent. As she quickly drew up her power, her body began to radiate bright gold as yellow and gold ribbons, like thin electric eels, spilled out of her fingers. She drew her hands to her chest then pushed them forward, sending the mass of ribbons, now shaped like thin spikes, in the intruder's direction.

The blow hit the intruder and its urthen, launching them off their feet and spinning them in midair before they landed with a grunt at the front of the tent.

The urthen growled—a deafening sound that radiated inside my body. I felt a sharp chill course through my skin and up my spine as I saw the creature tilt its head in my direction like it could sense me.

The figure's torch had slipped from his grasp yet still found its mark, catching the top of the tent with its flame. The dry canvas quickly became engulfed in fire. The leaves of the massive tree caught next, filling the tent with thick, white smoke, causing a haze that was nearly impossible to see through.

I used the timing to my advantage as I finally slit the canvas, enough for us to both crawl out and run. The urthen growled again and lunged right as my foot left the hole. Thankfully, the creature was too big to fit but was desperately trying to push its way through.

The entire tent was engulfed in red and orange flames within a matter of seconds, illuminating the camp and its surroundings. Fire crept up the giant oak tree that once was the center of our tent, charring the bark. The embers fell to the ground, catching the dried leaves around the camp and quickly setting them aflame. From the light, I could easily see there were more bodies laid across the ground and along the portico of the Rising Temple. Flames licked in between each of the columns holding the structure.

Soldiers and more urthens—some that looked like rabid and twisted dogs and others that looked like large reptiles—continued their carnage.

I grabbed Ora's hand and pulled her deep in the woods, leaving the screams behind us. Together, we ran until our lungs caught fire against the cooling night. The Blood Moon shone high above, giving us a faint light as we ran. And ran, we did.

I refused to look back, even when I felt the whips of branches stinging my skin and shredding pieces of the riding dress I'd never changed out of.

Both of our feet were bare, and I seemed to have found every damn pebble and broken branch that the earth could bless me with. The screams became more muffled the further we ran into the darkness of the trees.

A drumming noise grew louder behind us with every step we took.

I finally looked over my shoulder to assess the carnage, but I saw a Black Raider on horseback—well, on what looked like a decaying horse—gaining on us. Their sword was drawn, shining in the pale, red moonlight. Ora looked over her shoulder then twisted out of my grip, turning to face the approaching soldier.

I skidded to a halt, feeling something on the ground slicing through the skin of my feet. "*Ora!* We need to hide!" I turned as quickly as I could, tugging Ora to follow.

"No! I shouldn't be running! These are my people!"

"We have to get you to safety! *Please!*"

"I'm done running." Ora boldly stood still and let her magic rise to the surface again. Brighter ribbons of gold twisted around her arms and chest, illuminating her against the darkness. Her hair lifted in a phantom wind and swirled in unison with the magic that encircled her body. Sparks of magic emitted from her fingertips as she drew her hands in once again.

If the circumstances were different, I would have been in awe. The light was too bright for my eyes, forcing me to shield them with my hands and squint.

With her hands curved toward her chest like she was holding a ball, I watched Ora take a giant step forward and throw the ribboned energy straight at the Black Raider. In midair, the ribbons turned into glowing daggers, aiming true for the soldier.

In a swift motion, the Black Raider deflected the daggers with his black and silver shield, the force knocking him off his horse. I noticed the creature's decaying body had eyes that glowed red against its broken flesh and bone, while its hooves were encrusted in metal spikes the size of my fingers.

I knew the force of the impact alone would have caused some sort of injury that would slow down any rider. A broken bone, at least. The Black Raider slowly rose to his feet in a jagged motion and staggered a step toward us, pointing his broadsword.

"You'll have to do better than that," he croaked. The voice was both old and young. Broken and new. It pierced against my ears in a haunting way.

Ora snarled as she began a dance of various attacks of dagger-shaped energy, which the Raider continued to deflect and dodge. I could only stand there, feeling helpless but in awe at watching my sister's magic. I had never seen Ora's magic radiate in quite this way, or how effortlessly she Wielded it to attack and defend.

If the dance were not so treacherous, even the forest creatures would pause in wonder as the princess bent and glided, pulsating and radiating golden glows from her body and through her hands, finding their aim.

The Raider was relentless with his attacks and continued to rise from the ground, inching closer every time. Ora started to pant as sweat beaded at her temples from exhaustion, a precursor to the burnout. Each movement became slower.

My frozen feet finally found life as I ran to grab my sister's arm. I threw my small dagger toward the Raider, missing his shoulder by a wide margin. I pulled at Ora just in time as the Raider swiped his broadsword, nicking my dress and drawing blood from my forearm. Together, we spun to run but then Ora let loose a loud scream into the air.

I turned to see that the Raider had swung the sword again and sliced through Ora's thigh. Bright, red blood gushed from the deep wound and immediately soaked through her dress, dripping down to her feet. Ora fell to the ground, howling in pain, trying to cover the wound. The Raider, in two large steps, strode toward the laying princess and, in one motion, began to haul Ora over his broad shoulder.

Panic ensnared me as I screamed in frustration, grasping Ora for purchase. My fingers tangled against the delicate gold chain of Ora's necklace, breaking away its hold. I tried again, grabbing her by the dress and managing to pull her away, but the shift in gravity forced us to the ground. The Black Raider pivoted and reached for her again. A deep vibration sent a shockwave through me as I yelled again and struck the soldier with my fist.

Pain and fury encased my wrist. Instantly, a bright blue light radiated from my skin.

A sharp, shocking sensation traveled through my arms as an intense blue and silver orb-like force radiated around my body and pooled into my hands like quicksilver. Without thought, the force shot from my fingertips and toward the Raider, knocking him back to the ground with a hard *thud*.

My hands shook as soft, blue orbs like stardust dissipated into the air. The light around me dimmed back into nothing as I sat there in stunned silence. My heart beat like a hummingbird's.

I turned to find Ora staring back at me with wide eyes.

We were too distracted to notice that the Raider was already upon us again. He effortlessly picked Ora up off the ground. A scream of agony rose from Ora as the soldier tightened his grip and began carrying her away as she kicked.

I sprung forward, punching and kicking with all my might, but each attempt was futile. I questioned how the Black Raider was able to withstand all the hits from Ora's attacks, including the one I managed to give. He began to walk back toward the burning camp with Ora hung over his shoulders like a sack of meat. Blood covered most of her dress now and continued to drip to the forest floor. I looked at her in horror as I noticed her face becoming alarmingly pale from losing too much blood.

I scrambled on the ground to find any kind of weapon and came across a broken branch that I could wield.

Praying to the giants, I crept up behind the Raider and hit him in the back, careful not to hit Ora in the process.

In one motion, the Black Raider turned and sliced his sword through the branch in an unnatural movement, then forced a hit to my temple with the end of the sword before he continued to walk away.

Ora's cries slowly began to fade. The smell of smoke in the air began to fade. The light of the fires against the night began to fade. A trickle of something wet dripped down my face as my vision began to blur. My body hit a hard surface.

Then there was nothing.

CHAPTER 7

S weat pooled under my clothes as beams of sunlight pierced through the canopy of trees. Inhaling deeply, I smelled the forest floor mixed with tinges of burning wood in the distance. The stifling heat continued to rise as a small sting of skin, burning from the sun, forcing me to finally open my eyes and lazily focus on my surroundings.

Dirt and dead leaves clung to my face. Clumps of sweat-ridden hair rested on the forest floor. I slowly lifted myself off the ground but winced at the sting at my temple. Touching the tender spot, I pulled my hand back and saw a mixture of dirt and both dried *and* wet blood on my fingertips.

On my opposite hand, my knuckles had turned stiff. They ached in protest as I extended my fingers, finding my sister's necklace nestled deep inside my stinging palm. Tiny specks of blood bloomed from where the white stone had scratched and punctured my skin.

My vision slowly came into focus. The brightness from the sun above caused my eyes to sting. I shakily held up my hand, covered in dried blood, to shield against the relentless beam glowing down. The forest was quiet, with only the chattering of insects and a distant crackle of a fire breaking the silence.

Trees. Rows and rows of trees.

How did I get here? Where am I?

Gripping the necklace, I turned over to all fours and slowly crawled to a small tree, using it to climb up off the ground. I leaned against it as I sought to catch a breath. Each inhale sent a shockwave through my skin and pierced my skull.

Bruises. My body must have had bruises. My head pounded relentlessly, causing shadows to creep around the corners of my eyes.

Leaning on the trees, I made my way toward the sound of the crackling fire.

Must be hunters making a meal. They will help me return to Grianmore. I'm sure Mother and Father are worried.

My vision continued to blur in and out as I took unsteady steps forward. A root caught my foot, causing me to stumble before catching myself with another tree. On and on I went until I saw the source of the crackling fire.

Sobering clarity hit.

A realization so overpowering that my breath caught heavy in my chest. My heart raced as I took stronger steps forward to reach the clearing, steadily becoming more coherent as my mind worked to defog.

The shock of what I saw forced me back to my knees.

My vision took in the clearing in front of the temple where I remembered Ora and I making camp the night before...or was it nights? I couldn't tell how long I had been on the forest floor. My stomach instantly dropped. In the small setting where I remembered Ora's cot to be, nothing but burnt fabrics and ashes lay.

Rows of torn and broken tents laid in piles of ash, the contents charred. Bodies lay scattered on the ground with lifeless stares, many of them angled in unnatural ways. Their flesh was torn and burned. I recognized some of the features of the guards strewn before me, but most were unrecognizable as their heads and limbs were missing.

Acolytes, whose robes were once a brilliant shade of gold but now were stained a dark crimson, laid askew on the marble steps. Behind them, outlines of others were scattered along the floor inside the colonnade. Contents from my stomach made their way up, and I grabbed the trunk of a nearby tree to steady myself as I retched.

The temple, once white and sparkling like a star itself, was now black and gray from ash that floated in the sky and from the soft billows of smoke escaping from within. The edges of the marble roof were now dingy in color as a dusting of ash coated the faces and images within the temple's relief.

I rose to my unsteady feet.

My mind raced as I looked around to see if any of the bodies stirred, hoping for a single survivor. The horses were gone, and the carts and carriages were overturned and broken. The carriage meant for my sister was now burned; only a skeleton of the metal mechanisms and frame were left.

I tried calling out, but my throat was scorched from inhaling the smoke.

"Aurora! *Aurora*!"

My scream was a whisper. No one returned my cries. I yelled for anybody in the wild who might hear. I searched through the bodies to see if any were Ora, or perhaps even Sury. Some of the bodies had been cut brutally and left unrecognizable.

But I knew I'd recognize my sister and her golden hair from the masses.

The world became dizzy as I fell to the ground and began to weep.

Each tear rolled through the floating ash on my face, which settled like snowflakes. I yelled to the sky and cried enough tears to fill streams and rivers.

In my mind's eye, I saw dark rolling clouds above. Lightning struck in all directions before the clouds finally dissipated and allowed the bright sun to shine once more.

I wept until exhaustion overtook me and returned me to that sweet darkness from before.

***

A cool breeze sweetly greeted my hot skin and sent goose-bumps down my spine. I fluttered my eyes open and lifted my head to see if my surroundings had changed. If it had just been a terrible nightmare inspired by something I had read from a book.

The smoke from the ruins, now minimal, still flowed in the breeze. Once again, I felt a sharp sting in my hand. I forced it open with a gasp. A soft *thud* amongst the leaves on the ground caught my attention. Looking down, I saw where I had dropped Ora's necklace, the white stone now covered in shades of rusted red and gray ash.

Numbly, I clasped the chain around my neck. Its weight felt unbearably heavy against my exhaustion as I tucked the stone inside the bodice of my riding dress. The skirts were torn and caked with mud and giants knew what else. The sleeves were ripped along my shoulders and forearms. Blurry memories flickered through my mind, reminding me how the dress had come to be so damaged.

Memories continued to phase in and out. Ones of fire, urthens, someone laughing in the distance. That memory was new. Or was it a self-made recollection? Thoughts swirled around images of small, blue, glittery orbs that were overshadowed by bright golden shapes of spears piercing through the forest.

Before I realized it, I found myself shuffling down the path the riding party had taken to reach the temple just the day before. Or what I hoped had only been a day.

On the ground, I found the blade of a dagger, broken at the hilt. I recalled the dagger I usually kept tucked inside my belt and faintly remembered I had lost it. Knowing I would have to make do with the piece I found, I tucked the blade into the belt around my dress.

I walked without thinking, without feeling. Small, sharp stings occasionally brought me back to reality when my uncovered feet found pebbles or thorns from a creeping vine. The sun was steadily setting behind me, and the forest grew darker and darker.

Neither the growl of my stomach nor the sound of creatures tucked within the forest broke me out of my mindless gait. The darker the forest became, the clearer my mind grew. Glimpses of the attack flashed, and images of Black Raiders tearing through camp began to haunt me.

Then there were the misshapen creatures that walked beside the Raiders like they were trained pets. Trained to kill. Our father used to tell us scary stories of the make-believe creatures to make us stay in bed. But I saw the creatures with my own eyes. Urthens were *real*.

If anyone had told me that a year ago, I would have laughed in their face. But recent events had begun to open my mind. What else could be true? Did Father know that urthens indeed existed? Did they roam the forest now?

I took a small, chalky swallow as I stopped in my tracks on the path. I listened for what felt like ages, hearing only bugs chattering and the occasional deer walking through the brush—or at least what I hoped were deer.

I felt the blade wobble unsteadily as I unsheathed it from my belt, as if it were struggling to survive. After a few deep breaths, I gathered my courage and shuffled forward.

I tried to analyze and understand what happened. It was all so fast. Images of Ora, the Black Raider, and smoke filled my mind. Phantom screams pierced my thoughts each time I tried to string together the events.

The laughter. The laughter was the most out of place of all the flashing images and scenes.

I became too distracted to notice a low-hanging branch, and it whipped me in the face. Marks swelled with drops of blood and fell from my face, making my eyes sting from the acute pain I felt.

The throbbing made me think of the wound Ora had endured as she fought. The Black Raider's body never *showed* blood as Ora attacked, nor was there any sign of him stopping or slowing down. Like the Raider was a ghost encased in armor and a helmet. How could a spirit wear mortal clothing and fight like that?

Then, glimpses of my own attack came to mind—the awe and sensation I felt, the quick zap of energy that coursed through my body, and the foreign feeling of a hot and cold *force* escaping my hands. Orbs, in iridescent, glittery shades of blue and silver, reminded me of a toy made from a soapy solution and a grooved, circular wand I saw outside of one of the toy workshops as a child.

The images of the attack replayed over and over, of how I tried to protect Ora from the relentless soldier. Something that felt oh so familiar but also distant.

Hours passed as I trudged alone along the forest path back to the castle. My grip never faltered on the broken hilt of the dagger. I barely remembered hearing the roar of the Dolock River as I crossed the bridge leading back to Grianmore. I didn't stop to rest—my body seemed to move on its own.

Shock, I thought. *This must be what shock feels like.*

Sounds of crickets and birds grew louder as I moved within the blackness. After some time, I began to see small beads of light escape behind the trees and their leaves.

My legs ached, and my feet were numb from walking all night in the cold, but my heart felt a sense of relief the moment I broke through the forest to the field that stood between me and the fortified city on the hill beyond.

CHAPTER 8

The gate was open bright and early to let the sentries patrol, and for villagers to come and trade at the markets. The dirt and ash all over my cracked feet and torn dress made me appear as if I was simply a vagabond seeking shelter at the nearest city. My hair had become unbound with various twigs and leaves woven in. Parts of my braid had become plastered to my forehead from the dried blood at my temple and shielded over my teal-colored eyes.

Hardly anyone looked in my direction, too afraid to help a vagrant. But being ignored wasn't anything unusual, even when I dressed in my finest.

If it was a normal day, I would have thoroughly enjoyed taking a stroll amongst the stone city on top of the hill. White clouds idly rolled by as birds flew and cawed above. Buildings of all shapes and sizes nestled against the stone and brick pavement.

Some structures were three buildings tall and adorned with rooftop gardens. Others were smaller and had flared roofs with brick fireplaces jutting out from the top.

My feet found every damn broken crevice on the stone pavement, adding new thin cuts and stings as I walked. At one of the local missions, a small woman in a thin, gray robe thrust a chunk of bread in my hand as she told me about the giants' blessing. I barely registered what the woman said as I devoured the bread before continuing my path.

The chatter from the streets slowly began to wane the further I walked. These houses were meant for the courts and Royal Advisors from other kingdoms when they visited Grianmore Castle. Each court member held their own land and was responsible for their small territory within Gria, but also had a private residence close to the castle for when court was called into session a few times a year.

Before each home there was a private gate that led into a garden beyond. Large trees grew as tall as or higher than the homes and cast a deep relief of shade to the ground below. The coolness the shadows gave was a stark comparison to the sunbaked stones I had just walked on through the markets.

Vines with various colored flowers had overgrown the fences, offering another layer of privacy for the homes within. Almost like each residence had their own secret garden. From the quietness on the road, one could hear the faint bubbling of a fountain.

A sense of grief passed over me as I looked up to the white and brown houses with matching flared roofs. I had only visited these houses a handful of times, when Ora and I would visit Sury's family. I idly wondered what the deceased court members had left behind in these homes.

As I rounded the corner of the street leading to the castle, my breath caught. Closest to the castle gates was the Anmathios residence. On the outside, the house looked just like the other houses, but I knew once you crossed through the privacy gate, it was like you were in another world.

Sury's father had a strong green thumb—especially for someone who never Wielded an ounce of magic. Trimmed bushes and shrubs lined the short stone walls of the terrace. Behind a wooden bench was a square stone container filled with small herbs and flowers that emitted a spicy scent into the air.

Next to another wooden bench was a small wall with vines that overflowed to the wooden floor and bloomed the most beautiful shade of orange flowers I had ever seen. Cushions and blankets lined the benches and floors to make one feel the utmost comfortable when sitting outside.

I lightly smiled at the memories of Ora and me visiting Sury when we were barely adolescents, curled up on pillows and eating garlicky bread. The memory began to fade as I walked by the Anmathios home and felt how eerily silent the house was. How eerily silent the whole street was. A pressure behind my eyes stung as I bit back the tears.

I trudged through the city at what felt like a snail's pace and finally reached the castle doors. The world around me was calm and unknowing of the events that had taken place just a day or so ago.

Guards stood at attention at the grand mahogany doors that were miniature compared to the great architecture behind them. It took generations to build what was now before me. I stood in awe of the limestone and clay brick walls that housed various towers, courtyards, and large battlements that could hold wagons and carts full of supplies.

"Excu—" I began, but my throat was still on fire. I could barely raise my voice above a hoarse whisper. I tried again. "Excuse me, guards. I need to get inside. There's been a catastrophe, and I need to alert whoever I can."

The two guards just stood there and looked at me in confusion. One of the guards, who had reddish blonde hair, looked at the other one before speaking. "Citizens are only allowed in by appointment, and we haven't received notice of appointments today."

I huffed in frustration and pulled back my hair to reveal my face. The swiftness made my head throb at the touch and sent a slight sting behind my eye.

"I am *Princess Ophelia*! Our riding party has been ambushed, and I need inside to form a search party for the missing *queen-to-be*! You're wasting time! Now let me in!"

The two guards raised their eyebrows in shock before quickly escorting me into the castle's front courtyard, muttering apologies for not recognizing me sooner. They quickly led me inside the walls, where I was greeted with a cooling breeze to ease the rising heat from the sun. The stone and marble floors were cool to the touch, and I noticed tiny smears of bloody footprints trailing behind me.

One of the guards swiped a towel from a nearby closet to wipe the small trail while handing me a clean cloth to wipe off my feet, as a Healer was called. One of Nescoe's neophytes worked quickly to wrap my feet in bandages before I declined any offers for further inspection, desperate to get inside to talk to the Captain of the Guard.

We continued walking the halls. Bright light beamed through the stained glass windows from the sun shining above. Crafted wooden pillars also radiated the light and emitted a small amount of warmth from soaking in the rays. Through a series of doors and hallways, we finally reach the room that Aurora had set to be the meeting place for her court business. A massive buzz of people talking and moving quickly around the hall caught my attention first.

Down the massive wooden table, where I'd sat with my sister just days before, were spread an array of maps and papers. Lord Vovias leaned over one of the maps with Priestess Ariadne, both unscathed and unharmed from the attack.

I sighed in relief to see that part of Ora's court was still intact and that the two appeared to already be in deep conversation about a rescue for the princess.

"Lord! Priestess! Oh giants, it is so good to know you two are okay!" I ran to greet them, elated to provide any assistance I could to find Ora.

Vovias and Ariadne looked up from their map with shocked looks on both of their faces. Ariadne rounded the corner of the table quickly and clasped my hands into her own. She looked deeply into my eyes with coldness and concern, causing my chest to feel a heavy hum.

"You're not hurt?" Ariadne asked before letting go of my trembling hands and touching her own jeweled necklace.

"Only a few cuts and bruises, but I'll manage," I said before a servant quickly placed a goblet of cold water in my hand. I took long, soothing sips, instantly feeling the fire in my throat subside.

Vovias held the same scowl that always plastered his face. He rolled up the parchment that once held his attention and turned to face us. "What happened? What do you remember? Where is the princess?"

I steadily drew in a breath, trying to recollect the events that took place while calming my nerves. Ariadne poured me another glass of water from a pitcher nearby and encouraged me to drink. The liquid continued to cool the fire burning inside me and slowly helped reduce the dull ache in my head.

"Ora and I were in our tent, waiting for the ceremony to begin. A Black Raider with a silver insignia on his chest came into the tent to grab Ora. He had a..." I couldn't bear to say what else I saw, unless I wanted them to think I was mad. Surely,

I saw the damn thing on a leash, right? "I cut the canvas for us to escape and we made a good distance, but the Raider caught up to us. Ora tried what she could to fend him off. I tried stopping him, but I woke up on the forest floor surrounded by smoke..."

I took another sip of water, letting the night's images replay in my mind. Vovias and Ariadne looked at one another with a spark in their eyes.

"...when I awoke, everything had been set on fire. Bodies everywhere and smoke came from the temple where I thought... I thought *you* had been attacked?" I looked at Ariadne, who was staring at me. Her eyes narrowed.

"The question is, *princess,*" Ariadne leaned in close, mere inches from my face, "how did *you* survive?"

I looked at her in confusion. Surely, the blood loss was making my thoughts fuzzy.

Then reality hit me harder than the Black Raider's sword hit my temple. Two of the highest members of the court were here. No one in the city seemed aware that their princesses had been attacked, let alone that their future queen was missing.

I looked around the room, to the people who were talking and sharing notes on bits of parchment, not recognizing anyone around me. No one seemed like they were ready to make war or even a rescue mission. They walked about as if nothing urgent was happening and paid me no mind.

I tried recalling if I had indeed seen the bodies of *all* the court, but I couldn't remember the faces I *did* see.

Vovias leaned in close beside Ariadne, looking at me from head to toe, analyzing. The look in his eye forced my stomach to sour. He cleared his throat and spoke louder than necessary when speaking to someone directly. "Ophelia! *You* are a traitor! You orchestrated these events to overpower your very own sister! You've always been jealous that she was more powerful than you. This was your way of getting back at her for all the years you failed at *everything*!"

With each word, he got closer until he too was mere inches from my face.

I could make out every line and wrinkle in his aging face and the faint smell of smoke lingering in his hair. Fine lines of red pulsed inside the irises of his exceptionally bright blue eyes.

"NO! I would *never*!" I yelled frantically in confusion. "I would never do something like this to my own blood! *My own sister*!"

Vovias leaned in closer and spoke barely above a whisper. "It's a shame, really, that those fucking *urthen* things didn't finish you off. What good was it for them to bring the nasty creatures if they didn't finish the job?" A cruel smile plastered across his face.

Before I could speak, the very air I tried to breathe escaped. My chest began to tighten as I started clawing at my throat for air. Dark shadows crept along the corners of my eyesight.

Ariadne's curled hand held steady in front of me, pointed in my direction. She pulsed her fingers inward, tighter and tighter, working to steal more of my breath through her magic.

A strange magic I had never experienced nor felt before—that I didn't even know existed.

Fear pulsed deep within my stomach, and I started to panic.

A stinging sensation, like feeling the touch of static, rolled through every nerve ending, bone, and muscle in my body. Without any warning, a bright light flashed, and the static feeling ended as a deep wave of air expanded my lunges.

When I opened my eyes, I saw everyone in the room hunched over, shielding themselves from the light that came and went faster than the blink of an eye. Looking down, I found both Vovias and Ariadne looking terrified as they crouched close to the floor.

Ariadne lowered her shaking hand and looked into my eyes with a mix of icy terror and fear that quickly swapped to anger and wrath.

"Grab her, you fools!" she yelled as she struggled to get to her feet, like something was holding her down.

Without a second thought, I turned and ran from the room, slightly slipping with the bandages on my feet. The dull ache in my muscles and pain in my feet disappeared as I ran through the hallways, up the stone stairs, and across the banister walkway.

Fresh blood from the cracks in my feet seeped through the bandages, but still, I ran. I mustered any strength I could to hold myself upright as I raced across the freshly polished wooden floors before I found the door to my room down the hall.

I barreled inside and put the heavy metal lock in place. With difficulty, I managed to push the edge of my wooden dresser in front of the door just enough to block any intruders, buying all the time I could.

Scanning the large room, I found a pair of spare leather riding boots and stockings to cover my aching feet. Any other time, I would have put these items in the changing room near my bed—but this once, I silently thanked the giants for my messiness.

Faint shouting from the guards' commands could be heard from down the hall as they searched each room.

I crossed over to my bookshelf, overfilled with books and trinkets, and opened a small box that contained a pouch full of coins. I tied the small pouch to my belt and eyed another fortune of a spare cloak that was strewn across a chaise beside the bed.

Maybe the giant's blessings were indeed real.

A wave of a floral scent tickled my nostrils as I opened the glass doors to my personal balcony. The stone archway gave way to the railing that jutted outward over the royal gardens. I looked over the rail to plot my escape, but the sheer depth of the drop to the rocky ground by the garden wall below nearly made my stomach flip.

This can't be the end. This can't be the end.

I ran back into the room, looking for alternative ways to defend myself.

Then I remembered it. Beside my bookshelf, there was a large tapestry that hung on the wall.

A beautiful young king, riding into the meadow of his kingdom during the night. His hair was black as a raven, and his pale skin basked in the moonlight. The threads were made with the richest of colors and held their vibrant hues through all the years it had been in my room.

I didn't know how long it had been there, but it had always hung in this very spot for as long as I could remember.

The critical part was the door hidden behind the fabric. As delicately as I could, I lifted a corner and found the hidden door to a tunnel, half my height, that I prayed would lead me to safety.

The wooden door was old and barely big enough for a grown man to crawl through. I dropped to my hands and knees and pushed the door slightly ajar in hopes it would not make a scraping sound against the stone floor. Dust hit my nostrils, and I tried to stifle a sneeze as I pushed forward and into the small, crowded space.

The tapestry brushed back in place as it was before. With delicate force, I was able to close the door behind me and laid as still as I could to slow my breathing.

One giant's blessing. Two giants' blessings. Three...

The dark instantly took hold as I felt the air steadily growing warm around me.

As I began to crawl forward, a loud crash echoed from the room on the outside, and I jumped, hitting my head on the too-shallow ceiling. I quickly covered my mouth so I wouldn't scream from both the commotion and the scrape I'd just gained. Dust caked my forehead from the sweat and blood, both new and old.

Guards yelled various commands as they tore through the room. I heard furniture turned over, trinkets thrown, and what I could only imagine was the fabric of the bed being torn from a blade. Footsteps inched closer to where the tapestry hung but passed as they made their way to the balcony.

A man shouted, and the commotion stopped.

Faintly, I heard two men speak but couldn't make out the words.

One I knew for certain was Vovias from the snide tone alone. The complete snarl of betrayal in his voice sent a shiver down my spine.

That fucking asshole. A new layer of hatred for him was added to the never-ending list.

"The drop from the balcony should have killed her. Go check the gardens! She would have to be injured. Find her and kill her."

I bit into my palm to stop myself from crying from the emotional and physical pain, but mostly from the betrayal. My breathing gradually slowed as the thin air in the tiny tunnel felt like it couldn't sustain me for much longer. Despite the tingling in my head, I willed myself to stay still and breathe steadily.

Even after the guards left, I stayed there. Image after image of what happened—from the forest to the betrayal that took place in my damn own home—flashed through my mind. What was happening, and *why*?

Why are they working with *the Black Raiders of Dokvalon? If Ora was dead, who would take the seat if I could not?* I couldn't allow myself to ponder this further. Not until I had proof that my sister was dead.

No. They couldn't be working with the Raiders, right? We'd been enemies with Dokvalon for as long as I could recall.

Silence filled my ears, aside from my own heartbeat. Time slipped by as I continued to lay there and stare at the nothing in front of me, recounting the last handful of hours in all the details I could remember.

After what felt like enough time had passed, I slowly flexed my fingers and wiggled my toes, trying to muster any life into them I could.

Inch by inch, I brought awareness back to my body. It was time to move. Time to run.

As slowly as I could, I made my way into a crawling position, careful not to scrape my head again, and pushed forward slowly in case anyone could hear movement from inside the walls.

Inch by painstaking inch, I finally came to a halt when the other wooden door came into view, dimly illuminated around the edges from a light source on the other side. I pressed an ear lightly to the wood and listened for any movement on the other end. It felt like forever when I finally reasoned with myself that it was safe and slowly opened the door to another heavy tapestry.

I let a few more heartbeats pass me by as I listened for any signs of visitors that might be lurking. Then I opened it further and peeked around the heavy fabric.

Ora's room was still pristine, as if she had just left to go on a stroll somewhere.

Across the ceiling were ornate designs that matched her gold-inlay wooden bed and night table. Her dressers and miniature bookshelves held tiny baubles, gifts from local glass blowers and merchants, all hoping to find favor with an up-and-coming queen.

I rose from all fours to stand, feeling every ache in my bones, and groaned from my joints shouting in protest. I turned around to view the guarding tapestry behind me, the opposite of the one that hung in my room.

This tapestry beheld a large sun, filled with ancient symbols from the Olden Language that had been forgotten in time. Images of flowers in different stages of growth were brought to life by the large sun above. The golden threads were just as vibrant and glowing as the threads of the stars in my own room.

The sun outside had already begun to tuck itself behind the fields and snow-capped mountains in the distance as I briskly walked to Ora's changing chambers, the night sky taking over. I stripped off the torn and dirty riding dress before raiding the wardrobe and donned a pair of riding pants and a black tunic. I sent a light curse to the giants above for Ora having a considerably smaller waist than me.

I had always wished I had the same small structure as her and not the softer build I was given, especially at this moment when I desperately needed something to fit. Thankfully, the tunic was flowy enough to give my ample chest the space it needed.

Once Ora's necklace was safely tucked inside the tunic, I put the coin pouch and broken dagger in the pocket of the cloak.

I tiptoed quietly in my riding boots over to the balcony doors to see if there was an easier way to escape than the collection of rocks that were at the base of mine.

The balcony was almost identical to my own but hidden around the soft curve of the castle walls. Surely, if Ora could meet Sury in the gardens with their *undetected* rendezvous, then she had to have some way of regularly escaping her room—*safely*.

I'd never told her that I knew of her schemes and gladly looked the other way so she wouldn't get in trouble if they were ever caught. But I also just so happened to redirect any member of the Royal Court, or our own parents, to another part of the castle when I knew Ora was in the gardens.

Looking around the marble stone pillars, I saw the same ornate chairs, tables, and large vases that mirrored the ones to my own.

How in the world did she manage this? I wondered as I tried hard to think like my sister. I inspected each piece of furniture and could not figure out how Ora could safely sneak about the way she did. In the corner of the balcony was a series of large vases that held an array of flowers and shrubs. An empty one set next to the balcony railing, strangely by itself.

My eyes immediately rolled as I saw a piece of cloth tied tightly to one end of the railing and other bits of tied cloth placed inside the vase. "You sneaky rat. But how in the world did you climb back up?"

Inch by inch, I inspected the handmade rope Ora used to trail down the side of the castle and into the garden below. The rope dangled just above a shrub, which was a quick drop from the rope's frayed end. Sucking in a breath of air for good luck, I held onto the rope tightly and swung my legs over the railing, cloak tucked in tight under my arm.

Fire ripped through my hands as they resisted the dry cloth and the plunge down. Blood trickled from my palms from the burn. I steadied my weight and feet against the castle walls. I bit on my lip, trying to hold in my gasps and be mindful that my boots would not make a sound louder than a slight tap when the leather met the stone.

After a short eternity, my feet finally touched the ground below. I kissed the ground in thanks to the giants and inspected the fabric burns and cuts that had turned my hands cherry red. In the distance, soft murmuring grew louder as guards walked along in the garden during their nightly rounds.

Shouts in the distance plucked me from my thoughts as I continued to make my way through the garden. Deeper I went toward a wall of tightly grown evergreens, where I found a door I knew existed but had never explored.

The door was part of the securing wall that enclosed the castle, and it was overgrown with vines. The hinges were rusted from years of not being used or attended to. With great effort, I finally wiggled the rusted locking mechanism out of place and pulled hard on the metal handle.

Beyond the door and its wall was a vast field that went as far as the eye could see when the day's sun shone down, until it met the mountains in the distance.

But at night, it was an endless abyss of dark, illuminated just enough by the moon to see a few feet ahead at a time.

"Where do I go?" I whispered to myself. Everything I knew that had once felt safe was behind me. Now I didn't know what lurked behind those walls or wanted to see me dead.

But ahead of me was purely *nothing*. Just darkness and the faint glow of the waning moon above me. I scanned around the vastness and the castle walls as I tried to decide quickly where to run. My head swiveled as I noticed the moon's path on the ground and how it strangely lit up a part of Bainas Forest.

"I could start there. See where that could lead me," I said to no one. I needed to figure out how to rescue Ora—even if that rescue was done only by me. Figure out who was involved in the attack. Find allies.

My thoughts and courage grew as I took a step forward. I knew I would need to run wide into the field before making the slight semicircle to run on the outside of Grianmore's gates and walls. To head back to where everything started.

I threw on my cloak and fastened it tight before running as fast as my heart allowed across the field, back to the forest from where I emerged just hours ago.

When my life had completely changed.

CHAPTER 9

The trail was more treacherous than I remembered.

As my awareness returned, I couldn't fathom how I'd made it back to the castle barefoot. I also hadn't noticed how many damn rocks and roots jutted from the ground when we'd ridden through on horseback.

Occasional limbs and vines snagged against my hair, causing strands of my redone braid to loosen and stick to my dirt-caked face.

Creatures of the forest scurried past and paid no mind to me as I ran as fast as I could down the trail. I silently prayed to any giant that would hear my pleas not to let an urthen cross my path.

I wouldn't know what to do then.

Maybe the giant Ednos could bless the earth for me and toss away every loose rock in the path. Or maybe Guean, the giantess of the air, could do me a solid and give me a cooling breeze to refill my lungs. If the celestial twins, Aksyn or Nyska—mostly just Nyska's moon—could illuminate my path just a smidge, I could swerve around the low-hanging thorny vines that were ripping through my skin.

Even if something formidable crossed my path, I knew my small blade would be of no use, no matter the training I had—which wasn't very much to begin with since I usually skipped those sessions. My legs screamed for mercy to stop running. It would have been wise of me to keep to those training lessons with Hanovan instead of passing them off for my *studies...* The studies that usually included me burying my nose in some sort of book either deep within the library or curled up in my bed with my favorite sweets.

Each stride tightened the strain in my weak muscles until a sharp pain pierced my lower back, causing me to fall to the ground with a hard *thud*. I muffled a groan as I gritted my teeth and pulled myself back to standing. My blistered feet yelled in protest as each tendon and ligament caught fire from the strain of overuse. The palms of my hands had become thick with gravel and bits of twigs that felt sharp as knives.

I quietly thanked the giants above that I at least had shoes this time. Hopefully, the giant Iasis of Healing could grant me just a twinge of relief. I so wished I was as nimble as the dancers I watched at the theater instead of finding every knobbed root within the forest floor.

Alone.

I was absolutely alone and in the dark. I couldn't remember the last time I had felt this alone. I had always felt a sense of being an outsider but never truly isolated—Ora always did a good job with that. Standing absolutely still, I listened to the surroundings for any following footsteps or hooves coming down the trail.

Or anything worse.

Silence. Complete silence. I noticed that even the wind had ceased to stir around me.

My next step forward sent another shock wave of pain through the muscles that went deep into my back and down the backs of my thighs. I caught myself on a nearby tree and muffled a scream of pain. Agony ricocheted within my body and the unused muscles. Desperately, I tried to move, but my body resisted. Tremors vibrated up and down my legs, causing them to feel like bags of stone.

"Any fucking time, Iasis. Any relief will do!" I called out to the giant, practically begging.

Anger and frustration coursed through my mind, but I would reprimand myself another time. I had to keep going. Get far away from the place I once called home.

Using each tree as a leaning post, I staggered forward, continuing to follow the path to where I last saw my sister at the Rising Temple. It was risky, but I needed any clue I could find to understand what had happened—to piece the puzzle together.

My feet betrayed me once again as my ankles buckled.

I felt the anger swell and fill my chest and practically ignite a heat within me. With clenched eyes and fists, I beat the ground beneath me. I pounded the ground with all the energy I could spare. Small stones and whatever else that laid on the forest floor embedded into my skin, causing new scrapes and blooms of blood.

My anger turned into rage. My body turned numb to the old and new pain it endured. I beat and beat onto the ground, screaming until my voice turned hoarse.

I hardly noticed the sparks of various shades of electric blues flying into the air around me, like a blacksmith causing sparks to fly when hammering across an anvil.

I gasped as the light ignited around me and tried to see the person who'd thrown their Wielding toward me. I thanked the giants again for protecting me as I scrambled to my knees and quickly wiped away strands of loose hair from my face to see my attacker.

I fumbled for the broken dagger as I steadied myself on my feet. "Who's there?" I called out, but was greeted only by a songbird in a nearby tree. I frantically looked around, desperate to find a glimpse of anyone within the trees.

Then I felt it. The pulse deep in my hands.

A moonbeam peered down through the tree canopy and rested silently on my aching, empty palm. Little orbs of different shades and hues of blue and silver danced and slipped through my fingers, like tiny stars swimming in circles.

The sight left me in awe. I quickly sheathed the dagger and took a few steps toward a large sycamore, sliding down the rough bark and resting my aching back against its deep base. I brought my hands in closer, cupping them side by side, close to my face, as I inspected the tiny orbs of energy that continued to dance in my palms.

Each orb moved and radiated light, like a small waltz. I felt a strange pull within me that I had never experienced before. One that was felt deep within my core.

A steady hum was felt through me as the orbs continued to spin together and intertwine, holding their light and energy steady. Pulsing as if they were breathing.

I took a finger and tried to caress one of the orbs floating above my palm. The little orb jumped with what looked like excitement and twirled itself around my finger. It grew longer until it wrapped itself neatly around my hand like a bandage.

The sensation was both warming and cooling, like jumping into a lukewarm bath on a hot summer day as a child. I couldn't *feel* the orbs themselves, but I could feel a constant pull from them, like my hands were being led to magnets. The ache within my hands slowly dissipated.

Without thinking, my hand found its way to the cuts on my head from the injury I received in my attempt to help Ora. A small, steady stream of cooling entered my skull and dulled the ache little by little.

Surprise filled me again as I touched my forehead, feeling for the cut I knew was there, but I found nothing on my skin other than dried blood.

"*What* is this?" I gasped as I saw the light fading from one hand but still bright in the other.

Instinct told me to take the orbs that still shone brightly and place them on my lower back. The same cooling sensation crept along the strained and pulled muscles, allowing the sharp pain to disappear.

Looking to the heavens above, I let out a silent prayer of thanks to Iasis and sighed out relief.

At a distance, something snapped along the forest floor. I pushed myself harder into the trunk, shielding the fading light of my hands deep into my cloak.

Tales of urthens used to be far-fetched, simply ghost stories, but now they were tales come to life. I didn't know if urthens roamed this part of the continent or stuck to the dividing Shadowcraig Mountains between the realms of Gria and Dokvalon.

Could urthens sense magic? Sniff out a Wielder? Usually, stories and legends held some morsel of truth, but never once did I hear if urthens could do anything else aside from using their vicious teeth.

Silence again. I counted to one hundred before slowly rising from my spot and scanning the surroundings the best I could in the dark. As quietly and quickly as I could, I tiptoed around the tree and away from the main path.

I'll find another way to the temple, I thought as adrenaline pulsed through my veins. Maybe someone from the castle had followed me.

I felt a small sense of renewal now that the array of aches were minimal or gone.

Determined to get to the temple before daylight, I set out to find what I was looking for—then I would plan.

CHAPTER 10

The smell of smoke was undeniable and still clinging to the air when I finally found my way back to the ruined camp. Charred bits of wood and cloth made the scene appear as if it were war-torn.

To my surprise, the bodies that had been left lying on the ground were now gone, but a large pile of burnt wood and bone remained in the middle of the camp. I fought the urge to puke and stifled a cry as I thought of all the innocent people that were there to support my sister, now massacred.

Who did this to the bodies? Was this for honor or something more sinister? Each thought caused nausea to roll in my stomach.

As the light quickly rose against the trees, I scanned the area and the temple but saw and heard no one. Checking behind each tree as I went, I made my way to the half-burnt tent that we had shared that night.

I stepped onto the burnt remnants of clothing and furniture, and ash puffed upwards and into my nostrils, causing me to sneeze in a fit. I wafted my hand back and forth to clear the cloud and looked around to see what may have survived the fire.

The trunks we had brought were half intact next to the ramshackle bed frames. Bits of ash and leaf clung to my hands as I dropped to all fours to check under the frames for any item that might be of some use.

Two books I had brought with me were untouched by the fire, but one had pages that were destroyed or missing and would do me no good. I placed that book back on the ground and wiped off the ash from the cover of the other book in my hand, then froze.

My heart beat like a hummingbird as I peered down at the old, worn leather of the book I had read that night. It was practically untouched and barely had any evidence that it was even around a fire. I fumbled through the pages and found the binding still very much intact. My fingers skimmed through the pages and landed on the shadowy image that caused my breathing to falter.

I felt the same pull as before. Something within the pages called to me, and I forced my fingers to the page. Before I realized what I was doing, my fingertips caressed the image of the dark figure. I took a quick breath and quickly snapped the book shut, feeling my eyes regain focus.

I hadn't noticed that my surroundings had strangely turned gray as the sun's rays illuminated the charred tent. I checked it again and found my small, palm-sized dagger on the floor and attached it to the cord that wrapped around my tunic. Good—two daggers now.

"Phase one, done. Now to find a safe place for rest before I trek forward," I mumbled to myself and stepped away from the tent.

A snap echoed to my right. I pivoted quickly but found the head of an arrow pointed at me, aiming for my heart.

Sury stood a mere ten feet away with the arrow pulled tight against his bow.

"Sury!" I gasped. Relief flooded through me. I never saw who was killed in the raid and never had the opportunity to check the bodies before someone burned them. I felt the tears prickle at seeing him in the flesh.

Good. I have at least one ally.

"Did *you* do it like they said?" He spat, eyes burning with anger. "Did you set up Ora so you could steal her throne?" Each word grew angrier as he pulled the bowstring tighter.

Well, I thought he was an ally.

A tear escaped and fell down my ash-covered face, the reassurance suddenly escaping and turning into what felt like the beginning of despair.

"What?" Disbelief took root as I shook my head. "I would never. You know I don't care about the throne!" I swallowed hard as I watched his now-shaking hand.

Sury strained as he held his aim steady, his neck visibly tense. "How did you survive the attack then? They were after you both. I saw it. Then you were both gone." His eyes practically grew black as his hand shook more and he yelled, "How long have *you* been working with Dokvalon? You know you could have just come to her. She would have given you anything you asked for!"

Droplets of his spittle splashed on my cheek.

The book I held dropped to the ground as I slowly raised my shaking hands to the air. "We were *both* attacked by a Black Raider," I said calmly like I was trying not to scare a forest cat, keeping my eye on his arrow. "We ran into the woods, and I tried to help Ora escape, but I was hit in the head. The next thing I remember, I woke up on the forest floor. I swear it, Sury! You know me." I prayed he did.

Sury's eyes grew wild. "I don't see signs of a head injury." More spittle sprayed as he continued to talk through his clenched teeth, his knuckles white from holding his stance for so long. "Are you involved with Dokvalon? Answer me truthfully."

"No! I would never," I gasped as I felt the fear rising. Seeing Sury not only question me but also be willing to hold a bow so close broke my heart. I glanced at my raised hands. How could I explain something I so barely understood for myself?

"...And I think I healed myself? Just hours ago." I still couldn't believe the words that were coming out of my own mouth.

Sury scoffed. "Your magic isn't that strong. I've seen it. I've known you for a long time, Ophelia."

Fear crept within me as I worried his arrow would release, even if by accident.

"Sury, I can't explain it. I..." Realization hit. A thought struck me. It was a dangerous risk, but if I were to die, then I would have to know something first. "Wait, how did *you* survive?" Sury swallowed hard, the arrow shaking from his strain. "You're with Vovias and Ariadne. I thought you loved Ora! I thought we were friends! Why?"

"Don't you dare twist this on me. I *do* love Ora!" he spat. "I only just found out about *your* failed coup when you ran from the meeting hall. I tried calling after you right before Ariadne approached me and told me *you* were behind this."

My coup? He can't be serious.

Sury dropped his hands to ease his draw. The sun rose higher, exposing the dark circles under his tired eyes, the deep browns weary from fatigue.

"What is happening? Where is she?" he croaked as he tilted his head toward the sun's rays. A small tear escaped his eyes and left a small trail down his face.

Sadness ached harder within my chest for not only my missing sister but also for Sury. I had never seen him cry in all the years of knowing him, nor ever seen him so vulnerable. Until now. I lowered my hands and, in a few short steps, found myself embracing him as we both began to weep.

"What do you remember?" My words were caught in a pleading whisper.

Sury inhaled deeply, steadying his breathing. It looked like he was willing his tears to ease and dry. He pulled away and turned to hide his face as he wiped it with his cloak. Dirt and ash still coated his face and hair when he turned back to face me.

"I was sitting at my campfire when the Raiders came through. I had my sword nearby and tried making my way to Ora's tent, but there were too many, and they came in so fast." He held back a rage-filled sob. "Behind them were foot soldiers. All of them were impervious to the sword, like they were the walking dead. And then those creatures..."

He took another gulp of air before continuing. "The tent was on fire but then I saw her on the back of the Black Raider's horse before I could move. It was over so quickly. I couldn't find you and thought you might have escaped with some of the servants who made it back..."

I nodded, understanding. "Who else survived?"

"No one. I saw Healer Nescoe take a blade through the throat, then I saw Lady Samolson's head strung in those trees and her body on another. I can only assume Lady Simret's body made it to that pile." He pointed to the burn pile that was still smoldering. "Because she never returned."

Sury continued, "I raced back to the palace with the remaining horses as quickly as I could to create a rescue plan with the Royal Guard. When I found Vovias and Ariadne, they locked me out of the meeting hall. They said that *stronger* leaders needed to devise a plan, not a busted court with no power in their name or hands. Nothing a *Veik* could provide."

It was obvious that the sting went deep. Anger crept across Sury's face as he clenched his jaws tight.

Wrath burned deep within my belly, causing me to see red. "And they are making everyone believe that *I* did this? That I'm somehow in throes with a kingdom we've kept a distance with for decades? That's why they were shocked when I walked in." I said that last part more to myself. "They *hoped* that I had died. They *wanted* me to die. But why?" Each word made my chest burn in the familiar rage I felt before.

"That night, Vovias was stunned that I was still standing after the attack. I thought it was just my shock at first. I tried getting them to look for you, but Ariadne swore she saw you escape the attack on the back of a horse with a Raider. Wrong, of course, by the looks of you," he said with a light laugh.

I looked again at my palms. "I'm beginning to suspect that Ariadne was wrong about a lot of things." My gaze snapped up. "How could you believe them? After everything?"

Shame crested his face as Sury adjusted himself on his feet. He picked up the bow he had let fall to the ground, placing the arrow back into the quiver that was strapped tight across his chest. A short sword was sheathed to his belt. A phantom wind billowed through his dark cloak, revealing other daggers that hung close to his vest.

"I'm assuming your arsenal is for me?" I let out a cautious chuckle and smiled.

Sury replied with a smirk, "Unfortunately. I thought you really had betrayed Ora. Especially when I saw you run from Grianmore."

"But why?" The insult poured into a deep wound inside my heart.

"Vovias told me what he said they knew... I didn't think them to be true, but I fell into the lies. They were so...convincing." Sury brought his gaze up to mine. A soul-wrenching sadness weighed heavily on his face. "I'm so sorry, Phe. I've let you and your sister down. I was just so consumed in finding her that I just..."

"I forgive you." It was true. I knew how easily words and lies could etch deep within one's soul. "But," I started as I took a step his way and threw my fist as hard as I could into Sury's shoulder. The immediate sting in my wrist made me instantly regret the decision, but seeing the pain registering on Sury's face made me glad I did it. "That's for fucking doubting me, Sury Anmathios."

Sury rubbed his shoulder hard as he winced. "Point taken." He rubbed it once more. "Damn, you have a mean throw, but we need to work on your form. You'll break your wrist in no time with that mess."

I ignored his remark, even if he did have a point.

"Did you burn them?" I asked as I pointed to the pile of ash. Letting the bodies turn to ash was the proper way of setting a burial and not letting anything pick over the bones and sinew.

"Me?" He looked at me, bewildered. "I've been following you through the woods this whole time. I thought *you* did this." He turned to the pile, gesturing the smoke billowing in the air.

I frantically looked around the woods for anyone who might have stuck around. Surely the Black Raiders didn't honor the dead in this way, with how they obliterated the camp. Never mind thinking through the fact I had been followed by Sury since I ran from Grianmore.

Who else could have followed?

I turned to face Sury and noted the frustration building inside him just as he shouted at the heavens and unsheathed the sword at his side. He closed in on a nearby tree and struck it violently, releasing pent-up rage with each blow. I didn't dare try to stop him. Sury finally let out a long sigh and looked up again to the sky. Under his breath, he whispered a prayer and made a motion to his head and chest twice.

I stood in silence as I watched his breathing flow to a calming rhythm. I could only imagine the anguish he was feeling in knowing Ora was taken.

"So," he sighed again, still looking up toward the sun peeking through the tree canopy. "Two against what? Vovias? A whole kingdom?"

I rocked back and forth on my feet. No evidence of the sharp pain in my lower back. "This is our play," I said as I walked over to the dusty book that I had previously dropped.

"What is it?"

I turned to the page that had caught my attention the night of the attack. The shadowy creature in the cloudy vortex stared back at me, its white eyes glowing against the pages. "The Ancient One," I said without looking up from the page, my fingers tingling in response.

Sury shook his head and scoffed as he sheathed his sword at his hip. "That's just a ghost story, Phe. A tale told to scare children away from talking to strangers—to make them think that if they did, they might unleash a beast that would cause terror in their town."

"But where do tales like these come from?" I placed the book inside my cloak pockets. "Stories, folk tales, myths? They all derive from a kernel of truth. Look at the damn urthens! They were once ghost stories, too. Now we know full and well that they are indeed real."

"Fucking scary, too," Sury muttered.

"I thought about it as I *escaped* the castle...not *ran* from it." I cut him a look before continuing. "If the urthens are real, then why can't this be?"

"If this was real, how would this ghost, this *Ancient One,* even help us? Help defeat whatever it is Vovias and Ariadne have planned from all this?"

"By doing just that—defeating them."

"But we don't even know what the Ancient One is, other than remnants from a story."

"We have to try something! See if we can find what other Wielders might know. See if the Three Sisters know. See how we might be able to conjure it."

Sury's eyes grew big in surprise. "The Three Sisters are zealots! Their following are full of fanatics! We can go to my father and then write a letter to Beralt for help since he wasn't here. He has the second largest army in this realm. If we explain what's going on, he might be able to help! Take action *now*. Not put stake in a *story*!"

"It's not like I can just waltz to Lord Beralt's or your father's estates! If Vovias and Ariadne easily spread lies within my sister's own court and overpowered her with their deception, what do you think they might be able to do with the surviving and upcoming lords and ladies of Gria?"

"My father knows you and Ora like he knows me. He has governed Zonnagberg, the fourth largest city in Gria. He provided asylum from those who escaped the northern bordering realm of Mercyth that is unkind to Wielders. That is Anmathios territory. He still has loyal bannermen..."

"How do we know he's even alive?" I hated asking the question, but knowing just how close our families were, I wouldn't be surprised if he had been attacked, too.

Sury shook his head as I continued. "We hold off on their estates until we know more. We need something that will overtake Vovias without question." Another idea hit me. "If they tried turning your loyalty against me, a sister in spirit, then they'll throw slander against your name, too. The lover that sullied Ora from marrying a prince or king from another kingdom. Oh, don't look shocked as if you two hid it so well! If Vovias and Ariadne were truly clever, they would tell the entire kingdom that we betrayed her and wanted her throne! Would your father truly help with that kind of knowledge?" I spat out the last sentence.

Sury shook his head, "I would never!"

"How do you think *I* felt when *you* questioned me? Her own damn sister!"

Sury looked down at the brown leather of his boots. "I am truly sorry for ever doubting you." He scanned the surrounding woods. "But the Three Sisters? No offense, but isn't their way of Wielding a little *unconventional*? They're lunatics, according to the temple priests and priestesses. Zonnagberg is overrun with pilgrims who seek an audience with them. The tenants always complained about the overpopulation during Father's open council meetings. How do we even know they have merit in what they say?"

I looked down at my hands and saw the phantom orbs in my mind's eye. "I'm not sure, but we have to try something. Gain any intelligence we can and gather help. Figure out a plan in the process on how to get Ora back." I refused to believe she was dead.

Sury chewed on the inside of his cheek, lost in thought. "Before we do anything, we need to get away from this temple. I half suspect Ariadne will send soldiers this way."

"How did you know when I would escape?"

"Simple. I waited for you to make a move and I followed you. You're not so inconspicuous yourself. I know about the tunnel between the two of your rooms. I've used it my-damn-self."

I rolled my eyes, not wanting to know more of Ora's and Sury's escapades.

"Can you make it another couple of miles?" Sury nodded toward the northeast.

"If it means life over death, yes."

"It might be a risk, but there's an inn in the village that's not too far from here."

"I'll risk anything right now. We're no good running on fumes." As if on cue, a large rumble escaped my stomach. "And we need food, I suppose."

Sury nodded and led the way toward a deer path, leaving the burned temple behind, occasionally stopping and listening for any movement. I was absolutely useless here in the forest and hated to rely so heavily on his tracking skills. I never had the chance to witness his home myself, but I knew his family came from a long line of warriors and hunters that could track their enemies for miles. His father always boasted about the lush vegetation and thick trees in the north that were abundant with wildlife.

I followed closely behind, exhaustion kicking into overdrive the further we went. My mind wandered aimlessly as my eyes bounced between the ground and Sury's back.

Arjun and Father always went hunting when the Anmath-ios family would visit for court, and Arjun was practically like an uncle to my mother—he served my parents proudly. When news of my father turning ill, and my mother soon after, reached his ears, Arjun became terribly heartbroken for them. For us.

Before my parents passed, I never had the chance to wonder why he suddenly gave up his council seat for Sury to take, even when Sury had years before his father's retirement. Arjun simply told his son that he was growing old and needed Sury to be there in his stead and left the matter at that.

I found it humorous, knowing Sury as he is now compared to the small boy he was when we first met. My mind drifted back to that day in court.

***

I was seven as I watched Sury, who was at least two years older than me, be officially introduced for the first time to court. I sat next to my father's side of the dais, analyzing the boy next to his father, the former clad in bright greens and blues, bowing sophisticatedly to the queen. As if he had practiced it a hundred times.

A soft giggle on the other side of the dais, next to the queen, escaped a little girl whose blonde curls dangled at her sides. She wore a soft yellow dress that was fit for royalty with its intricate needlework.

Ora pulled in her lips as tightly as possible so another giggle wouldn't escape. She smiled brightly at the boy, who in turn blushed and scowled. He caught my glance as I lightly waved with a wiggle of my fingers so others wouldn't see.

Most children were kept away from the public and prying eyes. So any child who was made public before Her Queen and His King was a welcome sight for both me and my sister. I always looked for a new friend, while she enjoyed a new plaything.

We were excited to leave as soon as we were dismissed so the court could discuss things we thought boring. Ora skipped to the young boy and took him by the arm, directing him to lead her to the gardens. I shook my head at her boldness and quietly followed behind them.

***

My foot stumbled against a rock, shaking me out of my reverie, but my mind drifted back to the comfort of childhood memories the further into the forest we moved.

Through the years, we three were inseparable. Our imaginations took us to new heights each time we played. Our wild tales grew more intricate, and our stories were fit for the fables. I smiled thinking about some of the silly games we used to play.

Each season, when Sury left with his father to attend to their appointed land in the north, it became harder for us to separate. We would send letters to one another until the next season of court politics.

We learned how to ride horses and the proper teachings of court involvement, the latter boring Ora to the verge of tears. A new memory surged into my mind.

***

A thirteen-year-old Ora was half asleep on the floor next to the fire in our favorite room of the royal library.

Sury had already closed his book and was carving his initials into the wood of the sofa that I sat on, nose-deep in a book about numerics and magical law.

"This isn't a good look coming from a future queen," I muttered behind my book as I turned the page.

Ora rolled her eyes and tossed her book down toward the one Sury had thrown an hour before. "I would rather go riding and visit that nearby village that makes those carrot sweetcakes. Plus, I have plenty of time to learn this before I actually ascend to the throne. Mother has decades before she passes. No rush in learning the subject matter today, you worm!*"*

I shot her a glare as I continued to read. I hated to be called a worm, Ora's new pet name for me when I was stuck inside a book.

"Remind me again," Sury asked without pausing his etching, "why you would be taking the throne over Phe? Your Wielding law confuses the peasant Veik like me." He spat the insults. "Priest Awgar is the absolute worst at explaining anything. The dust bag needs to retire."

Ora quickly glanced over to me, while I pretended I wasn't listening and squinted harder at the phantom word that I was reading.

"Well... It's a matter of magic," Ora said delicately. She knew this was a sensitive topic around me, even when I paraded that it meant nothing to me. "In our kingdom, whoever is born from the crown that has the highest strength in power is the heir to the throne. Not the birth order."

"Yeah, but I thought you two might have been close since no one in the court really addresses it?"

"A few years ago, when I tested, I achieved the sixth circle, just like our mother," she said even more quietly. "And..."

"And I, the sister that everyone *pities, has only achieved the* first," *I interjected before Ora could finish. "And poorly, too, might I add."*

"Phe, I don't pity..."

I hastily continued, "Ora here achieved the highest levels of practiced magic at her test—the celestials. The raw magic to harness forces to her will. And passed with an array of bright colors. Quite literally might I add," I spat. "Not only did she pass the highest possible test we're allowed to take but she has shown abilities to fully *control other Wieldings in the process. Not just minor control. Something, apparently, no one in the kingdom has ever seen. Not even our Mother."*

"But I thought Healers had access to controlling the Elementis of Wielding too?" Sury scratched his head, trying to recall what old Awgar might have mentioned.

"They have a small amount of elemental control, but even that can be flimsy. If they don't practice regularly, they are bound to lose control of that element. They cannot control an Elementis in its entirety as strongly as someone who specializes in that element," I stated matter-of-factly before I continued.

"For example: Lady Simret is the strongest earth Elementis Wielder in Gria. She took control of the Loamil Manor, over her grandfather, at the mere age of twelve when she simply commanded an entire failing crop of wheat to return to its full glory, and then some, that fed her region for seasons.

"She is strong in that alone. Healer Calton can Wield it, just not as potently as her," Ora added.

Sury looked at me. "So, if you've completed the first test, that means you control Earthen sources, right? You could be as powerful as Lady Simret since you're sired from the Endromeon bloodline?"

"I can barely pick up granules of dirt from the ground," I whispered as I pretended to take further interest in my book than the conversation. I felt emotion swell in my chest as I counted in my head, choking down anything I felt.

I will not cry in front of them. I will not cry over this.

Sury looked at me with sympathetic eyes, but Ora knew better.

To the kingdom, magic was essential for our people to thrive. The reigning person imbued their magic into the land for prosperity and protection. Most royalty had higher levels of magic, with Ora being one of the most powerful at a tender age. To many, I was practically a Veik myself.

"Who has ever achieved the highest level? Does anyone know?" Sury asked in hopes to quickly change the subject.

"Seriously, do you pay attention to your lessons?" I slammed my book shut in frustration before glaring at Sury and Ora. "Priestess Ariadne is the highest magic Wielder. When she tested, it was said she achieved the Seventh Circle. The level of magic is so bold that the Wielder should rarely showcase it due to the toll it can take on the body and the mind. So, she refrains from demonstrating unless asked by the other priests and priestesses."

"She scares me, truth be told," Sury said.

Ora sniggered, threw a small pillow in his direction, and spoke in a mocking tone. "Future Lord Sury, one of the best hunters in the land, who has brought the queen some of the largest beasts from the surrounding forests she's ever seen, fears Priestess Ariadne? My, I guess we need to reevaluate your sense of horror!"

They chuckled together.

"Phe, forget about the nonsense people say about the circles. Forget what Ariadne has said about your power. Regardless of level, you're always going to be with me." Ora grabbed my hand, giving it a light squeeze that pulsed warmth through my arm.

"You mean more to me than what others might think, or even what you might think." She outstretched her other hand to grab Sury's. "This is all I need to be the greatest queen in our realm. Having you two by my side, magic or not, is all I need."

CHAPTER 11

The memory faded away when a twig snapped to our left. Shadows danced along the ground from the leaves that moved in the breeze above. I almost missed a movement amongst the boulders on the forest floor.

Sury lightly tapped me on the shoulder as he motioned a single finger over his lips, urging me to stay silent. Ever so gracefully, as if he had done the move hundreds of times before, Sury removed the bow from his back, nocked an arrow, and pulled the string taut, aiming it toward the boulders.

Nothing moved. Shadows continued to dance with the breeze and disappeared in between the rocks in the distance. I tried shifting my stance just a bit to relieve the tightness building in my muscles as Sury cut me a glance that signaled me to stop. I knew he could stand at the ready for much longer than I could with his endless practice of hunting.

If we hadn't already been looking in that direction, we would have missed the tiny movement. Up from one of the crevices flew a creature that made my heart rate race with confusion and anticipation.

With fur the color of fresh snow and *wings*, a small creature landed amongst the gray rocks. The tiny bundle of fur reminded me of a typical woodland rabbit with ears a little bit smaller than its brethren, but it had wings the same color and shape of a dove. The creature hopped to the side and gave a small flap of its wings before scrunching its nose and sniffing. It instantly reared to its hind legs and sniffed the air toward us, then paused.

Slowly, it went back to all fours and crouched, all while keeping its large, black, beady eyes focused on where Sury stood. I held my breath as I watched in awe. This was something I had only read about in my books full of tales.

"Is that...?" Sury began, his voice low in a whisper.

"Bratrian," I responded under my breath.

As soon as the word left my mouth, the winged-rabbit creature made a small squeak, signaling others to join it on the rocks. A flock of bratrian flew onto the rocks and landed with a soft *thud*. Small ones and big ones, all with stark white fur and the softest pink noses. Through the flock, tiny ones that could only be babies hopped alongside a larger one and snuggled.

I wiped my eyes, not knowing when the wetness had covered my cheeks. "I don't think they mean harm."

"They're still urthens. They're unpredictable," Sury said, with his arrow still taut.

Urthen. I still couldn't believe the creatures existed. Not until those dog-like creatures attacked our camp. If those existed, then what other urthen that were once "simply tales" were true? Why were we never told?

"Have you ever seen these near your home in the Northern Woods?"

"I've never seen an urthen of any sort until the attack. There were whispers, but I've never seen them. My father always claimed he saw one when he was a boy, but you know how he is when he talks."

Without taking my eyes off the small creatures nibbling on blades of grass, I extended my arm and gently pushed Sury's arrow down. He retracted but still held his bow and arrow close.

"Maybe not all urthen are as bad as we've been told. Maybe we were only told ghost stories of the kind of urthens that came during the attack."

Sury shrugged. "I'm not sure. Be careful, just in case." The same bratrian we'd seen before turned on its hind legs again, let out a resounding huff, then turned back to the flock.

I knew I could sit here for hours, studying the creatures I thought to be false. I still hardly believed what I saw but knew I needed to continue forward. I couldn't wait to tell Ora what we had seen, knowing full well Ora would want to capture one and turn them into pets to unleash across the castle. A deep pang of sadness hit me hard in the chest as I thought of her.

As I turned on my heels to leave the creatures at peace, a loud crash came from the right. The creatures all rose to their hind legs and turned toward the noise. With a loud squeal, each bratrian pivoted the opposite way to run deeper into the woods. The thing was too fast for me to see where it came from before it landed on one of the bratrian, causing it to screech. I flung my hands up to my ears to muffle the cries.

Its white fur immediately turned a bright crimson as its body was snapped between the larger creature's jaws. More bratrian tried running away, but the giant creature instinctively swiped with one of its large claws and forced a running bratrian against a rock, crushing its skull in the process.

"What the fuck?" Sury breathed, taking in the creature.

What the fuck indeed.

I remained frozen. The creature was another urthen of some kind and reminded me of what attacked us before, except this one stood on *its* hindlegs. Like the other, this creature's skin was pulled tightly against its muscular body, almost like a bear without its fur. With its back facing us, I could see the sharp outlines of its spinal column and rib cage, the back muscles working in tandem as it feasted on one bratrian while swiping at others with its free claw.

The claw was twice the size of my own hand and appeared to be more nails than flesh. Sury raised his bow once again, taking aim at the creature's back as I stepped behind him to stand out of the way. Leaves crunched under my boot, giving way to my footing, causing the creature to quickly turn toward us.

What the absolute fuck. Indeed.

Its jaw was large, with oversized teeth filled with tufts of white fur and sinew. This *thing* licked its lips with a forked tongue and appeared to...smile?

My heart pounded as the creature rose higher. The urthen had the structure of a bear but also looked strangely...human. An observer would think the thing looked weak and incapacitated, but the sureness of its steps spoke otherwise. A way to lure in its prey into thinking it was harmless, maybe?

Its bald skull had no eye sockets and small holes where the ears should be. Slits on its face resembled where a nose would normally sit. Keeping the twisted smile on its face, the creature took the claw that held the other dead bratrian, brought it to its lips, and inhaled. In one motion, the urthen widened its jaws large enough to place half of the bratrian in its mouth and clamped down tightly. Blood splattered everywhere. White feathers cascaded around it in a deathly aura.

It flicked its tongue with a quick hiss and stepped forward. On instinct, Sury let his arrow fly, finding its mark deep within the beast's chest. The urthen hissed as it used one of its claws to yank the arrow away, flinging a blackish liquid with it. Blood.

"Fuck!" Sury shouted as he grabbed another arrow, nocked, then released. He released again and again, each arrow finding its mark and landing deep. None of them seemed to phase the urthen as it crossed over the large rocks.

Sury threw down his bow and reached for the sword at his side. I had nothing but my damn Healer's dagger.

No! No! No! I felt the frozen fear of panic stab through me.

A shout echoed through the trees, shaking me to my core. Sury had made a successful swipe at the urthen and shiny, black liquid pumped from a gash deep within its chest. It surged forward before flinging Sury into a tree, where he collapsed on the ground. Sury's eyes tried to remain focused as he worked to regain his legs underneath him.

Desperation grew in my chest. I couldn't witness someone else I loved, loved like another sibling, be harmed. Scouring the ground, I found large rocks and began throwing them at the urthen's back. A few simply bounced off, but one found its mark at the back of the creature's head. It stopped in its tracks and turned toward me, cracked lips stretching over large teeth in a snarl.

The intensity of my panic was something I had felt a couple nights ago. My stomach dropped, like I had fallen from a cliff. Small bumps raised against my skin, and the hair on the back of my neck stood straight. A vibration hummed all along my arms and deep within my stomach.

I locked my stare on where the creature should have eyes and briefly wondered how it could sense where I was, but I figured that answer could come later...if later ever arrived. The wicked smile stretched wider as the urthen prepared to leap.

The vibration in my skin intensified as I felt the panic aim to swallow me whole.

Without having to understand why, I obeyed the calling deep within me. My hands flung to the sky. Tiny, bluish orbs escaped from my palms and thrust toward the urthen midair, the force of the impact driving me back a few feet, into the air and onto the ground.

I was sure that I cracked a rib or at least bruised one. My body remained stunned on the ground. My breath caught as I counted the seconds to see if the urthen would rise again.

I sensed Sury rise and stumble a few steps toward the beast. Something wet splattered on my face as I heard a wet gurgle and metal hacking into bone. I never took my eyes off the thing, even as I witnessed its head detach and slightly roll in the opposite direction.

"Best to decapitate it if a strike to the heart doesn't weaken it." Sury bent down and wiped the black-covered blade against the base of his cloak. I swept my eyes up and noted how Sury was covered in the same blackness. My hand trembled as I brought it to my face to wipe the remnants away.

"Fire," I said from the ground, barely able to find my words. "The tales say fire rids of them."

Sury nodded. "Can't be too careful then." He took a few strides over to where I remained frozen on the ground and helped me to my feet.

In a matter of minutes, we had collected enough wood to set the urthen ablaze. Neither one of us took our sights off the creature as we watched it burn. I thought I saw the creature's fingers move but hoped that was my imagination. Moments later, thick black smoke covered the woods. The smell was so rotten that it was almost indescribable.

I scanned beyond the smoke and fire and noted the white bits of fur still scattered along the rocks. My body moved on its own as I reached for the mutilated pieces and threw them into the fire, believing the poor things deserved their own funeral rites.

I just knew in my bones that the bratrian were peaceful, despite the general lore around the urthens. Maybe the tales were wrong and not all urthens were evil. Maybe some were good but had done well to hide in the shadows.

"Are we going to talk about it?" Sury asked as we watched the fire.

"There's nothing to talk about."

"That's an obvious lie."

"What do you want me to say?"

"How that happened. I thought..." Sury stopped, trying to find the words. "I thought your Wielding was...*different*."

He was right, wasn't he? My own questions swirled inside my head as I held myself tight, watching the flames burn the last of the beast.

"I don't know," I whispered.

"Can Wielding just erupt like that?"

I turned to Sury and looked him in the eye. We had been the same height since I was fifteen. "Maybe a good reason to visit the Three Sisters after all?"

Sury held a faint smile and nodded. "We've been still too long and I don't know what the smoke might have lured our way." He took the cleaned arrows and stuck them back into his quiver before turning toward the direction we'd been heading.

We continued to walk in silence. Sweat trickled from Sury's brow, but he refused to let it slow his pace as we followed a series of deer trails. I struggled to keep up, finding every damned rock and root under my feet—*again*. Just when my pride swelled for finding my balance, I found yet another root that stuck up from the ground and caused me to stumble.

My ankle twisted and forced me to topple into the base of the tree. Sweaty strands stuck to my face as my fury swiftly rose to the surface, the overwhelming sensation suffocating me. I screamed in outrage as I kicked the tree and the rocks on the ground. The pain barely registered as I struck a fist into the dirt beneath me. Without any warning, a fierce bolt of vibration escaped my clutches and ricocheted through the earth. Sury quickly grabbed onto a nearby tree as his knees buckled from the ground trembling in all directions.

"What the hell was *that*, Phe?" Sury huffed in my direction. "Earthen Wielders can't do that to the ground...can they?"

I was too stunned at my own display to find any words.

Where my hand had struck, tiny green sprigs erupted from the ground and bloomed delicate, purple flowers. I looked at them in astonishment. "I don't know." I had never done that before.

Sury stepped toward me and outstretched his hand, helping me back to my feet. "Let's hope no one else felt that."

A swift rush rose up from my stomach and into my chest once I found myself steady on my feet. I quickly ran over to the side of the trail and emptied the bile from an already empty stomach.

"Let's find water before we go any further," Sury said as he steered left.

"No," I replied as I hurled again. "I'll be fine. How much further do you think?"

"We need to find water before we make it to Wildegard. With all due respect, Phe, you look like shit, and we both need to wash up." After making sure I'd found my questionable balance, Sury continued walking forward, causing me to make haste, this time skipping over the jutting rocks.

I rolled my eyes, but could only imagine what I looked like since being away for at least two solid days and not having time to wash any of the dried blood off. I always liked the bond I shared with Sury and that he didn't address me as *Princess* or tiptoe around me. Aside from Ora, Sury was the only other companion I had known and he was comfortable in being himself. Anyone else would address me in a sneering tone, especially behind the queen and king's backs.

With Ora and Sury, I always felt seen. Included.

The trees steadily grew thicker and more dense. The ground beneath our feet turned from a crumbly, dry state to one that was rich and dense. We could hear the slight gurgling of a small stream. Water never looked so divine.

With meticulous caution, Sury inspected our surroundings before deeming it safe. He had admitted numerous times how he wished to live in the woods rather than rule his forefather's land. Each season that he returned to court with his father, he came back different. More defined. Determined. Resourceful.

Respect was synonymous with the Anmathios name, as many revered his father as a fair leader to the lands he had once ruled. Only Vovias and a select few followers had opposing views about Sury being too young and inexperienced, even though he was leaning toward the end of his second decade. Even with his rightly earned merits and honors, I still only saw Sury as an older brother that *could* be decent to be around.

The water was cool to the touch and instantly calmed my scorched throat as I brought my cupped hands to my lips. I could have consumed the entire stream if allowed but I knew that was a bad idea—I didn't want to be sick again.

I worked my dull Healer's blade to cut a small piece off the end of my cloak and dipped the cut cloth into the water, erasing the copious amounts of dirt and blood I had collected from my falls. My cheek throbbed, and my top lip was slightly swollen.

"Let me check your wounds." Sury inched closer but stayed at a respectful distance while taking my jaw, turning my head for him to inspect the damage. "I'm having trouble finding where the blood came from?"

"I *think* I might have healed most of it?"

"Healed? How?" Sury sat back on his knees and looked deeper into my scalp as if he'd missed something.

"I don't know!" My fingers began to pulse in the rhythm of my heartbeat as I felt frustration rise. A new rumbling sensation dove down into the pit of my belly. "I don't know why

141

they're targeting Ora. I don't know why Vovias and Ariadne are targeting me. I don't know anything about this magic. I JUST DON'T KNOW ANYTHING!"

Without warning, silver and electric-blue orbs formed at my fingertips and shot out toward the stream. One orb barely grazed Sury's ear. His hiss of pain matched the hiss coming from behind him as curls of steam rose from the water. A couple of small fish rose to the top, belly up, before being carried away downstream.

With a hand on his ear, Sury turned to see the steam dissipate from the water. He checked his finger to find a droplet of blood.

I clenched at my chest as a frantic breath escaped. "Sury! Are you okay? I didn't mean that!"

Anger flashed briefly on his face before he found his calm again. "Clearly, whatever this is, it's triggered by you getting frustrated or angry."

"Sury, I'm so sorry!" Even accidentally hurting Sury was too much to bear.

In one scoop, Sury embraced me as a brother would. He held me tightly as I felt a new wave of tears, followed by the silent ones I knew escaped his eyes, too.

"We'll figure this out. We'll find Ora. We'll figure out what's going on. She needs you to be strong and carry this torch. Stand on your feet. Be strong for her."

But I didn't know how to be strong. I knew the background. I knew the shadows. I knew being third best or even fourth best. This had never been asked of me. Even as someone who shared the famed Endromeon bloodline, I knew I would remain hidden behind the name.

"What's the plan from here, then?" I asked as I pulled out of Sury's arms.

Sury looked around, trying to find a certain direction, then he pointed.

"Just over there, up the stream a bit, is Wildegard. There's an inn there where I can gather some supplies and clothes for us. Even some bread. Hell, give me a loaf and a gallon of ale!"

"But won't they recognize you? Or at least know your name from court? It's the closest town before reaching Grianmore."

"No. I have an alias for when I book a room. So far, it's been foolproof."

"An alias? For what? Why do you need a room at the inn when the Anmathioses have the townhome and suite in the castle?" Sury made a grimace before turning away.

"Sury. *Why* do you have an alias for an inn?"

"You're not going to like the answer," he said as his grimace deepened before being replaced with a sarcastic smile.

I stuck my finger in his chest. "Why in the hell do you have an alias? For. An. Inn?"

"Well," he huffed a sigh, "it's so no one knows that me and Ora are there." He scratched the side of his head as he winced.

"And why would you and Ora be at the inn?" The answer hit me faster than I wanted.

Sury just shrugged and held a smug grin on his face.

"Seriously?! I knew you two snuck around to meet in the garden, but THIS?" I pinched the bridge of my nose and took in a deep breath to steady myself. "If the court found out about this, you'd both be ruined. You know that, don't you? They would force her to marry some crooked-nosed royal, and you'd probably be kicked out...or put to death."

"Well, I guess it's a fortunate thing for us that most of the court is dead then," Sury mocked.

I ignored the blatant sarcasm. "But how did you two leave the castle unnoticed? You know what... Don't tell me. This is an issue for another time. The bigger question right now is, won't they notice you're with a different woman this time? Will that screw anything up with your *alias*?"

"No," Sury said with another grimace.

"What?" I asked with a pointed look.

"She always turns her hair dark, almost like yours, so no one would recognize her."

"Well, that's just fucking great. Here I am, to show up as your courtesan and no one is the wiser. This feels disgusting."

"But like you said, no one would be the wiser, so it still works," Sury finished before heading in the direction he pointed.

"I can't believe you two would do such a thing. Something so risky. That you would ravish her away. That you..."

"Whoa there, Phe," he said as he made a pointed turn in my direction. "*She* ravished me. Let's get that story straight."

He chuckled and continued walking back in the direction of Wildegard.

I picked up a twig from the ground and chucked it toward him, missing by inches. I huffed with annoyance and followed behind him until we finally came to the village buried within the trees.

CHAPTER 12

I decided to stay hidden in a thicket as Sury collected what we needed from the Ivory Hare. Its wooden frame appeared as if it had been standing since the dawn of time, and it sported a slight lean to the right. The windows were mostly clear, aside from a dusty hue that clung to the glass. Little pink and white flowers sat in small boxes under the windows and bent in the small breeze that passed by.

"You two stayed...*here?*" I wrinkled my nose.

"Oh, the things you do for love." Sury chuckled. "And *other* things."

I didn't resist the urge to slap him on the shoulder, and doing so sent a small shockwave of pain into my hand.

"Hey!" Sury rubbed at the spot where I'd struck him.

"This is the best place you could find?" I whispered from underneath my hood.

"Matter of fact, this place was *her* idea," Sury whispered back, nudging my rib sharply with his elbow. "Your parents seemed to have paid little attention to this trading town, despite it being so close. What better place than somewhere the royals' eyes wouldn't look?"

"So, you two come here...often?"

"It's not all what you think, Phe."

"Not *all*?"

"Well, yeah, some," Sury said with a sheepish grin. "She wanted this to feel like a home away from home. A small retreat from the castle. An escape to just be herself. No expectations. No commitments. Here, she tries to be anything and anyone else other than 'the queen-to-be'."

His words stunned me. "What do you mean *be herself*? How is she not able to be herself at the castle?"

Sury let out a breath and continued, "The weight of the crown is heavy on her, Phe. She won't truly admit it, but I see it."

I stood in silence for a moment. "I thought she was happy. She always seemed confident about knowing she'll lead one day."

"She wears a mask, like she was taught from an early age, to hide any doubts or fears. Here, she can feel what she wants. Say what she wants. Do what she wants. All without scrutiny and the prying eyes of the court and servants."

My heart sank. My vibrant sister, who always wore a smile, was not smiling on the inside. How did I miss the signs? Why did she not reach out to me? I assumed the smiles and laughter meant she had everything put together. How could I have been so selfish through the years, pitying my own lack of magic and not truly seeing this?

"Why didn't she tell me?" I whispered.

"I'm sure she has her reasons. Ora kept parts of herself hidden even from me. It's something she's always done." He stuffed his hands in his dark brown trousers and shrugged.

"But apparently didn't keep enough of herself away from you," I chuckled and pointed toward the inn.

His grin broadened as he wiggled his eyebrows. I threw him an obscene gesture with my hand that forced us both to laugh.

"Wow, I honestly didn't think you would know that one since you're always buried in a book."

"Oh, trust me, I learn all *sorts* of things in my *books.*" I sighed.

I clutched my sister's necklace tightly as I watched Sury disappear among the wooden and stone buildings that lined the cobblestone roads. The windowsills were all decorated with small bits of yellow paper that were shaped into a bright sun. Garlands of all sizes and colors draped across doors and hung between homes. Banners with the royal crest flapped in the wind. Bouquets of rich flowers adorned large vases framed the steps to business and buildings.

This town, that I had never thought to bother with a visit, was preparing for Queen Aurora's coronation.

They don't know, I thought. Word of her disappearance seemed to go unheard. This could be good...or bad.

I watched the village members from the trees as they went about their merry business, while some worked to hang up flowers and paper suns. Others pushed or pulled carts filled with various goods. Could we ever go back? Would we even find Ora?

I stopped that train of thought before it could grow into a life-sized demon I wasn't ready to battle.

No, not until we sought counsel with the Three Sisters to see if there was any truth to the thing of ancient power we sought. Only then could I plan to rescue my sister from the clutches of the King of Dokvalon, where the Black Raiders hailed.

From there, I would take on Vovias and Ariadne. Fuck. Them.

Fuck everyone.

A shuffle against the fallen leaves on the ground shook me out of my thoughts.

Sury had returned with a canvas sack and chucked it at me with a soft *ooph* against my chest. He dangled a greasy paper sack in front of my face that smelled divine. "Provisions!" He gleamed as he picked out a freshly roasted fowl leg and handed it to me. My stomach roared as my mouth salivated. When was the last time I ate?

I didn't have any cutlery or napkins, and it was clear Sury didn't think to bring them either. I didn't care. I tore into the meat and nearly swallowed the thing whole.

"Holy hell," Sury said slowly with his own mouthful. "I don't think I've ever witnessed you being so improper before."

I took the last bite and chucked the bone into the woods. "I guess here, I'm not a princess either. Ora had the right idea with this place. Wish I could say the same to you and impropriety."

Sury smiled large enough to let little bits of meat fall from his mouth. I rolled my eyes and gave him a mocking, disgusted look.

"I've been thinking," Sury said softly, "you're banking a lot on the Three Sisters, and we don't know if the Ancient One is even real to begin with or if that's its true name. They speak in riddles! No one ever truly gets the answers they seek. Some pilgrims even come to my father's council to complain." He took another bite. "Look, if it's real, why hasn't anyone ever used it before? Why haven't wars been won in a day instead of years? Aren't you putting too much stock into this...this myth?"

I wiped my hands on my trousers. "It's a long shot. Yes. But seeing urthens validated my theory that this other creature could be real. Could it be some sort of urthen that people have forgotten about? Surely, we can tame it somehow, just like the soldiers did with those beasts on chains."

"Are you going to chain it up and feed it treats when it's been a good urthen, too?"

I flipped Sury an improper finger, only earning a chuckle as he finished his meal.

I knew I was chasing shadows, but I couldn't explain the feeling I got when I looked at the creature's eyes on that page. The pull I felt.

"I know this is ridiculous, but it's all I can come up with since I have no court backing. I don't know how to go against the Black Raiders alone or the king that owns them. My own kingdom will be against me because of Vovias's lies. The Grian Army is already in his clutches, and I cannot sway them myself!" I felt the pang of my nails digging into my palms from squeezing so tightly. "How did my mother ever trust him?"

Anger overtook my senses and forced me to jump up from the ground, clenching my fists tightly.

"Uh. Phe... Look at your hands." I looked down and saw the bright orbs dancing once again in my palms, interlacing with my fingers. Each orb burned brighter than the last and continued to pulse in the same fast rhythm as my heart.

They had grown like a well-fed worm. Instead of tiny shimmers, they now resembled small stars—the largest no bigger than my thumbnail. I lost track of how many swayed before me. Seven, maybe? Eight?

"Clearly, something in your emotions sparks these." I felt Sury closing in next to me to observe my hands and the tiny orbs that hovered and moved. "I've seen Ora's magic look like this, but she was always in a calm state. And more ribbon-like—not spheres."

I lifted my hand between us, both of us watching the orbs closely. They pulsed brighter, then dimmer, then brighter again as they twirled.

"She was taught to control hers the moment she Wielded her magic. Mine never evolved past the light specks of glitter. Not until the night when she was taken."

"What was different about that night?"

The question hit me harder than I ever thought it would. Why had this never happened before? Surely, I had felt anger or frustration before. I knew I felt fear the moment I realized our parents were beginning to *fade,* but even then, things felt muted.

We watched the bits of light slowly fade and dissipate into the air as I closed my hands and held them tightly to my chest. I had so many questions and couldn't pluck just one from my thoughts to concentrate on.

Maybe you truly didn't care when your parents passed. A sliver of something inky slithered across my mind.

That's not true, I pressed back to the voice in my mind. *I loved my parents very much.*

Maybe you weren't upset that Ora was taken. Maybe you were more upset that you'd have to pick up your sister's pieces.

That's not true. I wished for the inner voice to stop.

You won't be queen by your own right, but rather a simple replacement for someone who could have been better. You're the half-rate sister. The failure of a great line.

"Shut up!" I yelled to the air around me.

Sury jumped where he stood. "Damn, Phe!"

I shut my eyes as I felt an ache settle in my temples. "Sorry. I don't know what came over me. Probably the stress." I pinched the bridge of my nose with my fingers as I tried to take a steady breath.

Sury picked up the canvas bag he had brought and began pulling out fresh clothing and a mini arsenal of daggers. "Let's get a move on. It'll take quite a few moons to make it up north by foot," he said as he tossed me a dagger that was at least three times the length of my Healer's dagger.

We quickly changed, thankful for Ora's forethought in keeping extra clothes at the little inn. The new dagger fit perfectly within the sleeve inside my tunic, keeping it in easy reach.

"We'll find her," was the last thing Sury said as we set forth to travel deeper into Bainas Forest.

CHAPTER 13

On the third night, we chose to rest close to an open field. I stared at the white light beaming down on me and could almost feel its touch. A small smile rested on my face as a fond memory of me and Father walking in the garden one fall evening, gazing at the moon and stars, played in my mind.

At that moment, I imagined being rocked in my father's arms and drifted off into a peaceful sleep.

The next morning, I woke up to Sury nudging me awake with a firm finger over my mouth to keep me silent. My heart pounded heavy in my chest as I tried to keep my breathing calm. A large commotion could be heard off in the distance and through a thicket of trees to the south of us. Sury jumped to his feet.

"Dammit! Vovias's men!" He started to collect his things from the forest floor, careful not to let anything clink together.

"How do you know?" I mouthed, not allowing a peep of a whisper.

He pointed just as a golden glint sparked through the trees. "Grian Army. They've got one hell of a tracker. I know I've covered our steps to this point." He helped me to my feet. "Honestly, it took them long enough."

We could hear the muted shouting of orders while the beating hooves took off in different directions. With a series of signals, Sury motioned me to follow his lead and to stay close. Like the wild deer, we followed a series of paths and boulders that sat deep in the ground. One misstep would send us plummeting down one of their deep fissures and into the shadows below. Sury effortlessly jumped over the cracks and fallen tree branches, moving like a jungle cat.

I raced deeper into the woods. The forest floor almost betrayed me again with the vast amount of roots protruding from the ground, but this time, I was quicker and skipped over them. I came across a small creek bed and waited for Sury to catch up as I doubled over to catch my breath.

He was built strong. Growing up, he always looked too small for his stocky frame, but the years of hunting and training kept his body built with lean muscle and kept his footwork light. He could easily hold a steady pace and never appear like he was weary or tired.

As if he had done this a million times, Sury showed no signs of fatigue or sweat, even as he ran as fast as he could. "I don't think they saw us," he said in a steady breath.

I, on the other hand, was begging to every giant and giantess I knew to guide me in this journey in more ways than one. If Ednos, the giant of the earth, could do anything to relieve the burning in my calves due to the constant walking on the uneven forest floor, that would be wonderful.

It's not that I didn't enjoy being outside. I would sometimes find myself tucked into a hidden alcove of the royal garden, next to my favorite pond filled with tiny orange fish, buried within another bizarre tale. I was good at hiding in the shadows, but I had always been more adventurous in my mind and within the pages of a book than in reality. I felt at home and safe inside my own little world.

As I walked through the forest now, I gasped for air, trying desperately to fill my lungs. The thick air made it harder to breathe and caused me to choke a bit.

Sury gave me a light pat on the back, like any old friend would, and started walking again. "Stand up straight. Raise your arms above you and rest them on the top of your head. You'll be able to fill in your lungs much easier than being hunched over like that."

The feeling of fire scorched my throat as I breathed. "Your wild man skills have paid off I guess." I huffed and stood to take in a large gulp of air, like Sury instructed, before catching up and meeting his gait. "Do you know where we are?" I hoped Domesis's, the giant of fortune, blessings didn't only go so far.

"Lucky for you, I *do* know the way back to the Praesid Manor. You know, the place where I was born?" Sury called over his shoulder. "Trust me, Phe."

I flipped him the bird as I walked behind. "Can never be too careful," I muttered.

Praesid Manor was an old home, deep in the forest, that bordered the neighboring kingdom of Mercyth. I had never visited Praesid Manor on any of the diplomatic visits but admired the stories Lord Anmathios or Sury would share of their home. It bordered the land that once belonged to the mystics, or so they said.

Folklore and fairy tales seemed to always stem from those lands in the north. Even the tales of urthens. Strange things happened in those woods. Unexplainable things. Ironically, that realm now found no kindness to anyone who Wielded. Maybe that's why urthens were never seen. Maybe they had been hunted and went into hiding.

I could only hope that if we weren't accepted at the Sisters' Keep, we could find solace and regroup at Sury's home undetected. Surely Vovias's snare couldn't reach through all of Gria? Only time would tell.

Every so often, we would slow our steps, both listening for any hooves or men shouting in case we had been heard or followed. Only the rustling of leaves followed our path.

"We need a plan in the event we get separated or if someone comes after us," I huffed, still trying to catch my breath. "What do you and Ora do in case something happens when you're at Wildegard? Do you have a safe word or place or anything?"

"Surprisingly, no, but I agree that we need something. Know any bird calls? It's effective when I'm hunting with a party."

I shot him a look. "Do I look like someone who knows bird calls?"

"Eh, it was worth a shot. Figured you might have read it somewhere. I'll teach you an easy one."

As we passed tree after tree, Sury taught me how to maneuver my fingers around my mouth. With a few tries, I started to sound more like a convincing dove over the squabble of a dying goose. Even though what we endured was a serious manner, we both couldn't help but occasionally laugh at how awful I was at bird calls. But the laughter was a warm welcome to lift our low spirits.

For miles, we walked. I was silently more grateful than ever that my little sister was more cunning than I ever gave her credit for. Still, I had never witnessed Ora change her appearance before, and the thought was unsettling.

Changing one's appearance was considered an element of dark magic. Graevick's magic. A magic that was forbidden. That no one even liked talking about because of the vile nature that was embedded within.

Graevick was a prophet who was said to receive the Original Blessing of Wielding from Mother Giantess herself. According to the stories, he went mad with greed and turned dark. It's said he even turned from his original following and established dark followers known simply as Graevicks.

The thought made me shiver.

"You said Ora would change her appearance to disguise herself when you two went to the inn? I've never seen her practice that kind of magic before. Where did she learn it?" I tried hard not to lose my breath as I kept up with Sury.

"Only her hair," Sury said, shaking me out of my thoughts. "She only did it sparingly because she could never master it. Said it made her feel...off. She was only ever able to turn half of her hair dark, which was helpful that she could do the front and cover the rest with her hood."

I wanted to be surprised that Ora dabbled in magic Ariadne had taught to be off-limits—the kind of magic only dark lords and priests ever dwelled in. But then again, Ora always had been known to be mischievous and rarely listened to any rules but her own.

"But don't worry. She never showed signs she was turning into a Graevick. She felt guilty in the little she tried and never ventured further than that."

A faint glimmer of memory trickled into my mind. I remembered overhearing our mother arguing with Ora about rules and policies and such for a queen, and then Ora storming off.

"She's just like you, you know?" I heard my father say to Mother.

"I know. And that's what worries me!" the queen replied tartly.

There was hardly a way to tell how much time had passed the farther we walked. The dense canopy above our heads only allowed small rays of the sun to greet the floor. Neither of us dared to stop for fear that Vovias's men or the Black Raiders might somehow learn of our path.

Sury was careful in covering our steps the further we walked, only stopping occasionally to pluck a few berries from various bushes. We mostly walked in silence, with an occasional lesson on edible plants and which mushrooms to avoid.

By the sixth nightfall, Sury halted to make camp. I could have cried to Domesis with how grateful I was to rest my feet. Sury argued against a fire to eliminate any risks the flames might bring us. Through the cluster of trees, a few oaks with wide, gnarled branches greeted us like a shield for protection in the night.

Birds of all kinds rested on the limbs or called from the other trees. We sat on the forest floor and slowly ate what I was able to scavenge from Sury's lessons.

"It's been kind of fun sleeping on the ground," I mused as I nibbled a rosehip.

"Eh, it's not that bad as long as you don't get a twig poking you in the back or a rock nudging against your ass."

"Speaking from experience?"

"One time," Sury started to chuckle, "I went out with my father's hunting party. I was maybe nine? Ten? One of his men thought it would be funny to place small rocks inside my bedroll. Like I would never notice. Well, sadly for them, I saw the whole thing as I dangled my feet over them from the tree we rested around—a lot like this one." He pointed skyward as he continued. "Later that night, after I got out all the rocks and twigs, I took the asshole's waterskin and decided to play a little game."

"No, you didn't." I couldn't tell where this story was going, but my instincts just *knew*.

"It may or may not have tasted like rabbit piss. And he may or may not have woken with a dead rabbit in his bed roll."

"Sury!"

"And those men thought twice about the next time they wanted to play tricks on a young lord." A saccharine smile stretched wide across Sury's face.

"I bet you made Lord Anmathios proud."

"Matter of fact, he got a good chuckle as well and said that no one should underestimate a youth. Just because they're smaller doesn't always make the older men the wiser."

"That does sound like something your father would say." I looked out to the trees and watched two squirrels quarrel over food. "My mother and father loved him, you know? They always talked in such high regard about him."

Sury's laugh deflated. A moment or two passed before he spoke. "He was heartbroken to learn when your parents got sick. He sent for Healers from the Wild Country. The ones who are said to know great Healing Wielding. But none would have been able to make it in time. Especially when he learned his couriers were intercepted and beheaded in Mercyth."

Sury leaned over and grasped me on the shoulder. "He would have been at their funeral if he could. It almost killed him that he couldn't make it. He loved your mother like family."

I could only nod as I blinked back the tears. I gave Sury an encouraging smile before turning my gaze toward the grasses on the ground. No one could fault Lord Anmathios for not making the trek to Grianmore. His own health had been steadily declining over the years.

"Do you think she's okay?" Sury didn't have to look up for me to sense his concern for my sister.

"I know she's strong. I know she's a fighter." I wouldn't allow myself to think otherwise.

"I will kill any and every fucker that has laid a finger on her. Wielder or not. I will kill them."

"And I will help you burn the bodies." We clinked a raw mushroom as a toast and a promise. "This is already an act of war. It's just an army that we need to find."

We sat there eating as Sury continued to share stories of the various hunting trips he'd taken with his father. While he talked, a thought pounded within my mind, instinct nudging me to bring my aching feet closer, as if I could observe them from within my boots. I stared hard at my shoes, wondering if there was any magic I could pull from to help dull the pain. Anything to maybe help the throbbing.

I nudged my fingers forward, stretching them toward my target. A featherlight caress touched my belly as I continued to point, following a thought that entered my mind. A thought to summon the orb forms.

But nothing came.

I clenched my brow hard as I tried again by tightening my belly, forcing another pull. A silent growl rose in my chest, filled with frustration. Then, as the magic fell silent, a spark of energy surged from my hand faster than I could catch it. The orbs transformed into a glowing ember, igniting a dead leaf beside my boot.

"Shit!" I cried and extinguished the flame with dirt.

Sury looked at me with a raised brow but said nothing as he continued to sit there in silence, nibbling on the small cache of boletes.

CHAPTER 14

The days were the same as we crossed through more forests and plains, steadily making our way toward the border and the Three Sisters. Sury never showed signs of slowing down despite the rising heat, while I did my best to keep up. I'd never seen a soul more determined than Sury.

The sun came and went. Each night, the moon showed she was waning and that we would soon be encased in pitch black by nightfall. The constant murmurs of the stream we chose to follow were our only comfort. I couldn't stop the dread that lay heavy on my chest. Would the Three Sisters provide guidance or know anything of Ora's fate?

Are they on our side? I asked myself but stopped that trail of thinking. Someone had to be on *our* side.

I stopped counting the miles but knew we were getting close as the forest thinned. Hope steadily increased with each step, but I kept the notion to myself. Just in case I was wrong.

"Here. We just crossed the Anmathios border." Sury pointed to a cluster of rocks with the Olden Language carved into it, signifying the new territory. "There's no way in hell my father would side with Vovias. We'll be safe here if we cross any of his bannermen."

"You mean *your* bannermen. You're the official lord here," I reminded him.

"While I became the official lord a few months ago, many of these men still see my father as the head of the estate here. In time, I know they will be just as loyal to me."

We both resumed our regular motion to set camp again for the night. Edible flowers and berries were all we could nibble on, though Sury was able to snag a small trout for us to share next to the small fire we braved.

He kept his bow close but never wanted to risk losing an arrow on a grouse, nor lose time hunting. I craved a substantial meal but was content to forage along the way. This luck of a trout was a reward in itself.

Night turned strangely cool as we sat. It had been days, on the verge of weeks, since our encounter with those Grian soldiers close to Wildegard. We'd never braved any other inns but occasionally snuck into a farmer's barn for the night before heading out before sunrise. My body shook with exhaustion and it was taking its toll. Sleep evaded us, no matter how hard we tried, even if we took sleep in shifts. I felt too heavy, too weak, to practice any magic from my own command and not by emotion—especially anger or fury.

I nestled up against a broken log before closing my eyes. The warmth of the fire and the coolness of the breeze created a strange but welcomed sensation. It felt like autumn was on the cusp of the season, but we were entering the throes of a warm spring. Everything felt off.

I lost myself in thought and felt the drift of coming sleep right before Sury rushed to stamp the fire out. Within a few heartbeats, I rose up from the ground and held my breath, trying to hear any sound within the forest. I didn't need Sury to articulate what made him jump—I sensed something too. My heartbeat thrummed rapidly in my chest, and the fast *swooshing* within my eardrums drowned out my hearing.

The leaves on the trees turned frosty as our breath curled in front of us. I instinctively pulled my cloak tighter around me. "What is it?" I whispered to Sury, who drew his sword and dagger.

"Silent. *Too* silent." He scanned in every direction. The way he tilted his head back and forth as he looked through the trees reminded me of a hawk stalking its prey.

No sound of crickets or frogmouths sang into the night. The silence was deafening. A cold and icky feeling crept along my spine, and the hair on my arms stood on end as the sky and forest grew darker around us. A shadow snaked through the limbs and along the forest floor, snuffing out the embers.

A foul stench wound through the air and wrapped itself around our senses. The same foul, decayed smell I remembered the night Ora was taken. My swift panic forced my breathing to become rapid, despite my efforts to find calm.

Black Raiders.

I attempted to warn Sury, but he was already on the move and yanking me into a run. I chanced a look over my shoulder as I heard the whining of a mule and a stampede of hooves beating the forest floor behind us. I didn't know how the Black Raiders were able to stay unnoticed or how they even tracked us. We had been so careful about the paths we took. Black Raiders had never been seen this far north. Numerous territories would have struck them down first.

They *should* have struck them down.

But this was a different time. We were in an unseen war.

And I would be damned if a Black Raider got their hands on me tonight.

The minor giantess, Cisoi, who governs death's door, could fuck right off before ushering me to the other side without getting to see Ora again.

Pain seared through my lungs, which were fighting for air, as Sury and I continued to sprint, our panic building with each stride.

Don't let them get to you or Sury. Breathe. Be smart, I repeated, over and over.

But you were never the smartest, were you? The dark thought tickled the back of my mind as I continued to sprint behind Sury, unable to close the gap between us.

I looked over my shoulder again to see how close the Black Raiders were. The trees and tangled limbs blocked the direct sight of them, but the crashing hooves were getting closer. The rhythmic beating ricocheted off the trees and echoed around us, sounding closer and closer.

The air was knocked out of my lungs as I ran into something hard and stumbled back a few steps. Sury had come to a complete halt, his own breathing rapid. A small, silver orb of light, no larger than a coin, appeared dramatically in front of his face.

Another orb popped up in front of my face, almost blinding me. It pulsated a soft glow and was encased in wisps of silver light. Both orbs danced together and bounced onto the ground a few feet ahead of us, zigzagging through the trees, leaving a small glowing trail behind.

Sury grabbed my arm again to change directions, away from both the Black Raiders and the mysterious orbs. Before he could take another step, another orb zipped in front of his face and into the same direction as the other small two.

"I'm going to go on a whim here and say they want us to follow them." I gasped for air. Before I could sprint in the direction, the orbs were traveling. Sury grabbed my cloak and yanked me back.

"We can't trust them, Phe! They could be more urthens. Ones that might be controlled by the fucking Raiders that are headed this way." He pointed his dagger in the direction of the coming horses.

I couldn't explain it. The pull that grew in my chest and a tiny whisper in my ear telling me to follow. The whisper felt light and ethereal.

This way. You need to come this way.

I pulled out of his grasp and turned to run toward the whisper. "Trust me!"

"Phe! Wait!" Sury hissed, but I was already running. Sury stayed nimble on his feet, catching up in just a few steps, all without a misstep on a rogue tree root.

More little orbs and wisps sprung into the air and illuminated the path at our feet, guiding us through the thickening grove of trees. A few more gathered in a pulsating line and whipped across the ground before...diving below the earth?

Before I could understand what the guides were communicating, both of us fell forward. Our momentum forced us to slip down a muddy bank into a bed of tangled roots. Sury screamed out in pain and clutched his shoulder tightly as we slid to the ground below.

Tiny orbs twirled around my hand, which felt aflame from the scrapes from the fall, and tugged me forward before zipping into a large crevice of exposed roots from the trees above. I pulled Sury by his tunic and pushed us into the roots. We pinned our backs to the damp earth floor, as far underneath the tree and within the tangled mass as possible.

As fast as they appeared, the orbs disappeared to leave us in pitch black once again. I felt the air around us turn to ice, a rapid sensation against the fire in my chest. The air curled like smoke as if we had been thrown into the depths of winter. Tiny ice crystals formed along the dangling roots, encasing the earthly pathways in a sheen of frost.

We huddled closer. A soft beating of hooves could be heard above and through the dirt floor. The smell of decay swirled, filling our nostrils again. I glanced at Sury, noting how he held his mouth, probably to withstand emptying the contents of his stomach. I wouldn't blame him. The smell practically swallowed us whole. My own breath turned erratic through my mouth, desperate not to smell anything.

The dark forest grew black and the trees before us vanished out of sight.

If it wasn't for the physical touch of Sury's arm, I would have thought I had blacked out into an abyss. The foreign feeling slithered inside my head as a screeching whisper filled my ear. Harsh words collected in my inner thoughts—voices in my head from the riders above.

"*We know you're out there, Princess and Lord of the Hunt. Oh, how sweet the queen-to-be tastes. How our brothers have all laid their eyes upon the sweetness and tasted the living.*"

I felt the hard squeeze of Sury's hand on my arm, guessing by the force that his knuckles had to be turning white. I shot him a look and silently shook my head, grabbing his hand in hope to comfort him but ultimately to keep him silent. Or from doing anything heroic...or stupid.

"The work will be complete, Princess. The queen-to-be will be the Queen to the Dead and the Damned. Don't you care for your sister? Don't you care for your lover, boy? Come to us."

"Stop this game. Finish them," another shrill whisper demanded before a hoof stomped the ground.

Trepidation took hold. I could feel each beat of my heart on the verge of bursting, the valves within growing agitated with the force of the blood it pumped. My stomach cramped with each beat. My breath slowly dissipated, and my head felt heavy.

My whole body began to vibrate and shake as I tried to remain still and silent. I heard Sury hold back a grunt as we both did our best to cover our ears. Anything to drown out the high-pitched screams that came from nowhere and everywhere.

Up from the earth, more orbs formed. This time, they were larger and brighter and the most beautiful shades of blue I had ever seen. Bright and dark blues, like a lightning storm, pulsed as they multiplied into a giant sphere of light. Then, like shooting stars, they burst into the air and flew toward the riders—shaped like daggers.

The Black Raiders screeched before galloping away at a deadly speed in the opposite direction. The blackness rippled away from the forest as crickets chirped once again in the distance. Sury gently released his hold and slid down further into the tucked crevice.

"What the fuck was THAT? Please tell me you heard that too."

I could only nod, still too frightened to speak. Each vibrating cell inside my body became still, leaving behind a numbing sensation along my skin. Sharp prickles tingled along my fingers and toes as blood rushed back into my extremities.

Tiny orbs, like the ones before but just bright enough to illuminate my palm, rotated in little circles. My eyes grew wide as I watched them hover and spin along the scratches and, one by one, close the skin, leaving only small traces of the dried blood behind.

I guided my hand toward Sury and gasped. A thick, black arrow protruded from his shoulder. The tip dripped in blood.

"Sury! You're hurt!"

"No shit," he said in between his panted breath.

I ignored his remark as I assessed his wound and the arrow that had shot through his skin and muscle. His shirt was already soaked in blood. My stomach lurched at what we both knew needed to be done.

"Phe," Sury said in between gasps, "Break the arrow. Pull it out."

The orb in my hand vanished as I shifted to my knees, aligning myself beside him. I placed one hand gently on his shoulder to steady him, the other hovering over the arrow's shaft.

"Oh, and be easy, eh?" he added with a nervous laugh.

"Take a deep breath," I commanded, forcing myself to do the same. "And bite down on this." Without allowing his protest, I shoved a piece of tree bark in between his teeth.

I didn't count down to give Sury time to brace for the pain. It took all my will to snap off the fletching. In one swift motion, I dropped the broken piece and carefully pulled the remaining shaft from his front, avoiding the tip.

Sury bit back his agony and pounded into the tree crevice above with his uninjured arm. I tore a small piece of my cloak to tightly tie off the wound around his shoulder to lessen the bleeding. A blessing from Iasis would be wonderful right about now.

"We need to find some willow and chaseflower before we get to the next town. It'll help until we can get you to a Healer." I stepped out of the crevice and looked into the forest. My eyes strained against the night in hopes I'd see a small orb reappear, but none came.

Sury grabbed my hand and squeezed tight. "Be careful."

I counted a few heartbeats before I found the courage to lean out of the rooted crevice and begin searching for any willows or the small pink flower—careful not to stray too far from Sury. Healers were often summoned for matters kept behind closed doors by the courtiers, but when a guardsman was injured during training, I'd usually sneak close enough to watch the Healer work and jot down quiet notes.

I remembered willow always being kept in a vial, and the flower's stems stored in the pouches Healers carried to ease pain from wounds. Desperation clawed up my spine as I searched the dense forest for those telltale, picturesque swinging branches.

To my right, a small chirp trilled at my feet. My dagger was drawn and ready faster than I realized as my ears strained against the silence. The trilling chirp sounded again but this time closer. I took a step back and poised the dagger in the direction of the sound. No horses' hooves were heard. No clinking of armor. Was it still a signal from a Black Raider?

A third chirp sounded, this time right beside me. I snapped my head down to a lone, fallen tree trunk from where the noise came. My knuckles turned white as I gripped the dagger tightly, holding its aim to the log.

A rustle of leaves on the forest floor shifted, followed by a small little trill. Up on the log jumped a tiny fluorescent green *thing*. In length, it was no bigger than my middle finger and reminded me almost of a caterpillar. The thing inched forward on its six fuzzy legs that looked as if they belonged to another forest creature. Its tail was a curled collection of fuzzy, faux leaves.

In a blink, the green creature rose on two back legs and looked up as if looking *at* me. I blinked to make sure I wasn't hallucinating. Ears of a rabbit with a face between a fox and a barn cat, two paws lifted toward its face. The middle set of paws held something brown.

With a little shake of its head and white whiskers, two jeweled beetle-like wings quickly flapped behind it before settling back down again. The color was of freshly sprouted spring grass with small highlights of the brightest orange against its ears and the tuft around its neck.

The whole thing could fit neatly inside of my palm. "What are you?" I breathed, the dagger still clutched tightly in my hands.

The thing shook its head as if giving a knowing look. Another flap from its wings and the thing trilled again. On command, dozens more replied and flapped or jumped onto the log. All with the same brightly colored fuzzy coats that glowed against the night sky. Their tiny, knowing dark eyes blinked in tandem as they looked up at me.

I noticed they were all carrying something small and brown in their paws. I gently tucked away my knife and stretched out my palms to show I meant no harm. I half chuckled to myself that I must be going crazy, or maybe I'd hit my head at some point. I racked my brain to think of what creature I might have read about that fit this description. If this wasn't a hallucination.

A thought struck. "Hibryds?" The little creature shook its head as if it understood me. "Whilens? No, that's not right. It doesn't appear you have fangs." This was absolutely insane. "Are you *rurons*?" A collective trill sounded as the apparent leader nodded its head. "A raggle of rurons!"

The ruron flapped its wings once more and dropped the thing it was holding down to my feet. I noticed the edges were rough, while one side was smooth.

"Is this...is this tree bark?" The ruron nodded again as it flapped its wings three times, signaling the rest of the rurons to drop their treasures at my shoes.

I scooped up the pieces and observed them the best I could in the darkness. As if knowing my thoughts, the ruron lifted into the air to hover over my hands, allowing its soft glow to illuminate the bark.

My heart dropped. "Willow. You brought me willow bark! For Sury!" My smile stretched wide across my face. "And chase-flower stems!" The ruron nodded again and let out another series of trills. On the command, the rurons lifted into the air in unison and bent their bodies into a low bow before turning and flying into the dark to disappear.

"Thank you," I whispered and pivoted my heel to run back to where Sury sat in the crevice. I wasted no time in using the back of my dagger to grind the bark and stems together as much as possible in a hollow limb. Then I sprinkled the mixture into the wound in hopes of staunching the bleeding.

"How did the Black Raiders even find us?" I retied the bandage around his shoulder.

Sury shrugged his good shoulder and looked as shocked as I imagined we both felt. "Those were not the same Black Raiders that your family has fought off for years. This is different."

This *was* different. How could they travel so silently? How could they slither into our thoughts?

"Did you happen to see who helped us? There wasn't any trace of a Wielder in the woods."

"I didn't. All I saw was blackness."

Surely, there would be some sign in the woods. Why wouldn't they stay to help us?

"Speaking of help—I saw rurons earlier. They brought me the bark and stems for your wound."

"Rurons? Actual rurons? The fuzzy bug-like cat creature?"

"Yes! Even better, a whole raggle of rurons! Just like in the stories! Except these were more green than yellow." I couldn't contain all my excitement to see more urthens.

Sury only shook his head in disbelief. "Better than the beasts that have been known to lurk into the night, right? Like the crested walkers. Nasty things. Their nails drip with poison, and they play with their prey." He wiggled the fingers of his uninjured side to emphasize the creepiness. "Let's hope *those* are at least stories."

Thoughts trickled inside my mind as I tried to process what had happened with the Black Raiders and the orbs.

As grateful as I was for the help, where did it come from? I sensed a familiarity that could not be explained, but how did the orbs know where we were? When to help? How did the rurons know what I was looking for?

"Why now?"

"Hmm?" I glanced at Sury.

"Why are urthens coming out now? I have hunted these woods for over two decades and have never seen anything like the stories we've been told."

"I'm just as lost as you. Something must have changed for them to grow so bold." An unsettling thought crept through my mind. A myriad of images of Ora in Dokvalon's clutches, created by my imagination, played over and over in my mind.

Sury snapped his fingers to bring me back to the present. "Let's keep going but further off the path we were following. We need to stay on the move in case they decide to come back and finish the job. It's not that much farther."

I helped him to his feet and ensured he was steady. Carefully, he sheathed his dagger and clenched his arm to hold his shoulder as we continued our endless walk into the night.

CHAPTER 15

Small dew drops emerged from the ground below and coated our boots as the daylight grew. Trees turned thinner and through the smaller clusters we could finally make out a large clearing and the township beyond.

Zonnagberg.

I let out a sigh of relief to see it after walking for days. I was eager to seek out an inn for a warm meal that consisted of something much heartier than cattails and dandelions.

If I have to eat another damn mushroom, I might just have to punch something.

I could make out the white flags on top of the city walls as I squinted into the distance. Each one had seven interlocking golden circles painted on them. Wielder's Circles. A beacon to a safe haven for pilgrims who came to seek rest and restoration on their journey.

Zonnagberg was known for being peaceful and welcomed all people, Wielders and Veiks alike. Many came to better understand their own magic and draw strength from one another. Others sought knowledge from the Sisters, or their acolytes, if they weren't accepted to study at the High Seven Temple.

By Ariadne.

"We're almost there." I could taste the hope rising in my chest, wondering if every pilgrim felt the same. "Are you sure no one will recognize you here?"

Sury shook his head. "I rarely visit Zonnagberg." He continued, "Are you sure you don't want to go to Praesid Manor first? Maybe devise a plan? It's not even a full day's walk…"

I shook my head. "We're here, and I don't want to waste any more time. After we visit the Three Sisters, we can head there. Talk with your father."

The Sisters' Keep was unsanctioned for teaching Wielding and was condemned by the priests and priestesses of the High Seven. They were often called zealots and accused of spreading heresy about Wielding and its creation. Those who came to seek their guidance were either fanatics themselves or very desperate.

At least, that's what I had been taught my whole life.

Sury scanned the field and the city's walls beyond. "I don't see any of my father's usual guards near the gate. Stick to the tree line before we make our way in. Just in case Vovias or Ariadne have sent their own guards." We ducked back into the forest and walked around the outside of the fortified walls.

"You said no one else survived the attack, right?" I huffed as I matched my pace with Sury's.

"Right. They even thought I had died until I entered Grianmore."

"No one knows what Ariadne is truly capable of. Paired with Vovias, they are now some of the most powerful people in Gria. No one in a new court would dare to oppose them." I huffed at the mental image of the pair tarnishing our mother and father's thrones and Ora's rightful place. "They've had to be planning this for a while." I kept diving deeper into thought.

Sury nodded, but the rage that radiated off of him was palpable. "And no telling what lies and tales they have spun to keep people from asking questions since festivities for a coronation would have happened by now."

With light steps, we crept to the township's walls that climbed high into the bright sky. Turrets and pillars looked like thick tree trunks covered in bright white mortar and bricks. Sury stopped in his tracks. I bumped into him with a loud *oomph*. He turned and held his finger to his lips to silence me. A light breeze brushed through the bright leaves on the branches above and mimicked the swooshing sounds of a river. Other than that and the occasional murmur from across Zonnagberg's wall, all was silent.

I don't hear anything. I did my best imitation of speaking with my hands. If anyone had seen me, they might have thought I was losing a battle with a cloud of gnats.

"I think we're clear," he continued to whisper. "If Grian soldiers were already here, we would hear them because of their armor. But just to be safe..." He motioned his hand to an approaching group of pilgrims with their wagons.

They were all dressed in various styles of clothing, some tattered from the long journey they had taken and some wearing their finest. They were singing songs of joy and peace, and it seemed there was so much excitement about visiting the Three Sisters.

Sury continued his walk along the border and to the front gate as he motioned for me to put up my cloak's hood in the hope it would hide some of my identity—just in case someone in the group might notice that a royal member was within their party. We locked arms with one another to blend in and hummed to the easy tune the travelers sang.

The front gate was plain and large. Nothing special about the brick and stone that held the wood in place, but the metal frame that encased it held intricate designs of seven interlocking circles. Any person who could see could tell that the ironsmith took great care in their work.

I kept my head down low as I walked through the front gate and gingerly looked around as if I were on a pilgrimage myself. Zonnagberg practically glowed against the bright sun in the sky. The buildings within were whitewashed, like the city walls, and looked much brighter against the dark wooden boards that lined the walls and the windows.

Flower boxes sprouted along the buildings, holding vibrant shades in every color. Some even could rival the royal gardens with their hues. Sky blue overhangs lined various shops and businesses, offering small bits of relief from the sun for their customers.

But what caught my attention the most was the waterway. Sapphire blue water trickled through the center of the city, with walkways on either side. Bridges and fountains lay one after another, the latter displaying a prism of colors in the sky as droplets of water fell back into the river.

Gray cobblestones lined the streets and forked in different directions across the town. Vendors and merchants lined up and down various roads, selling small trinkets that were said to help amplify a Wielder's magic. A fool's hope. Other vendors sold small and large silhouette sculptures of the Sisters as keepsakes for the pilgrims and students to take back on their journey. Carts with food and spices peppered the streets and filled the air with a delicious aroma. The smell alone made my stomach growl.

Toward the end of a busy street sat a quaint-looking inn that held a tiny sign for the Alba Inn. The inviting exterior matched the buildings around it, except for the greenery growing on all sides. Vines crept up the walls and shadowed the windows of the rooms. Lush flowers and herbs crowded the boxed containers. A true hint of an Earthen Wielder's talent. Sury gave me a comforting nod before we headed in the inn's direction in hopes of a spare room.

A small overhang of blues and golds shaded the front door. Wooden tables and chairs were scattered under another awning, this one identical to the one shading the door and connected to the Alba's exterior walls, protecting patrons from the sun.

Inside was moderately crowded with more patrons who were all in deep, but loud, conversations and some even singing merry tunes as they clinked their tankards. Eyes of yellows, oranges, emeralds, and blues were spread throughout the room.

Sury gave me a knowing look. He, too, concluded that no one had heard about the future queen or her fate.

The interior was bright thanks to freshly washed windows, and the floors had been recently scrubbed and carried a scent of pine. Chandeliers, and candelabras on shelves, held long, white candle sticks that were dimly lit by someone's fire magic. Despite being such a quaint inn, the owner knew what they were doing when they picked this spot for the sun to shine through as it did. It gave the space a cozy and comforting environment. A stark contrast to the Ivory Hare in Wildegard.

A barmaid to our right was busy cleaning a table and collecting empty tankards. I leaned on a wooden support column and lowered my head as Sury strode over to where the barmaid was hard at work.

"Excuse me, miss, is there a room available?"

The barmaid looked Sury up and down and gave him a small wink. Her curly blonde hair was bound, but small slivers escaped their place and hung around her face. I noticed her apron was clean, and the top of her dress was deeply unfastened, revealing the large crest of her breast.

"O'course, love." Her thick northern accent was deep and sultry. "We even have rooms that come with special services...for extra."

I could almost claw the barmaid's eyes out myself for Ora. Sury smiled his rakish smile and nodded in my direction.

"As much as I would love to know more about these *services* of such a fine establishment, you see, I'm traveling with my companion, and she might get a bit jealous." He topped it off with a wink that could make any woman swoon.

"Cheeky bastard," I said under my breath as I pretended to find interest in the dirt under my nails.

The barmaid nodded in my direction and rebutted, "For a small upcharge, we can make sure she's not jealous, love."

I blushed hard in embarrassment. I had never heard this kind of exchange before and didn't know what to think of it. No one talked like this amongst the halls or rooms within the castle. Or at least, I had never heard them.

"Maybe another time... She's not experienced in the ways of the *threes* just yet. But we will inquire about washing our clothing and the service fees for fresh linens." Sury winked again.

"Your loss, love." She took the tankards and her towel over to a large wooden desk by the door that was littered with full and empty dinnerware.

Sury handed her a meaty coin in exchange for a key and a set of fresh linens before making his way to the stairs, with me close in tow.

"What in the hell was *that?*" I hissed.

"Save your breath. Act the part so we go unnoticed," he growled under his breath. "No one has spotted me yet. Let's keep it that way."

"You call that *going unnoticed?* She practically had sex with you with her eyes!"

"This is the real world, Phe, not a book. If you open your eyes, stranger things might happen to you in life." Sury stopped in his tracks and peered over his shoulder with a grin. "Or maybe read a *different* kind of book." He forced a laugh as he continued walking forward.

"I'm telling Ora," I huffed under my breath as I followed Sury up a couple flights of stairs and into a room. It smelled like cedar, and a small desk held the wash basin and a couple of extra blankets.

"Home sweet home," Sury said as he sat on a plush chair next to a tiny window overlooking the road below. "Until we can get to Praesid, at least."

I took off my cloak and proceeded to wash my face in the basin. "Too bad I'm not with a better companion because in the books I *do* read, a single bed in an inn is always a treat."

"Too bad you're stuck with my ass, and I have no issue sleeping on the floor," he said with a smirk.

Though my face felt clean after days on the road, I studied my tunic and the dirt and grime that had made a home within the threading. "We need new clothing before we call an audience with the Three Sisters. I'll peruse the shops and see if anyone is selling tunics that we can change into."

"Knock yourself out. I'll take something dark." Sury proceeded to tuck himself deeper into the chair and pulled his cloak's hood over his face right as I noticed the dark circles pooling under his eyes.

"I'd like to have a look at your shoulder before I go."

Sury only grunted a response for his approval.

His face was pale, and sweat beaded on his brow. I gingerly placed a clean hand on his forehead and felt his skin in flames under my touch. With nimble fingers, I pulled back the cloak from his chest and found his tunic and the bit of cloth I'd used to tie off the bleeding were both soaked in dried and fresh blood.

His skin was red and swollen where the arrow had punctured, but what worried me the most were the thick, black veins that now webbed out from the wound's center, and pulsed inky remnants across his shoulder in tiny lines that felt ice cold.

"You need more willow and chaseflower." I pulled the remaining bits the rurons had given me and forced him to consume the grounded bits with the last of his water in his waterskin.

I grabbed a clean cloth from the basin and began to gently clean the caked blood and some of the infection that oozed out onto his skin.

Sury hissed in pain but didn't move from his spot. Using another clean cloth, I gently wrapped it around the wound and tied it off. I thought through years of past lessons on the basics of Healing and what could help an infection that was starting to fester. "The Three Sisters will be able to heal this in no time," I said as happily as I could muster. "Just hang on a bit longer and get some rest, alright? I can find something in the market to help with the pain in the meantime."

Sury waved me off as he drifted to sleep with his boots still on, exhaustion finally taking over.

Without another word, I clutched my waning coin purse tightly and headed for the market on the street below. Eagerly, I made my way down the polished, wood steps and through the heavy oak door before the barmaid could say anything to me.

I didn't allow myself to care that I must look, and smell, like a woodland creature since my goal here was to remain unnoticed. With a few bits of hair tucked away in my braid, I hoped I simply looked like a traveler looking to seek accommodations for my stay.

It was almost quite freeing in a way—pretending to be someone else. Is this what Ora felt when she and Sury escaped to Wildegard? For as long as I could remember, pity and sympathy were the looks I would receive from the many in Grianmore or the temple, as if I were a wounded animal. When the pity faded, eyes always diverted to my royal parents or Ora. Making me invisible to who I really am.

I always thought I never minded it, especially since my family was far more important. I never knew the difference of being noticed for something else instead of for what I lacked.

But this felt different. No one knew me here. I could use this to my advantage.

I quickly shook the feelings aside. The local vendor carts and wide array of shops along the streets caught my gaze. A loud commotion came from down the street, grabbing my attention. An older man with a graying beard and balding head had set up a wagon full of different kinds of fruit, with some I had never seen before. He stood over a spilled basket of red produce as he yelled at another man with wild hair, shooing him away with a large walking stick.

"Filthy beggars. No respect!" the merchant yelled at the man who scurried down the road in tattered pants and a half-torn shirt. I watched the beggar turn a corner before I turned my attention back to a beautiful silk dress in a shop's window.

"Eyeing something you like, my dear?" A short, middle-aged man with dark hair sprinkled with wisps of gray stood in the doorway of the little shop. "We have fine silks and other materials, all imported. Some even from Elethia itself. Why, I believe we have something that would..."

I stared back at the man, about to politely decline, until he interjected. "My! Those eyes! I bet you have all the young lads running in your direction with that beautiful hue. I have just the perfect shade of a purple dress that will make those teals pop! Come in! You must come in!"

I blushed at the compliment. I'd only ever received them from my parents and Ora, or occasionally Sury...whenever he was prompted *by* Ora.

"You're too kind, sir, but I only need to buy tunics today."

"Tunics! Why! A lady needs to be dressed in the finest. But alas, if you wish, come inside, please, and I shall obtain what you need."

I followed the man inside the well-lit shop. From top to bottom, wooden shelves were lined with bolts and rolls of various materials in different shades, patterns, and colors. In the center of the shop was a glass case filled with small pieces of cut gems in beautifully crafted bangles, earrings, and the like. I could see Ora requesting to try on each piece.

"Tunics are this way, my dear!" Following the sound of his voice, I found the man in a large armoire, wrestling out an array of clothes.

"Oh, just a couple of dark ones will do, sir! Perhaps two black ones, if available? And trousers, too. One for me and a male companion—similar height."

I heard the man make a slight huff and wrestle himself out of the armoire with the cloth in hand. "I will not let you walk out of here with such drab colors, dearie. No, I will be happy to grant you at least one black one, but I must insist on this beautiful shade here. It will do your eyes justice."

The little man pushed a soft, dark, sapphire blue tunic into my hands. The color was stunning and dark enough to hide parts of my body I always worked to keep hidden.

"Oh...well, thank you. I appreciate your kindness."

The shopkeeper simply smiled and took the things to wrap them in a delicate paper, tying them off with a simple cord of string. "You know, I have seen many Wielders over the years but not many who have your shade. It reminds me of what I've heard about one of the princesses back at Grianmore..." The man stopped and tilted his head, taking me in. He noted my clothes. My hair. My boots.

I held my breath. Surely, he didn't know who I was. The look on my face must have given me away, but he finished tying the parchment and smiled. "Of course, that would be silly. Wouldn't it? A royal wandering this far north." And he winked.

I exhaled slowly and nodded as I smiled at the man in thanks. Hopefully, for his discretion, I handed him a few extra coins as I took the tunics and new trousers before continuing on my way. The streets bustled with people of all kinds. Aside from the whitewashed walls of the buildings, the familiar feel of Grianmore made me feel right at home. A small rush of homesickness filled my belly before I spotted a sign for an apothecary.

Healers were becoming rarer over the years and were revered by any community they resided in. Most of the wealthy hired a personal Healer, if there were any around, and Grianmore had their select few to serve the nobles and dignitaries that came to visit. It was like the Healers themselves were disappearing. But to be in a place like Zonnagberg, or near the Three Sisters, the owner of the apothecary must have a strong Wielding in Healing magic.

Inside the apothecary, the walls were much darker than the tailor's shop. A thin haze covered the room with the smoke of an incense burning across the room, smelling something heavily musky with a hint of vanilla and citrus. The smell was both overpowering and inviting.

Shelves held various bottles, some empty and some filled with interesting contents. Baskets of fresh cloth for wounds, herbs, and utensils lined other shelves and hung neatly on the walls.

The banisters above held little cords of string that were bound to drying plants and flowers, all of different colors. At the back was a half wall that was cut off from the rest of the shop with a locked door that came up to my waist. I peered over the wall and found an empty clinic, practically untouched. Hanging near the entrance where I stood was a wooden sign with bold painted letters reading:

ATTENDING PATIENTS. OUT OF CLINIC. BE BACK SOON.

Well, shit.

There goes getting a Healer. Without wasting time, I collected what I needed and asked the shopkeeper for a mixture of herbs to help fight off Sury's wound and growing fever.

The Alba Inn was only a few streets over from a vendor stall that held fresh breads and meat pies that made my stomach growl. I purchased a couple before finally making my way back. I didn't know if it was the sun, the meat pies in my hand waiting to be devoured, or the vibrancy of the village we were in, but I began to feel hope. Real hope.

Hope for my sister and a better future.

Sury was sound asleep when I returned but quickly sat up as I placed all the packages down on the table next to him.

"I bought meat pies from a local vendor," I said as I stepped back to the wash basin for a proper cleaning. "Would you like to eat outside with me? It's a pretty day."

Sury kept his head down and shrugged his good shoulder as he leaned back in his chair. He would never admit how exhausted he was, but his demeanor was revealing.

"Turn around! I smell like a squirrel and want to bathe before I eat." Sury rolled his eyes and laid back in the chair but placed the hood of his cloak over his head to keep his face hidden.

We took turns to wash and dressed in the new clothes, Sury taking a bit longer than usual.

I buried my nose in my new tunic, noting how the cloth faintly smelled of fresh lavender. How did the man make the clothes smell so good? I left my thoughts to ponder as I re-braided my freshly washed hair into a simple plait that laid long over my shoulder. "I bought some supplies to help tend to your wound. Can I see your shoulder again?"

Sury grumbled. Water droplets fell from the ends of his growing hair and splashed onto the wooden floor. His face looked almost sunken from the length of hair growing on his face.

"The beard looks good on you." I chuckled.

"You think?" he asked as he scratched his fingers through the hairs. "You think Ora will go for it?"

"Not a chance." I laughed as I laid out the supplies next to the basin and instructed Sury to sit on the bed. The cloth I had tied onto him just hours before was already soaked in fresh blood. Little spots of infection and a black substance stuck against it.

Sury's skin was still warm, despite the rustic treatments. I did what I could with the supplies in hand, noting how the black within the veins seemed to pulse as I placed some of the new herb mixture into his cleaned wound before wrapping a fresh cloth around his shoulder. He did all he could to hide the pain, but I could sense it with each touch I delicately placed near his wound.

I couldn't help but place my hand as close as I could, wishing I had the same power as the Healers. I wondered what Spiritus felt like to Wield. I imagined that I could see the medicinal properties of the herbs releasing into his bloodstream and fighting away the infection and whatever the black substance was.

My mind's eye pretended that a delicate blue glow intertwined against the shadows within the blood vessels. The soft hue danced like silk blown away in the wind, wrapping itself amongst tree limbs.

And then it pulled.

My fingers began to twitch uncontrollably. A hiss escaped my mouth as a pain like I had never felt before seized like lightning in my skin. White hot but ice cold. I felt the sharp tinge of my teeth gritting as the pain ricocheted against every nerve in my body before it suddenly stopped.

The remnants left just enough evidence of a tingle before calming again. I pulled back my hands to study them like I was seeing them for the first time.

Within moments, Sury took in a deep breath and let out a sigh of relief.

"Wow." The tone in his voice lightened and sounded slightly more energetic. "My shoulder feels much better. Those herbs must have a giants' blessing to kick in so quickly."

I didn't look away from my bare hands. Was my mind going crazy at what just happened? Maybe the lack of rest was finally catching up to me.

It took me a second to find any words as I finally tore my eyes away from the hands I'd known for twenty-four years. "The herbs should help with the infection and the fever. The Healer was out, but the shopkeeper said it'll only be a temporary fix based on the minimal details I gave them. I didn't know how to exactly explain how we had Black Raiders following us and shooting poisonous arrows." I shrugged at the last bit.

"Hmm, probably for the best you don't mention that to anyone."

"I don't think many people would refrain from asking us more questions. So, the minimum it is. The fact that no one has noticed *you* around here is a miracle in itself."

"Must be the beard," he said with a rogue grin. "Or maybe Domesis has found favor for us."

That would be the day.

"I mentioned we were trying to seek the Three Sisters for help, so they gave me enough mixture to last a few days until then, or until one of their Healer neophytes could help."

Sury rotated his shoulder a few times and massaged around the bandage, color already coming back into his face, before sighing another breath of relief.

CHAPTER 16

The overhangs kept us moderately cool and provided enough shade to where we wouldn't get burned from the midday sun. Patrons were seated at the surrounding tables, talking and singing in merriment. Some more so singing in drunken delight.

It seemed that happiness was contagious in this town. A thought made me wonder why patrons didn't seem this happy when visiting the High Seven Temple to learn about magic. The same thought quickly escaped me as I scanned for some empty tables and saw a small one next to the inn's wall.

From behind, Sury walked up with two tankards of ale and sat opposite at the rickety table. We settled beside each other along the road and silently gazed at the walkers and vendors as they made their way up and down the street.

"So," Sury said as he sipped from his tankard. "Do you know what you will say?"

I took in a gulp of my own ale and almost choked at the stale taste. "You actually drink this?"

"Sometimes you have to drink it fast," he said as he took another giant swig and began to study the meat pies, sniffing each one intently.

I was not as cautious with the pie as I was with the ale. The bite immediately melted in my mouth. The crust held a delicious balance of butter and spices. Potatoes and onions, swimming in a rosemary gravy, and with chunks of lamb. I swear I had never tasted something so divine. Thank the giants there wasn't a mushroom in sight.

A noise must have escaped my mouth based on the way Sury looked at me.

"Calm down there, Phe. It's just a meat pie." Sury poked fun with a smirk.

"Sorry." I blushed. "I wasn't expecting it to taste this good!"

I took another bite and savored every morsel that bounced across my tongue.

He rolled his eyes and practically swallowed his meal in just a few bites. "Plan?" he asked as he washed it down with another swig from his tankard.

"From what I've read," I said in between bites, trying to hold my manners as my tastebuds wanted to devour the food, "we simply request their presence to hear our pleas. From there, I'm just as lost as you."

"Is it not the same as when someone visits the High Seven Temple?"

I shrugged my shoulders and continued. "Ariadne rarely mentioned the Three Sisters. If anyone brought them up in our lessons, she would say they were wasting their breath speaking about *inferior beings*. She said they're blasphemers of magic who disregard the rules of the Circles. She would say their ideology was toxic to Wielders and they only wanted to spread discord between us and Veiks. Disrupt the balance between us."

"Balance?" Sury scoffed. "Since when has there been balance between us? But you suspect she's been lying about them?"

"I'm beginning to suspect she fears them. Why not let us talk about them? We were vaguely taught of the pilgrimages and only learned pieces from the visitors that waited for Ariadne's audience." I waved my hands at our surroundings before continuing. "She always taught us that the High Seven Temple was *the* highest honor and made it seem like this town was no more than a field outside a dirt hut."

"Makes sense why she wouldn't let my father speak much about Zonnagberg. He would easily call her bluff."

He was right. I'd never heard Arjun speak much of the town itself. Only when small matters of the Sisters came up. Did my father or mother know the truth?

Sury sat back and took in the surroundings. Zonnagberg almost resembled the abundance of Grianmore and the townspeople. People of all kinds were laughing and dancing in the streets. There was a feeling of joy around every corner, a feeling of prosperity and life.

***

We decided to rest before setting out for the Sisters' Keep the next day. With Sury's shoulder in question, I had insisted that he take the bed to properly sleep while I slept on a small pallet of extra blankets on the floor, even with his protests.

The rhythmic breathing from the bed was the only tell that Sury was still fast asleep, even as the sun now rose. Good. We were tired, but the wound was draining him.

We needed a Healer, or at least one in training.

I quietly rolled off of my pallet and climbed to my feet before tiptoeing out of the room with boots in hand. Sury's light snoring covered my steps as I peered into the hallway, instantly greeted by the smells of someone cooking in the kitchens below.

Some patrons were already sitting at the long wooden tables, half awake or still up from the night before. I chuckled at the thought. Others were clad in their traveling clothes, and some were huddled around tables, all dressed in beautiful sage and silver robes. Acolytes.

I stood there, taking it in. I saw them with their beautiful, glowing-colored eyes signifying the typical Wielder in study, but the most fascinating of all were those with plain-colored eyes—all dressed the same. Some conversed amongst themselves next to the inn's windows, while others held the hands of weeping patrons.

The High Seven Temple's acolytes wore white and stayed within the confines of the temple walls, only tending to those who were granted acceptance to visit the temple itself. Come to think of it, I didn't think I'd ever seen an acolyte within Grianmore's walls.

Magic hummed underneath my skin as thoughts swirled at what the visit with the Three Sisters might entail. Would they accept us for an audience? Would we be turned away like so many who sought an audience with Ariadne?

How would you win against Ariadne and Vovias's game? the inky voice whispered. *How will you take on Dokvalon with no army? The Ancient One is pure myth told in ghost stories to keep naughty children in line. Calling on the Sisters is even more foolish.* It hissed the last sentence.

But urthen, I reasoned with myself. The urthen had been just as fictitious once, so maybe this wasn't a fool's hope after all?

You're a fool all the same.

A light clearing of the throat caught my attention. Thank Domesis for my good fortune that a different barmaid entered from the back curtain. She had placed two bowls of sweet porridge and fruit onto a large tray to take back to the room.

When I returned, Sury was awake and sat up straight in the bed rubbing his eyes, exhaustion still heavy on his pale face. A look of surprise and relief crossed his tawny features once he saw me enter the door. As graceful as a mountain cat, he jumped off the bed and then...roared.

"What the *FUCK*!" He crossed the room in a few quick steps. Even though we were similar in height, he did his best to look down his nose at me. "Do me a favor and let me know the next time you decide to leave! I don't need any extra worry these days of you disappearing without notice." The whites of his eyes faded to a light crimson, then turned white again. The veins in the whites pulsed brightly in comparison.

"Good morning to you, too," I huffed. "I only went to get us something to eat." I shoved against his good shoulder and walked across the room to set the tray on the small table. I took one of the bowls and forced it into Sury's hands. "I need to check your bandages before we leave."

I was not taking no for an answer.

"Oh. Thank you." Sury's stature shrank a few sizes as he looked down at the bowl. Shame blanketed his features before he smiled an emotionless smile. "Add this to your collection so I know you're safe next time you wander the fuck off."

I looked down at the dagger he held out. It was a little bigger than the one I carried but still large enough to be lethal. I took it and quickly sheathed it inside my boot.

"Now sit," I grumbled before opening up the small flap of his tunic to inspect the wound. The heat still radiated from Sury's skin as I unwrapped the bandages I'd set the day before.

The black spider webbing of veins continued to pulse and vibrate under my touch. I held back my gasp as I noticed how the veins had crept out against his skin and closer to his heart. Without a word, I went to the water pitcher to clean the infection before applying more of the herbal mixture.

"Phe," Sury started. He clenched his eyes shut tight as he struggled to work through his words. "I didn't mean to sound like an asshole. With Ora gone and this mess that we're in, I don't want anything happening to you, too."

"Focus your energy on finding her and feeling better," I clipped. His anger was still palpable.

"Thank you, Phe. I mean that."

"Of course. You're practically my own blood. Although I would rather not do any of this again."

"I was going to ask her to marry me, you know?"

My fingers stilled, waiting for him to elaborate.

"After the coronation, of course. A few months before they passed, I had received a partial blessing from your mother and father, but they said she had to marry an officially titled nobleman." He smirked.

We sat there in silence as I continued tending to the wound, both of our tensions finding their way back to as normal as they could be.

"Is that why your father stepped down so quickly to make you lord?"

"Possibly. His motives were always multifaceted," he said with a small smile. "So...did that one barmaid hit on you as you got breakfast?" Sury snickered.

"Thank the giants that it was someone else this morning, and she barely bothered talking to me." I smiled in return. "There. All done." I helped pull his tunic back above his shoulder. "What do you say we enjoy our meal outside again?"

We changed before I made a quick effort of my braid to look half groomed for our day. As we worked through our meal under the inn's overhang, I continued to watch in fascination the people who walked down the streets. There were more acolytes than the day prior, all clad in their robes. Some walked arm in arm, while others stopped to talk to random citizens at their carts and stalls.

The town was still sleeping for the most part. Most of the shops still had their doors shut and locked, while the carts around the streets had canvas sheets over them. But in the distance, blacksmiths could be heard sharpening and pounding metal, while cranking and sawing against wood was heard close by. Even the smell of fresh-cut pine danced in the air.

An artist's district was nearby and had an array of shops and studios and a small amphitheater for performances of different kinds. I wouldn't mind seeing the small bookshop that Sury described, which was around the corner on our way to the Sisters' Keep.

"When should we start making our way over there?" Sury asked as he ate another spoonful of porridge.

"As soon as we're done. Luckily, our clothes don't smell yet, and we look decently presentable." I shrugged as I watched an acolyte motion something with her hands to a frail woman with a cane.

"I say if they see as many pilgrims as there are in this town, then we have to be some of the cleanest travelers they've seen. A lot of those here smell like they could use a strong bath. Or five."

"That's funny coming from you. The man who would rather live in the woods than his family's estate." I chuckled as I popped a sliced apple into my mouth.

"There are still such things as washing oneself in a stream every now and then. I'm not a *complete* barbarian."

"Remind me as to why my sister decided to pursue a romantic relationship with you? I mean, there was that one vizier..."

"Well, Phe, when you are the size of a..." Sury nonchalantly pointed down to the inseam of his trousers.

"Stop!" I threw my hand up in protest and shivered. "I was only joking and do not want to know *anything* more about you two than I already know!"

Sury clanked my cup of tea with a smile as he drank deeply from his own. The tables around us steadily became occupied by other patrons and visitors chatting over their own mugs of brewed energy. I finished up the remnants of my bowl, savoring the sweetness that filled my stomach.

"Let's say just for shits... What do we do if the Sisters decide not to accept our audience?"

"Then we try again! Ora wouldn't give up easily, and neither should we."

"No. Your sister doesn't give up at all." Sury smiled as he drained the remaining portions of his tea.

I chuckled at a memory. "Remember when she was relentless with that one visiting lord...Teakin, I think, from Mercyth...who acted like he knew *everything*, but Ora continued to prove how right she was in *everything*?"

"Oh yes. I remember hearing how your mother gave her a good scorn for a week after that. You know, propriety for diplomacy and all that."

"She's never been diplomatic," I said with a laugh. "Never mind that she was thirteen. She still didn't give up!" We smiled at one another with the memory, feeling a renewal of hope.

"Ready?" Sury asked. I only got to nod once before we heard a voice speak up.

"Oh, there will be no crossing that bridge today." A deep, raspy voice came from behind Sury, who whipped around, ready to face one of the Black Raiders or one of Vovias's men. I hardly registered the dagger he pulled from his belt, ready to strike.

Instead of a soldier, our eyes met the gaze of the wild-haired man I saw being shooed away from the merchant's cart. His long brown hair was unwashed and matted against his temples and down his back, and his left ear was pierced with bright silver hoops, reaching up to the crest of the arch. From the dirt on his face, I couldn't tell just how old he was but guessed maybe a decade older than me.

His eyes were brilliantly bright, especially against the dirt on his tanned skin, and were the sharpest shade of silver I had ever seen. It was like looking into freshly polished silver candlesticks. The man cracked a small, sideways smile that almost reached his cold eyes.

My magic seemed to hum as I felt my heart flutter at his gaze. The sensation of something old and foreign flickered across the inner walls of my mind, but also something deeply curious and strangely familiar as I took him in. The man's smile stretched just a hair higher as he cocked his head to the side, studying me in return. I didn't realize I had stopped breathing before snapping back into the moment. The inward flickering subsided.

"Who are you?" Sury said, with his knife still angled out in defense. "What do you know?"

The man's clothes were just as filthy with holes peppered across the material and his trousers worse for wear. Upon further inspection, he was completely barefoot, and his feet were caked in mud. The man sat on the bench behind us, eating from a bowl of cherries that I could only guess he must have stolen from a stall.

I noticed underneath his rugged beard that his cheeks were sunken in. Matter of fact, all of him looked completely starved. Like something was eating him from within. Eating his very soul. But the light inside his eyes glowed fiercely. I realized I had never seen another Wielder with silver eyes. Bright golds, and hues that rivaled gemstones, yes, but never *silver*.

"Sit down before you draw attention to yourself," the wild-haired man said as he continued to eat cherries, one by one, spitting the pits on the ground. The juice ran down the sides of his mouth and covered his chin and torn shirt, like a rabid dog who had been caught feasting on its prey with blood still on his face.

He turned his gaze toward Sury before turning back to me. A flicker of energy radiated down my spine, and my fingertips tingled before the feeling disappeared again. "Just passing along friendly advice," the stranger said as he popped another cherry into his smile, juice splattering more.

Through his torn shirt, one could see there were four equally thick blackened bands inked across his right forearm. Curiosity urged me to inquire what they meant, but instinct told me to keep my mouth shut.

"I think we'll manage just fine, *sir*." Sury turned back toward his chair and sheathed his dagger into his belt before sitting back down.

The stranger tilted his neck, releasing the sound of an inner crack. "You might manage. But will she?" the man said again with another tilt of his head, only piquing my interest that much more.

His stare pulled deep within my gut and chest, causing my magic to stir and surge to the surface. Small shadows crept along the ground and hovered over my feet. Something was so curious about this man and his eyes that I forgot about my surroundings. He felt like an old acquaintance that I hadn't seen in decades. But I had never seen this man other than the day prior.

"What do you mean?" Sury said through his teeth, in motion to rise from the table again.

"*Sit down!*" I quietly hissed. I looked around to see if any of the other patrons were looking our way, but most were either busy in conversation or deep into their meals. The shadows retreated.

The wild-haired man winced as he threw another cherry into his mouth and popped the juice and pit to the ground next to Sury's feet. "Yes, *Lord*, please sit down." Sury shot the wild-haired man a pointed look, ready to pounce without question.

I sprang to my feet and pulled on Sury's good arm for him to sit down to face me. I looked across his shoulder and at the man behind staring back at me. "Who are you?" I asked, trying to sound as menacing as I possibly could. I knew I failed when he merely chuckled and answered in his raspy, deep voice. A sound similar to when someone goes hoarse from screaming, almost a whisper.

"It's not that hard to guess who he is with daggers such as yours. A house's insignia is carved into the handle. Only the Lord and Ladyships of Gria have such fine pieces for a blade. Unless you stole it." Good. He doesn't recognize who Sury is, who in turn gave me a look of warning, slightly shaking his head, before the man continued. "With the closeness of you two, we suspect you are lovers looking for the Three Sisters' blessing to get married, since the daddy of the *Little Lord* wouldn't give it. Unfortunately for you two lovebirds, soldiers of Gria are blocking the bridge."

I laughed inwardly in relief at just how wrong the stranger was and felt a small sense of relief that my identity and intention were still hidden. I relaxed my shoulders a smidge as I leaned closer to Sury to help play up the ruse. Which also felt wrong to do.

"Well, you are all-knowing! Pray tell, how do you know that it's the Grian Army that is here? Why stop people from visiting the Three Sisters? Truly, why waste those resources in calling on the realm's army for a *Little Lord*." I tried to sound like a damsel that had just been caught in a mischievous plan and even batted my eyelashes twice. At least, a *different* mischievous plan.

"We saw them as we passed by the river. They barked orders about a fair maiden with teal eyes. And from what we gather, that would be *you* since many Wielders around here don't have your hue; mostly greens and golds."

"He's delusional," I whispered just low enough for Sury to hear.

"Maybe we are. Maybe we're not," the man replied with a simple shrug as he popped another cherry into his mouth. "We heard the order from an older man who sent soldiers this way to inspect Zonnagberg, just in case."

Something told me I didn't want to bet against what this man said. A shadow flickered and pulsed inside of me, wanting to question him more. A heartbeat later, a chaos of shouts and neighing horses were heard just three streets over.

Fuck.

Sury grabbed me by the arm and pulled me inside the Alba and up to the room we shared. Without words or thought, we both grabbed our things and began the descent back down to the front door as we heard footsteps and horses march along the stone paths now two streets away.

The stranger now sat where we'd just been, eating scraps out of the bowls we left behind. I tied my cloak around me and threw the hood over my head to conceal myself as much as I could.

We scanned the road in front of us for any sign of danger. Through the crossways, we saw foot soldiers stop and question everyone they passed on the street, all looking for the *fair maiden with teal eyes*. Sury tugged on my arm to pull me to the right. Both of us turned on our heels to escape down another side street and away from the inn.

"You don't want to go that way," the man called out, drinking the last remnants of ale from another empty table's tankard. "They have all the entrances blocked. But one."

"But one? Where the hell is it?" Sury marched up to the man and grabbed him by the collar of his torn tunic. He forced the man up and out of the chair like he weighed nothing. "Better yet, show us." Sury grabbed a dagger and forcefully pressed it against the man's neck.

The stranger revealed a wicked smile, as if he enjoyed the game.

"We don't have time for this!" I cried to deaf ears.

Something red flashed across Sury's eyes. "Clearly, this man knows more about us than we know about him. I'm not taking any chances. Not with them so close," he spat. "Now, you will lead us out of this place, unharmed, or you will wish your death to be a painless one."

"Oh, how we wish for death already," the stranger whispered as his eyes flashed wide, grinning maniacally. The man fully straightened, towering over Sury, and took steps forward with Sury still clutching his tunic, forcing the dagger to press closer to his skin. One wrong move from either one of the men and the stranger's throat would be cut, despite his obvious height advantage.

In a swift motion, the stranger twisted from Sury's vice grip and turned Sury's arm up and inward, making his own dagger press tightly against Sury's ribs. "Be careful who you point that dagger to, *boy.*" And just as quick, the man released Sury and stepped aside. "As long as you don't mind getting dirty. This way." And just like that, the man turned on his heels and quickly went around the back of the Alba. We stayed rooted where we were as we questioned our next moves.

"We can't trust him, Phe." Sury shook his head, the red haze in his eyes still there, the veins in his throat throbbing.

"Do we have any other choice? He didn't have to tell us about soldiers being here."

"He could be leading us to a trap and into Vovias's hands, desperate for money!"

"We'll be dead either way then. But at least I died taking a chance. A chance to save us and my sister."

I took off after the man as I watched him climb over a wooden fence behind the inn's back alley. I took a few steps forward, ready to follow, but I felt an emptiness behind me. I looked over my shoulder for Sury but found him still at the mouth of the alleyway, standing deathly still.

No. I felt my heart drop, thinking the worst, but then I saw a woman in a sage and silver robe standing in front of him. Her hand was clasped loosely between his nape and jaw while her other hand held firm near the front of her brocaded robes. We didn't have time for this.

They looked as if they were in deep conversation, except Sury said nothing, only nodded and looked down at his feet. She let go of him just as she turned her head and looked toward me. She was stunningly beautiful, and her eyes were a beautiful deep shade of gold. Quickly, she turned back to Sury and spoke a few more words before moving around him and walking down the road.

"Sury?" I whispered as I began walking toward him.

He never responded as he looked up to the sky, mumbling unheard words, then pivoted toward me like nothing had ever happened. I planned to pry later.

"He went this way," I said as I scaled the same fence as the man. Sury was just a foot behind me when we reached the man waiting for us at the base.

"Took you long enough," the stranger said as he shook his head like we were wasting *his* time.

I felt a rising panic but forced it to obey, for now, as we continued down the darkened alley. The walls were too close for my comfort. Near the alley's opening, I could make out the shop where I'd bought the tunics. Good, I knew where I was. Kind of. A flash of silver and gold glinted ahead, forcing my feet to come to a quick stop.

Grian soldiers.

I clutched Sury's shirt and pulled him up against the wall to hide behind numerous crates. We stood there and watched as soldiers banked the steps of the shop and pounded on the door. The stranger also stopped and peeked over his shoulder as if he sensed we were no longer behind him. He tilted his head again, studying me, before casually pivoting and resting against one of the alley's walls like he belonged there.

We watched the soldiers in their usual gilded armor, but something about the way they moved and behaved struck me as odd. One of the soldiers, a tall and broad woman with stark white hair pulled tightly in braids close to her head, beat on the door again. The small man who owned the shop fumbled in unlocking the door and quickly pulled it open.

"The shop is not yet open, my dear lady, but perhaps if you come back another time..."

The woman clearly didn't hear the man or ignored him as he spoke. I decided it had to be the latter. "A fair woman, black hair, Wielder, teal eyes. Have you seen or sold to anyone that matches this description?"

The man, clearly nervous, fumbled with his hands and looked at each of the towering soldiers. His lower jaw quivered as he tried to find the words and nervously looked around. My heart sank when the man's eyes wandered to mine and narrowed. His spine straightened just a bit, and he cleared his throat. "No." The man spoke with forced confidence. "No, I have not seen nor sold to anyone who matches that description."

The woman shook her head and turned about-face to walk down the steps. Each soldier followed her lead, but one remained on the top step next to the shopkeeper. Before anything could be done, the soldier reached toward the man, who doubled over at the same time. No words were spoken as the soldier pulled back a sword. A deep red glimmered in the rising sun and dripped onto the steps next to the shopkeeper's feet. Blood.

A squeak rose up in my throat, but before a noise could escape, I felt Sury's hand against my mouth. My eyes widened as I locked them with the dying man's and started to shake. I glanced back to watch the soldier walking away, the clink of armor echoing against the stone steps as he walked down to follow the others. The shop owner's hand, covering the wound at his gut, was coated in blood. His once cream-colored tunic began to turn to the color of rust as the wound seeped. His dulling hazel eyes turned toward me again right before he landed on the top step without another breath.

Tears formed in my eyes for the man who could have been truthful and saved his own life. Wondering why he did such a thing entered my mind, but the thought was interrupted by a raspy voice.

"We have to move," the man called from down the alley with a softer look in his eyes before he took off once again.

He motioned us to snake behind him as we crept behind buildings and over fences. His motions were fluid and fast. I wondered how he was able to move so quickly, given that he looked as if he hadn't eaten a solid meal in months. He moved like a hunter. On second thought, more like a predator. Quiet. Quick. Every step was surer than the last.

His arms and wrists bent out at slightly odd angles when he climbed, and his legs and feet bent out with each step. The eerie sight sent a chill up my spine that caused a light rumble of my magic deep within my gut, like my magic was being challenged.

When we finally reached the northwestern portion of the city's wall, we were greeted with a dead end. Behind us, we could hear shouts from the soldiers inching closer to where we were now trapped. My breath quickened as I searched for any way to scale the wall or the building opposite in hopes of finding a quick exit.

You're trapped. You trusted a fool and now you're trapped. The same inky voice slithered across my thoughts just as the stranger turned toward me and pinned me with his stare, his eyes momentarily flared. My heart raced unwillingly.

"I knew it. This bastard led us to our death!" Sury withdrew his sword and placed the blade next to the stranger's torso.

The stranger's eyes grew wild, and another maniacal grin spread wide on his face as he took Sury in. Slowly, he leaned forward into Sury's sword, causing the blade to prick the skin on his frail-looking chest. A tiny trickle of bright, red blood dripped down and landed on his dirty tunic.

"This way, *Little Lord*," he said as he made a deep bow and kicked on a metal grate at the base of the stone wall, making it clink in its place. The grate was thick enough for two men to lift, but the man lifted it with ease and placed it next to the opening before he dropped into the ground below.

"What the fu—?" Sury sighed to the sky as he sheathed his sword. "Giants help us."

I passed Sury in silence as a strange sensation of instinct took over, only to be pulled back by my arm before I made it closer to the hole. "Are you sure?" he asked as his eyes pleaded. "I don't feel good about this. Everything within my being is telling me this is not a good idea."

I grasped his good shoulder. "I can't explain it, but we have to follow him."

"How can you be so certain?"

I wasn't. This was all pure madness. Everything about this situation we were in was madness. Everything I was willing to chase was madness. But like a magnet pull, I just knew.

"Trust me," I said as I turned and dropped into the hole.

The world instantly became dark. It took a few moments for my eyes to adjust to my surroundings and the dimly-lit griminess, illuminated only by the hole above. The air was a lot colder but held a thick moisture of stench.

I steadied myself on a stone wall and dry heaved until I could cover my mouth and nose with my cloak. Neither helped much. Dead and decayed animals, bits of food, and who knows what else floated in the questionable waters that came to my ankles. At least the water didn't go into my boots, but it did soak up a few inches of my cloak. Dammit.

Sury sprang down behind, steady on his feet, taking in the surroundings as well. "Where the hell are we?"

"From the smell, I'm going to guess the sewers."

"This way." We heard the deep whisper from a darker tunnel. A flash of silver iridescent animal-like eyes blinked once before disappearing around a corner. I unsheathed my dagger and held it close to my side in case my wits were wrong and this was indeed a trap. I knew better than to throw all my trust into a stranger, but I also knew I had very little choice. If Vovias had found us, then our fate in his hands would be far worse than in this stranger's.

I still couldn't pinpoint why I had the strangest curiosity in the man we followed, though. Sury was in step with me as we continued down the dark tunnel, only illuminated by the occasional beam of light from the grates above. Our feet echoed as we created small splashes in the water. Steady trickles could be heard in all directions as an occasional squeak from an animal echoed in the distance.

The deeper we trekked, the easier the air became to breathe. I felt sweat trickle around my hairline and fall down my spine near my trousers. Steadily, the tunnel grew lighter as we neared a giant opening at the end, which was closed off with thick, tightly fitted bars. Another dead end.

I ran past the stranger and to the bars. I shook them violently, hoping at least one was loose for us to escape. Just beyond the opening, I could see the trees and a clearing ahead. Harder and harder, I pushed the bars, but nothing would budge as I let out a frustrated cry.

"Enough of these games!" Sury roared at the man. "Get us the hell out of here!"

The man turned and looked me in the eye. He held my stare for a brief moment and squinted, like he was trying to see something that wasn't there.

"Not everything is as it appears, is it?" he whispered just low enough for me to hear.

With his foot, he tapped the far-left bar, which popped loose and fell, creating a large enough gap for a person to slip through.

"Thank you," I breathed and watched the man push through and into the forest. We followed close behind, all running like hell.

CHAPTER 17

The fresh air was a much-needed remedy to the grueling smells within the sewage tunnels. The tall evergreens and sycamores shaded the forest floor and provided some relief from the sun's bright rays. We slowed to a moderate pace. Behind us, I could hear the faint shouts of soldiers off in the distance.

I doubled over to my knees, trying to catch a breath, cursing the giants for a body failing the endurance I needed. Time was not on our side. We had to keep moving.

"Where are the bannermen? Guards?" I asked Sury as I wheezed for breath.

"I don't know. That's what concerns me. Anmathios foot soldiers should be used for searches. Not soldiers who looked like they're from Grianmore."

"We need to hurry. I don't think we have a lot of time before they expand their search." I breathed in deeply as I stood and turned, walking right into Sury's back.

The stranger stopped running altogether and stood before Sury with his hand out in front of him. His chin lifted high with a small smirk on his lips. "We got started off on the wrong foot," the man said. "Peiro." He breathed as if he'd only taken a light stroll.

Sury eyed him and cautiously shook his hand. "Sury." His labored breath drew out each syllable. Regardless of his paling face, I sensed something else was off. His stance was rigid but loose, like he was forcing himself to stand.

Peiro turned to face me and placed his hand over his heart before giving me a slight head nod. "Phe," I said, breathing hard through the pleasantries, "and thank you again. Your kindness will not go unnoticed."

Peiro gave me a small smile. "You're eternally welcome."

"Now what?" I directed the question to Sury. "Where do we go from here?"

"Let's keep moving. Those soldiers are trained to move quickly, and my father's estate is a day—"

"We can't get your father involved. We don't even know for sure if..."

Sury's pale face flushed with color, bringing his bronze skin back to life, even momentarily. "Don't you *dare* imply my father is a part of this. He loved your mother and father! He loves your sister as if she were his own daughter!" Spittle sprayed the higher his voice carried.

I jumped at the outburst, trying to find the words to tell him that I didn't mean that how it had come out. "Sury..." In a matter of a few blinks, his eyes turned from red back to their whites.

"If we may," Peiro cut in, stepping in between us, "we know of someone who lives not too far off from here whose land is warded and remains undetectable by those with ill intent. It's no more than half a day's walk from here if you need somewhere to rest and think of a new plan for your nuptials or why-ever-the-hell Grian soldiers are chasing after you.

"Or we could walk through the forest back toward Zonnagberg. There's another way to the Sisters that many have forgotten about...but that might take more than a day, and by the looks of you, Little Lord, I don't know if you have the time."

"Why are you so keen on helping us?" Sury stepped toward Peiro, his hand finding his dagger once again.

Peiro saw the threat and stepped forward, tensing his back, ready to spring.

"Seriously, you two! You both are so quick to draw blood first, ask questions later!" I pulled on Sury's good arm, trying to draw him back, but was shaken off like a fallen leaf.

"We can't trust him, Phe!" The whites in Sury's eyes reddened again. "We don't know him or why he's helping us!"

"You're right, but he's helped twice now. He got us this far." Desperation clung in the air.

"Listen to her, Little Lord." Peiro bent his neck side to side, joints popping. "You would not have made two steps out of Zonnagberg on your own. Your pride and inflated sense of self-worth would have gotten you caught as soon as you stepped away from that inn." I stepped around Peiro to stand by Sury. I noticed his bright eyes flashed a bit as he continued staring Sury down. "We've known too many worms like you in our time. Listen to the wisdom the lady has given you. You can either trust our hand, which has gotten you this far into safety, or follow your own sense that's drawing you back to your master." Each word he spoke came out lower and harsher, driving his points home with deliberate force.

The men were leaning in toward one another—Sury with his dagger within reach, Peiro's hands flexing open and closed. I needed to do something to stop possible bloodshed between the two.

I felt myself start to panic. Nerves and rage tightened and squeezed in my core, the magic shifting to a mind of its own, reacting to something I couldn't see. A pull drew up and out. Silver orbs danced in my left hand as I pulled out my dagger with the right. The sun overhead dimmed a fraction, lessening the rays that speared down in between the tree leaves. Shadows along the ground started to vibrate in place, trying to crawl forward.

I took a deep breath as I faced the man. "Peiro, show us out of this forest and no harm will come to you. If you try to harm me or my companion, extreme measures will be taken." I hoped and prayed to the giants above that I looked convincing this time.

Sury knew my temperament and that I could never hurt another person...intentionally. He raised his eyebrow slightly, but not enough to show Peiro my bluff. He knew that my power wasn't strong enough to use for fighting but probably also thought I was insane enough to attempt a bold move against the stranger.

I expected to be met with malice or rage, but Peiro looked at my hand with fear in his eyes. He clenched his fingers to his temple and twisted his face in agony, screaming in a silent plea. He fell to his knees quickly, bones cracking on impact, and began to convulse on the ground, twisting grotesquely at our feet. His mouth stayed open in that silent scream as the edges of his mouth lined with white foam.

"Phe! What are you doing to him?" Sury passed a worried look to the man and back to me.

"Nothing! I just touched my magic at its surface! I'm not...I'm not doing anything! I can't even move a leaf with this little draw in my Wielding!" I quickly dropped my hand and absorbed the magic back into my skin, feeling a slight cooling in my fingertips. I raced to Peiro on the ground and flipped him to his back.

His eyes were out of focus as he held his gaze on the trees above him. Despite the dirt, and what I suspected was weeks from a proper bath, he smelled oddly sweet, almost cloying to my senses. Peiro lay there, catching his rapid breath, and finally fixed his focus on my face above him. The brightness in his eyes had dimmed to a dull, sterling gray.

"What are you?" His raspy whisper thickened his deep voice. His fingers trembled as they reached for my face.

"We have to move, *now!*" Sury quickly shouted.

I heard the cry of a horse just beyond a ridge of trees and the light thudding of soldiers' feet stomping in the distance. The Grianmore men seemed to be moving at a speed I didn't think was possible.

I helped Peiro to his feet. He stumbled forward, catching himself against a tree to regain his balance. "This way," he said without turning back, and began sprinting through the thick trees as if nothing had happened. He moved with surprising grace and speed, especially for someone whose body looked so frail.

Sunlight caught glimpses of the silver in his ears as he bobbed through the thickets and dense bushes growing closely together. He quickly scrambled up another ridge ahead and stood by the base of a tree, waiting for us to catch up.

We struggled to find our breath as we finally crested the top and turned to overlook the dense forest below. Peiro was picking wild berries from a nearby bush while I doubled over and dry heaved from the exertion. The air in my lungs clung to every cell, not wanting to let go.

Sury's face bore a couple of droplets of sweat, while Peiro surprisingly looked like he was within his own element. "We're about to enter the densest part," he said as he threw the last of the blackberries into his mouth. "Everywhere is covered in thick vines and ferns. I need something sharp to help chop us all through." Peiro outstretched a hand to Sury in demand of his sword or a spare blade.

"Not a chance," Sury huffed as he handed me his quiver and bow, and pushed in front of Peiro, drawing his sword to begin chopping through the trees with his good arm.

"Are you going to make it?" I felt Peiro's shadow cascading down on me as I tried to gain my composure. I tensed when I felt his fingers brush the small of my back. Peiro's eyes widened, and he pulled back his hand like something had bitten him.

"Apologies," he mumbled.

He was two heads taller than me, with my head meeting his chest, and looked thin under his worn clothing. There was no telling how long he had gone without a proper meal. I felt a sense of sorrow and sadness for him. Deep lines were etched around pained eyes that looked intently at me.

I felt my magic stir deep in my gut, itching to come back to the surface. A silent gesture or warning I didn't know. Steadily, I pushed it down with each calming breath and guided it back to its holding place. I looked at Peiro and simply nodded that I was fine.

I took in a deep inhale to calm my breath. "Are you sure we can lose them in this thicket?" I said, more so to Sury than to Peiro.

Sury shrugged. "It seems it's the best we can do for now," he said, then proceeded to chop through the greenery to create a narrow space for us all to walk through.

I followed closely behind with my own dagger in hand, hoping to help provide any protection where I could from any soldiers who might find us, or the stranger. I argued inside my head at the madness we were in.

You were always known not to think for yourself, and when you do, the decisions aren't the brightest.

Your sister was always the critical thinker of the two. Maybe that's why she's the queen-to-be and not you.

Shut. The. Fuck. Up, I seethed to the inner voices.

Footsteps and sounds of soldiers and horses became steadily quieter as we hiked. Sury occasionally held up his hand to stop us all where we were and listen for anyone following us.

While the forest protected us from the searching soldiers, the unforgiving greenery slowed us down to a grueling pace. Sury was now covered in sweat and frustration, even after adjusting his cloak to allow some sort of relief. I sensed the fatigue setting in and knew his shoulder was adding to the toll.

"We need to rest before going any farther. Even for an hour," I pleaded for Sury's sake. I didn't know how long before the poison would take another grasp on him, and I had accidentally left the herbs to give him comfort.

"We need to cross the river," Peiro gruffed. "A little farther, then you both can rest."

It felt like hours with our grueling slow pace to the small clearing and the roaring river beyond it. The Dolock River nearly slices the country into two parts. Aorr, the giant of water, made the river look angry with its swift current and small white caps.

Peiro pushed past Sury to lead the rest of the way to the water and simply walked through the waist-deep looking river without caring about being pulled under. Sury and I removed our cloaks and tightened our weapons before following the man's steps.

The clear water was cold and crept up into my boots as I carefully stepped forward, trying to avoid any loose rocks. The unforgiving flow did its best to topple me over and carry me downstream. Any other day, I would have simply enjoyed reading a book on the bank and let the river's words carry me into a sweet sleep.

I bit my lip to muffle the discomfort from the vast sensation of my skin turning from hot to cold and wiggled my toes to bring in new life before trudging forward. Each step brought the water steadily higher until it was just below my chest. Sury, only a few steps behind, moved at a slower pace than I anticipated from him but, nonetheless, appeared to be welcoming the cool water as it whipped past and splashed onto his tunic.

I saw him struggling to find his own footing with each crushing push of water. He paused momentarily as he tried to gain a new breath with each step. The current took an angry turn as if sensing Sury's passing and pushed harder against him. His feet stumbled forward. I twisted my body quickly to catch him by the shirt, pressing on his wound to hold him upright. Sury yelled out in anguish and lurched forward again. The river continued to press on us to force us off balance. He grabbed at the quiver's strap I had tightened around my chest. The leather snapped, releasing its hold on me and floated away too quickly for me to catch.

My panic quickened as I tried to hold Sury, while making sure I was still on even footing. The tingle in my toes refused to subside and only amplified as I dug my feet into the riverbed, trying to find any hook to steady us from going underwater. For no rhyme nor reason, I shot my hand out in front of me as if I could shove away the rising current.

I felt the surge of the river against my fingertips. A stammering pulse calming to a gentle beat.

What the hell? I thought to myself.

The roar of the river momentarily turned to the steady calm of a babbling brook. I pulled back my hand to pull on Sury's good arm this time and hold him upright, taking advantage of the current's collected mood. We found our way onto the pebbled beach with calculated steps.

I felt my legs shake uncontrollably, begging for any rest I was willing to give them. Once on solid ground, we dropped to our knees and drank our fill of the cool water. Each cell in my body felt revitalized while I thanked Aorr for not killing us.

Even with the sun high in the sky, I felt an incurable chill from the water. I silently cursed it and Aksyn, the giant of the sun, to hurry up and dry my clothes and hair. Chills ran up and down my spine, leaving tiny bumps in their wake. A cold breeze answered my shivers, and I started to shake as we begrudgingly resumed our grueling pace on the rocky riverbank.

Peiro had already made great strides, searching for small pieces of dried wood, and he worked quickly to build a small fire next to a soft patch of grass. His movements were the same as if someone had simply taken a light dip along the river and not just waded through rapids.

I walked up to the grassy part of the embankment and plopped down next to where Peiro set up small sticks.

He pointed to the tiny bits of tinder. "Here. Start this."

I looked at him in confusion, not entirely understanding.

"Your Wielding. Start the fire. I can tell you're cold."

"I can't," I answered.

Peiro's bright eyes intensified as they narrowed. "Can't? Or won't?"

I returned his glare, even matching the straight lines of our mouths as I crossed my arms over my chest. "Can't. It's not my level."

He arched his brow as he continued to assess me. Did he have a look of disgust? Irritation? My chagrin blossomed as I watched him turn with a grunt to find something to start a fire by hand. I felt another wave of shame.

You have failed so many and now you even fail the stranger who has graciously helped you this far. Why should he even bother? I heard the inky voice say. I clenched my eyes shut, trying hard to force back the thoughts.

I didn't notice the warmth in front of me until I heard Sury step across the rocks and sit with a *thud* beside me. I opened my eyes and found Peiro squatting across from me. His eyes practically glowed against the growing flames he worked to start.

I quickly looked away to redirect my focus to Sury. "Aren't you freezing?" I asked as my teeth lightly chattered.

Sury flung his wet hair back and forth, splashing droplets on my face. "That actually felt quite refreshing." He laid down in the grass, resting and stretching his back. "I've been burning since we arrived at the Alba."

"I'll find us food. This man looks like he's about to keel over," Peiro said quickly as he stood and walked over to an opening in the trees that led into the forest behind us.

I looked down at Sury and noted just how pale he had become. "How? We don't have arrows?" I called out, pointing to the now broken bow.

"Easy," Peiro said as he walked deeper into the forest.

The sun slowly descended. I continued to feed the fire with tiny sticks and blades of dried grass, finally drying my clothes and hair. I could feel my muscles and bones ache in protest from sitting on the hard ground. A grumble came from my stomach to remind me that we needed to find something to eat.

"Where do you think Peiro's gone? Should we help?" I turned to ask Sury, finding him fast asleep. His clothes were now dry but his skin had turned to almost gray in color. "Sury! Are you okay?" I shook him hard on his good shoulder to wake him up, careful not to dig my fingers into him. Sury sprang up with a jolt. He gasped for air and clenched his chest before shaking his head and taking in the surroundings.

Tiny black lines on Sury's skin crept up from underneath his tunic and toward the hollow at the base of his throat. I blinked twice to make sure I didn't see them actively climbing.

"How long have I been sleeping for?" He rubbed his eyes and winced at the setting sun. "Has Peiro caught anything? We need to keep moving."

"Not too long, but you need to stay and rest. I can forage for berries before we leave." I climbed to my feet, reluctant to leave Sury by himself.

He rose to his feet, demanding that he help, and stumbled up to the path Peiro had taken into the woods. Even against my protests I watched him disappear into the tree line. Food—he needed food. I made a quick search up and down the river's edge and hit the jackpot with some gooseberries.

"YOU STUPID PIECE OF SHIT!" I heard Sury yell through the trees. My heart raced as I dropped the cache of berries and ran in the direction of his shouts. The fear setting in felt cold. How did the Grian soldiers catch us so quickly? We would have spotted them first. Wouldn't we?

You're an imbecile. This was a trap all along, the voice whispered.

I grabbed the dagger from my boot right before I saw his body on the other side of the thick trees. "Sury! What happened?"

He was partially doubled over, holding himself upright using a limb, standing over Peiro's body, who seemed to be half asleep against the base of the tree. The pupils in his grayish-silver eyes were heavily dilated and drifted from side to side, looking at nothing above him.

"What happened?" I called out again as I stood next to Sury.

"This waste of air is messing with us! He's a *user*, Phe! Users are liars and thieves! He's not out here to help us! He probably doesn't even fucking know who he is or where we fucking are!"

Valley gilliflower. What's highly addictive the desperates use to escape whatever demons, real or not, chase them. Sure enough, beside Peiro's still hand lay a tiny wooden pipe that held a brown, sticky substance at the end. I smelled the same foul, sweet essence I had smelled on him earlier.

I felt a slight tinge of pity mixed with rage. His face appeared more at... Was it peace? His softened features were less rugged than before and the lines around his mouth were soft and framed his lips beautifully.

What could torture a man so much to cause him to mask his pain in such a cruel way?

A dark cloud loomed over Sury's face as he peered down at the wasted man at his feet. A palpable rage rose to the surface as I noticed the unnatural red color take over his eyes again. Sury bellowed out in anger and kicked the man in the side over and over again. The sound of bone cracking echoed against the trees.

Shock matched my own fury.

"SURY! Don't you DARE!" I yelled as I jumped over tree roots and pushed Sury away, careful not to slice him with my dagger. Little dancing orbs emerged from my hands, sending a slight shock into his skin as I pushed.

Sury gasped as he brought his hand to his chest. He pulled back his fingers and looked at them in confusion, as if expecting to see something on them. His eyes snapped up to mine, reddening with each passing moment.

"What is wrong with you? Is *this* the man my sister loves?" I hissed between clenched teeth. I had never seen him stoop so low. I knew he was better than this.

"Don't defend him!" he snarled. "He's sending us on a fucking goose chase! For all we know, we're absolutely lost! And you're too fucking blind to see it!"

His words felt like a slap to the face. I took a deep breath to hold my composure, hoping it would not feed off his rising emotion. "You're angry. I get it. I'm angry! But we *do not* do this to people." I pointed to Peiro who laid unnaturally still, blood dripping from his nose.

"He's wasting our time, Phe! Time I don't have!"

"What do you want me to do? I'm doing all I can with what I know! I'm trying my damndest to figure out where my sister is while the Grian Army, *my family's* army, is after my own fucking neck!"

"We're following fucking breadcrumbs! I have to get to her... to see her! One last time." An emotion I couldn't quite grasp flashed across his face before smoothing back to bitterness. "Before it's too late."

"I don't see *you* coming up with any ideas that could help us other than drawing your damn sword at every turn!" It struck me mid-sentence. "Wait...what do you mean *one last time*? You *will* see her. We both will! We have to stick together and work through this."

Sury dropped his head and slowly shook it, letting a quiet sob escape his mouth. "She told me I would die before I get to see her again." His shoulders drooped forward.

"What are you talking about? *Who* told you this?"

Sury looked up, his eyes brimmed with tears. The strange red in his eyes was now gone.

"The acolyte in the street. She said she studies under the Sister who knows what is to come. She told me, '*You will be greeted with death before being filled with life. You will die before seeing the love of your life.*'"

My heart fell. "Maybe she was mistaken?" I tried to come up with a million reasons to justify the mistake, but my thoughts froze as I watched tears crest over and fall down Sury's cheeks.

"I said the same thing. She said she knew I had questions about your sister, about my shoulder and the poison within it. She said she could sense it."

I stood there a moment before turning back to Sury. "Why didn't you tell me?!"

He shook his head and looked into the trees in the distance, having trouble finding his next words. My blood boiled as I felt my rage rise within my chest. I felt my Wielding come to the surface but paid it no mind.

My sister's lover, my own friend and brother through a bond.

This was too much. I couldn't do this without him.

I hardly had time to notice small shadows at my feet as Peiro howled out in pain, shaking the silence around us. My eyes flew to where he lay as he began to convulse and shake on the ground. Bits of foam escaped his mouth. His eyes fluttered open and then rolled to the back of his head, showcasing the whites.

The shock settled my anger and dissolved the magic that was my hand. As soon as it disappeared, Peiro stopped seizing and lay completely still, breathing erratically. His body was slightly contorted with his legs bent underneath him in odd angles.

I watched in horror as he flickered his eyes open and adjusted himself to lay flat on the ground, gasping for air before catching his breath in deep inhales and exhales.

I willed my feet to move and step toward him to help just as he softly began to chuckle—a chuckle that built into a roaring laughter. I watched as his eyes pulsed between a dulling and glowing sterling silver.

"Ah, so we see you two have caught us with the *sticky sweet*," he said as he looked blankly into the leaves above him. "What will you do now? Throw us into a workhouse in the middle of nowhere?" His laugh sounded contorted. "Gallows it be for us. Swing a day or two, then try again."

Sury's eyes grew wider as he stomped over to a leather pouch that lay next to Peiro's boots and swiped it off the ground. "I know what the hell I'm doing first."

Peiro tried but failed to scramble to his feet to stop Sury from taking his only belonging. "No! We need it! For the love of giants and peace to them, we need it!"

He struggled to take it out of Sury's vice grip. Without a second thought, Sury threw a hard punch with his uninjured arm and landed his strike into Peiro's jaw, causing the latter to topple to the ground, blood spilling from a newly split lip. His head crumbled to his hands. "Cisoi find me, *please*."

"This is what you wanted to defend, Phe?" He pointed to the lump of a man on the ground. "We don't have time for this!" Sury bellowed and began walking back to the river to dump the contents. "He's toying with us!" he called over his shoulder.

I peered down at the man who now lay at my feet, slowly moving to regain his composure. His shoulders hung low as he kept trying to find a steadying breath.

"Tell me that you're telling the truth about where we're going. If you so much as whisper a white lie to me, I will bring forth my magic again and not stop. Are we clear?" I made each word a roar.

Peiro halted on his knees and looked at me. I couldn't explain the slight hitch in my breath as I took in his dulling gray eyes. But in the next second, a dark shadow crossed over his gaze. His eyes steadily turned brighter and clearer against his rugged skin, accentuating the silver and gray flecks within his irises that made his eyes appear illuminated. Like full moons against a starless sky.

He dropped his head and blinked a few times before finding his words.

"On our honor and even on the Mother of the giants," he said as he held a hand over his heart, "you are being led to a safe place. Not many are aware of its existence."

I stuck my hand out to help Peiro to his feet. "To the giants and all things above, you better pray to them for mercy if you lead us astray. And not just from my friend, who I will not hold back next time, but from me."

In a swift motion, he took my hand and held it tight. As he stood, he pulled me in closer, peering down to my face. His face was so close that I could still smell that sweet, intoxicating scent on his lips.

Despite all the reasons my mind screamed at me not to, my heart skipped at his closeness, and I felt a warming tingle I had rarely felt before. Curiosity roared inside me.

"What are you?" he whispered. "Thuvina? Giantess of death?"

I tried to find the words to ask his meaning, but came to my senses and let go of his rough hand. "I don't know what you mean," I said as I turned on my heel to leave him in the woods and head back to Sury.

I sheathed my dagger right as I spotted Sury pacing the river bank, muttering to himself. "Want to talk?" I called out, testing his emotions.

He turned his gaze to me and, in a brief moment, I saw his eyes flash the same strange red before returning back to his dark browns.

"I'm fine," he lied. "I'm worried about Ora and if this shithead has made us endure a longer detour... Does he even know where he's going?"

"I really do think we can trust him."

"How? How can you absolutely trust this complete stranger? A *user* of all people? They're the lowest of the low! They cheat, they lie, they steal—we're following him blindly, and he talks as if he's multiple people! By the giants, how am I even allowing this?" Sury pulled at his hair. He looked at me with menace in his eyes and closed the distance between us in just a couple of easy steps.

Every instinct in me screamed that a threat stood before me. My heart stammered as my body shifted into a fighting stance, ready to defend against any incoming blow. Just as I moved, the sun dimmed. Shadows from the tree line crawled forward and slithered along the ground. In our wake, the vibrant green grass dulled and curled like blades in a drought. My fingertips tingled as I flexed my hands closed and open again.

"I knew I should have left you at the Rising Temple," Sury said through his teeth, his skin tinging red as his breathing quickened. "I knew I should have done this alone. You've never been good at anything except for taking up space. Ora is better off without *you*."

As if my body were not my own, I stepped forward and smacked him hard in the face. The pain seared my hand and traveled up my arm. As soon as my fingers touched his hot skin, I felt a sense of pressure release within me. The sun turned back to its bright glory and pushed back the shadows. Even the grass turned back to green.

His eyes widened in shock as he clenched his burning cheek. His paling face crumpled. "Phe, I'm sorry!" Another red shimmer passed over his eyes, and his shoulders sagged forward. He dropped to his knees, still holding his cheek. "I'm so sorry. I'm so sorry," he repeated over and over, each word turned into a whisper.

I knelt down beside him and took him into my arms and held him the same way a loving sister would. "I miss her, too. You *will* see her again. I promise," I whispered into his ear.

CHAPTER 18

We sat by the riverside with the small fire dying beside us, deciding to camp for the night. We knew we needed to get moving, but traveling at night would be a fool's gamble against robbers and sharp-toothed urthen.

Peiro returned from the tangle of trees and walked over to the river's edge to wash the blood from his face. I felt it again. The same strange pull as before. My body forced me to get up from my spot, with berries in hand, and walk over to where he sat.

"Just in case you're hungry," I said as I gently held out a small handful. He gave me a look and studied my hand. "Gooseberries. They're not poisonous. See," I said as I popped one in my mouth and chewed before dumping the rest in Peiro's hand.

"Thank you," he said, never taking his eyes off mine.

I found Sury staring at me in disbelief. He narrowed his eyes as I walked back toward the fire. "Your heart's too big, Phe. When will you see this isn't one of your stories?"

I let the night pass in silence. By morning, my body ached in discomfort and my feet felt as if they were melting into my boots as we sat.

Deep down, I felt that we were heading in the right direction, but I could never figure out how to explain it to Sury. I looked back to the tree line, watching Peiro now sitting at the base of a tree as he stared at nothing across the riverbank. His head snapped in my direction, catching my gaze right before he jumped to his feet, signaling us to follow.

I followed behind Sury and watched my footsteps as we climbed over fallen limbs and trunks in the forest. I was growing quite proud of myself for not tripping, and I smiled while pretending to be a small fairy bouncing from stump to stump. Anything to help keep my mind from wandering to Vovias and Ariadne or the Black Raiders and their lies.

Sury stopped his trek and turned to face me. He gave me a small smile as if to say, *You're right. It's going to be alright. We're going to save her and end all of this.* And what clenched my heart the most was his look that said, *I'm sorry.*

"Oh, how the love is in the air," Peiro teased over his shoulder with a twisted smile.

"Shut. Up." Sury gritted out as he turned to bare his teeth in Peiro's face. The same shimmer as before shifted over Sury's eyes, growing colder. "Probably plotting where to kill and dump our bodies."

"For the love of Aksyn's sun, Sury, please!" I began, but I was cut off when Peiro stopped in his tracks and turned to face us.

"Well, that's not very nice, now, is it?" Peiro jabbed Sury in the chest, causing the latter to hiss in pain. "If we wanted you dead, you would have been gutted and thrown from that ridge the moment you drew your sword."

Even with both men having bodies that needed a Healer's attention, I was still amazed at the hubris of the male ego.

In one swift motion, Peiro snatched one of the daggers from Sury's pocket and pointed it toward Sury's neck. He cocked his head and quickly threw the dagger faster than Sury could react. The blade flew through the air and stuck with a dull *thud* into the trunk of a tree directly behind me.

A small trickle of blood appeared from a cut on Sury's ear where the blade had barely grazed him.

"Count that as repayment for the slice to our chest," Peiro growled before turning to push further into the thicket.

"You sliced your own damn chest, you crazy fool," Sury said through his teeth, then grabbed the blade that was pinned deep into the poor tree.

"For the busted lip, then!" Peiro called over his shoulder. "Or maybe the nose. Or the rib."

Before Sury could throw out another verbal punch, he howled in agony and fell to the forest floor, writhing in pain. He clutched his wounded shoulder tightly and started scratching at his throat, gasping for air.

"Sury!" I yelled as I dropped to the ground to peel back his tunic and the cloth covering the wound. The spiderweb of black veins now stretched higher up his throat in needle-width marks. The blackened veins had inched closer to his heart, nearly encircling it.

His body was still hot to the touch, and small bits of flesh showed fresh lesions around the wound entry. Dry, gray skin flaked away as if it was actively dying in front of my eyes.

Sury clawed harder at his throat, choking to find air. His eyes fluttered and closed as he faded into unconsciousness in my arms.

"Sury! SURY! Breathe!" I cried in a frantic plea as I tapped on his face to wake him up. "I don't know how to help him!"

Think, Phe. Think.

I tried to recall the herbal medicines I had learned about in books or from the Healers. My thoughts swirled into overdrive from all I had read about Healing magic, but I couldn't pin any thoughts on what I needed.

Doesn't matter though, does it? Not like you can touch Healing magic. He's as good as dead, you fool. I squeezed my eyes tight, wishing the voice would disappear and find a better time to taunt.

"When did he get this?" Peiro knelt beside me to inspect the wounds.

"Before Zonnagberg. We were attacked just before arriving. It's some kind of poison."

Peiro leaned down and sniffed the wound. "We know what this is," he rasped deeply as he bent down and scooped Sury up into his arms. "Cut through the trees to get us past this thicket. And be quick. He doesn't have much time."

I did as I was told without a second thought as I picked up Sury's sheath and sword to cut through the forest. Peiro followed closely behind before pressing forward once the trees thinned. Eventually, we came upon a grove of birch trees. Their white trunks were a stark contrast to the bright green leaves that created a beautiful canopy above.

"This way!" Peiro called out. He began running with Sury in his arms, leaving me behind like he carried nothing but a light package.

I fumbled with my shaky fingers as I worked to sheath the sword and swung it across my back. I barely had enough time to register that Peiro was already a great distance ahead, running as hard as he could. It wasn't possible for anyone, even for someone in good health, to run as fast as he did.

I frantically looked and listened for any sign of Peiro as I kept running in the direction where I last saw him, praying it was the right way. Sweat dripped from my brow and into my eyes, causing them to sting.

Don't panic, I told myself. *Don't panic. You'll find them soon.*

I began to panic.

Not only did I not know where Peiro had gone, but I was also lost and alone in the woods. I didn't know this area well enough to know who could be friend or foe, let alone how to get out of the grove. Each wave of panic made my heart beat wildly and climb into my throat.

Just as I wiped the sweat out of my eyes, a fluorescent green thing popped up to my right. I looked over my shoulder to notice a tiny ruron flying at an impossible speed beside me before zipping to the right. I didn't question it and immediately changed directions. One ruron turned into two. Two turned into a raggle that clung to a tree a few yards ahead.

As I ran toward them, I noticed they were all beating their legs against the trunk in a rhythmic motion. A strange sound, the mix between a bird's caw and an oxen's groan, came from the sky. A bratrian soared overhead, then barreled to the ground before continuing to run forward as the rurons disappeared.

I changed course and followed the white bratrian as it dodged the base of each tree. Something flashed beside me while something else flew overhead. I ducked just in time and saw four bird-like things, all a beautiful iridescent shade of lilac, flap their wings together. They followed the bratrian's course, guiding me with their bright color against the stark white bark of the trees.

In the distance, I saw a bright clearing through the trees with a small wooden cabin in its middle. The bird-like things and the bratrian immediately stopped and circled back. As I got closer to the clearing, I noticed the cabin was large enough for a single room and a stone hearth.

I could barely make out that Peiro had laid Sury on the small, rotted porch next to the doorstep, as if he was waiting on something. He pounded on the door right as I caught up to the grove's edge. I leaned against one of the trees and tried to hold myself steady. My legs ached and wobbled with each breath I gulped down. Bile climbed up to the surface as I worked to slow my breathing.

Peiro began beating against the door once again, almost forcing it off its hinges. The half-rotted door quickly swung open as a large, dark-skinned man with white dreadlocks pulled behind his shoulders exited the cabin's door and peered down at the men at his doorstep.

His white hair and beard, the latter cut short, were a stark contrast to his skin and shone like fresh snow in the sun. He appeared mightier than the door frame to his cabin. Each step on the porch made a wooden board creak beneath his large feet. I half wondered if he needed to bob his own head down in order to enter through the doors safely.

"Using again?" the man's voice boomed.

Peiro quickly shook his hand. "You can scold me later!" he hissed.

"What is this?" The man's voice boomed loudly, almost echoing off the trees that encircled the clearing of his cabin. He easily towered over Peiro by a few inches.

"Death arrow." Peiro looked at the man, who nodded in understanding. "Dokvalon."

The larger man nodded again. "Get him inside, quickly."

The man opened the door wider to let Peiro through with Sury in his arms.

"And you need some tea to calm your nerves," the man said to no one in particular but then turned his gaze directly toward me. "I can feel them from here." His bright, iridescent green eyes were wide and bright. Wielder's eyes. Eyes that always seemed to glow. The man turned around and entered his cabin, leaving the door open.

I didn't try to talk myself out of entering this stranger's home—not with Sury at their mercy. I ran inside.

The wooden cabin was small and worn on the outside, but just over the threshold, the inside was somehow much bigger than I could fathom. I had heard of such magic but had never witnessed it. I took in all the rooms and the two sets of stairs, in the shape of a horseshoe, leading to another floor above. A large oak tree stood in the center as if it had always belonged there.

The inside was grand and cozier than what I could have imagined the cabin to be. The room to my right had a roaring fire, and the walls were lined with bookshelves, overfilled with books and scattered pages. A drawing room of sorts.

A long hallway to my front extended further than what seemed possible, but then again, my small world had been greatly disrupted between what was and what is possible. The walls were paneled in a rich golden oak that mimicked the floors. Large red rugs lined the length of the hallway.

The immediate room to my left, sporting pale wooden walls and a stone floor, held a long, solitary wooden table in its center.

A large window let in the sun's rays and a view of the birch tree grove. From the outside, I hadn't seen a window.

I heard the two men speaking and followed them in.

Various sizes of cabinets and shelves hugged the walls, all holding odd trinkets and various artifacts. One of the tables held a litter of glass bottles, all cleaned and free of dust. An iron pot sat on another table's corner with an earthy-smelling goo bubbling—without the help of a fire.

Dark wooden beams above my head held an array of flowers and roots, all perfectly dried. I spotted remnants of lilac root, wolfsbane flowers, and a pretty dried yellow flower that looked like a cross between a rose and a daisy.

Peiro had set Sury down on the table in the middle of the room like he was told. The large man cut through Sury's tunic with a sharp blade to reveal the wound had grown more. I held my breath upon seeing the black veins webbing wider than just moments ago. Now, the inky trail dipped below his breastbone and crawled closer to his navel as the ring around his neck had grown a shade darker.

Lesions peppered Sury's skin and swelled into blisters. They had climbed across his chest and up his neck while the black veins now encircled his barely beating heart.

"Do everything you can, old friend," Peiro said as he clasped his hand on the large man's shoulder. "He's important to her."

The man nodded and turned back to his assessment.

I watched as the large man called out for different herbs and roots that were needed for a salve and tinctures. Without hesitation, Peiro moved about the room collecting the items from drawers and bottles. He knew exactly where everything was.

I watched in awe at the harmony these two men had as they worked to ease Sury's pain. The large man, seeming to have everything he needed, barked more orders to Peiro for another concoction of dried leaves and boiling hot water.

Following orders, Peiro set off into another room and quickly returned with a chipped porcelain cup. He sprinkled the leaves inside the cup and poured the water over them, allowing them to steep.

"I need a moment alone with this poor soul. I can't work properly with a mother hen running loose," the large man called out as he shooed us both away. "You know what to do."

Peiro took me by the elbow, balancing the cup of amber-colored liquid in his other hand. He guided me outside the room to the hallway, despite my protests to stay.

"Drink this." Peiro shoved the cup into my hands.

I looked inside and saw the tiny leaves and flower buds swirling in the liquid. "No."

"If we wanted to kill you or your companion there, don't you think we could have done so sooner? Why go through all this trouble just to kill you now?"

"Are you going to kill me?" I asked softly.

Peiro's gaze bore into mine and subtly shook his head. "You are more apt to do us harm than we to you."

I eyed him and the cup intently. The warming scent of nutmeg and clove lifted from the glass and into my nostrils. I eyed the contents carefully and stared at the small chip missing at the top of the rim. A small crack descended from the chip, making me wonder how much longer this glass would hold.

Despite my better judgment, I took a small sip of the warm liquid and felt something soothing course through my veins. I took another sip, then another. My stomach eased as my shoulders began to unwind. Emotional knots unraveled when I drained what remained. My senses steadily grew calm, and my nerves dulled almost instantly.

"Thank you," I said, and handed the cup back to Peiro.

I looked at the surroundings again, and the sun shining down on the clearing in front of the cabin. Only then did I realize I was staring out of two huge bay windows that were set firmly next to a large oak door, with a small stained-glass window at its top.

"Where are we? What is that man going to do to Sury?" Questions spewed out of my mouth before I could reel them back in.

Peiro took a deep breath and looked out the windows before speaking. "Fyom is a good man. The strongest Healer we know."

"How do you know this man?"

"It's complicated." Peiro winced slightly at the question. "But we've known him for quite a long time now."

"Why do you keep saying *we*?"

Peiro turned his gaze, locking his piercing eyes to mine. A small shiver ran down my spine as I stared into the cold, silver eyes. "It's complicated," he answered again before returning back inside the room.

"Can you tell me why my magic caused you so much pain earlier?" I called after him, following close behind.

Peiro said nothing as he kept walking.

"Give me something, dammit!" I called out, desperate for any answer. My magic stirred and rose to the surface.

You're a dense girl, the voice snarled.

Peiro squeezed his eyes shut and held his temples with his fingertips. "Shut your mouth, you stupid thing."

"Excuse me?" My eyes narrowed.

His, in turn, widened before he growled and slammed the door in my face.

I huffed in frustration before barreling in, feeling hot and angry. "Don't you *dare* slam a door in my face!" The gall of this man. The tension in my shoulders crept skyward as I felt a tingle across the palm of my hand.

"You whine like a pompous princess," he barked.

"I do not!"

"The whole walk here, you did nothing but whine to that man about what you call a *lack of power* compared to who-ever else." He hovered down, inches above my face. "Accept who you are!"

"You don't know anything," I sneered right back. "Or anything about me, at least."

"You don't either, it would seem."

"BOTH of you can cease your bickering. I'm trying to *concentrate*!" I jumped at the shout and cut my glance to Fyom. He walked around the table where Sury lay and stood next to the wounded side. "And drink this to knock that shit out of your system," Fyom barked to Peiro as he thrust a heavy-looking mug of steaming contents into his hands. "Stupid fool."

"You. Come." He pointed a large finger at me, beckoning me further inside the room. Baskets filled with different roots and herbs were scattered around the table and in between Sury's clothed legs. Bottles of different shapes and sizes, even colors and smells, were scattered around him. Many of the smaller tables were pulled in close and holding strange utensils.

"Will he be alright?" I whispered as I peered down to Sury's still body.

The small rise and fall of his chest was the only indicator that there was still some life in him. His skin was losing its sun-kissed glow. His once shining black hair had now lost its luster.

"Is this the only spot where he was hit?" Fyom asked as he assessed more of his body, adjusting him only slightly.

"Yes. I tried to pack it with willow and chaseflower when I could. It took us a few hours to get to Zonnagberg before we could clean and treat it."

"An infection set in on top of the poison that's trying to reach his heart. If you'd waited any longer, your spouse would surely be dead. You're lucky Peiro was able to get you here so quickly."

"I cannot thank you enough for being willing to help him. You see..." What could little bits of truth hurt? I had observed through many of the courts that the best way to keep things hidden was to tell small remnants of honesty. "He's my sister's lover and my friend." I felt myself fumble to find the words. My hands began to shake again. "And we were on our way to her." I didn't know how much to reveal or if I had already put our lives in jeopardy. With the Black Raiders having crossed our borders, could these men be trusted?

I felt my heart grow desperate. I needed someone, anyone, who would be willing to support me without giving away where I was. I locked up my fear before it could take a deeper hold.

The large man looked at me with an arched brow, sensing my hesitation. He strode around the table to where I stood and held out his hand for me to take. *Giants*, his hands looked like they could hold two of mine in one. I gingerly placed mine in his and felt the rough calluses that were embedded in his palms.

His hands were large but felt so gentle. He gave me a kind squeeze, sending warmth through my hand and up my arm. "Fyom. I am Fyom." He looked like he was nearing his sixth decade.

"Phe."

Fyom revealed a soft smile filled with bright white teeth. "Your friend should be okay. I believe I was able to stop the infection just in time." He looked Sury over again and checked his herbs.

"You knew it was from Dokvalon?" I asked as I pointed toward Peiro. "It's not a poison I've seen before."

Fyom sighed deeply. "From what I've tested, it looks like a perverted strand of magic embedded in some sort of nightshade that is known to grow in Dokvalon. I counteracted the nightshade component, but I'm still figuring out what magic was in the arrow." He flickered his eyes to Peiro then scratched the short length of his beard. "Tell me, did he exhibit any odd behaviors after being hit? Were his mannerisms different?"

I didn't hesitate. "Yes. But he's been wounded. That could make anyone act differently."

"Not what I mean. Did he ever act erratic?"

"He kept getting so angry—that wasn't like him. And his eyes—they flickered red a couple of times."

Fyom nodded, not taking his eyes off his new patient. "I will need a few days to study it and watch his symptoms. It's a shame the Black Raiders have crossed our borders unchecked." He turned his bright green eyes to mine. I practically had to crane my neck up to see him.

Seriously, how did he fit inside this room?

"Do you know why he was shot with a Dokvalon arrow? They shoot to kill, so how your friend managed to survive is a miracle on its own." He questioned.

I hesitated, uncertain of how much to share. "I don't know why." I felt the words fumble out. "We were on a pilgrimage to see the Three Sisters. When my sister became lost, we were hoping the Sisters could give us answers on how to find her."

It wasn't all a lie. I held my breath and hoped the man wouldn't pry further. Fyom gazed down at me like a bird about to ingest a bug. He scratched his white beard with his fingers and crossed his arms, thinking.

"You're lying. Dokvalon doesn't simply cross the Grian borders and shoot pilgrims. Unless they're after something. Dokvalon is known to be more methodical than *shoot first, ask questions later.*"

Peiro snorted from the corner.

Fyom turned around to a large cabinet standing by the wall and rummaged through the contents.

"Not a lie! We were on our way to see the Sisters!" I stepped closer to Sury and gently moved my hand to my waistband and the dagger hanging there. The tension around us suddenly rose.

"Pilgrimage, you say?" he called out behind him. "The Sisters send their acolytes to those who do not Wield, and clearly the poor, almost-dead soul on my table is *not* a magic Wielder." Fyom turned around with a box and another teacup in his hand. "Or he would have died already. This death magic would have tainted his own and fed the infection faster... Not to mention his eyes don't match a Wielder's."

Shit.

"So what? I was seeking an audience with the Sisters." I stumbled to find my words, trying to find ways to bend the truth. Peiro sat quietly in the corner with his arms crossed and legs planted firm on the ground, watching me intently. I noticed his face was already flushed with more color than before. Whatever Fyom gave him was clearly working to cleanse his body.

"Where did you say you learned your Wielding?" Fyom asked.

"The High Seven."

What could that piece hurt? Many magic Wielders found education and ranking there.

"Ah, I'm sensing some truth now," Fyom said as he crushed wolfsbane and dandelion roots and added a broad green leaf before pouring in steaming water from a kettle nearby that hadn't been there before.

"Yes. And making a pilgrimage." I repeated.

Fyom opened a box and revealed a large set of crystals, all different colors and intensities. "An accepted Wielder of the High Seven making a *pilgrimage* to the Sisters. I smell a lie again. No one that's been through the High Seven gives the Sisters a second glance."

The crystals were shaped like icicles, each with a sharp point. He studied them closely and pulled out an intense-looking blue one. The veins scattered and pooled in various shades of white and gold. With the blue crystal in his hand, he grabbed another cup of steaming liquid and stood in front of me.

I noticed he was blocking me from the door.

The inky voice made its appearance again. *Now you've done it, you half-wit. May you meet Cisoi.*

Fyom peered down at me and put the cup on the table, next to Sury and within my reach.

"We're about to find out who you are and why you're lying to us." Before I could move, Fyom grabbed my wrist and pushed back my tunic's sleeve to reveal my pale and dirty skin.

I fumbled for my dagger with my other hand but couldn't get it free from its sheath. "No!" I yelled as I struggled to pull my arm free from the man's vice grip. His fingers practically overlapped over my forearm.

"No one *just happens* to run into Dokvalon Raiders. They always have a purpose to their plan."

My mind raced while my heart stammered with my life practically in this man's hands.

Vovias or Ariadne's lies have already traveled up north, and I'm his prize. He's going to kill me, I just know it, I thought.

"Dokvalon is nothing but vile intent and disease. Who's to say *you* aren't one of their spies pretending to seek refuge until you're able to find the rest of your pack?"

Wait, did he think *I* was with the Black Raiders?

"Death to Dokvalon!" the man seethed.

Before I could catch his meaning, Fyom quickly made a thin slice across my arm with the blue crystal and drew a tiny stream of blood along my skin. My magic rose to the surface and hummed violently at the threat. Blood nestled next to the point on the crystal and soaked into its base. Fyom took the steaming cup and mixed the bloodied crystal with the contents. In a swift twirl, a faint, gray smoke rose from within. Fyom took a deep swig before setting everything to the side.

His eyes rolled back in his head, revealing the whites, and a small trickle of blood escaped the corner of his mouth. He stood over me, his body shaking and convulsing. I tried to wrench my arm free, but his grip only tightened.

He exhaled deeply and began to cough before emptying the rest of the cup's contents into his mouth. His hand still gripped my wrist tightly as his eyes fluttered and shook. Finally, his gaze landed on me. Hard. His body was as rigid as a bronze statue.

What did he see? What was he looking for?

I gulped as his bright green eyes dove deeper. A tug at my soul. I felt something foreign touch my magic, making it stutter at the intrusion. The room darkened around me as if someone had snuffed out the lantern in the room. Cold sweat formed along my neck and shoulders as I felt pure, unfiltered fear sink deep within me.

He was going to kill me. I needed to leave. I needed to escape. My hand buzzed and tingled. Shadows crept forward and rose high above the man who towered over me. In my peripheral vision, I saw the shadow of something sharp angled high toward the giant of a man, and in the distance, someone groaned in pain.

Before the shadows could move, Fyom's body slumped forward, shrinking in size. His green eyes softened as he regained consciousness and formed into a wide stare of confusion right before his dark face paled.

He gasped as he dropped to his knees and placed a fist over his heart. "Princess Ophelia."

Peiro's eyes grew wide as his stare pinned me again. A look of pain coated his features and he tensed, knuckles up by his temples. His eyes flickered briefly before softening, and he slowly lowered himself to his knees in reverence at my feet, his fist pressed over his heart.

CHAPTER 19

I stared as both men knelt on the floor with their heads lowered. *What the hell just happened?*

"You don't have to kneel!" I stammered. The flip from accusation to allegiance was too much.

"Utmost apologies for the intrusion, Your Royal Highness," Fyom stammered, still looking at the floor. "When you said you were being followed by Dokvalon Raiders, I thought you might have been an agent of theirs. For, you see, there has been word they have crossed their borders, and one cannot be too careful of spies..."

Fyom, the colossal man that I'd initially found a bit intimidating, was still sputtering his apology and explanation as he continued to kneel on the floor. "...I would never intend any harm on an Endromeon..."

"Please do not apologize!" I noticed then that Peiro was still kneeling with his head bowed. I didn't know what to say. My mind was reeling from the truths that had just poured in, and how Fyom was able to obtain them. I couldn't shake the feeling that something had caressed my magic in the process. "What did you just do?" My voice was barely above a whisper.

Fyom looked up, confused. He hesitated as he rose to his feet. "Why, Your Highness…"

"Just call me Phe," I said, to knock away the formality.

"Apologies, ma'am…uhm, Phe." His hand still rested over his heart. "Through your blood, I was able to see bits and pieces of who you are and what you endured the last few days."

"Through just a few herbs and a crystal?"

Fyom raised his eyebrow in confusion. "That is simple Healer magic to help understand diagnoses we cannot physically see. Maybe even mastered by sixth years. Did they not inform you of this at the temple?"

I mentally noted that he didn't reference the High Seven Temple's formal title. "No… And you could sense my magic?" I gulped, keeping my eyes pinned on him.

"Just that you are an Endromeon. But everyone knows the Endromeon family comes from a long line of powerful Wielding." He spoke slowly and quietly, like he didn't want to spook a wild rabbit. "Was sensing another's magic not a part of your lessons?"

My cheeks grew hot. "No," I said again. "They liked to frequently remind me that my Wielding has always been…on the lower end. So, I'm sure that particular knowledge was considered above my level." I spat the last part out with old visions of Ariadne's retorts of inadequate magic.

"That's a lie." The gruffness of the voice surprised me. I had forgotten that Peiro was in the corner. He was practically hidden behind the wall of a man in front of me.

I watched with furrowed brows as Peiro slowly rose from his kneel and gently released his hand back down to his side. The silvers of his eyes had dulled just a smidge.

"I beg your pardon?" I hissed at the audacity. He knew nothing about me, yet he acted as if he did.

Peiro completely ignored me and continued talking to Fyom. "We've seen it, Fyom... *Felt* it."

"Felt it?" Fyom turned to face Peiro, and the two stared at one another for a long pause, as if silently communicating.

"What *have* they taught you? About Wielding?" He turned his gaze back to me and softened his expression to curiosity.

I recounted all I had learned during my time in the temple, and explained how everyone had assumed I was a late developer since my mother's name had carried on so proudly for generations. Until Ora had advanced quickly for her age, showing her control for Sixth Circle of Power, the celestials, like our mother. Eventually, the conclusion had become that my First Circle of Power, Earthen Wielding, must have been a mistake—until the years passed, and my Wielding ability would not advance like every other Endromeon.

Many chalked it up to a magical deformity, which stunted my own Wielding abilities, prompting Ariadne to personally oversee my studies for years.

"I guess all there is to learn for a First Circle Wielder. Basic herbal and atmospheric knowledge. Some incantations grounded through the earth," I said with a small shrug. "I've gotten quite skilled at making vines grow and flower petals bloom in vibrancy, but they tend to die afterward. I can sometimes get small herbs to grow in potency to help with the Healers' needs."

Fyom scratched his groomed beard. "It's been a long time since I have stepped foot in the temple to pay homage. Quite a long time. Who is now in charge?"

"High Priestess Ariadne. She even has the Seventh Circle of Wielding and has been the Special Advisor due to her high ranking."

"Ariadne? *Priestess* Ariadne is running the temple, you say? And she's tested you and claims this is where you are?"

I felt my annoyance rise. I felt so exposed to his knowledge of who I truly am, and now he was questioning me about my magic Wielding like I didn't know what I was talking about.

"I'm sorry to disappoint *another* inquisitive mind on what I should and shouldn't be!" I chewed on my bottom lip to keep in my anger. Keep in my failure.

But you did fail. Look at you, only a miniscule part of the Endromeon line. No one will remember your name. Well, they might remember it as the poor girl who ended up letting her sister die.

My eyes strained at the pull of tears that I fought against. *I will not cry. I will not cry.*

Peiro cocked his head as he continued to silently observe.

"My deepest apologies. I didn't mean to offend. You must be exhausted..." Fyom's deep voice whispered softly.

I couldn't hear what else he said. My blood boiled up and roared in my ears, producing a loud ringing noise. Light gray swirls clouded the corners of my sight.

I hardly heard Peiro speak as he said, "Fyom. We can sense it." He gently pulled the man's arm to put distance between me and them.

My thoughts raced uncontrollably. I was ranked second best to my younger sister when no one cared to know who *I* was outside of magic. Outside of my sister's shadow, when Ora so clearly shined.

Every emotion, both known and unknown, came rushing to the surface. Frustration, followed by anger and sadness, compounding with exhaustion and confusion. I felt my senses going numb. My vision blurred.

Yes. Let your emotions get the best of you.

I'm so tired of explaining myself, I said back to the voice. *So tired of no one understanding. I'm so alone.*

I couldn't stop the outpour. I couldn't contain it.

A rolling release from within my body reached the surface and tingled my skin. The feeling amplified and sent tiny pricks along my arm in a sensation of sewing needles scraping across my skin. The muscles in my hands spasmed closed before opening again. From the middle of my palms, the bright blue, glowing orbs radiated and hovered above my hand.

The light grew brighter with each wave of emotions that seemed to pour into them. Inside them were beautiful, tiny streaks of light and glowing stars.

A piercing scream echoed in the back of my mind. Awestruck, I watched the orbs within my hands. My vision snapped back to clear as I saw Peiro contorting on the ground before me. I barely had time to register Fyom Wielding a shield of green light over Peiro and himself as he sent something green toward me, slashing into my orbs, almost snuffing them out.

Spiritus.

The iridescent green of his shield shifted in a magnitude of color as it expanded over them. Any observer would have found the shift to be remarkable in how it mimicked the color of a reptile—if that observer weren't in the process of defending themselves.

My orbs spun fanatically in and around my hand, forming jagged shapes that resembled Sury's hunting knives, but the fluidity looked like a silk ribbon lost to the wind. I couldn't stop the motion as the shapes took solid form and flew forward.

Like hot steel cutting through cloth, the orbs pierced through Fyom's shield, shredding it to pieces. The edges curled back like paper caught on fire, giving way to the force behind the orbs' magic.

An instinct told me to push forward but I tried pulling back. My breath hitched as the orbs listened to instinct and not my reason. My fingers trembled uncontrollably. Each jagged-shaped orb arched toward Fyom and Peiro, like a viper ready to strike its prey.

"STOP THIS! WE MEAN NO HARM!" Fyom's deep voice boomed loud and wavered as he steadily lost grip on his fraying green shield.

"I can't stop!" I yelled at the top of my lungs. No matter how hard I tried, I couldn't stop it from pouring out of my palms and toward Fyom.

In a swift motion, Fyom released one hand from his magic shield, weakening it further as my magic continued to plunge toward him. With his other hand, he grabbed the chair that Peiro had sat in and pushed it across the room in my direction. It hit its target and knocked me off balance, forcing me to slide backward, pinning me to the wall. Fyom released his shield completely the moment my orbs disappeared and continued using the invisible force to pin the chair against me.

My arms were stuck to my sides and immovable. The surge I had felt quickly disappeared, and a hollow feeling formed inside my chest. A strange fog in my mind dissipated as I tried to understand what just transpired. I had never felt that kind of rush before, as if my magic broke through a dam and couldn't be contained. The feeling was divine and intoxicating. Both fear and excitement coursed through my veins.

I wiggled hard against the chair to push it aside, but failed. I watched as Fyom finished an incantation with his hands just as an invisible rope snaked around my wrists and waist, tightening them further to my sides.

"Let me go!" I shouted across the room. Shock and fear poured out of his stare as Fyom's eyes locked onto mine. He turned to Peiro, whose breathing was shallow as he remained unconscious and bent in odd angles. Guilt twisted inside my chest as I watched Fyom quickly dance around the room, collecting herbs and roots and a musty box full of bottles that held various liquids.

"Will he be okay?" I found myself trembling. My heart ached at the thought of hurting another. The deep lines in Peiro's face had softened, and his usually tight lips now relaxed into a beautiful flush. He looked as if he were in a deep sleep.

"For now" was all Fyom said as he quickly worked to restore the man's health.

Silent minutes passed before Peiro's eyes suddenly fluttered open. No one spoke as Fyom gently helped him to his feet and guided him out of the room.

My hips throbbed where the chair pinned them to the wall. With every fiber in my body, I fought against the exhaustion threatening to take over to keep my guard up. Through the window to my right, stars steadily began to twinkle across the sky, becoming brighter with each passing minute. I kept a brave face, trying desperately to stay courageous for both mine and Sury's sakes.

But the familiar doubt took its hold.

Look at him, girl. Look at the dying man beside you. You did this.

I watched Sury's chest peacefully rise and fall.

Loud footsteps echoed down the hall as Fyom reentered the room. His stature was similar to Peiro's, both tall, but Fyom was much wider. I watched as he ducked his head underneath the door's frame before entering the room.

My nerves pitched when Fyom walked over to check my wrists before turning to Sury. He positioned his hands underneath Sury's legs and back, then effortlessly carried my friend from the table and to the doorway from which he came.

"Leave him alone! Where are you taking him?" I screamed as I thrashed against the invisible bindings, anything to break their hold to get to Sury.

Fyom ignored my pleas and left the room. I used all my might to try and break away from the invisible shackles. Sweat formed across my brow as I tried to tear through the restraints. I felt my shins and knees bruise as I desperately tried to kick the chair away, all to no avail.

Fyom's heavy steps echoed from down the hallway. If only I could summon a weapon of some kind. Use anything in this room that appeared to be an examining room. My fingers trembled as I attempted to call forth my Wielding but the dregs felt empty.

"Where is he? Where did you take Sury? I demand to know!" A small trickle of blood slid down my hand as I tried to push the chair away, bearing all my weight against it. My nails dug into my palms as I wiggled and pushed against the force that refused to budge.

Fyom's bright green eyes lit up as he stepped into the room, closing the distance between us in just a couple of steps. I barely reached his breastbone in height. He raised a hand to his chest, and the green shield materialized before him, covering most of his body while tiny green wisps pulsated through the opaque light.

The force that radiated off his shield pulsed through my veins as he neared. My shoulders were pinned and my nerves pinched, all feeding an unspeakable fire around my spine.

"No one comes into my home and attacks me, regardless of royal titles," he spat. "No one with your level of training, as you *claim*, can achieve something like *that*. Explain yourself!"

"I don't even know what I did!" I sputtered. "Is Peiro okay? Where is Sury?"

Fyom stayed a healthy distance away but close enough for me to take in his dark features and the deep lines across his face. His green eyes shone brightly with small specks of yellows and creams around the pupil, intensifying them to look as vivid as fresh moss in the sun.

My heart pounded against my chest and my breath was bound to suffocate. I felt too much like a small animal trapped in a cage, the hunter observing the snare.

"How could you not know? No one possesses that kind of power and does not know about it!"

"I'm not lying to you! I swear! Let me go!" I struggled against the invisible bindings again. Fyom eyed me carefully and stepped closer, keeping his magical shield in place. Tears betrayed me as they lined my eyes. I fought hard to keep them from falling, but a lone tear ran down my cheek. "Do whatever it is you did earlier to detect if I'm lying or not! You'll see the truth. I'm not as powerful as you think!" I frantically shook my head.

"Not powerful? Is that what you think that was? As you tortured the man in cold magic?" he asked in disbelief as he pointed to the corner where Peiro had sat. His eyes bored deeply as if he were staring directly at my soul. I could feel the anger radiating off of him as he drilled for answers. His upper lip quivered and showed small flashes of his bright white teeth.

"If you are telling the truth, what did Ariadne tell you at your testing? *How* did Ariadne test you? Tell me now. What did you manifest?"

"Just small control of simple granules of dirt."

"More fucking lies." He snarled. I watched as the giant man took a step back, fighting against his bottom lip with his teeth. His clenched fingers worked themselves open just as his shoulders worked out of their tense hold. I was too scared to look away. Too nervous that I might miss another attack, regardless of whether I could defend myself this time.

But none came.

Instead, I watched the man's breath return to a normal, slower rhythm just as the intensity within his eyes shifted to something I knew all too well. His demeanor shifted from ferocity to something akin to somber as he called back his shield, instantly turning the room darker with the withdrawal of its ethereal glow. Only the flow of a small candle encased us in its light, but it was enough to see his pity.

And I hated it.

CHAPTER 20

"What do you mean?" I pleaded, begging to understand what he meant by there being more lies. The shame engulfed me in such a way that I didn't notice when the invisible bindings left my hands, or when the chair moved.

Fyom studied me, perhaps anticipating my next move, and handed me a cloth to cover the cut in my skin.

"Come. You must rest," he said calmly with commiseration in his eyes, and turned to leave the room. "We can discuss more in the morning." I flexed my hand to test my movements before following behind him.

We walked in silence down the long hallway while I held a cautionary distance. The hallway was lined with many doors on either side, and strategically placed sconces held a single candle each to guide us through the dark.

Fyom stopped at a door and pointed to another across the hall with a gentle gesture. "Your friend is in there. He is under a Healer's Rest, granting him peace until I find a cure. You are more than welcome to stay with him, or this room is also available. My home is your home, Princess." He lightly dipped his head as he continued, "Accept my humblest apologies for earlier. Please know I was only protecting my home and those within it."

I nodded in understanding as I uttered my own apology. He turned to walk farther down the hall before disappearing around the corner.

Immediately, I lunged toward the door to Sury's room and quietly slipped in. The room was larger than I expected but still had the same wooden theme as the front of the...cabin? Whatever magical structure this was. Sury lay on a large bed tucked under cotton sheets in the middle of the room.

Fyom had said he'd magically induced sleep to hold off any physical pain Sury endured. The dim light from the small candle on the table next to his bed illuminated the tiny droplets of sweat collecting at his brow. I took a small cloth from the table and gently swiped the beads away.

My heart pained as I watched my brother-in-spirit sleep. Though he looked at peace, I saw the small black lines now stretched toward his jawline. I felt the flow of tears as I gently threw my arms over him and wept on his uninjured shoulder, feeling my sister's necklace cut deep into my chest as it wedged between us.

"I'm so sorry, Sury! I don't know how to make this right, but dammit I will! Dammit, Sury! I *will* make this right. I will claw the eyes out of every person responsible for all this hurt!" The candlelight glowed brighter and then flickered as a faux wind passed through the room. Time felt as if it stood still, with only the melting candle giving away the moments that slipped by.

I couldn't tell how much time had passed before I finally pulled myself away and curled on the floor next to his bed. My head grew heavy and my eyes strained as I wept into the crevice of my arm. The sweetness of the dark enclosed me, giving me the peace of sleep.

***

The sun's rays maliciously shone through small holes in the room's curtains and into my eyes. I growled at the sun and was rubbing my swollen, sleepy eyes when a light knock came from the door.

Fyom gently poked his head inside the room. "I figured I might find you here. Next time, feel free to grab extra blankets and pillows from that wardrobe there." He winked. "No need for a princess to sleep like a pauper."

"I had everything I needed but thank you for your continued hospitality." I stretched my neck and shoulders as I pulled myself off the floor. If only Ora could see me now, could see how I've made the forest floor my bed—and now this.

"Nonetheless, breakfast is ready when you are." Fyom started to slip out the door.

"Thank you," I called out, "for everything." Seeing the warm glow in the giant man's eyes warmed something within me that I couldn't explain. I knew I was safe in this stranger's home. Fyom nodded his head in acknowledgment.

"Do you know how long we have for Sury?" I asked to help break the silence. Fyom opened the door wider and stepped in. In just a couple of steps, he closed the gap between the door and the bed. His light green shirt played perfectly with the hues of his eyes and the white hair that hung loosely to his broad shoulders.

He lifted the cloth to inspect it further, then pulled out a small jar of salve from the bedside table. He rubbed the contents on the cloth before reapplying it to Sury's shoulder. "It's hard to tell. Dokvalon's poisons work differently than the ones I'm accustomed to."

"You're so sure that it's Dokvalon? We've been at peace for over eighty years. We would demolish them with our army."

Thoughts swirled in my mind as I tried to connect the pieces of the puzzle.

Fyom looked at me with gentle eyes and sat at the edge of Sury's bed. "I vow to you that this home is yours for as long as you wish. Tell me more about why you're this far north and why your companion here has been struck."

I looked at him and calculated my odds. The same warm feeling nudged me, telling me I could trust him and his word.

So I recounted all I knew, from the moment Ora was taken to now, sitting in this very spot.

"If it was indeed Dokvalon that took her, then why hasn't there been any word across the kingdom about the queen-to-be being taken or the Grian armies marching west?" Fyom was lost in momentary thought. "Nonetheless, we cannot take on the world without a bite to eat." With a flick of his eyebrows, he turned to leave and left the door open.

I turned to squeeze Sury's hand as hard as I could. "I will make this right. You will see her again." Then I followed Fyom down the hall.

I hadn't noticed the grandeur of the hallway the night before. Brilliantly cut archways appeared every few steps and housed numerous doors on either side. Sunlight came from the grand windows ahead bounced off the stone walls. Intricate blue and tan rugs clung to the floors and were in perfectly placed intervals.

Silly, I thought, *him claiming his home to be a humble cabin when it's more like a wooden estate that would rival some of the lords of Gria.*

"How can your home look like this when the outside looks different?" I called from behind, trying to sound simply curious without being insulting.

"It has developed a mind of its own over the years," Fyom said over his shoulder.

Mind of its own indeed.

Through the last of the arches, I reentered the grand room—the entrance to his *cabin*—and took note of the two large spiraling wooden staircases that went to a whole other floor. At the base of the stairs stood the tall tree. Its green leaves shook in an unseen draft as their branches tore into the roof, supporting the ceiling.

Around the base, on the opposite side of the tree, stood another large room. A single fireplace set within a stone wall had remnants of an old fire. Leather chairs were placed on either side with a leather sofa to match. Between them were simple wooden tables holding various lamps and trinkets with a few scattered books.

Beyond the fireplace were open sets of grand windows that overlooked the circle of birch trees and into the mountains beyond them. In the far distance, past the mountains, pillars of black smoke lingered in the sky and formed gray clouds.

The clouds never traveled from their spot, but continued to build.

"Dokvalon," Fyom said as he walked to the windows and observed alongside me. He towered over me but humbly had his hands held in fists behind his back. He must have sensed my tension because he added, "You and Sury are safe here. Only a few know about this place."

I turned my worried gaze from Fyom and back to the Shadowcraig Mountains.

"I didn't realize we were so close." In my mind's eye, I quickly tried to reassess my geography of the kingdom to familiarize where we could be.

"The curse of Dokvalon is always too terribly close. Come, let's enjoy breakfast. I suspect it's been a while since you've had a whole meal."

"If I have to eat one more bolete, I think I might punch something."

The man chuckled. "It's a good thing I'm all out then." He winked and turned down a small passageway that opened up to a spacious kitchen and seating area too large to be a nook but cozy enough to be a small dining room.

The tall ceiling housed large, spacious windows to allow the sunlight to filter through. Tightly wrapped along the wooden beams that crossed through the open space were bright green vines with small flowers pointing in the sun's direction. A small cabinet clung to the wall holding various plates and cups, along with more peculiar trinkets.

The dining table was overflowing with different kinds of bread and plates of butter and cheeses. Fresh fruits lay in overfilled platters. A large metal container held different styles of sausages and bacon that still sizzled, and in the middle was a giant kettle of brown liquid with fresh steam escaping the top.

My mouth watered as I took in the feast laid before us. Fyom pulled aside one of the large leather chairs and ushered me to sit. I took in the sight of the three long windows opposite me and the sunlight radiating inside. Fyom sat next to me, at the end of the table, and poured the prepared tea into a cup.

"This is my special blend. Much better than coffee. Three times the amount of energy it can give you, without the jitters." He chuckled, clearly amused with himself, and filled his own cup to the brim.

I took the cup and brought it to my nose, inhaling deeply.

The scent alone was invigorating.

Small wisps of rose petal and orange, along with other notes I couldn't quite place my finger on. The moment I took a small sip, my tastebuds came alive. Energy surged through me as I took two more giant sips of the tea. My eyes lifted, the heaviness practically disappearing, and all the while my hunger panged deeper.

I tried to hold back my eagerness for the food and to mind my manners from all my royal training, but hunger won. Suddenly, my plate was filled with slices of bread, all slabbed in butter. Fresh pieces of fruit and scrambled eggs piled on. The bacon hardly had a chance to hit my plate before I snatched it and stuffed it into my mouth, where it melted deliciously. A little moan escaped my throat as I took another bite. If this is what it's like at the giants' gates, I didn't want to come down.

"I take it that breakfast is good?" a deep, husky voice said. "Or you're just that hungry because I know Fyom can't cook worth a damn."

I opened my eyes, not realizing I had closed them at some point, and locked eyes with Peiro, who carried a sarcastic smile on his face. He looked more alive and full of energy. His once stark silver eyes had dulled into a soft gray that hinted at a borderline brown.

I was instantly aware of how overstuffed my mouth was and grabbed a napkin to cover it as quickly as I could, all the while trying to chew without choking. Peiro sat down opposite of me, his own plate stacked high with enough food to feed at least four people.

"Glad to see your appetite is coming back," Fyom said as he poured his second glass of tea to the brim.

Peiro gave a small chuckle as he added a third piece of bread to his plate. The closed side-smile worked naturally on his face, and interestingly, he looked years younger than the night before. His tanned skin was now fuller and flushed with color. The lines on his weary face had softened and the skin around his cheekbones had filled out, leaving them not as sharp as before.

In fact, his chest and shoulders had also filled out and were much broader. The shirt he wore clung tightly to his chest. The sleeves were rolled up to his elbows, showing his corded forearms and the four black tattoos that encircled the right.

The once-wild brown hair, full of knots and tangles, had been cut shorter, to the tops of his shoulders, and combed back into a smooth half-braid. His beard was now clean and trimmed down to a stubble. The lines at his jaw accentuated the fullness of his lips, and the muscles radiated down his neck with each bite he took. The only thing that seemed utterly familiar about him was the hooped silver earrings that glinted in the sunlight and the ink on his skin.

"I see you're feeling better," Fyom said as he took a deep sip from his mug.

"I am," Peiro agreed as he piled on his fourth piece of bread. He had clearly been starving too. He laughed at a joke Fyom told—what the punchline was I wouldn't know— and his laugh was deep and smooth and hung delicately in the air.

How did he go from looking like he was an inch from death's doorstep to someone who looked remarkably healthy and vital?

And how was he so beautiful?

Peiro caught my gaze and tilted his head to the side, raising a singular dark brow in the process. "Do I have something on my face, Princess?"

I didn't realize I was holding my breath and quickly refilled my lungs. "Uhm...sorry. I was staring out the window behind you." I scampered out the excuse as I simultaneously recalled that it's been ages since I had proper a bath, let alone a look in the mirror, and I silently died a little on the inside.

Nonchalantly, I smoothed wild hairs and tucked back loose strands of my braid behind my ears. I kept my eyes down on my plate as I listened to Fyom and Peiro's friendly exchange.

"Never take that shit again. Do you hear me?" Fyom gently rumbled from behind his mug.

"We can talk about that another time," Peiro said in between chews.

"You look *different*," Fyom said over his piece of buttered bread topped with cinnamon and raisins.

I had another word in mind for how the man looked, but clamped my mouth shut.

"I don't know how to explain it, but your tea hasn't helped me feel this like before. Did you use something different?"

Fyom cast me a small glance as he shook his head at Peiro. "Same recipe I've always used."

"Whatever you did has made me feel the best I have in ages. I might try to swing a sword. Do you still have that one I gave you?" The excitement in his eyes shone brightly, and a pleasant smile spread wide across his face.

"Peculiar." Fyom eyed the man skeptically with a brow raised.

"Don't be a gloom, old friend! This is something worth celebrating! I can think again. I can *feel* again."

I watched the men exchange more looks before Fyom narrowed his eyes and Peiro continued to pile another serving of food onto his plate. It dawned on me that he said *I* and not we. What was in that tea?

"Princess Phe." Fyom shifted his body toward me.

"Please just call me Phe," I said in between chews and behind my napkin, as if I were sitting at a royal dinner. Each bite was painstakingly smaller than what my stomach wanted it to be.

"Phe." Fyom beamed. "We have much to discuss today. After I tend to Sury's wounds, I would like to meet with you in my study. You can share more of your story with me and tell me how a humble servant such as myself can help." He continued, "Your magic is fascinating to me. I'd like to assess it as well."

"Assess it?" I looked back and forth between the men to garner an understanding. Peiro shrugged as he shoveled three pieces of bacon into his mouth. "I'm not sure what all there is to assess. I told you everything."

"May I be frank, Your Highness?"

"No, but you may be Fyom," Peiro said as he softly chuckled into his cup of tea.

Did he just make a joke?

Fyom paused for a moment and then boomed with laughter. The exchange between the two was like that between a father and son, clearly unserious and finding any room for a joke—despite the aura of seriousness that cascaded over Fyom.

I chuckled. "Yes, you may be frank, *Fyom*."

He took another sip before continuing. "While it's true that it has been several years since I myself have tested, your situation sounds...unusual. And from what we all experienced last night..."

Peiro shot me a look.

Guilt and shame coursed through me as images flickered through my mind. His scream. His body contorting. Him lying on the ground unconscious. I couldn't bear to look him in the eyes.

Fyom continued before anything else could be added. "All that to say—something just isn't adding up. But this will be with your permission, of course."

"Of course," I said. Heat rose to my cheeks and guilt edged further into my chest. "I would like to take a moment," I looked down at my dirty tunic and wrinkled my nose, "and wash up."

Fyom chuckled. "Of course. Every room here is housed with a bath chamber. There is also a fresh change of clothes prepared for you as well."

"But how did you—?"

"Fyom is filled with all sorts of magics and mysteries, as well as this house," Peiro said with a smile. "The house itself might know what you're thinking before you do." He finished with a light laugh before popping a piece of fruit into his mouth.

I nodded and excused myself from the table. I made my way back to the large tree in the grand hall before returning to the passageway that housed the bedrooms. I checked in on Sury, who still seemed at peace, and wiped away more sweat from his brow before leaving to enter the room meant for me.

It was identical to Sury's, down to the placement of the wardrobe and decor. This time, I paid attention to the room itself and the three large windows that lined the opposite side of the door. A giant bed in the room's center looked deep and inviting, with too many pillows and blankets to count. In front of the bed was another fireplace that had been cleaned out and was ready for cool weather. A huge fur rug lined the floor and took up the majority of the vast room.

What kind of creature would have this much hide?

The door in the corner opened to a large bathing room, with walls that were lined with white birch bark and smooth, ash-colored stones, and iron chandeliers filled with flames that flickered brightly. On a large vanity was a metal platter holding small vials of various oils. I picked up a light red one that emitted scents like dahlia and cherry blossom, with a small hint of calla lily.

It reminded me of Mother and her favorite light red dress she would wear. I took the vial and walked over to the large stone basin set in the middle of the room. It was large enough to comfortably fit two grown adults.

As I placed a few drops of the oil into the bath, I was surprised to see that it was already filled with steaming water. A large metal hook bolted into the wall held a fresh cloth for drying and, to much amusement, a fresh tunic and riding pants—just my size—were at the ready inside a large linen cabinet. I chuckled with a hint of embarrassment to see fresh underthings waiting, too.

The water caressed my skin like a warm blanket and sent soothing waves across my sore muscles. I melted further into the bath, allowing the water to flow over my submerged body, and simply stayed there to feel nothing. Silence greeted me. No thoughts of family. No smells of the forest. No inky voices in the back of my mind. Nothingness surrounded me.

I almost forgot I needed to meet Fyom and hastily set to dry myself and get dressed. I put my fingers to quick work braiding my wet hair into something functional.

I checked myself in the mirror and noticed my rounded cheeks had grown into sharper angles since I last saw my reflection. Even my neck and arms were slightly slimmer, accentuating my breasts more.

But my eyes. They still held the same bright teal and steady glow behind them, the tell trait of a born Wielder.

I peeped back inside Sury's room, noting the fresh bandages and new vials on the nightstand, before setting off back down the passageway. It took me a moment to look around and guess which room was Fyom's study. I finally heard his great voice echo from above, "Up here."

Once at the top of the large steps, I found a large open room that rivaled some of the rooms at The High Seven Temple. My jaw dropped. The room expanded over what I could assume was the length of his *cabin*, and the walls were lined with shelves and books from floor to ceiling. A thick wooden ladder clung to the shelving rails, eager to please the next curious mind.

I rushed to one of the shelves that housed books on magic I had never seen or heard of before. Curiosity and excitement filled my heart, and I suddenly felt the urge to curl up on one of the soft couches and dive into reading. Each book was bound in brightly colored fabrics and deep brown leathers. My fingers traced along the spines as I perused each title.

"My personal collection," Fyom's deep voice softly rumbled as he walked toward me.

"I've never heard of some of these, and the Grianmore Castle's library rivals the Seven's. Where did you find these?" My gaze was still fixated on all the books.

"I've traveled far and wide across our own continent and to others around us. Some have been gifts and some have been, uhm, permanently borrowed."

I gave him a quick eye and smirked as I continued to read the various titles on other shelves.

Realization hit. The magnitude of this collection would be considered an offense to the temple. A large collection of tomes and education on Wielding, outside of the temple or the castle, was considered *too* dangerous without the proper authorities—according to Ariadne.

"You mentioned that Ariadne was the High Priestess? Ariadne Terrigan, correct?"

"Yes."

Fyom stroked his beard. "It's been quite a while since I've had the pleasure of visiting the temple. I forget what she looks like. Could you describe her to me?"

The question was peculiar, but I obliged his curiosity. "Well, she has very fair skin. Almost like snow. It makes her bright red hair look like a flame in comparison. She also has golden skin markings that she says tell the story of how she became appointed as the High Priestess, being the only Wielder in years to reach the seventh level."

"Seventh level, you say?" His eyebrows rose as he dropped his chin.

I nodded as Fyom led me to a giant desk that was at the back of the room, in front of large curtained windows. The desk overflowed with stacks of books and papers and scrolls. A little scale sat in the corner, collecting what looked like dust. I couldn't help but play with a small bauble that swayed back and forth on a stand.

"Why do you ask?"

Fyom walked to another large desk in the middle of the room and rearranged various things before he answered, "Simply trying to recall things from my old memory. Sounds like I need to get out of my home more often."

I stood next to Fyom and observed that the desk had two small boxes, various bowls and cups, and a pitcher of water. Fyom opened one of the boxes and pulled out a collection of dried herbs. He placed them into one of the bowls and used a grinding stone to turn them into a fine powder.

In the other bowl, he placed his hand over the empty basin and let his fingers dance above it. Steadily, a faint trickle of water began to rise from the bottom and fill halfway, while the water level in the pitcher began to diminish.

I smiled. "You make that look easy."

His eyebrows furrowed in concentration. "Years of practice," he said with a smirk and began mixing in the crushed herbs. He opened the other box to reveal small vials containing various liquids. A small pink one was chosen, and a single drop of its contents was mixed in with the herbal concoction.

I watched every movement in fascination and tried to name each herb as he swirled the cup in front of him. My eyes wandered before fixating on the same large blue crystal Fyom had brought out the day before. I felt my body fighting to seize. I quickly backed away from the desk and brought my arms in close. I could feel the cut he'd made earlier start to throb against my skin.

Fyom noticed my distance and held his hands up to show he meant no harm. "This will be different. If you would allow me, I want to see her Wielding influence from when she guided you through testing. It will help me understand your Wielding more." He gently reached for the arm I held with an open hand. "Your choice."

I subconsciously clutched the stone of Ora's necklace—I refused to take it off until I found her. "Tell me what I have to do."

He held the crystal in his hand and extended it for me to take. "I only need the smallest of pricks on the finger and a drop into this cup."

I hesitated for a moment. "But you're doing blood magic. This magic is forbidden. This is the magic of Dokvalon."

"So they would make you believe." Fyom's eyes were soft and patient as he watched me contemplate my next move.

"And what exactly will you see? Didn't you see enough when you cut me yesterday?"

"My deepest apologies, again, for that intrusion." He bowed his head slightly. "This allows me to see how your magic moves and what might have caused you to lose control. This is a common practice to see how diseases and viruses move against one's blood or magic. Very similar to your friend."

"Last time, this triggered something." My face reddened from embarrassment as I felt guilt rise. Images of Peiro's pain came to mind. "I don't want to hurt anyone," I whispered.

"You won't as long as *you* are okay with this. We can find other sources, but it might take longer. And we don't have the time we crave."

I stood there with my arms tightly clutched and tapped my lips with my fingers. Without another thought, I took the crystal from his hand and brought it close to inspect it. I imagined the deep golden veins pulsing across the brilliant blue and throbbing against my hand.

How much was I ready to reveal? Did I want to see what I already knew?

He'll find nothing worth noting. One drop and he'll discover just how useless you are.

Ignoring the thought, I quickly poked my finger against the sharp point of the crystal, drawing a single bead of blood, and allowed Fyom to guide my hand over the cup to let it drop.

A warming sensation webbed from the prick on my finger to the cut on my arm as Fyom's hold on my hand increased slightly in pressure. Both wounds began to glow like the moon was trapped beneath my skin. I rolled up my shirt's sleeve to find the cut was gone and replaced with smooth skin.

The workings of Spiritus. Of Healing.

"Again—my apologies," Fyom said before working with the contents inside the bowl.

He quickly added other ingredients before swirling them together and pouring them into a cup. Nothing happened as we stood there in silence for a moment. Fyom then took the cup and sipped the liquid.

"What are you doing?" I waited anxiously for him to say something, to say anything, but he just stood there with a blank look on his face. A quiet moment passed before Fyom emptied the rest of the contents into his mouth and stood there in silence.

I wasn't sure what to make of it. Fyom twirled his cup like it was nothing more than your average tea and looked down at me quizzically. "Most interesting indeed."

"What's wrong?" The insecurity started to rise again, and a multitude of questions and doubts swirled in my head.

He can taste your weakness, girl. That voice scraped across my mind like a nail over flesh.

"There's a fog. Your magic flickers in and out. I can't quite read it."

"What do you mean? Should we try it again? Maybe you need more blood."

Fyom walked to one of his many shelves, pulled out a dark red book, and flipped through the pages. "That won't be necessary. We might have to try another option."

I stood there and waited for him to explain.

Fyom shut the book with a snap and turned on his heel to face me again. "How would you feel if we tried testing your magic? Like at the temple?"

"What do you mean? It's already been manifested and tested."

"I mean, truly *test* it," he said with a shake of his head. "I have suspicions and theories, but I'd like to find a place to start."

"How will this help Sury and my sister? I can't waste anymore time!"

"Helping you will help them." Fyom spoke with a pinched thumb and index finger as he explained. "We will only know more once we figure out what could be causing the fog in your readings. Why you can't find the control you're needing." He scratched his face and tossed the book onto his desk. "Who even placed that fog in the first place. They clearly don't want something seen. Your control could give you enough power to save them."

"If it might help, then let's do it," I said with confidence to mask the doubt settling in my chest.

The echoes from the shadows when I first tested crept into my mind. *She's the fall of the Endromeon line.* The whisper was as strong as if I had just heard it yesterday, not almost two decades ago.

"Give me a moment to prepare. I will meet you outside in front of the cabin." Fyom walked toward a giant oak hutch built into the wall on one side of the massive room.

"I love how you call this extravagant place a *cabin*. This room alone looks like it could rival those of the Scholars that I've read about."

Fyom stiffened for a moment, then gave a hearty chuckle and turned back to his shelves to search for the book.

CHAPTER 21

I headed down the large stairs to the great hall, where the sun sat high through the front windows beside the large entry door. The outside air was cool and the ground was still covered in dew that sparkled in the sunlight.

I took in the beauty that I hadn't caught before—the surrounding forest of birch trees that encircled the cabin. Verdant ferns tickled their trunks and bloomed flowers in bright colors, but what caught my eyes the most were the delicate blue-green flowers scattered along the forest floor and into a small, open meadow in the distance.

The floorboards of the porch creaked and moaned and looked as if they hadn't been attended to in decades. I turned back to look once more at the so-called cabin. To any observer on the outside, Fyom's home did indeed look like a moderate circular hut with layered wooden shingles on its top that desperately needed to be redone. Or was this part of the facade?

Curiosity got the best of me and I decided to explore the surroundings and around Fyom's home. As I wandered, I picked a few small stems of the delicate blue flower and placed a small one in my hair above my ear. I knew I had walked to the side where the dining room windows should be, but I was met with dry-rotted pinewood and cracked, hardened clay. Maybe it was the other way?

Echoes of loud grunts and the shrill of clashing metal bounced off the cabin's walls as I continued to walk on light steps. The sound of something being beaten grew louder and ricocheted against the forest's trees. I quickly grabbed my dagger from my waist and held it just like Sury taught me when we practiced in the woods. My heart raced in panic, wondering how anyone could have found us here, given I wasn't exactly sure where *here* was.

Tiptoeing around the bend, I gripped the dagger tightly and jumped, ready to strike. Warm relief coursed through me the moment I realized it was only Peiro, with a sword in hand, violently attacking a wooden structure with a makeshift target on its chest. I was mesmerized as I watched his feet move magically across the ground, swinging his sword high and low, striking true to his target.

The sun shone across his shirtless, tanned skin, which looked darker and fuller than before. Dark lines of ink trailed over muscles that intrigued me, begging to be studied. He seemed to have gained half his size in muscle overnight. His trousers hung low on his waist, and a thick leather band with its sheath rested loosely at his side.

Each strike tensed the muscles of his hard body and caused beads of sweat to flee from his torso and back. He wielded the broadsword with meticulous ease and flipped his wrists in graceful movements, as if his body were remembering the steps to a violent dance.

An internal temperature rose deep in my belly. I continued to clutch the dagger tightly as I watched him practice over.

"Are you going to keep standing there, or did you come out to practice, too?" Peiro called out as he slashed into the wooden structure again and again. He turned around, showcasing those darkened silver eyes that were a stark contrast against his golden skin.

My jaw clenched as I quickly looked away from his body and acted interested in trees off to the distance. The very *far* distance. "I'm just waiting on Fyom and decided to wander around, was all."

I didn't register how fast he closed the distance between us. I gasped at the quick movement and the wall that was now in front of me. I could see the beads of sweat collecting on his chest and shoulders.

Look anywhere but at him. *Look anywhere else!* I repeated inside my head.

"They match your eyes."

"What?" My eyes betrayed me as they looked into his. The lines in his face were still faint from the other day, framing his smooth face with wisdom.

Peiro used his strong calloused hand to gently raise my fist, which still squeezed the stalks of the flowers, crushing their stems in my fingers.

"Oh, thank you," I stammered and pulled back my hand. "You seem to be enjoying your morning and chopping away at that poor creature there." I nodded toward the pell.

He chuckled. "Yeah, well, it had it coming."

"How are you feeling?" I shyly asked. Quick images of his contorted body and magic flashed against my mind and forced me to wince.

A hint of a smile flashed across his face. "I feel great. Fyom has always been a remarkable Healer and a master at his own tonics. I haven't felt this good in ages. I think I finally got a good night's sleep for once."

I lifted a solitary dark brow. "You don't remember last night?"

"Last night?" He looked off toward the trees, staring for a moment. "I remember you and Fyom boring me, then going to sleep after Fyom gave me his tea. I woke up feeling a way I didn't think was possible again." He stared off again in wonder, a small smile creeping across his face.

My heart clenched at just how strong of a hold the valley gilliflower must have had on him. Whatever Fyom created to detox his body must be state-of-the-art. Not many Healers have been able to help users in the way I'm witnessing for Peiro. It takes weeks for many to gain their weight back and months before they even feel stable enough to live on their own.

Peiro raised his hand and lightly twirled a dark strand of my hair around his finger. My stomach dipped as my breath hitched. His face tilted up as he took in a quick smell of the air. "Your perfume."

"It's dahlia. Like my mother wore." I swallowed hard.

"Hmm. It's wrong."

"What do you mean?" I sputtered, clearly confused.

He met my eyes, holding my gaze for a heartbeat that sent my stomach spinning. "You smell like moonlight and jasmine. Don't hide what you are."

I could only blink as the sensation continued.

His hand dropped from my face, fingers trailing along my waist as he raised his sword hilt with the other. "Come," he rasped. "Show me what a Princess of Gria can do."

I took a shy step back and glanced between him and the pell. "I don't want to interrupt what you're doing..."

"It was a bit late for that when I felt you ogling."

Heat rose to my cheeks. "I was not *ogling*." I tried my hardest not trace the ink with my eyes.

"Hmm. Right. Well, then, get to it. Show me."

"I don't know how."

Peiro scoffed. "What do you mean *you don't know how*?"

I looked down at my boots as embarrassment kissed my cheeks. "I only had a handful of lessons, but never with a sword."

Peiro's sword hand dropped to his side as he wiped his face with his free hand. "You mean to tell me a Princess of Gria doesn't know how to wield a sword? Back when..." He stopped and rubbed his chin. "How did the king and queen expect you to defend yourself then?"

"Most Wielders rely on their magic. But many also run. Rely on the armies," I said as I sheathed my dagger.

"Is that what you are, Princess? A runner?" *Yes.* I always ran away from conflict. Never found an interest in fighting. "From what you told Fyom, you have no army. Who are you going to rely on now?" He took a step back. "It's best you start creating calluses on your hand, girl."

My head snapped up at that. "Girl?" Anger brewed deep. "This *girl* is a woman. And a part of the family that rules over this kingdom, so you'll show some damn respect to this *girl.*"

A wide smile slowly etched across Peiro's face, showing his white teeth. "Prove it."

"Prove what?" My teeth were bared, holding back the energy that desperately wanted to rise within me. My fingers involuntarily tremored.

"That you're someone that doesn't need saving. That you're someone I can pridefully bow before. Get on my knees for." A wicked glint flashed across his eyes. He was clearly finding which buttons to push, but damnit, my body did something funny as his grin widened. He held up his sword hand again. "Prove. It."

I couldn't hold back what happened next. My anger mixed with annoyance and straight exhaustion from losing my parents to losing my sister and now having my friend on his deathbed. Everything within me surged before I could take my next breath.

The emotional dam I had molded into place began to crack.

The orbs barely had time to form as a whirlwind of energy forced me to bring my hands before me and expel an unseen power toward Peiro. In a flash, he was picked up off his feet and hurled into the air by an invisible gust of wind. His body went in one direction, the sword another.

He hit the solid ground with a hard *thud* and landed in odd angles. The energy subsided within my skin as I noticed I still held my hands before me while gasping for air. Panic took over when I observed the body lying on the ground.

I was frozen as I watched the steady rise and fall of Peiro's chest. Slowly, he adjusted his arms and legs and rolled over to all fours, coughing. He rose, wiping his mouth with a hand covered in dirt. He turned his head side to side, cracking his neck in the process. He rolled his shoulders as he turned, showing his lip had split a little, evidenced by bright red blood beginning to pool. He used the back of his hand to wipe it away and smiled.

His eyes dulled darker to a dark gray-brown.

"That's more like it." He winked and walked over to the sword lying on the ground. In a few strides, he covered the distance between us and raised the sword over his head.

I moved just in time as his sword swung down. "What are you doing?!" I backed away, watching him turn and twist with grace.

"Figure it out, Princess!" Peiro sing-songed before charging at me with surprising speed. I ducked and rolled across the rocky ground, wincing as stones bit into my shoulder. I sprang back up just in time to dodge his next swing

"You're crazy!" I yelled. How could he have looked so frail and weak just the day prior, and now he was wielding a sword like he'd never missed a day?

"I've been called worse. Now figure your shit out!" He took another swing. "Will you stand on your own two feet, or will you fall?" The force caused me to stumble. As I fell, I caught sight of a wooden rack near the pell with notches that held different-sized blades.

I scrambled to my feet, hearing Peiro close behind as I ran to grab a blade to defend against the oncoming attack. With both hands, I seized one that looked manageable and spun just in time to catch Peiro's strike from behind. The impact jolted through my hands and arms, forcing me to give way just a bit.

His blade was mere inches from my face as I held steady and locked eyes with him. I pushed with all the strength I had, barely budging him back.

He peeked through the crossing of our blades and smiled. "You're a quick learner. A little rusty on your turns, but with practice, they'll even out."

"I don't want to fight you," I said between my teeth.

He pouted—actually *pouted*—when he said, "Is this what you'll tell the Raiders next time they shoot an arrow at you? *'Please, no. Stop. I don't want to fight. Let's discuss war over tea and crumpets.'*"

Rage bloomed. I pushed my shoulder deeper into my defense, forcing him back an inch.

"Look around you, *Princess*." He never took his eyes off mine as he pushed back. The force made me stumble again. "No one is going to rescue you or your sister. You're better off dead if you wait for someone to save you."

My hand and blade began to hum.

A sharp sting of vibrations speared up through my hands and into the blade, causing them to shake slightly. The rusted blade started to glow as a shrilling sound rose around us. The oxidized spots on the blade shrunk in size as the glow burned brighter and the metal turned hot, almost molten in color.

Peiro's sword began to give slightly where it met mine. He looked at his blade with bewilderment in his eyes.

"That's a good start," he said as he pulled away. The force of his absence caused me to back into the rack. My hand felt frozen, my muscles unable to release my grip.

I looked down at my sword, seeing the light fade, leaving behind a metal that looked as if it were newly crafted from a smith.

"What the hell?" I panted each word between breaths. Peiro simply stood a few feet in front of me, placing his sword back on the rack, seeming unphased. "You could have killed me!"

I noticed a small bend in the sword where it had…melted a bit? I barely had a moment to register before he grabbed me by the nape of my neck, forcing my face upward. The act itself didn't hurt but ignited something within me that felt familiar. Like I was in the presence of an old lover.

My breath caught as he peered into my eyes. I took in the lines of his face and noticed just how beautiful he was. His gaze lowered to where our lips almost touched. My heartbeat raced in anticipation.

"If I wanted you dead, Princess, it would already be done," he whispered. "I told you before that you are far more capable of bringing me harm than I am of harming you." I felt the heat of his breath caressing my lips. I swallowed hard, my body wanting to betray me and longing for something that felt forbidden but desperately needed. "You're stronger than you think you are. Even the most beautiful flower can be a poison. The moon also has a dark side."

"You don't know me."

"I don't have to know you. I can sense it." He gently let go of my neck and stepped away.

I was about to speak again when Fyom appeared around the bend. "There you two are. Peiro, how is the training? Looks like you never missed a day."

"Feels like it did when I was younger. Much younger," he laughed.

"No headaches this morning?"

"None." Peiro shook his head.

I took note of Fyom passing a small vial into Peiro's hands when he said, "Get off that *vine*."

Peiro smiled as he walked back toward the pell. "I feel like me! You should be happy. Whatever you created is working!" His excitement grew with each step, and he picked up his sword once again before resuming his violent dance with the wooden target.

We left Peiro behind while wood chips still flew in the air from his attacks. My curiosity grew insatiable, and eventually, I couldn't resist the urge to learn more about the man with the sword. "Does he come to you for help? Is that how you two know one another?" I asked as I followed behind Fyom.

"We're old friends. But why he comes to me is his story to tell." We continued walking until we were back by the meadow where I had picked my flowers. I recalled there was one still in my hair.

In the clearing sat seven metal stands arranged in a circle, each with a small clay bowl placed on top, just like at the temple during testing. Quick images of a scared seven-year-old girl wearing a simple white gown and shoes crossed my mind.

"You mean you want to *test* it, test it?" I came to a halt a few feet away from the center of the circle. "I thought only the priests and priestesses knew how to, and that we couldn't test again."

"And this is what Ariadne has told *you*?"

That was an odd question. "Well, yes."

"Does she tell all her students this?" Fyom adjusted a few bowls to the center of their stands.

"Of course," I assumed.

Fyom turned his gaze and sighed. "I'm afraid this *Ariadne* might be lying to you. She may have even lied to your mother."

I already had my suspicions but hearing them from someone else helped my validation. "What makes you think that?"

"Tell me what you've been taught about the Seven Circles of Wielding."

"Well..." I thought back to my lessons from when I was seven years old. "The higher circle means higher power."

"That is true for us now, in the grand hierarchy. Yes."

Frustration built. "The more control you have of your Wielding, the more important you become. Which is why when someone comes of age and has proven to have strong control, they can join the court." I kept going. "Not many noble lines have kept the Elementis in their names. Anyone can be the strongest Wielder in an element and gain power in court. For better or for worse." I thought of Lady Simret and Vovias. "This is why the fifth and sixth levels are also revered, and usually only found in the old noble bloodlines. But there hasn't been a seventh in centuries, aside from Ariadne."

Fyom gave me a questionable look. "Does Ariadne test for the seventh level for all the students?"

I thought back to my testing day, to Ariadne stating that the testing for the seventh level is prohibited, but that she was the anomaly when she manifested. "Well, no. It's forbidden. Hers was just happenstance."

"And what does the Temple Council say on this manner?"

"Other priests and priestesses? I only saw Ariadne at *the* test. She leads the Council, too."

Fyom stroked his chin and gave me a sarcastic smile. "In the Temple of the High *Seven*, there's only *one* guide for those Wielding magic? *One* priestess?"

I stood there in silence, thinking about his question. "Of course, there are tutors that train the students in certain Wieldings, but it's always been this way. My mother only recalled one priestess when she tested."

Fyom let out a deep sigh. "Ariadne has soured many minds with her lies and thievery, I'm afraid. The woman you described, *the fair maiden with bright red hair*, was a young priestess when *I* tested."

But that wouldn't make sense. She would be close to a century old, or over it.

"Is there a chance you're wrong?"

Fyom shrugged his left shoulder. "Perhaps. But not likely."

His pride was astounding.

"There is supposed to be a priest or priestess, one for each level, with the seventh only there for pure tradition, to guide the manifestations. Ariadne didn't hold resolute power but simply stood in that space." Fyom stopped and gingerly scratched his stark white beard. "Probably more so to kill anyone who might have risen to that level."

"How can this be?" The idea played slowly in my mind and I wondered how it could even be possible. It couldn't be. Could it?

"My theory is blood magic, but that is a theory I will share later. First, let's try to understand if it was indeed Ariadne and why she placed a fog on your Wielding in the first place. Come to the center, please."

I stepped into the middle of the circle, the stands and bowls encasing me within. Flashes of the child version of myself bounced back and forth, and the shadows whispered.

Fyom walked the perimeter of the bowls with his hands clasped behind him. "The original Scholars state that Wielding came from one place. A gift from the giants. Wielding is like the veins in our skin. While there are different trails they take, they are all connected to a single, beating heart. Six interlocking circles, all connected together to work as one. Working *within* the essence of life and death."

My nose wrinkled in confusion. He was telling me the exact opposite of what I had been taught. Even the mention of *Scholars* was surprising. No one talked about the enemy to the temple from some war that was caused ages ago.

"We only know of the *illicitus* through stories handed down from the Temple Council and their notion that no one should be able to Wield life or death. The only example they have is from ancient stories that have been misconstrued during the time of the Scholars. Fear drives them. We don't know the true extent because we can never see it."

"Except Ariadne."

"Exactly. And why is that?" Fyom continued walking. "It was said that when the balance of Wielding magic became broken, that allowed the essence of life and death to enter the fold and to be Wielded just like any other power. Regardless if it's right or wrong, it is now a part of our magical makeup." But how did he know all of this? He spoke with so much certainty. "Magic is meant to function in unison. A working community. Someone who Wields at the Fifth Circle is meant to be no more important than a First Circle, as it's been taught. They all have a role to play in the realm of magic, equally."

The words hit me in the heart. Flashes of memories echoed the harsh words said of my *lowly* magic. I began to think of all the students who had crossed Ariadne's path and wondered if the same dark words were embedded in them.

How mighty words could be to the mind.

"Each Wielder specializes in the element they Wield, but as you know, many can only draw on their element when they're near to it. This is why those who have the strongest control are revered. They need less assistance to Wield." Fyom finally stopped his pacing and stood right in front of me, facing me over the first bowl. "It was once said we were strong in the Wieldings we were blessed in without the need of a source. So I, a Healer, wouldn't need to have the Elementis so close to perform the Healing arts. But since the balance was broken, now we have the Seventh Circle, control of life or death. The *illicitus*. The forbidden level.

"Yes. They have unique roles but all are *equally* important. And according to the Scholars, as time has gone on, Wielding itself has become greatly weakened. Each generation becomes less impactful than before. That's what's been interesting about the Endromeon bloodline... Your great bloodline. It has stayed strong enough to be in power for centuries." Fyom looked down, as if reading the echoes in my mind. "Now, come to the first bowl, please."

I tried to mentally digest what I was just told. From Fyom's words, it seemed that Wielding was meant to be a unified practice—free from the hierarchical status that plagued the court and kingdom. Vovias demanded inequalities simply based on his *power*.

It was true he needed only the tiniest spark to ignite a blaze. But just because he showed great control didn't mean anyone should be beneath him—even the others who Wielded fire. Even the Veiks he despised. The thought overwhelmed me.

I cautiously stepped toward the first bowl and the single blade of bright green grass, noting the vibrancy matched the green in Fyom's eyes. I saw a flash of Ariadne standing in front of me with her wild, curious eyes pinned on me like a fox hunting a hare.

"Earth," Fyom spoke and snapped me from my thoughts, "might appear docile, pliant...controllable." Each word grew more serious. "The very essence of life itself roams through the grasses or digs in its dirt. It's essential for us and other living beings to prosper. However, earth has its dark side. We know it cannot be controlled, but it merely grants us permission to live boundlessly. We must respect it and know our place." Fyom placed a large outstretched hand over the bowl, motioning me forward. "Allow the earth to be Wielded as *you* both wish."

His encouragement warmed my heart. Just as before, a small tingling sensation crept over my hand and up my arm, coursing through my body in a serpentine motion, and emitted tiny orbs at my fingertips. Just then, the little blade of grass split into two. A small smile crept up my face as the Wielding of earth I had grown to know remained steady.

"Do you feel that? Your Wielding swelling in the pit of your stomach?"

I was surprised by the question and let my hand fall while I nodded, causing the fidgeting blade of grass to still. "Yes. Is it supposed to?" I couldn't recall if I felt the magic *swell* like it did just moments ago on the day I tested. I had only felt the tickling sensations in my hands that I thought all Wielders felt.

Fyom said nothing as he moved to the next bowl, which held a small feather for Wielding the air. My excitement faded. Echoes of Ariadne's harsh words rang in my mind, telling me to take command of the source, the source I already knew to be a losing battle. My nerves prickled as my mind found comfort in the racing thoughts that something must be truly wrong with my Wielding.

How was my family so powerful yet I held nothing compared to them?

Like I've always said, girl, you're weak, the ink whispered. *This is a waste of your time, and you know it. You're wasting time on finding your sister. If she's dead, then the blood is on your hands.*

I felt tears prickle as I blinked rapidly, refusing to let them form.

"Don't," Fyom's voice barked.

I was shaken out of my thoughts by the complete surprise of the outburst. "Don't what?"

"Don't allow your mind to do that."

"Do what?"

"Doubt. You are much stronger than you have been led to believe."

I placed my hand over the next bowl, with a small feather inside. The images of old temple walls and whispers from dark corners flickered into my mind. My hand lightly tickled, but it faded as fast as it came. I placed my other hand over the bowl to try again. Nothing happened. Only the hairs on the tops of my knuckles seemed to react to a faux breeze.

Before Fyom could speak, I stepped to the next bowl, which held a small drop of water. I threw my hand over the bowl in angst and waited for anything to happen. My blood pumped viciously through my veins and rang in my ears. *Pity.* Ariadne's words sliced through me just like they did those years ago.

See? You never listen to me, girl, the voice said right as I stamped my foot in frustration and yelled out in anger.

"Do you call this doubt? When you can see for yourself that I cannot do it? That I am *not* as strong as you think I am? I'm not a strong Wielder like my mother or sister, and that's the fact! Everyone in Gria knows that the *great and powerful* Endromeon bloodline has a weak and unfit princess. Has a flaw."

Fyom's form towered over me as he leaned down to meet me at eye level. "Even if you were *weak*, if you didn't fit someone *else's* definition of strength, that does *not* mean you are less than. You can still make a difference. You only have to believe it!"

I shook my head as I placed a palm to my brow, trying to find a calming breath.

"Even with that in mind, how would you begin to explain last night? We both saw what you did, and that's a Wielding I have not seen. A *strong* Wielding," Fyom softly asserted.

"I had an unexplainable anomaly, but I'm sure you can find the explanation in your books." I tossed my hand toward the bowls and stands. "This isn't going to work. And there's nothing more I can prove to you or me."

"But Phe..." Fyom extended his hand to stop my fleeting footsteps.

"No buts! My Wielding has always been questioned, and this is utterly humiliating to show you what I already know. I'm useless. I'm worthless. I'll never be able to find my sister, let alone save her!" My eyes swelled as tears started to pour.

I ran back inside and down the hall to Sury's room. He still lay there, soundlessly asleep, and didn't budge when I slammed the door. Tears fell uncontrollably as I rested my head on the pillow next to his and sobbed.

"I thought I had the strength, but I don't. I need you to wake up so we can work this out for Ora's sake." I clenched his shirt in an effort to wake him up with soft shakes. "Please, please wake up. I need you. Ora *needs* you."

I lay there and let the thoughts and hurt swirl like a thick shadow. Every thought of Ora's rescue diminished into a storm cloud and washed away. Hopeless. Everything was hopeless.

CHAPTER 22

A day passed before I worked up the courage to poke my head out the door. I heard neither Fyom nor Peiro as I tiptoed my way to the kitchen for something to satisfy my hunger and soothe my thoughts. As I later turned the corner to return to my room, I heard a large voice boom warmly from above.

"Feeling better?" Fyom stood at the banister of the top floor, overlooking the grand entry. A soft smile that stretched across his features. "Come. I have something to show you," he said as he turned around and headed back into his study.

I climbed the stairs to the next level and found Fyom standing next to his desk, which was now littered with more books and scrolls, all piled high. All seemed to defy the laws of gravity as they slung over the sides.

I rolled my eyes and reluctantly followed, catching my appearance in the reflection of a glass bookcase. My eyes were red and swollen and strands of hair fell out of my loose braid. I quickly smoothed my hair and wished for the giants to help my eyes. Embarrassment tinged my cheeks from my outburst earlier.

"I'm sorry." The words came out as a hoarse whisper. I cleared my throat to speak louder. "I shouldn't have acted in that way, especially after all you've done. I know you're only trying to help."

Fyom's soft eyes looked up from a scroll. "Phe, you have nothing to be sorry for. Your mind has been soured against not only magic, but also against itself."

I knew the words were meant to be warm, but I felt them fall into the pit inside my chest where my heart was supposed to be.

"I want to know why," Fyom continued. "Why sour your mind, especially as someone in the royal family? Why place a fog across your Wielding? What is Ariadne hiding?"

I tucked a strand of hair behind my ear and looked away. "You said she was the High Priestess when you tested? And there were six others?"

"Come, let me show you." Fyom pointed to a scroll that was flat on his desk. The paper was frail and brittle, and the lines written across were deeply faded. "This is one of the first scrolls of the High Seven Temple, written partly from the Scholars, about their philosophy on Wielding. How magic Wielders have a duty to the realm of magic and to the non-magic people of the land. Protectors. Servants. Not mighty power Wielders above all."

"How do you have something from the Scholars?"

"Never mind that."

I ignored the dismissal and looked across the writings and the names of the first seven priests and priestesses. "What happened? What caused the shift? Do you know?"

Fyom shook his head and pulled a large gray book from under a stack of others. "When I was a boy, my mother took me to the temple to learn more about my source. Wielding was a rare gift in my family, with only my grandfather and sister showing the ability, and no one knew how to help my particular Wielding grow. During my years there, the priest or priestess would teach and embody the original teachings and philosophy when the temple first began."

I watched as his eyes moved around the text before he flipped through the pages.

He continued, "I remember a woman then, Ariadne, just as you described. Through the years, the priests seemed to become sick, but no one thought of it at the time because they were indeed some of the oldest Wielders in Gria. Usually there is a newly appointed priest or priestess to take their role."

My brows furrowed. "Are you sure it's the same person and not just someone else with the same name?"

"I have a feeling it's the same Ariadne. When I first used the crystal to find out who you were, there were essences within your memories I couldn't put my finger on. Remnants of something old." He scratched at his beard. "I was sitting here, trying to understand your magic. I remembered feeling the same essence before, and as I've been sitting here, recounting the days of my youth at the temple, it clicked."

"Essence?"

Fyom tapped his chin. "The best way I can describe it is like a beetle crawling at the back of my brain. I felt it when she was around the students as they studied, and never again since I've left."

"What does this mean then?" I waved my hand at the things littering his grand desk.

"Somehow, in some way, she's taken over the temple for her purposes and has gone unnoticed."

"But why?"

"Simple. Control."

"Control for what, though?"

"Power. Influence. You said it yourself—she was practically your mother's right hand." Fyom looked up from his text and into my eyes. "You."

Confusion and curiosity struck hard. There was nothing special about me. Why would Ariadne be interested in me?

"She's hiding something," he continued, "and you're in her epicenter."

"But there's nothing special about me."

"But there is. Why else sour your mind? Why else force you to believe, after all these years, that you're weak when you've so clearly demonstrated you're not?"

"My mother also thought I was weak," I whispered as I twiddled the stoned necklace.

"Do you truly believe your mother, the great Queen of Gria, would believe her own daughter, flesh and blood, would be weak in *any* sense?"

I couldn't answer. While my mother never said anything of the sort, I could always sense it. Like she was trying to figure me out in some way. She always looked at me like I was made of glass.

A thought dawned in my mind so suddenly and so quickly, I wasn't sure why I hadn't thought of it before.

"It could be possible she tried to sour my mother's mind." I clutched the necklace harder. I pondered the thought as I dropped into a nearby leather chair, the cushion sinking in. "But how is she getting by unnoticed, and for so long?"

"Ah, that was the point I was getting to earlier!" Fyom brought over the large gray book and placed it in front of me, pointing to the text and a large black skull on its page. "It all points to her dealing in dark magic. Blood magic. Graevick's magic."

"But that was outlawed, and the original priests burned those books centuries ago. No one practices that unless they crave a death sentence. Even the Temple Council!"

"This is exactly what I had heard, and from the same source as you. From *her*."

Things began to click in the back of my mind. "Then she knows how to tap into unnatural Wielding. If she knows this, then there's no telling what all she might know and what she could do. What she might do to Ora." Worrying thoughts swirled faster. "But why target Ora the way she did? Why take *her* and risk a whole kingdom?"

We absorbed the silence as we let our minds travel deep, connecting the pieces of what we knew to those still unknown.

"It is possible," Fyom led, "that maybe she wasn't the correct target."

CHAPTER 23

A little noise escaped my throat.

My knuckles throbbed from clutching Ora's necklace tightly as I dove into my recollection, recounting to Fyom every detail of the night that felt like both eons ago and yesterday. The storming of soldiers, all dressed in black—a few on horseback—and the large urthen creatures that were under their command. Ora fighting and being taken away.

"And then you were on your way to the Three Sisters to find her?" Fyom carried his gaze to the window and beyond it. Stars now peppered the night sky and cast a silver glow over the tops of the trees.

"Well..." I began, quickly calculating how much I felt Fyom needed to know, but the weight was becoming too much to hold on my own. He needed the full story of what set Sury and me on our journey. "I have a theory, and I needed the Three Sisters to help me confirm it."

Fyom stood in silence, still staring out the window, waiting for me to continue.

"I know it's a long shot and potentially just a myth, but I have a theory that finding the Ancient One will help my cause." I held my breath at the last part. I knew I was grasping for straws, but it was all that was giving me hope. Seeing the urthens with my own eyes had solidified that maybe not all fairy tales were just that—tales. A single kernel of truth had to be embedded in those stories.

Fyom turned quickly on his heel. His illuminating green eyes stared deeply into mine. "What do you know of the Ancient One?" His whisper was barely audible.

I had been so regularly scoffed at whenever the nighttime story was mentioned as a remote possibility that I was shocked Fyom—amid his sea of knowledge—didn't bat an eyelash.

"Just what is shared to children as a bedtime story. A story to make them behave."

"But..."

"But that it's a being that can control the darkness. Turn any innocent Wielder into darkness and...that it'll steal your candle at night if you don't listen to your parents...or something to that effect." I blushed at the idea as I spoke it out loud. I truly was an idiot.

"And to what purpose do you feel the Ancient One would help? If it wasn't a story?"

"I'm not really sure. I just thought there could be something to it. Maybe. I have no army, but maybe I could ask it...or command it...to go and save her on my behalf."

"And you think such a thing could be *controlled?*" A rough voice asked. My stomach dipped as I felt his presence close in behind me. I craned my neck over my shoulder, eyes locking with the depths of dark silvers staring back at me. Something tumbled and twirled deep within me as I fought to take another breath.

I licked my lips to ease the dry skin. "It's a guess."

"If the stories were real?"

I nodded, swallowing hard.

Peiro walked toward me and towered over me, but my body leaned in, inviting his presence into my space. His hair was wet from a bath and he smelled of bergamot and mahogany. His strong jaw tensed as his gaze continued to bore into me. The same gaze that I could become lost in or that could utterly consume me. "If you could control it...would you also free it?"

His question confused me. I furrowed my eyebrows as I fumbled with my answer. "Free it? Out in the open? If it's as dark as the stories say, then it's better that it stays locked up. Used when needed. Maybe even destroyed. If that would be an option."

Peiro nodded, never taking his eyes off me.

"You know," Fyom interjected as he turned toward a series of dusty bookshelves, "there is always some kernel of truth in the fables our parents told us." He caressed the spine of a dark leather book. "Let me see if there is something that we can find.

I'll need a moment to read. Oh, and Peiro," Peiro snapped his attention to Fyom, "a word with you, please. In private."

I took that as my cue to leave and headed back to Sury's room. His breathing was still steady from the magical sedation, and the blackness in his veins had turned to a dull gray, the edges a mix of silver.

"I hope this is a good sign," I whispered. "Fyom said he'll research something to help us, but...I don't know if I can do this without you." I took his cold hand and clutched it tightly. "Only time will tell, but in the meantime, please rest," I whispered and turned to leave the room. "For Ora."

***

Nights passed as I waited for Fyom to share anything he found worthy of sharing. The morning dew of the tall grass tickled my boots as I passed through the endless sea of birch trees that set the perimeter of the cabin. I let myself get lost in my thoughts as I wandered, picking small wildflowers as I went.

The fact that you are seriously thinking you're able to get to her with a story is quite entertaining. Fyom knows nothing and will be of no help.

Yes. She could be dead, and you're wasting time on more nonsense.

That's all you ever truly have been—a waste of time.

I shook my head as I warred with the inner voices. Clouds of thought entered my mind and I wondered if I would, or could,

324

make the hard decision and carry on without Sury. Let him heal and get the rest that he needed so badly.

The days flew by amidst Fyom's hospitality. It had to be Domesis's blessing that I had been able to find somewhere safe as Sury recovered. Where I could think of a plan. My fingers twitched, feeling the pent-up energy coursing through my veins. Itching at me to do *something*. My feet were moving before I realized they were carrying me around the side of the cabin, toward the pell.

It half surprised me that I didn't see Peiro chipping away at the poor wooden block that now held deep grooves. It also occurred to me that I hadn't seen him since a few nights ago. I looked over my shoulder, half expecting for him or Fyom wandering around the corner, before I found the courage to pick up a sword off the wooden rack. I selected the same shortsword from when Peiro decided to play his insane game to test my strength.

The grip was a worn, smooth leather, with bits of string binding it together, though it was coming undone and frayed. I tightened my grip around the handle and lifted it straight in front of me, testing the weight that felt comfortable. Reassuring. I stepped up to the poor, dilapidated pell as my mind's eye set to work, trying desperately to recall the basic movements Sir Hanovan attempted to teach all those years ago. Footwork was the most I could remember. I inhaled, feeling my lungs expand and then rapidly release my breath as I struck.

Deep vibrations rang through the tip of the blade, through my hands and up my arms, jostling all my joints. A string of tears crested my eyes from the dull pain of the jarring impact. I tugged on the handle to wiggle it loose from the notch I'd created. I swung back and hit it again.

And again.

And again.

And again.

Sweat crested my forehead, loosening a single bead to drip down into my eye. My hands became numb, and the sword grew heavy the more I tried. The frustration grew as I tightened my hands around the pommel and threw all my weight into the swing of the sword, which found its mark on the pell but violently bounced off, forcing me to stumble backward.

"Fuck," I whispered hoarsely. I peeled my hand off the pommel and cradled my shoulder.

"Your footwork seems bearable, but the form in your elbows needs work."

I whipped around to find Peiro leaning against the wall, eating what looked to be a persimmon. His light-colored tunic framed his broad shoulders perfectly. A little too perfectly. His dark trousers fit loose and lightly stretched as he had one ankle crossed over the other.

"How long have you been watching me?"

"Long enough." Peiro took another bite, wrapping his lips around the plump fruit, and chewed. I paid too much attention to the juice that coated his lips.

"It's quite rude to walk up behind a royal family member unannounced." I straightened my shoulders as I inclined my head.

Peiro's half-smile grew. He placed the remainder of the fruit on the window ledge beside him and walked forward, closing the gap in easy steps, standing mere inches away and lowering his head.

Heat radiated off his body and seeped into mine. His breath mingled so close that I could taste the tangy sweetness from the fruit. My heartbeat rapidly rose as his presence seemed to engulf mine, welcoming the closeness.

"I'm here, Princess." His gruff whisper made my breath hitch as a small tingle cascaded down my spine. Molten heat pooled below my abdomen.

His eyes had changed again. The hue now leaned to dark gray and lined in a faint silver ring.

"Don't call me that," I managed to say, barely above a whisper.

"What? A princess? Isn't that what you are?"

"Yes. But..." I felt foolish as I fumbled my words. The title feels more like shame than anything anymore. "You can call me a little doe for all you like..."

He stepped into my space, all-consuming, and tilted my chin up with his thumb and forefinger. "You see yourself as weak? Docile?" He *tsked* as he slowly shook his head. "You're anything but."

My breath caught. No one had ever seen me, let alone told me they saw me, as anything remotely strong.

Peiro leaned in further, searching my eyes. "Then I guess," he continued in a volume barely above a whisper, "I shall have to find something else to call you." His thumb hovered over the crest of my lips before pulling away. "We didn't start off on the right foot during our first meeting." The wink in his smile and the warmth of his tone radiated through my skin. "My name is Peiro. Nice to meet you."

"Ophelia, but everyone calls me Phe." I smiled in the mock greeting. "Nice to meet you, too." I extended my hand and felt his warmth grasp mine. The muscles in his hand tensed against my skin, sending a small shock. I didn't realize how close I had leaned in until our breath practically became one. My skin tingled and grew hot as I glanced between his eyes and lips, which still carried the sweetened fruit on them.

Just a small nudge forward and I would be able to taste the persimmon on his lips. My tongue gently ran along my own in anticipation. A strange courage overwhelmed me. Just as I began to move forward, to appease my curiosity, Peiro took a large step back, granting us space.

I shuddered as a coolness swept over me upon feeling the abrupt distance. My cheeks singed with embarrassment as I smoothed my hands on the front of my tunic. I blinked rapidly to cool my senses and found a new grip on the sword as I turned to advance toward the pell once again.

"Can I help you with something?" I said over my shoulder, wishing I could die right on the spot and not have this embarrassing exchange. Maybe he didn't notice what I was ready to do? Maybe it was mere coincidence that he decided to step back?

"I was only observing what the sovereign family of Gria could do with a sword."

I felt a rise of shame and anger. "So you came to mock me then."

"Never."

I jumped at the nearness of his words and looked over my shoulder, finding that he once again stood close. I quickly turned my head forward, looking at nothing in particular, but I was acutely aware of how close he was behind me.

"May I?" Peiro asked as he gently moved his hand down my arm and rested it upon the wrist of my sword hand.

I nodded, a storm of mixed emotions swirling inside.

"Your footwork needs dusting, but in time, you'll get there," Peiro said as his body shadowed behind. "But your hands need reassurance." His other hand moved down my free arm, sending shock waves, and rested above my opposite wrist.

Gently, he guided my free hand to the hilt of the sword, nudging for me to place one hand on top of the other. Suddenly I was encased in his presence. Both of his arms wrapped around mine, his hands held a firm but gentle grip. His broad chest rested against my shoulders and brought in an overwhelming feeling of warmth.

I couldn't help the small smile that grew on my face.

"You need strong but loose joints," Peiro said into my ear. He took control and moved my arms, mimicking a strike. "Strong enough to feel the force of your strike but loose enough to where you don't feel the pure energy of the strike reverberate."

Together, we practiced various swings. He'd call out the names of footwork stances I remembered and together we would step forward or slide into the mimicked strike, annihilating the faux enemy before us.

Peiro demonstrated several techniques, and eventually let go to grab his own sword to illustrate certain angles for me, directing me on when to keep my elbow or shoulder in. The fluidity and grace of his wrists and fingers could make even the most beautiful swans envious.

"You were a Grian soldier, then?" I asked after a much-needed break.

Peiro took a deep swig of water and looked down into the swell of his cup. He nodded. "I was a soldier. Yes."

I smiled, wiping more sweat off my brow with the sleeve of my tunic. All my muscles ached in places that were equally delicious and bothersome. "Well. My sister will be lucky to have a soldier of your caliber, if you choose to serve again." I took a small sip from my cup. "I'm sure we can have you promoted to a lieutenant or even a captain, if you prefer."

"I appreciate the gesture," Peiro said as he hung up his sword on the rack.

"Are we done?" I was surprised at how eager I was to continue to learn. I felt my hope rise with each strike and step I practiced.

At how I felt so much closer to rescuing my sister, even if that meant I might have to leave Sury behind.

"For now."

"Shall we practice again tomorrow?" Something giddy rose inside my chest.

Peiro nodded. "Until then, *Ophelia*." He bowed forward before pivoting on his foot and walking around the bend of the cabin.

I continued to practice on my own until I felt my stomach growl in protest. I took that as a cue and hung up my sword to find something to eat. The cabin was eerily silent and, once again, the kitchen and dining room empty, although the large table was littered with trays of meats, sauces, and vegetables. Once my stomach was satisfied, I grabbed a small cookie filled with almonds and coconut and set out for the front porch to watch the darkening sky.

I passed through the great hall and the tall tree in its center and halted in my tracks as my hand hovered over the front door's handle. Escalated whispers carried over the empty space above me. I turned to the landing that entered Fyom's study.

"She deserves to know."

"And why is that?" I knew that voice.

"You at least owe it to..."

"I've given enough." Peiro's harsh whisper echoed in the empty space.

"Hardly," the other voice said.

"You know nothing of the sacrifices I've given." His whisper rose an octave.

"This could end. You just have to admit it...if you want it to end."

"Of course I want it to end!" the voice sneered.

"If it's what you said, then she could do it. And if she can do it, then you owe her far more than what you're willing to give." Fyom's voice carried.

"You don't think I know that?"

Who were they talking about? Not wanting to be caught eavesdropping, I left the men to their heated conversation in favor of sitting on the rickety porch. Even the post where I sank down and rested my back while finishing my dessert was surprisingly sturdier than it appeared.

I sat there in silence, letting my mind overwhelm me with thoughts.

The moon was full and bright in the sky as the sun set beyond the trees and the meadow. One by one, the stars danced into the night, shining and pulsing their steps to a well-orchestrated rhythm that's carried on for centuries. I watched, mesmerized by the stars and moon above. I could never explain to anyone, including my sister, that my heart longed for and pulled every time I saw the moon, especially when it shone so brightly like this. It always invigorated me. Called to me.

"She's beautiful," a deep voice said from the shadows.

I straightened and fixed my eyes on the spot where I heard the voice. Goosebumps ran across my skin, and I knew it wasn't because of the coolness of the air.

"That she is," I said, slightly above a whisper, and turned my face into the moonlight. "Do you ever think that Nyska stares back down at us?"

"I wasn't talking about the moon." Peiro stepped through the shadows holding an armful of firewood. His hair and face were clean once again, his tunic hardly stained. I subconsciously inhaled the scent of bergamot and mahogany that clung to the air.

Warmth radiated through my chest as a small smile bloomed on my face. "I thought you were inside." I quickly nodded to the bundle of wood in his hands to change the subject. "This place needs fresh-cut firewood? I figured Fyom had the cabin enchanted to do its own."

"It gives me something to do." A small smirk grew on his face that glowed from the porch lanterns. "Plus, I needed to let go of some tension."

"Tired of beating that poor wooden man into smithereens?" I mused.

"One can only take a beating for so long." Peiro chucked the firewood next to the cabin's steps and sat beside me, looking into the night sky.

"Is that where you sneak off to most days, to chop firewood?"

"That. And to pick this." Peiro positioned himself against one of the rickety-looking support beams as he neatly tucked the stem of a flower into my hair behind my ear. Once settled, the toe of his boot lightly rested against mine. The acts were so juvenile and simple, but it still sent an anxious swarm of butterflies through my insides.

"I know I haven't said it before, but I am truly sorry about your sister." His eyes, which had grown a shade lighter and the ring around the edge more silver, looked deep into mine. The image of two stray stars looking right at me.

"Thank you," I said with a lump in my throat. A force flipped deep into my belly and tingled against my skin.

We sat in silence for a moment, simply enjoying one another's company.

"Ophelia," he said in a low whisper as if he were trying to find the right words. Slowly drawing out each sound. "I'm also sorry about your friend. I know I owe him a bit of an apology." A slight smirk crept onto his face. "Maybe."

I chuckled. "You think you two will be able to speak without challenging one another?"

"He wouldn't be the first one that doesn't see eye-to-eye with me," he mused as he turned his gaze to mine for a few short heartbeats before going back to the stars.

"*Naa'n le'ya,*" he whispered.

Puzzled, my brows bunched together. "I've never heard that before. What's it mean?"

"It's an old tongue. Translates to *moonlight*. Or simply *naa'n* for moon. The moon is commonly thought little of, but it holds more power and mystery than most care to see."

A small smile formed as I practiced saying it, feeling the foreign movements across my tongue. "Is it commonly spoken where you're from?"

"Used to be."

"Where are you from exactly?"

A sad look flashed across his face. "Far away."

"Do you miss it?"

"At times." Peiro turned his gaze as another flash of emotion crossed his face. "You mentioned you wanted to see the Three Sisters." He was clearly changing the subject. "Why come all this way when you have more resources at home?"

I took a moment to think of the words I wanted to share. But something about admitting my needs felt right. "Well, it turns out, those that we thought we could trust could be the very ones against me." I paused, waiting for Peiro's response. When none came, I felt my thoughts spew out in words, "Why does Dokvalon need Ariadne? Vovias? What do they want?"

"Is it possible that those two could be lovers?"

"Maybe." The thought provoked me and burned in my core. Anger coiled through the pit of my stomach and slowly built into a pulsing rage. "He was my mother's trusted advisor," I said between my teeth. "I always knew he was a snake...a virus. It makes sense the snakes would form a pit to devour my family." How long have these games been played against my loved ones? They didn't seem eager to sit on the throne when I found the two in the court hall after Ora's failed ceremony.

"Seems like the game of politics refuses to change," Peiro said into the night sky. "Politics, even where I come from, was full of snakes. It took a long time for me to understand this but what I always told myself is this: *Only I can decide how they affect me. You can choose how you want to be treated.*"

The words washed over me in a wave of understanding I had never thought of before. They felt not only encouraging but like an invisible weight being chipped away off my shoulders.

"How would the Sisters help your cause?" Peiro inquired. "Are they not a neutral source in the kingdom of Gria?"

"They are. I was needing their help on a different matter." Peiro turned his body to allow his back to rest against the opposite post, giving me his full attention. "It might be a folly of an idea, but I wanted to see if there was a sort of weapon I could use against Dokvalon. Something more powerful than any Wielder. Something that I can use to grab my sister and run..." Hesitation was present, but I pushed past it. "Fyom said he would help me look through his books. Said there might be something within the lore. I wanted... I wanted to see if there was any lost truth about the Ancient One. Anything I could use to save Ora."

Peiro stiffened at the name, then settled back into his easy posture. "How can a fairy tale save your sister?" His tone grew rough and short.

The unsettling tone shocked me and made me cower. I pulled my foot back and straightened my spine. "I'm... I'm not sure. I know it's a long shot but..." I found myself needing to explain once again. I always felt the need to explain myself to anyone I talked to.

Because no one believes in you.

"Your plan *is* folly!" His eyes flashed silver faster than I could comprehend. "Fyom should have never picked up that torch for your search. You're thinking of a suicide mission using a fairy tale." Peiro turned his head and took a deep breath before continuing, his tone icy and cold—but his eyes told something softer, kinder. "You're better off taking your friend and forgetting about your sister. Go rally the queen's men elsewhere."

The bite behind Peiro's tone made me jump.

My nerves rattled as fear reverberated through my bones like I was only eight years old. I saw the faces of my parents, my mentors, and Ariadne, all screaming at me. "But I don't know what else to do!" I hissed. "I have to save her somehow! I'm risking my neck being *here*. Talking to you. I don't have anyone aside from my dying friend in a stranger's home." My heartbeat raced as the nerves turned into frustration. "I thought it was a fool's errand at first, I did, but I've seen true *urthens* since that night so maybe there's truth that can help."

I sucked in a sharp breath, finding the courage to continue. "If you're so quick to point out my flaws then enlighten me with a better idea! I can't just sit here and speed train with a sword all day." The force from earlier flipped again, beating against the inner walls of my very being. "Why don't *you* go get her on my behalf then?" I commanded.

Peiro's body briefly tensed as he huffed a deep sigh, annoyance rolling off his shoulders. "How about *not die*? You're playing a dangerous game, Ophelia. One you know nothing about. This story has already made people before you sacrifice so much. I wanted to help but I'm not going to put myself in the hands of Dokvalon and his Raiders. Have your parents and priests not told you about their horrors? Do you think it's a mere coincidence that those very mountains are the thing that separates those two kingdoms?"

I narrowed in on the fact that other people have searched for this thing, too. Could it be possible? If others have sought this sort of power then it has to exist. I chewed on my fingernails at the thought.

Heat radiated off of Peiro's hard body. His eyebrows narrowed, intensifying the brightness of his eyes even more. "Do you not pay attention? Your sister is probably dead, or she will wish she was before the king gets his hands on her." His lip twitched slightly after each pleading sentence as he leaned in, gripping my shoulders with a soft but firm hold.

He's right, you know. You're already too late. And why would anyone follow you? What do you have to offer?

"Open your eyes, Ophelia," he continued his plea. "Consider it a blessing you got out before anyone else got to you. Go live your life while you still have it. Leave this story behind you."

I batted my eyes, trying to hold in the tears that were forming. Hope was all I had until now. As I peered deep into his glowing eyes, something fierce within me clicked.

"No."

Wrath. Burning white hot in my very muscle fibers and bones.

Peiro pulled away fast, hissing as he grabbed his temples, his eyes squinting shut as if trying not to yell out in pain.

He might have meant well but I felt the tang against my skin. "Who are *you* to dictate what I can and can't do for me or my own sister? You don't have to follow me and that's fine. But don't you dare act like you know me or who I am."

My inner mind's vision became blurry with all the anger that swirled. Voices of different kinds echoed in my mind. Voices that were heard through the years.

You can't do this.

You're not allowed to do that.

You're not like your sister.

You're not strong like your mother.

But then the echo of a much softer voice carried forward, ringing the words that Peiro just shared...

You can choose how you want to be treated.

"Enough!" I screamed at the thoughts in my head, my voice carrying into the trees. "I'm so tired of you telling me what I can or can't be!"

Each thought carried a kernel of heat that fueled the inner fire within me so hard that I felt my very heart changing.

How can you say you're trying to save your sister? You can't do anything to save her.

I tried to control each emotion that came, but failed. Who could reign in a storm?

Turn back. You're useless and Fyom knows it. Peiro knows it. Sury knew it already.

Tiny fissures cracked along my emotional shell. The grief for my parents was overshadowed by my sister being taken—leaving me utterly alone. The deception by those I thought were loyal. The anguish of not knowing if my one and only lifeline to the reality I once knew was going to pull through his sickness.

The fissures spread.

I felt myself shake uncontrollably. The shell I had crafted from years of harassment and torment inside the temple. The maelstrom of emotions that I held, year after year, finally reached its breaking point.

Who are they to question me? I seethed.

The fissures spread wider. Cracked deeper. The heat inside my chest rose higher. Layers of lies, hurt, manipulation cracked from the surface and my inner fire burned through them all.

For too long have I been pushed to my edge.

Metaphorical ashes of doubts drifted away into the wind. Instead of the night sky full of twinkling stars, I only saw ashes and the faces I wanted to burn.

My heart, ablaze and anew, forced me to scream. "NO MORE!"

I was finished following everyone else's rules. I was going to get to my sister. Alone or not.

The edges of my vision blurred into various shades of silver and white. I let the anger and frustration pull me to my feet and walked aimlessly toward the circle of bowls Fyom had set earlier.

My body vibrated, desperate to Wield again.

.

CHAPTER 24

"If no one will help me then I'll help myself. Damn anyone who stands in my way," I said as I threw my hand over the first bowl containing a small flower like the one I had in my hair.

Waves of raw emotion, both familiar and not, coursed through my veins as I felt tiny tickles across my palm and up my elbow. I closed my eyes, letting the feeling take over as a new coolness crested over my internal flame.

I moved my hand back when I felt the small delicate flower dance in an ethereal breeze. A light tug behind my ear caught my attention as the other flower from my hair floated in front of me and danced with the other. Something I had never seen before, no matter how often I practiced my Earthen Wielding.

My excitement grew as I moved the flowers using only my mind, causing them to twist in the air like two lovers sharing a private dance. My hands and fingers twirled together as I continued to manipulate the stems in midair. Each pull and push of my Wielding into the flowers erased a faint haze within me. I ever so steadily poured more of my Wielding into the petals until they glowed the fiercest shade of violet anyone had ever seen.

My feet shifted to the second bowl.

I had been told my whole life the Earthen circle of power is where I would always stay. But when I peered down to the lone robin feather that rested against the bowl's curve, my palm felt a swift gust across my fingers. The feather, like the flowers before it, rose up before me and began to twirl in a hidden wind tunnel before fluttering away into the darkness of the forest, taking more of the foggy haze with it. My mind became a little sharper.

Nothing could stop the smile from dancing on my lips. My inner fire climbed higher as I moved on to the third bowl that held a single dew drop.

Black inklings of doubt echoed again and tightened their grip on my mind. *So you played with air. You'll never Wield higher than your sister. Than your mother. Do you truly think you're better than they were?*

In my mind's eye, I imagined my fire striking the deep chamber where the voice was hidden. I could have sworn I heard an audible hiss.

I closed my eyes, embracing the sounds and smells of the forest around me. Crickets and beasts echoed their songs of the night. With a deep inhale, I placed my hand over the tiny droplet and felt...nothing. I waited and felt the haze trying to re-thicken. Forced myself to keep my breathing under control, to listen to the welcomed silence in my mind.

The air in my lungs screamed to be let go. I pushed back against the haze that wanted to form, feeling my inner mind's foothold starting to slip. The inner fire dying as the swell of my Wielding dwindled.

But then, the sweet voice of my mother echoed through my mind. *My tiny moon. Though people may not always see your greatness, know you're always in the sky, high above them all.*

A trickle of water caught my ear, and in that exhale, I opened my eyes and looked into the bowl where the single droplet had grown and overflowed to the ground below.

Tears swelled as I watched the water pour, observing a small glisten across the tips of my fingers, feeling the cool wet-ness across the pads. Once again, I placed my hand over the bowl—the inner hum of what I now knew was my Wielding calling to be used—and stopped the trickle. With a dance of my fingers, I turned the drops upward to reach my hand, splashing water against my palm.

In a fluid sweep, I pushed the water high above and motioned it into an endless wave before sending it crashing into a nearby tree, releasing shards of the haze with it. Small droplets bounced back and coated me in a small mist.

My heart would have taken flight if it wasn't caged inside my chest. After another cleansing breath, I moved to the next bowl of burning coals. Hot tingles pricked my hand and shot up my arm as heat burrowed into my skin. A small flame, no larger than a candle's, appeared in my palm and burned steady as I turned my hand skyward.

The tiny flame pulsed ever so slowly but then began to dim. My heart wanted to sink as the flame was close to being gone forever. I closed my eyes and focused. *Let me in,* I whispered. Instantly, the lick of the flame grew and erupted into a fireball, hovering above my hand. The surprise of the sudden burst of energy caused me to jump.

While essential to life, fire can also be a means of destruction, I heard Ariadne's voice say.

"Destruction indeed." A smirk played across my lips. Images of burning Vovias played in my mind as I pushed and pulled both hands together to make the flame grow bigger and shine brighter, illuminating every shadow that had crept the circle.

Another layer of the haze turned to ash as my inner fire licked higher. A creeping satisfaction that I had been able to touch all the Wieldings of the Elementis caused a wicked smile to play across my features.

With another dance of my fingers, I coaxed the flame back onto the coals before stepping to the next bowl. The bowls that began to test Spiritus.

Another robin's feather lay in its center, but this one was broken into two jagged pieces. I wiggled my fingers, stretching out the dull ache in my hand as I gingerly hovered my palm over the two fragments. The light hum tingled within my skin before spreading once again to my fingertips. The sensation felt as if my hand had fallen asleep and was desperately trying to wake up.

As the hum intensified, the two pieces of the feather jostled together before intertwining, like the flowers earlier. They twisted and turned, faster and faster, until the two pieces finally became one single feather. A smile danced on my lips as the pulsing hum finally subsided from my palm. Remnants of the haze continued to dissipate.

I felt a clarity I had never felt before as a tiny wiggle in the back of my mind urged me to keep going.

To break free.

I stepped to the next bowl to find a sunstone and a moonstone that faintly glittered against the shining moon above. Each piece was shaped like a dewdrop that curved into the other, displaying equal and utter balance. One could not outweigh the other.

I knew the sunstone was meant to represent the elements of the sun with endless rays that shine brightly in the daytime. How large it sits in the sky and how much life depends on it for warmth and growth. My mind recalled the day Ora finished testing and found that she could harness the celestial Wielding of the sun—something powerful and magnificent that could bring joy to those around her, but also something to be deeply respected, as the sun could burn.

Deep in my soul, I knew I didn't have that essence. That I was different—but that didn't mean I had to be less than.

Regardless, I wanted to know the extent of my magic's reach now that I felt free from the broken words that had once bound my heart. The desperation of knowing for *me* carried my newfound strength.

I flexed my fingers over the smooth sunstone to see if my Wielding was like my mother's or sister's, or if I could even test at this level at all.

Give it a try, my heart whispered. That was all I needed to hone in my focus on the glittering gold within the sunstone. A faint vibration coursed inside my bones but the stone barely moved—just glittered ever so slightly with a hint of magic. Again I tried but the stone refused to be moved. Beside it, the iridescent flecks of light in the other rock twinkled against the dark.

"Does this mean...?" I caught myself saying as I flexed my fingers over the counterpart, the moonstone. The stone meant to represent not just the moon itself, but the greatness within the unknown. The mass of the space above and around, and the uniqueness to the role it plays in the very world I live in. The force that can shine brightly or creep in the shadows.

With a flick of my fingers, a strong vibration surged deep into my bones and knocked through every joint inside my body. Tiny orbs of faint blue and silver light emerged from my fingertips, like it did that very first time in the forest. When I felt the rawness of my emotions so clearly.

So similar to the rawness I experienced now.

My hand shook uncontrollably as more little orbs formed and grew, dancing in between my fingers. I pulled and tried to find control with my other hand, but the orbs only danced to the other palm and wrapped tightly around my wrist. The soft pressure grew and vibrated deep within my body...my soul.

More of the haze shattered into tiny pieces and dissolved into nothing. The orbs danced and multiplied, encasing me in a vortex of spinning energy, all different hues of blues and silvers. A silent gale erupted and carried my hands up to the sky to meet the fullness of the moon. Strands of hair pulled and whipped around my face.

Realization hit me. Everything clicked into place so neatly then. The Temple Council *had* lied. Ariadne *had* lied. I was far more powerful than what they set me out to be. But why?

The vibrations instantly stopped, my body going completely still as my rage resurfaced.

"No more will I let the thoughts of others dictate my life," I whispered. "No more will their lies impede my nature. I won't let anyone tell me who I am and what I know I can be. No more will I allow others to hold that kind of power over me." Heat grew in my chest. "They held me down because they. Are. Afraid. Of. *Me*. They're afraid of *my* greatness. Now they will know what I am capable and worthy of," I roared into the night sky.

In that moment, when I felt the well inside me had filled to its brim, my Wielding burst into a great force, sending the orbs toward the sky and around me. My magic poured out like an uncontrollable waterfall met with fresh rain, illuminating the sky with tiny, bright dancing moons.

The sensation of finding the inner release sparked in me something anew, like a weight I had carried for far too long had lifted.

A smile whispered across my features as I took a deep breath and sucked in the dancing orbs, absorbing them back into my body on my command. With a flick of my wrist, I sent the same orbs back into the sky to dance again, feeling the moon caress my skin in anticipation as if she approved. With a wave of my fingers, I sent the force to play amongst the trees and entwine with the shadows. The forest floor was illuminated by the white glow and the once-teal flowers glowed in a phosphorescent hue against the light.

A cascade of tears fell down my cheeks. Each one a symbol of relief and renewal. My heart had never felt as light as it did in this moment. Years of an invisible weight continued to lift as I manipulated the orbs in whatever manner I wished. I picked flowers with them, caressed the feathers of a watchful owl, and rode the wings of a firefly. My world was now full of possibilities.

I didn't know how long I spent under the moonlight. I didn't care what came next. I had found a powerful source of magic I'd been told my whole life I would never attain. Something I knew I could use to save my sister.

Ora. I gasped.

In one final swift motion, I tightened my fingers into a tight fist to pull in and absorb every orb back into my skin. A cooling feeling gave me goosebumps as the force nestled back into my body.

I closed my eyes and opened my palms in front of me as I dove deep into the pit of my stomach to feel my Wielding in its raw state. The feeling was foreign, like stepping into a room that had been locked up for so long.

Deeper and deeper I dove, recounting all the vile things I had been told from the *mighty priestess* and the whispers of those around me. With each remark that hurt and stung, I found another orb of magic and built it on top of another—until my inner hold was set to burst.

She'll be nothing like her sister.

I can't believe the queen keeps her in public view. They have to be disgraced by her.

She is almost as low as a commoner.

Even the First Circle Wielders must be ashamed at the abomination she calls Wielding.

And just like that, I threw my Wielding into the air once again and let it explode. My whole body illuminated like the full moon above. Tiny tingles pricked my skin but I welcomed them. They were my reminders that the words hurt, but I am greater than those words.

My eyes opened as I felt them intensify to everything around me. The air became crisper, the sky more clear, and the trees began to talk to me in hushed whispers. The wind twirled around me with glitters of burning coals and water droplets.

I stood there for what felt an eternity, taking in the new sensation.

Shadows serpentined around my feet and ankles as a faint scratching sound caught my attention from a bowl beside me that I had completely forgotten about. Over my shoulder I watched a tiny seed rattling from an unknown source before beginning to sprout. Steadily it grew into a simple white blossom, each petal uncurling from the bud and stretching out wide.

I turned to see the flower rise up and hover above the bowl by a few inches. It hung in the air ever so silently before the beautiful petals began to shrivel, each one falling off as if it were being plucked by unknown hands.

A singular dark shadow crested over its bright center as it began to fold in and fall off the browning stem. Just as soon as the center decayed, the leaves shriveled and dropped back into the bowl.

A bloodcurdling scream pierced the night sky, sending my magic back into my body in a single heartbeat. Utter darkness wrapped around me, like someone had snuffed out the moon itself, sending a *swoosh* of air into the forest. My lungs strained against my chest as I sought air to breathe.

A commotion made me twirl on my feet to find Peiro still on the porch, lying on the floor with Fyom leaning over him, trying to keep him steady. Peiro had his head buried tightly in his hands, writhing in agony. He lay prone, his muscles frozen in place, practically turning him to marble.

I lurched forward on my feet, covering the distance in quick strides and kneeling down beside Peiro. "Not again! Not again!" I felt my panic grip me as I saw Peiro's skin fading from the warm tones to the pale glow of the moon. His hair glowed between a dark brown and dusty color as a few strands came undone from its tie.

Fyom pulled a small vial out of his pocket and emptied the contents in Peiro's mouth. Within a few short heartbeats, his body started to loosen its grip as he dropped his hands from his head. His muscles rolled in twitches throughout his body. He sat up painstakingly slow and his breathing remained ragged as he shook his head to regain his senses.

Fyom inspected him once more, pulling down the soft skin around his eyes and peering in before turning his gaze straight to me. "She *can* do it." I barely heard Fyom's whisper.

Peiro gruffed, his gaze turning to me as well. This time, his eyes had darkened but still shone brightly against the night sky. "That must mean her sister..." His eyes widened as his features softened, like a droplet of hope then despair settled into his heart. They suddenly intensified and narrowed. The look of anger and frustration creased the lines on his face as he jumped to his feet and stormed inside the cabin, slamming the door behind him.

"Peiro!" I called out and ran toward the door to follow, but Fyom stood in front of it with one hand, blocking the entry, the other holding a large book. "Let me tell him I'm sorry! I don't know how I keep hurting him." A small sob settled in my throat.

"Phe, do you know what you just did?" Fyom completely ignored my pleas and pointed to the bowls behind me. Urgency was tilted in his tone.

"What?" I looked to the bowl that held the small moonstone, still sitting there, now faintly aglow. "I don't know. I just felt this pull within me and went through each bowl. I felt a connection with the moonstone." The moonstone! I smiled at the thought of Ora's reaction when she found out I held a celestial like her, like our mother.

"No, Phe—*that*." He stepped off the porch, grabbed my wrist, and pulled me back to the center of the circle. He pointed to the seventh bowl holding a withered flower stem. "*No one* has seen this in a long, long time."

I was confused by the question and looked at him and the bowls. "I must have done too much of something when I tapped into the Earthen Wielding. I've done it before," I said with a light shake of my head, thinking of all the times I've turned beautiful petals into something grim.

"Phe," Fyom said, dropping my wrist as he inspected the bowl further, "I placed a seed in this bowl." He sounded borderline exasperated. "You took that seed—the sample of life, which came alive—but then Wielded it to *die*."

I turned to the bowl traditionally placed as a symbol and inspected the dried, withered flower. Nausea coursed through my veins at the possibility. I didn't command the flower's life to end. Did I?

"I didn't do anything of the sort! I focused only on the moonstone. I swear it!"

Fyom picked up the frail flower stem, inspecting it like a new discovery.

"You didn't have to *test* for it, it seems." He turned around to look at the bowls, each one glowing bright and still in motion from my command. My control. "It would seem that this power has always lived inside you. You hold the power to Wield *all* of the seven interlocking circles of magic." The revelation was more so for himself. "You can control them all, even death itself." The last words came out barely above a whisper.

The reality of what he was saying hit through me. "But that's preposterous!" A light chuckle escaped, as if he'd just told me the earth was square. "Just moments ago I could only control the earth, and barely at that. Now you're saying I control *all* the levels of magic?"

Of course you don't. There is some kind of mistake, you fool. The voice deep in my mind struggled to resurface and sounded like a faint whisper.

I ignored it.

"There's not a soul on this earth that Wields higher than Ariadne. No one has that kind of Wielding!" Each word sputtered faster than the next. "Not even Ora has this kind of magic and she's been a prodigy since she was seven!"

"But has anyone *seen* Ariadne do what *you* have just done?" Fyom turned toward the glowing windows of his cabin before turning his fierce green eyes to me. I felt my body cower.

"You're placing a death sentence on me if that's true. If anyone, aside from that priestess, who Wields this power is sentenced to die, thanks to the precious Scholars you seem to enjoy referencing." I spat.

"Who here would condemn you to die?" Fyom took a step forward, his frame towering over mine.

Silence shook between us. My mind was swirling with the new revelation, not quite believing what was happening. I tilted my head up as I tightened my lips and stared back at Fyom. That this had to be some sort of dream. Or nightmare. The shadows of my ever-present doubt climbed through the edges of my mind but felt more dim than before.

I took a small step back and turned away from Fyom. "Even the tales reference that whoever can Wield an *illicitus* eventually turns mad. They're as good as dead anyways." How could I go from barely Wielding any magic to becoming something I had never dreamed? Something potentially lethal. Something that could drive me *insane*.

"That might not be the case." Fyom's voice turned soft, like someone who was trying to coax a frightened animal.

"Then what do you know?" I felt my hands tremble slightly as I raised them to my face, inspecting each swirl on my fingertips as if they were foreign. "I never came across a book or tome on the *illicitus* that explained it in detail. It's barely spoken of, aside from what Ariadne would share."

I tried combing through the archives of my mind, through every book I had come across that might have mentioned the *illicitus* Wieldings, but I couldn't recall anything in particular—other than that it was outlawed centuries ago. My mind scowled at my inner thoughts and at the weight I felt.

Just moments ago, I was elated to be my sister's equal, and now I felt like something that needed to be hidden once again. My joy soured, crumbled into dust, and withered away.

"I read in a journal once, long ago..." Fyom looked into the distance and toward the dark mountains. "That it was the original priests who viewed this as too costly for anyone to control, even if their hearts were pure, because hearts can be *tainted*. But from what I read, no one has actually seen it in full power other than one instance by a Scholar centuries ago. Either they killed those who can Wield it, or those who were smart enough went into hiding. Probably went too insane to Wield it and were dismissed by those around them."

Excitement grew at the same rate as my shame at what my fingertips could potentially do. If someone got their fingertips on *me,* what would *they* do?

No one would fool with such a silly girl. You're not worthy of this power. Do not delude yourself. You'll always be in her shadow.

The voice continued to edge on. I kept ignoring it.

Fyom continued looking into the beyond, his brow burrowing as he dove deeper into his thoughts. "There is a story, much like the ancient entity you're chasing. There is a rumor. A piece of folklore. A legend that says there was a key. A key, given to us by a giantess, that unlocked the power to Wield life and death. But its very power caused our Wielding nature to become imbalanced and was outlawed just as quickly. Those details seemed to have been written out of the history texts—more than likely by the ones who outlawed the *illicitus* in the first place. What if this were true, too?"

I shook my head, not understanding, as I pointed to the withered stem. "There has to be a mistake. Maybe the answer is as simple as me overpowering myself in Earthen and making it wither. Or I lost control around the water content and made it dehydrated. Or..."

Fyom's eyes heavily fixated in the direction of the dark mountains. "Something has changed. I can sense it in the air." He briefly turned his gaze back to the glowing bowls.

I pointed to the book he was still clutching tightly in his hand. "Anything new? Does that book have something to do with the Ancient One?" I asked, pulling Fyom out of his reverie and hoping to change the subject.

He looked down at the big book in his hands and shook his head. "Folklore has specks of truth. But *which* side of the truth can be hard to tell. As far as the ancient entity, no. Nothing of use in my collection. Unless..." Then he abruptly stopped.

A storm came across his eyes but suddenly vanished. "My apologies. I'll keep looking for anything that might give us an explanation for this. But please, have some dinner—you must be hungry. Something fresh is on the table." And like that, he turned on his heel and reentered the cabin, leaving the door open. "Oh, and congratulations on being more powerful than you could ever realize," he called back, laughing over his shoulder, before disappearing.

***

I felt both light and heavy at the same time. Each step toward the door held growing elation yet also a mix of exhaustion. And, I was ravenous. The dining room was once again empty, lit candles in their sconces, glowing above trays of meats and vegetables. I sat down and pulled food straight from the trays, without adding anything to my plate.

The hallways remained eerily silent as I went to check on Sury. I rounded the bed to where he remained asleep and sat next to him to switch out the medicated bits of cloth with new ones.

"I wish you and Ora could have seen it outside." I spoke as if my friend were awake to listen to my day. "According to our host, Ariadne has been lying this entire time, it would seem. Oh, Ora would love to have a row with her. You know how she can be." A soft chuckle escaped my lips before letting go of a deep sigh. "I wish you both could have experienced that with me. But I'll show you when you wake up."

I continued to work the bandages around the wound, careful not to inflict any pain. "I think you'd like Fyom...or maybe not, with the collection of books he finds enjoyable. I know just how much you *love* to read." Another chuckle escaped me before the sadness crept in and landed in my heart.

Muffled shouts overhead caused me to jump where I sat. I looked up to the ceiling and could only assume I was under part of Fyom's study. Faint voices yelling about lies and fairy tales. Was Peiro yelling *to* Fyom? *At* him?

"...she'll find out one way or another..." one of the voices said, but I couldn't make out who.

Stomping echoed from down the hall as someone raced down the stairs and into the entry hall before a loud slam from a door reverberated through the walls. I pushed the strange encounter from my mind as I continued to look over Sury and the veins that were still sickly black. A small thought crept into my mind about what Fyom had said just moments ago.

They called it a death *arrow. If I can manipulate death, then maybe I can help Sury.* I took my palm and hovered it over the thick black veins under Sury's skin, then concentrated on the pull deep within my stomach. An orb, the size of a grape, appeared from my hand and held steady as I readied my mind, directing it on what to do.

As told, the orb dove into Sury's chest and disappeared. Keeping my mind's eye on the orb, I commanded it to expand and push back against the sickness inside his veins. All of a sudden, Sury's body tensed, and his coarse breath stopped at the same time the veins grew darker and expanded further across this body.

"No, no, no!" I breathed as I demanded the orb to reel in at once. On cue, the orb emerged from his skin, leaving no trace behind. The black webs began to recede and eased Sury's tense body. His breath withdrew back into its slow rhythm.

I held my own breath as I witnessed each of the deep black veins turn lighter in color and shrink back to where they started. Faint silver marks etched further across his chest, where the blackness had once crept and receded. I looked at my hands, as if seeing them for the first time, and studied them for a few heartbeats. "I didn't mean to hurt you," I said as I felt the panic rise and quickly took to my feet to leave him in peace.

You fool. You could have killed your only ally. You have no control. No business thinking you can Wield such precious power.

Why would you even think you could try something so drastic when you only saw the fraction of power in that flower? You think you're like your sister, don't you? Think again, girl.

"Shut up! Shut up! Shut up!" I yelled to the inner thoughts as I slammed my bedroom door.

I sat on the bed and stared at my hands, letting thoughts roll and crash into one another. How do I keep hurting those around me? What is this force beneath my fingertips?

The stars twinkled and faded as a distant light rose in the sky. I continued to pull and push my magic to the surface and let the orbs move around the room, burning brightly like an eternal blue and silver flame. My heart felt fuller than I ever dreamed it to be. The feeling of finding a missing piece within myself consumed me.

I finally felt whole.

CHAPTER 25

The sun shone through the bedroom window and I found myself sprawled on top of the covers of the bed. I didn't know when I had closed my eyes but guessed the continuous draw of Wielding must have drained me enough to find sleep.

Peaceful sleep.

In one lazy move, I removed myself from the soft mattress and headed toward the bath to wash. The water was deliciously warm, and inch by inch, my sore muscles from training with Peiro found relief in the steam. Images of silver eyes and fingers caressing my hot skin flickered across my mind and vanished.

The fresh scent of soaps filled the air. My unbound hair rested halfway in the water, framing and covering my chest. The image reminded me of the old tapestries that hung in the royal library and told stories of urthens that dwelled in the forest in nothing but the skin they were born in.

Now I wondered if those were real or, indeed, just stories.

After filling my lungs with air, I submerged myself completely underwater. Without much effort, I willed the water to roll, tiny bubbles caressing my skin and raising goosebumps across my body. My lungs started to catch fire, but the sensation of feeling the water move around me on my command kept me distracted.

I pushed myself back into a sitting position once my lungs screamed for air and moved my soaking hair behind me. The water continued to roll and move like a sea caught in a storm, but with a wave of my fingers the tiny orbs rotated over the water, causing it to still.

The smile on my face never faltered as I continued to bathe.

Afterwards, I stood in front of the looking glass, now in a fresh dark tunic and matching breeches, to observe my mass of wet hair. A wild thought clicked into my mind as I brought my hands up before me and commanded the tiny blue orbs to explore and manipulate the air around me.

Immediately, a gust of wind twirled up and swirled around my wet strands in a couple of swooshes and let the dark, wavy strands land in neatly dried pieces around my shoulders and down to the midline of my back. When was the last time my hair was free of pins or leather ties?

"No wonder Ora is always able to get ready so quickly. I can get used to this." I beamed before heading out of the room to check on Sury once again.

I held my breath this time as I opened his door, praying to Iasis that he was okay. The thought of hurting him haunted me. To my relief, he remained still, in his peaceful slumber, the dark veins receding a fraction from the night before and leaving more silver scars in their wake.

Too close to killing your friend. *Then you just leave him there? What would he have to say if he found out?*

I shook my head at my doubt and left him in his sleep to head down the hall.

The house was still eerily silent as I entered through the kitchen and into the dining room. Fyom was sitting at the end of the table, in his usual chair, reading over a tome that looked as if it were ready to disintegrate. His tired eyes squinted over the text but he acted completely unphased to me clumsily sitting in a chair beside him.

I took the metal carafe that held the precious awakening liquid from the table and noted that it had long grown cold as I poured some into my cup.

"If you'd like to practice," Fyom said as he continued reading the text, "my mug could also use a warming up." And he nonchalantly pointed to his own that was half full.

Fyom acted as if my newfound Wielding were an everyday occurrence. Like everything that had taken place within his home over the last few days was nothing out of the ordinary.

I set my cup down and brought my orbs to the surface of my fingertips.

"Eventually you'll find that you don't need the physical representation of your Wielding," Fyom said without looking up from his book, "and can simply command it to be."

I remained silent as I sent my glowing orbs to dance across both my and Fyom's cups, willing them to heat to the contents within, before they disappeared from where they once came. I scooped my cup into my hands and took a deep, invigorating inhale of the steaming liquid before taking a sip.

"Ouch!" I spit the liquid back into the cup and set to soothe my burning tongue with a cold piece of fruit.

A soft chuckle emerged from Fyom. "Looks like *a lot* of practice is in order." With a wave of his hand, he sent a faint stream of cooling air over both cups, then took a sip from his own.

"Thank you," I said as I slowly tested the heat of the liquid with my lips before taking another sip. The contents ignited my nerve endings. With another sip, I felt awake and refreshed.

"It's rather quiet this morning. Is Peiro outside practicing?" I looked down at my mug and whispered, "I need to tell him I'm sorry that I keep hurting him. I swear I don't know how I'm doing it."

Without so much as looking up from his book, Fyom replied, "He left this morning."

I snapped my head up to look at Fyom, who continued to look at the tome. The memory of overhearing the muffled encounter replayed in my mind. "Oh. Did something happen?" I was surprised by my own shock of him leaving and worked to contain the emotion. "Did he say when he would come back, or...?"

Fyom shrugged and went back to reading, turning a page. "He does that. Comes and goes as he pleases. Sometimes days and sometimes months at a time."

An odd anger sparked within me at the thought of him leaving just when I felt vulnerable enough to ask for help. I knew this wasn't his fight, and while I hadn't outright asked him for help, I still had hoped something within him would want to. To help save his queen, at least.

Why would I even think that a complete stranger would help me? Perhaps I misread him. Maybe I only assumed he would be willing to help.

Why would he help you? You have nothing to offer. He isn't loyal to anyone but himself.

"But he helped me this far. I thought maybe he would have helped again," I quietly whispered to myself. "Coward."

Old feelings of helplessness crept in like growing shadows, ready to put me in a chokehold. Who I had thought were allies in court had turned. My own friend was on his deathbed.

"You were saying something?" Fyom asked as he raised an eyebrow.

"Oh. Nothing." Why was I so angry at Peiro for leaving? He never said goodbye. I tried to dismiss the disappointment in my heart and adjusted my thoughts to a welcomed distraction. "That looks like a good read," I mused.

"Finding details about a very old law from some time ago has become quite tedious. But utterly necessary in understanding how *illicitus* became accessible. Not just for your sake but also for the sake of this kingdom." With a snap, he shut the tome and turned his gaze to me. "Dokvalon has to have some ideas. That must be why they attacked."

"Tell me how to help." I kept my voice even, but my desperation grew with each word. "I can't sit here idly and wait for a miracle."

"Come with me." In one large motion, Fyom set to his feet and headed toward the stairs. In a few short steps, he eased up the staircase and into his large study. He directed me to sit at a table as he pulled a number of books and scrolls from various shelves and dropped them in front of me. I lightly dusted off the first book in the stack, *A Brief Glimpse into Ancient Runes, Volume 42.*

"Research!" Fyom exclaimed. "We need to research more about the *illicitus* to see how you can control it. Wield it. Then, once we find that, we'll practice."

I was glad Fyom's back faced me so I could roll my eyes.

***

Despite doing the very thing I enjoyed—reading and learning—frustration built, page after page, as I scanned the eighth book before me.

"How is this supposed to help? I've wasted too much time. I need to get to her! Now," I said hours later. My mind ached after reading over the mathematics of rune laws and incantation instructions for growing a cat an extra set of whiskers.

"Don't you want to understand the very power you possess before waltzing into a rival kingdom without an army? How to harness it?" Fyom called out from behind a stack of books. "Would it not make sense for a swordsman to learn and hone his skill before being called into battle? Time is of the essence, but we cannot afford you losing your head as soon as you step onto Dokvalon ground. You need a plan. Not a whim."

I rolled my eyes at his remark, annoyed at his undying wisdom.

"HERE!" Fyom barked from the corner of the room.

I raced to where he stood with a leather folder still in my hand. Fyom was pointing to something on a dusty page. The words were too pale to read without leaning in close, and most were mixed in with runes I had never seen before.

"What am I looking at?" I asked.

"There's the kernel of truth. Your story is based on an ancient entity from the northern isles."

I knew the region and the land he referred to. "The Killing Bones Islands. Where the privateers had their base a few hundred years ago. How do you know? I can hardly read the words on the page."

"Never mind that! Do you know what this means?" He looked down at me with a light in his eyes before turning back to the book. "Give me a moment to keep translating."

I did—there was hope that what I was chasing was real. Fables and myths of urthens were real, and now here was a sliver of truth about an entity in the gulf that neighbored three kingdoms. "I'm going to go get some fresh air." I dropped the folder in the chair beside him. "This is good work!" I squealed, feeling invigorated.

The air was warm with welcoming notes of lilacs and lemongrass. My feet wandered toward Fyom's garden where he mentioned he finds solace and peace. The worn, narrow path was lined with small rocks and pebbles that outlined designated spots for his various herbs and flowers.

Everything was in full bloom as I took in the bold hues of dahlias and the crisp leaves of vines that tangled themselves along a covered trellis, allowing small rays of sunlight to slip through and decorate the worn ground beneath.

A small wooden bench, encased in a growth of wildflowers, sheltered me as I idly tried to find a sense of calm to think straight. My legs bounced and shook and forced me back to my feet to wander around the cabin once again.

Muted voices rolled against my mind. *You're wasting time. She's as good as dead at this point.*

Why are you even staying at this stranger's house? He doesn't have a clue how to help. He's stalling you. Probably just as scared of you and this Wielding power and is trying to figure out how to encase you...like Ariadne did.

I grabbed onto my sister's necklace, sending a silent prayer to the celestial twins of the sun and moon, Aksyn and Nyska, wishing for their help. Around the corner, I spotted the pell Peiro had used to practice with his sword. A sense of anger seemed to be expelled every time he drew his sword against this wooden opponent. Something that drove him. Released him.

Moments passed as I recounted the steps Peiro taught me with a practice sword. In my mind's eye I saw his hands holding his sword. The same lethal hands also holding mine, guiding me. The gentle caresses of his fingertips against my hands as he instructed me in the right ways to hold a sword. I quickly shook my head, thankful for the spare leather strap I kept in my pocket to tie back my hair, and began moving my body, giving my mind reprieve.

For days I continued this cycle.

Sweat formed on my brow as I repeated the steps and strikes and defenses. Step. Strike. Repeat. Step. Defend. Repeat. My muscles shook as my grip grew numb and frozen around the sword's handle.

Unwanted images of Peiro practicing alongside me repeated across my mind. I mentally recanted how his grip was firm but soft as he guided me. The wall of muscle of his chest when he held his arms around me, guiding me where to strike.

The way his eyes looked into mine, exploring. Wondering. The way it heated my chest.

The soft smirk and the fullness of his lips each time he studied me when I sat in Fyom's study or simply wandered around the grounds. The memory of his voice as he softly spoke into my ear when we practiced, or as we sat and spoke together, sent a radiating combination of longing and anger down my spine.

I recalled the urgency behind his words when he wanted to know if I was someone he could follow. *Prove that you're someone I can bow before. Get on my knees for.* His words echoed across my mind.

I stopped mid-swing. The sword fell out of my hand.

Prove it... I heard it again as I felt my chest cave in. An ally I thought I had was gone. No matter the efforts, no matter what I was trying to do for the sake of my sister, I couldn't even prove to a common man that I was worthy enough to follow.

So, he left. Fury ignited again.

In a single twist of my wrist, I cast my hand toward the wooden pell and set it ablaze. Black smoke rose in swirls as the flames encased the wooden figure. I envisioned the creature to be the Dokvalon Raider that took my sister and twisted my hand further, engulfing the wood in a furnace. While I had never laid eyes on their king, I could easily imagine setting him on fire and watching him burn.

Sweat kissed my brow as I poured more fury into my Wielding and the fire before me. My hand shook to the point of exhaustion before it fell limp by my side. I closed my eyes and took in a steady breath, forcing my emotions to find their center. My anger and frustration slowly ceased like the ocean waves, steadily crashing into a rock. Ever so slowly, receding little by little, until the waves came to an end.

I felt the magnetic pull of my Wielding that I was growing to know. With a movement from my fingers, I turned the fire into water then to wind. All with their own steady control. The wood, now charred, looked unrecognizable—more like an old stump than a practicing tool.

I needed to clear my head and walked back to the hard dirt path of Fyom's garden. I chose to sit on the ground next to brightly colored echinacea and took in the aroma of the blossoms around me. With a small twirl of my fingers, I played with a small green stem and Wielded it to grow bigger and taller, until it began to bud and flower into deep pink petals.

Across from me, I took a small yellow coneflower into my palm and began to manipulate the petals ever so slightly. With a small touch of force, I bent and folded them to the middle and back out without breaking or pulling.

"Fyom's right," I muttered. "I need to sharpen my blade before I go into battle." I took another deep inhale. "I'm no good to anyone if I don't know what I'm doing."

And with that, I continued to practice to the point of exhaustion.

CHAPTER 26

The days looked the same. In the mornings, I would help Fyom search his text for answers or other clues about the entity before ending the day by practicing with a sword or magic. I still refused to touch the *illicitus*. It fell too foreign and wrong and shameful to try.

So, I put my focus elsewhere.

Fyom allowed me to help as we checked on Sury's progress. He would create various concoctions and encouraged me to imbue my Spiritus ability into the medicine, making it more potent. A few tries and only one exploding bottle later, I was able to get the hang of creating medicinal tinctures.

Balms, tinctures, and salves littered Sury's room as he continued to sleep. The wound had closed a bit, but the black veins made painstakingly slow progress. I listened intently as Fyom muttered incantations and drew Healing runes over Sury's bare chest and across the wound, hoping all of his work would not be in vain.

One night, as the moon waned to its crescent formation, I sat outside in the meadow, letting the breeze kiss my skin. I sat still, focusing on my inner well, and felt the moon take hold of me. The sensation was like the gentle embrace shared with a friend.

I focused on learning control but played along the rim of the inner well of my magic, just seeing what I could do. Using the moon's force as a guide, I forged the orbs into new shapes and sent them further and further into the trees, tracking them with my mind before reeling them back in. I even mimicked the motion of a hand wave to a black moth that fluttered by.

As my intuition and control built, I began to practice forging my magic into shapes of various weapons. I recalled the night I'd watched Ora turn her magic into daggers to fight off the Raiders and wondered about the amount of training she must have undergone to forge something so beautiful and vicious.

Nonsense. Ora was able to master a simple feat of magic before she had her first bleed. For you to scratch the surface, it will take years.

"Enough!" I commanded the voice to quiet, feeling it hiss in retreat, and focused on the physical blade Sury had given to me with its lines and sharpness. Then I closed my eyes and envisioned it in my mind. Using the moon for extra strength, I pulled my magic to the surface and commanded the orbs to take the same shape.

I set to work controlling and aiming the blue-tinted, glowing blade at a nearby tree. Day after day, I practiced. I even began wielding a true blade while also Wielding the one from my magic. The spirit of the celestials taking solid form.

My muscles ached as I maneuvered again and again, one hand on a sword, the other controlling the blue-tinted Wielded blade. Both found their targets simultaneously in opposite directions.

I practiced the control until I felt it. Felt ready.

"How do I get into Dokvalon...preferably undetected?" I piped up one morning at breakfast.

Fyom's head snapped up from his book. "Are you sure you're ready?" he pleaded. "I feel close to uncovering..."

"It's now or never. I can't simply stay here while she's out there in their hands. It's been weeks already and I must act. I *have* to be ready. I don't have a choice."

Fyom gave me a steady look and sighed. "If you must."

"I do. I have to. There's no way of knowing when Sury will be well enough to travel. Every minute I stay here is another minute that Ora is in harm's way, and who knows what she's already endured."

Fyom gave me a knowing look. He knew he couldn't talk me out of the idea. "I'll check a map for a path through the mountains into Dokvalon. Of course, it might be a little outdated."

I gave him a snickering smile. "All the more time for me to practice along the way."

The next day was a blur as we planned for Fyom to look over Sury and to keep looking for more clues while I took the two-week journey to Dokvalon. I wore my riding leathers and boots with a simple black tunic when we met on the porch, my cloak in hand and hair braided tight. Fyom produced a small travel sack, magically curated by the house, it seemed, as it was full of everything I needed. Extra daggers and bundles of cheese and bread were packed carefully.

"Don't forget about which common weeds can be used to your advantage for healing," Fyom instructed. "And don't make your fires too high..." He was the definition of a mother hen.

"I know, Fyom," I said as I went over the pack one more time.

"There's a small pot in there to boil your water. But you could probably boil the water in the air as you collect it..."

"Fyom. I understand." I softly grabbed his forearm and smiled.

Fyom looked down with an emotion I couldn't read. He seemed reluctant, as if he had more to tell me. Like there was something deeply unsaid.

I leapt forward and gave him a surprisingly tight hug around his middle. Fyom stiffened briefly, then gently laid his hands around me in a tight embrace. The gesture made me think of my father and how much I missed his warm hugs. A small tear swelled.

"I cannot thank you enough, Fyom," I whispered into his shirt while shedding the tear. "You have become a true friend, and I thank you."

"We have much work to do, so this is not a goodbye, Princess Ophelia."

I pulled back and smiled at the gentle man's eyes before looking toward the direction where I was to begin my travels. I stepped off the porch for the forest with the travel sack secured tightly across my back.

A light shuffle and crashing sound came from the trees in the same direction. I pulled free the dagger Sury had given me. A deep force of Wielding thrashed against my insides, begging to come to the surface as I commanded my Wielding to form the blue-tinted blade in my opposite hand. I glanced over my shoulder to see that Fyom had also turned to the trees with his green-iridescent shield in place.

Fyom had sworn no one knew where he lived and that stragglers never wandered onto his land. I hadn't even seen any urthen creatures venture close, other than the day we first arrived. The odds of someone finding us were small, but nonetheless, my heart mimicked a hummingbird flapping its wings.

I crouched low and stayed light on my feet, recalling Peiro's instructions, and dropped the supplies down beside me. From the shadows through the trees, a figure came forth and staggered toward the clearing. The sun shone down on their filthy feet. Their garment was tattered and torn. Light illuminated the intruder's face as they stumbled forward, out from the shadows of the birch trees.

I didn't hesitate. I ran hard and fast toward the stranger and dropped the dagger while I commanded my Wielded blade to disappear—right before I scooped the intruder tightly into my arms.

Tears poured from my face with every breath.

How was this possible?

Time in that moment moved so slowly as I held onto my sister.

My soul knew this wasn't a trick. On the contrary, a very piece within me felt like it had become whole, as if some force had filled in a gap I didn't know was there. I didn't think I would ever let go.

We fell to the ground, both of us sobbing into one another's shoulders as we rocked back and forth. I reluctantly pulled back and pushed back the hair that crowded Ora's face to look into her dull, honey-colored eyes. Her hair was matted with filth, and her very essence looked as if it had been taken away from her.

Yet she was here in my arms.

In a single sweep, I looked for any signs of cuts or bruises, noting her skin held a deathlike pallor. Dirt and grime lay thick across her skin and gown—the same one from the night she was taken.

"Thank Domesis you're here!" I whispered into her ear as I rocked her lightly back and forth.

"Thank the giants indeed," Ora replied. Her voice was hoarse, barely above a whisper.

I unwillingly let go and climbed to my feet. "Here, let me help you up. Are you hurt? Injured?"

Ora shook her head ever so slightly. Her grip was weak and her stance wobbled as she struggled to find her footing. Her knees were more prominent, and the tendons stood out from the sunken skin in her hands and arms.

I clutched Ora's face between my hands softly. "How did you escape? How did you know to come here?" Time moved once again when another rustle came from behind the trees. I made sure Ora was behind me, but was still hesitant to let her go.

I brought forth my Wielded blade in my free hand while I grabbed her wrist to keep a protective hand on her. The slightest pressure felt like I might snap a bone if I clutched too hard.

Parry. Dodge. Wield, I repeated over and over in my head as I waited for a Black Raider to emerge from the inner shadows of the forest, ready to reclaim their prize. I would be ready, and this was the moment. No one was going to harm my sister again.

I lifted my hand, and my Wielded dagger spun, ready to be thrown. I arched and launched my blade right as I saw Peiro emerge from the forest. His tunic was travel-stained and clung to his chest with dirt and grime. Just as quickly as I released my blade, I pulled back the force and commanded it to veer to the left, missing Peiro by inches.

He turned his head, looking at the scorch mark of Wielding next to the tree where he stood, and then looked back to me and *smirked*.

After making sure Ora was steady on her feet, I broke my hold on her and ran to Peiro. Time slowed down again as I embraced his welcoming body, feeling his muscles shift as I held on tightly. Peiro wrapped his arms around me and squeezed as he rested his cheek on the side of my head. I drank in every inch of him that I could.

"I see you've been practicing." He caught me by the arms and looked deeply into my eyes. The bright glow had now intensified to almost a blinding white in the sun. As bright as the day of our first encounter. "Is this payback from our first lesson?" he asked as the smirk grew. The lines on his face dug in deeper from when I last saw him, and his hair appeared dry and brittle as it was pulled back into a loose half-braid.

I made a mental note to ask him about it later, but for now all I could do was whisper "thank you" before the tears began to fall. So many questions formed within my mind. *How?* That one question kept bubbling to the top.

Peiro looked into my eyes, understanding. "You commanded me. So, I went." He nodded toward where Ora stood.

My heart fluttered, but before I let myself ponder his words, I turned on my heel and hurried back to Ora, who stood in the clearing, drinking in the summer sun. My breath caught at how my little sister looked so defeated and drained. Like a lost little girl who doesn't know where to go. I took Ora by her thin shoulders and brought her into a side embrace before ushering her inside.

Fyom's mouth was agape as he stared at Ora and kneeled down on one knee. "My Queen. It is an honor to have you. My home is your home. As long as you wish."

Ora stopped and looked at the man "Thank you…" She halted and looked to me for help.

"Fyom, this is Fyom. He has been a great friend in trying to find you. We've been working together on how we can defeat Dokvalon."

"Rise, sir," Ora said softly. The usual ring of confidence had escaped her voice. Fyom's large body rose and towered over us, yet his demeanor and face remained softened as always. "Thank you for helping my sister, and for sending your friend to my aid."

Fyom shot a questioning glance to Peiro, who now stood a healthy distance from the porch, looking in awe at Ora.

"I'm going to take her to my room."

"I will make her a Healing tea," Fyom said, "and send a platter of food to your door."

"Thank you." I gently squeezed Fyom's arm in thanks before taking Ora inside.

She walked like the undead. I kept her tightly curled in my arm but held her gently—too afraid I might accidentally snap my sister in half with her newfound frailty.

"Can I help you with your gown?" I asked quietly as we halted in front of the steaming tub.

Ora only nodded. While I had no idea what she'd endured, I still wanted to grant her some level of decency. I made quick work of the soap bottles on the counter, pouring a light-scented one into the water. With a small wave of my fingers, tiny blue orbs dove into the water and swirled together in a circle. The act caused large bubbles and foam to rise and skim the surface for extra privacy. I grasped onto Ora's hand to steady her as she stepped into the water and gingerly sat in the tub with her soiled dress still on.

She hissed as her face tightened into a grimace before easing away. She pulled her knees up to her chest, wrapping her arms around them and resting her cheek on her knees.

"I'm going to help take your gown off, okay?" I whispered. The foam and bubbles came up to the crest of Ora's shoulders. Knowing she could be fully covered, I assessed the material, noting the stains of blood, and selected one of the many holes that allowed me to easily rip the fabric apart.

My heart tore.

Deep lines, too many to count, were embedded on Ora's back. I couldn't tell if they were from whips or chains or some sadistic bastard who enjoyed sharp objects. Cuts of various sizes ate her body. Red, angry flesh with welts and wounds seemed to touch every inch of her skin. A lump formed inside my throat.

Then an anger of a new breed emerged inside of me.

It took all my concentration to control my boiling rage as I delicately washed Ora and cleaned her hair before helping her into a simple dressing gown. We sat together on the soft bed as we drank the tea Fyom had made, me helping Ora take the sips she needed.

The cheeses and bread were sliced small, but I still tore the pieces into smaller bites for her to slowly nibble on. After she had her fill and her eyes grew heavy, I helped her lay back on the bed, where she almost immediately fell asleep. I didn't care to take the dishes back or even change my own clothes. I just climbed on the bed beside her and rested my head on the crook of my elbow, watching the rise and fall of Ora's breath, too afraid to close my eyes, fearing this was a dream I would wake from too soon.

Day turned into night and back into the day.

I lazily opened my eyes, seeing Ora still asleep.

The cuts that were along her neck and face had grown considerably smaller. The angry red flesh had simmered into a bright pink. Her skin gained back some of its fullness and colors, the tendons not so prominent in her hands.

I rolled off the bed and went to the bathroom to tend to my needs before exiting the room with the plate of dishes. I completely disregarded my fallen braid as I quietly tiptoed to the kitchen, but stopped in my tracks as I saw Fyom and Peiro quietly talking in the dining room.

I kept my head down, hoping not to disrupt them as I placed the dishes into the sink. Turning toward the cupboard, I found Peiro leaning against the doorframe. His presence was all-consuming and seemed to suck the air from my lungs.

"*Naa'n le'ya.*"

No other words were said after a few heartbeats. What could I say, after all? *Thank you* seemed too small for the gratitude I felt. Should I apologize for doubting his loyalty to his queen? It was the obvious reason why he risked so much. His loyalty would grant him riches beyond his imagination. It's what drove most of the nobles in the court. But I was also still angry that he had left without saying goodbye.

How did this turn so complicated?

Peiro looked down into his half-empty mug before looking back at me. His gaze made my body tingle like a million fireflies were trying to escape. The rings around his irises were sparkling silver. It was strange how his eyes continued to change. I had never seen a Wielder's eyes do as such.

"We, uhm, I—"

"Thank you—"

We started at the same time.

Peiro chuckled a little bit. His half smile stretched across his face.

"'Thank you' doesn't necessarily grasp it, I know." I scrambled to find my words. "I don't even know how to begin to thank you."

"You don't have to."

"How can I not?" I took a couple of steps forward, placing myself a few inches in front of him. "You did the very thing I set out to do. Even when you told me not to. What made you do it?"

The lines in his face looked deeper. His sleek brown hair lost some of its luster and looked broken in some places. The weariness from the travel must have worn him out.

"I knew that we...it needed to be done," he spit out slowly. Not in a way that was malicious but as if he were struggling to find the words.

"How did you even get to her? And so quickly?"

Peiro paused. "We'll sit down and tell you everything." Something heavy laced over his voice.

"You'll be rewarded, you know." I stepped forward. "I'll make sure you receive the amount of gold of your choosing and..."

"I don't want gold," Peiro cut in. "That's not why we..." He stopped. Without thinking, I grabbed his hand with mine. The touch was shockingly warm and soft, despite the calluses on his palms.

We stood there for a heartbeat, both trying to figure out what to say next.

"Thank you," I murmured again.

"You really don't have to keep saying that..." he started, but then suddenly stopped when I left him with a soft kiss on his cheek. Like his hands, his face was warm, and the rough stubble of his beard lightly scratched my lips.

I pulled back and gazed up into his silvered eyes. "Just say 'you're welcome,' okay?" I felt the corner of my mouth tilt upward, the fireflies wreaking havoc against my stomach.

Peiro brought his empty hand up toward my face, delicately wrapping his finger around a strand of hair that had fallen forward and tucked it behind my ear. His hand cupped the bottom of my jaw, slightly tilting it up.

I bit the inside of my lip as my gaze flickered back and forth between his lips and eyes. Slowly he inched forward with his lips hovering delicately over mine. My body hummed in anticipation.

A soft patter of footsteps was heard to my right. "Ophelia?" a soft whisper spoke.

I turned my head as Peiro let go of my jaw and stepped away from me. I felt cold from the instant shift of his body.

Ora had dressed herself in a large tunic and a spare pair of leggings from one of the dresser drawers. Her once-bright, golden blonde hair was now pale as it hung loosely around her small frame. She looked frail with sunken cheeks, making the angles in her face visibly sharper.

I took only two steps before I brought her into a tight embrace. I could feel her shoulder blades too prominently, her arms too frail. I stepped back and placed Ora in an arm's-length hold, assessing her, and noticed the formerly vivid red flesh on her neck was greatly dull, now only showcasing deep green and purple bruises.

"Aurora, here, let me help you back to the room..." I used a sister's firm but gentle tone when she meant business.

"No," Ora whispered. "I'd rather not be in a small space right now."

She didn't have to explain herself for me to grasp the understanding. I only nodded. "Are you hungry? There's breakfast on the table if you like. Or if you want to eat outside, I can grab us a tray."

"The table here is fine." Ora motioned her head in a light nod toward the window.

I heard Fyom leave the table and enter the kitchen through another doorway before rummaging through various cabinets.

I held onto her as we walked the short steps to the dining room, too afraid to let go for fear she might fall. The tunic and leggings practically swallowed her and made her look like a child playing dress-up. Peiro remained stoic as we walked past him and into the next room.

Ora sat down at the opposite end of the table from Fyom's chair and looked out the window. Her gaze was empty as I set to work on adding easily digestible fruits and breads onto her plate. I didn't have any idea when Ora's last meal was, but if the state of her body was any indication, it had been quite some time.

How could anyone do this to a queen? To any human? I vowed to myself that whoever did this to her would pay.

Fyom entered the room with a mug of steaming liquid in his hand and gently sat it down in front of me, nudging me to give it to Ora.

"More healing tea," he said as he turned to grant us some space and sat in his normal chair at the other end of the table. Peiro didn't linger and followed close behind him, sitting in his usual spot. The two men said nothing to one another and simply looked out of the window.

I grabbed onto her hand, feeling the tiny bones flex. "You're safe here," I said as I followed her gaze, seeing the Shadowcraig Mountains that bordered Dokvalon and Gria. "They can't get to you here. No one knows where we are."

I looked down at Fyom, who gave us a reassuring nod.

"And we made sure to take paths that Black Raiders would not be familiar with," Peiro said softly behind his mug of coffee. Offering a small sense of comfort.

I nodded and looked back at Ora. Her eyes slowly shifted and turned down to her plate before turning to me. "I... I... Uhm..."

"You don't have to talk about anything right now. But when you're ready, I'm here," I said with a small smile.

Ora nodded and turned back to her plate to nibble in silence.

CHAPTER 27

I found myself sparring with Peiro with both a physical sword and the one I Wielded, his presence ever radiating with confidence and authority. Fyom sat on a wooden bench next to the cabin's wall, reading another large dusty tome, stating he was much closer to uncovering more about the stories of the strange entity, while Ora rested.

I parried Peiro's assault and rolled into the dodge. As I sprang to my feet, I pointed the end of my Wielded blade toward his neck, where it hovered so closely that the force that radiated off the glowing sword slightly ruffled the ends of his hair like a breeze.

"Someone's been practicing, *Naa'n le'ya*." Moonlight. Peiro stood still, his form towering over me. I was acutely aware of how close our bodies were. If I took a deep inhale, I knew my tunic would brush against his. He slowly backed away from the Wielded point and smirked.

"I got tired of sitting around, doing nothing," I said as I called the Wielded blade to disintegrate into the air.

Fyom mumbled something behind us about reading not being a waste of time. "What do we do now that we have the queen back?" he called out as he turned a page.

Peiro mockingly bowed in my direction before turning toward his canteen. He took a large swig before handing the rest to me. Our fingers lightly brushed, which sent a kaleidoscope of butterflies through me. "Fyom does pose a good question. Your main objective was to get your sister."

I stood there for a moment. I hadn't been able to talk with Peiro alone yet, so he could explain how he accomplished such a feat in finding my sister. And alone. Not many lived to tell the tale of entering the Shadowcraig Mountains and returning, let alone returning unscathed with a fugitive in tow.

I had been so consumed with learning more about Wielding my power or seeking the Ancient One to rescue Ora that I didn't get to think much about the next step. "Well. Capturing a queen is an open act of war. Now that Ora is back on Grian soil, we must rally her men. Restore her rightful place on the throne."

"But what about the broken court and those who conspired against her?" Fyom asked, lifting his eyes from the dusty pages. Ever since I had told him what happened, he hardly wanted to talk about the court members. He held a sense of empathy when their lost souls were discussed.

"That's true." I thought for a moment. "Most of the court fell at the temple," I said carefully when I spotted Fyom's eyes narrow. "At least Lord Beralt wasn't there."

I tapped the edge of my sword against the insole of my boot. "Those who had fallen would have been replaced by now by magical law, but I'm not sure who would have taken their positions and if their pockets are lined with whatever Vovias might have promised them."

We continued to talk about plans and strategies. Outrageous ones that involved asking the king to the north, the Chronicle King, for help. It was widely known that he detested Wielders and had once stated he would rather eat his own boot than to give a Wielder a water.

"Why not just go directly to the people? Why not tell them what's happened?" Peiro asked after we debated for what felt like hours.

"Use your head, boy. You above all else should know that would attract too much unwanted attention." Fyom's eyebrow arched high.

Peiro slowly turned his head toward the giant of a man and pointed with his sword, "You know better than to call me *boy*."

Fyom chuckled as he sat. "And what will you do about it? Rather I call you *old man*?"

I ignored the odd exchange. The two continued to bicker as I looked up into the bright blue sky, noticing something move out of the corner of my eye. I whipped my head in the motion's direction while pulling my Wielding to the surface, clearly on edge.

Ora slowly walked around the bend and in our direction. Whatever was in Fyom's tea worked miracles, as most of the bruising and cuts along Ora's skin now looked almost nonexistent. Only small pink and silver lines remained, and the bruising had faded to a very faint yellow. Her skin had returned to its lively color while the hollows of her cheeks were now full.

"Aurora!" I called out as I left my sword on the rack and closed the gap between us. "How are you feeling?" I didn't hesitate to grab her by the arms and observe her features.

"Better," Ora said with a small smile. "Considering." A returned spark lined her voice. A hint of energy coated in sadness.

I matched her smile with my own and looped her arm through mine. "Come. I haven't properly introduced you to our host." The two men continued to bicker back and forth but stopped suddenly as we approached. "Aurora, this is Fyom. The man who lives in this...*cabin*."

"A nice cabin indeed," Ora said with another small smile. Fyom nodded with a spark of amusement in his eye.

"He has been a most gracious host," I continued, "and I believe is too wise for us." I snickered.

Fyom rose from his seat, setting the tome in his place, and lowered his large frame to one knee. With one hand he covered his heart and bowed his head, looking to the ground. "I am here to serve, My Queen." He looked up to Ora's face. "May this home be of service to you for as long as you need."

Ora nodded. "Thank you," she said, and signaled for him to rise.

I looked to Peiro next. He too knelt where Fyom had and placed a hand over his heart. "May my sword and body fight for your kingdom always." He cut his eyes to me as he said, "I will serve you. Always." The spark in his eyes sent shivers down my spine.

Ora nodded. "Nice to officially meet you both." She motioned for Peiro to rise. "I cannot express my gratitude enough for all you must have done for my sister. For me."

Fyom swatted his hand casually. "My Queen, it's truly—"

"Ora, please," Ora cut in. "I'm assuming we're all friends here."

Fyom chuckled. "I guess you two are more alike than I originally thought. Anyway, it is truly an honor to have you as my guest."

Ora turned to me. "What were you all discussing?"

"Well, what to do next now that you're back and safe. But you don't need to worry yourself with this just yet."

"I would very much like to hear these ideas," Ora said. Anger pierced her small smile. Something glistened across her eyes.

"We will, my sister, after you've rested," I urged.

"I'm fine." She shook her head with a clipped smile. "What is the current state of things since...since the incident?"

I glanced at the men as I took a deep breath. "Well, I strongly believe Vovias and Ariadne are behind this. Most of the court fell when...when everything happened." I almost choked on the words as I said next, "I saw many of them in the aftermath. Well, as much as I could see."

Ora said nothing as she crossed her arms over her body and stared down at the ground.

I reluctantly continued. "Obviously, Lord Beralt wasn't there, but we don't know where his allyship lies. Telling the people of Gria outright about what happened without any court backing might cause too much panic or could be easily twisted by whoever Vovias might control. We can't rally any help from the northern territories past the Northern Woods. And we don't know who claimed lord or ladyship of the other territories within Gria after the...*incident.*"

"So, in other words, we're stuck," Ora cut in.

I shrugged. The gesture was meant to be comforting but fell short of convincing. "We'll think of something. Vovias is *not* getting away with this." Anger brewed with each word.

"What about Sury?" Ora whispered. She held herself tightly as she kicked the dirt under her boot.

With everything happening all at once and only small changes in Sury for weeks, guilt threatened to eat my heart at the fact I didn't mention him sooner, but knew it wasn't right to withhold them from one another for another moment. "He's here," I said shakily.

"Sury's *here?*" Ora all but bounced on her feet.

"He is," I said hesitantly. "But..."

"Why haven't I seen him? Take me to him!" Ora hurried around the cabin and to the door, grabbing the handle. I raced around her, blocking her from entering. Ora gave me a rightful bewildered look and tried to push past me.

"Aurora," I said softly, instantly gaining her attention by using her full name. "I need you to listen to me." I gently grabbed her shoulders as I struggled to find the words to explain Sury's state and that he'd knocked on death's door. I inhaled deeply.

"Is it bad?" Ora whispered.

I briefly closed my eyes as I exhaled. When I reopened them, Ora stared back at me, intently waiting. "He's hurt. Real bad," I continued. "As we headed to Zonnagberg..."

"Zonnagberg?"

I nodded. "Yes. I can tell you more about that later, but when we were close, we were ambushed by Black Raiders." Ora stiffened. "As we were running, one of their arrows found their mark in Sury's shoulder."

Ora dismissed me. "Then it's just a flesh wound, right? You told me that Fyom is a Master Healer. He should be able to heal him up fine, right?"

I let go of Ora's shoulders and took a deep breath again. "It was no ordinary arrow. Fyom believes it held some kind of dark magic called the *death arrow*. It's spreading in his body. Fyom has him in a deep sleep to slow the spread until we can figure out what kind of treatment can help."

A soft whimper escaped Ora as she drew her hands to her mouth and began nibbling on her nails. Hope and then despair flashed across her features. She shook her head and released her hands from her mouth to straighten her spine. "Show him to me."

I could only nod. "Of course."

I turned to open the door and motioned Ora to follow down the hall and to Sury's room. Nothing had changed inside the warm room where Sury slept. His bed was still neat, and the hutch and drawers next to the bed still held an endless supply of bandages and tinctures Fyom and I had concocted.

"Sury!" Ora gasped as she pushed past me and knelt on the floor next to his frail body. I silently thanked the giants that Fyom had overlapped the collar of the tunic Sury rested in, covering the lesions and blackened veins across his body.

Ora scooped one of his resting hands into hers and began to weep. I turned to leave to give Ora a moment, feeling like I was violating a desperate moment between them.

"Don't leave," Ora said between bouts of tears. "Stay. Please."

I nodded and shut the door. I sat on the divan, staying present but also giving Ora a moment to herself. The sun set and cast dark shadows over the meadow as we sat in Sury's room, allowing Ora to empty her well of emotions. I managed to grab a small tray of food to bring back to the room, where we both sat on Sury's bed, Ora next to him and me at their feet.

We sat there for hours and shared parts of what had happened to us during our time apart. I shared what I could about the Ancient One being based on a real entity lost from long ago, how Ariadne had placed a fog on my Wielding, but didn't elaborate further—not sure how to explain the fullness of it all. Not yet.

Ora held her stare on Sury's still body and planted a tiny kiss against his temple. "Thank you for trying to help. I do like to make a good mess of things, don't I?" she teased.

"I'm thankful you're here. I don't know how Peiro found you."

"Truthfully, it's all a haze," Ora said. "But he's rather quiet, isn't he? A man of not very many words. Stoic. But rather handsome, right? In a rugged kind of way?"

"I haven't noticed," I said nonchalantly, nibbling on an apple.

"And what would you call what I saw between you two in the kitchen earlier?" Ora asked with wild excitement in her eyes. "Are you smitten?" Excitement in her voice grew with every question.

"What? No!" I shook my head. "I barely know him."

"Aside from all that, I say rescuing your sister shows a pretty big interest."

"He's committed to his kingdom. He's showing loyalty."

"He didn't have to do it. You told me how the way you and Sury came about him was random. I don't believe in randomness. There's a reason his path found yours."

I took another bite of my apple, wishing desperately that Ora would turn to any other subject.

Ora smirked with a matter-of-fact response. "You know, Mother and Father didn't trust one another at first, from what I've heard. But they grew to love one another—their love was evident."

I rolled my eyes and looked off to the moon high in the sky. I turned to take Ora's hand in mine then looked at Sury. "We will find a way to make him better. I don't care what it takes or who we have to threaten or convince, but we *will* make him okay. That I promise."

"And make Dokvalon pay for what they did to me," Ora said as she stared in no direction in particular.

"That too." I hesitated with my next words. "Do you want to talk about what happened? We can wait, too. All in your time."

"Not yet." Ora shook her head. "But you truly didn't send Peiro? He acted like he was there because of *you*. I mean, he didn't say much, but when he did talk, he always mentioned that he knew you. Even gave quite the description of you and your magic. I thought you sent him to save me."

My brows furrowed. "I actually thought the opposite, that he wouldn't help. I even asked, and he said rescuing you would have been a fool's errand. But I'm glad he was wrong," I said with a small smile.

"What changed his mind?" Ora asked.

I could only shrug because I didn't have an answer. It was whiplash from him urging me to give up on my plan to him following through on his own. We sat there in silence for a while, simply happy to be back into one another's company.

"Do you think he'll be okay?" Ora whispered, breaking the comforting silence. She looked down to Sury again and inspected his wounds. The magical coma worked hard at keeping him stable as we raced to find a cure.

"I want to tell you yes, but I don't know. I so deeply wish I knew. Not just for his sake but also for yours." I grinned, changing the subject. "He's told me that you two had *time* together at the inn, but aside from that, I can tell he really loves you, Ora, from the way he talks about you. And his sacrifice helped me get here."

"He *told* you...? About...?" Ora's face began to turn bright red as a sheepish grin spread across her face.

"The cat's out of the bag. I mean, I always knew you two had feelings but didn't know about *that* until recently." I waved my hand in the air.

"You know I've never been much about following the rules, Phe." Ora chuckled.

"Yes. That I have always known about, which makes it more ironic that you'll be the new *ruler* of an entire kingdom. If only our people knew just how unruly you truly are!" We laughed together.

The smile on Ora's face started to fade as she began to ask, "But, how do we get past Ariadne and Vovias? Reclaim our blood right?"

"That might be a question for tomorrow. For now, let's focus on you resting. Today has had enough problems on its own." I got up from my seat on the bed and began to collect our plates.

"Sister?"

"Yes?"

A little smile danced on Ora's lips. "If it's okay, I'd like to sleep beside Sury tonight."

"You don't have to ask me for permission."

Ora looked like a small child, not knowing how to say the proper words for what she wanted to say next. "Thank you. Truly."

"Never thank me. I'm your sister. It's my job to take care of you. Giants know what trouble you'll cause next," I said with an exaggerated eye roll and then bid her goodnight.

***

Sleep evaded me. My body hummed to be outside and to bask in the moonlight. I finally had my sister back. Sury's healing still needed time with no answers in sight. Fyom was pages away from finding out more about the entity in the north where the Ancient One stories came from. For the first time in weeks, I felt the delicate string of hope strengthen.

I sat within the tall grass and wildflowers of the small meadow adjacent to Fyom's trees that faced the looming Shadowcraig Mountains.

A soft shuffling came from behind. I turned to see Peiro walking toward me, his eyes shining brightly against the night sky. His large frame gracefully folded with ease as he sat next to me, looking up at the stars. His small finger brushed against mine where it rested in the grass. The small act ignited the butterflies again, as I bit my bottom lip to hold back my smile.

"Can't sleep?" Peiro asked, keeping his gaze upward. I turned to face him, noting how the moonlight danced beautifully against the harsh planes of his face.

"No," I said, drinking him in. "I strangely feel more energized at night these days. You?"

Peiro's gaze cut down to mine, a smirk curling up his face. "Me and sleep aren't the best of friends."

I turned back to watch the night sky, taking in the constellations of Aorr holding his water pitcher and Ruheia, giantess of the hunt, holding her seven-star bow. "They're magnificent," I said, nodding to the stars.

"You are magnificent." His voice was rough. I turned to look at him and saw he had extended a delicate white flower with a small smile on his face. "I picked this for you," he said, trying to contain a chuckle.

I smirked knowingly but simply said "thank you" before taking the flower and smelling the center. Nothing could stop the smile that grew wide on my face at this new, regular occurrence.

"That night," he continued, "when you tested, wholly tested, I've never seen anything like it." I was very aware of how close Peiro was sitting next to me. "Your eyes were closed, so I assume you had no idea, but you radiated like a star."

"I-what?" I quickly turned my head to Peiro, bewildered by this revelation.

"You were beautiful. You pulled down the moonbeams, and then small stars fell and encircled you. You looked like the embodiment of Nyska and her moons. Your face was at...peace."

He turned his gaze to meet mine. The bright silvers and grays bore into me, seeing something I couldn't quite put to words. "Beautiful."

I quickly cast my eyes to anywhere else but his as I felt heat course through my body. "Thank you." I felt my cheeks redden at his compliment. It felt strange to capture someone's attention, let alone someone whose energy seemed to pull me closer every time I was near him. Suddenly the middle of the small flower became very interesting.

"You created a beautiful purple and teal aura, much like the color of your eyes." Peiro nudged a finger under my chin, forcing me to look at him. The heat inside my body radiated wildly, the air felt charged. "It reminded me of the celestial lights you can see up north, near—"

"Why did you help us?" I blurted. "After saying my plan was a fool's errand?" I wanted to focus on anything else besides the warmth creeping through my skin and the heat settling low in my belly. "The real reason why."

Peiro's face became sullen as he pulled back. His fingers landed in his lap and interlocked and released over and over. "Because I realized something changed."

"Like what?"

"You can help me."

I scoffed. "So you only planned to help me so I could help you with something? As a repayment system? Even after knowing that I desperately needed to save her? That *this kingdom* desperately needs its queen? I had already promised that you would be repaid." Anger surged through me, cooling the heat only slightly.

Peiro sighed and closed his eyes, turning his face toward the moon. "We're not... I'm not explaining this right." A small twitch ricocheted down his body.

"Then explain it," I snapped.

"It's not that easy!" Peiro softly growled as his body tensed.

My body betrayed me by wanting to draw him closer. It seemed to have a mind of its own as I felt my fingers intertwining with his. The anger dissipated slightly as my fingers felt the calluses in his palm.

"Hmm," he said as his hand enclosed mine. "You have warrior hands now. Much different than when we first met." He gently turned my hand over to uncurl it, stroking my own newly-formed calluses with his fingers, never letting go of my hand.

"You sometimes speak in *we*. Why" I whispered.

A shadow passed over Peiro's face as he inhaled deeply. "It seems to happen when the shadowed memories of Dokvalon enter my mind." He continued with his soft strokes against my palm.

"Memories?"

Peiro nodded, warming my body with his gentleness. "For years, I was enslaved to their kingdom. Did whatever bidding that was asked from the king."

I let his words digest within me. "You were an assassin?"

"That." Peiro nodded again, still edging his fingertips against my skin. Each stroke stoked the growing fire in me. "Amongst other things the king might have use for." He never looked into my eyes as he continued. "Assassin. Entertainment. The court's whore. Slave." After a steady breath, he continued.

"After an attempt to escape, they forced me to be a prisoner within the Shadowcraig Mountains. It's where all the people that the king finds valuable are sent. If he didn't want you prisoner, or found no further use for you, then you were simply dead. But then I finally escaped and have been running ever since."

Silence passed as I grew to understand everything he had just told me. He could have simply kept this story to himself and not shared such vulnerable parts about himself. He didn't have to prove his loyalty, or prove anything at all.

"That's how you were able to rescue Ora? Because you knew exactly where they would be holding her?" My heart swelled.

Peiro squeezed my hand back and nodded, meeting my gaze. "I've known these lands for a long time. I know the routes that keep you hidden."

"You risked everything to get her, knowing they're searching for you? You could have been caught."

"It was something I had to do." He said, simply nodding again. A strange glint passed over his eyes and quickly disappeared.

In a swift motion, I threw my arms around his neck and squeezed as hard as my muscles would allow. "Thank you, for everything," I said as tears rolled down my cheeks. I pulled back and looked into Peiro's silver eyes and smiled. "I don't know how I could ever repay you."

Peiro's hand cupped my face under my jaw, tilting it up slightly. His eyes glinted as he shook his head. "You owe me nothing. I already know I am in your debt forever."

Before I could stop myself, I quickly brushed my lips against Peiro's to thank him, but found them warm and inviting. I pulled back in shock from my actions, hoping I didn't just frighten him with my boldness. Heat rose to my cheeks as I looked away in embarrassment.

Peiro made a low rumbling sound as he pulled my jaw forward, hooking his finger under my chin again, and took my lips to his. The stars aligned and crashed around me as my heart and mind swirled in a dreamy abyss as I closed my eyes. His lips were soft yet in control, and they sent shockwaves through my body.

His tongue parted my lips and delicately danced with mine as I felt his other hand cup the side of my face as if he wanted to drink me in. The pace increased, but only slightly, as he pulled me against his hard body. He never overpowered me and the precipice of control was in my hands to see if I wanted this.

Oh, how I wanted this—to drink him in just as he pressed toward me, as if called to me. The hand that was on my cheek moved to the nape of my neck. His fingers interlocked with my braid, tilting my head back more for easy access.

I found his shoulders, broad and strong, and held onto him as if my life depended on it. Each stroke of his tongue made me drunk with emotion. The muscles low in my belly tightened and coiled as he delicately nibbled my bottom lip, applying just enough pressure to make me crave more. My body longed to be touched.

With a soft command, Peiro steered my body over his with both of my legs bent over his hips, as he continued sitting. Our forms were still hidden within the grasses as our tongues swirled and danced in a frenzy. I pressed against him harder, desperate to ease the growing tension deep within me. Traces of his hardened length pressed against my inner thigh. I was lost in the cosmos.

He pulled away, the absence feeling foreign. "Ophelia? Look." His breath was strangled like he was gasping for air. I immediately pulled back and opened my eyes to find the same little orbs I saw weeks ago dance and jump around us. Only this time there was a small reddish tinge to the outside that bled into a strong purple glow.

The glow cast an iridescent shine on the blades of grass and flowers around us. The once-white birch trees illuminated with a faint purple shine as if a nebula had descended from space and shifted around us.

"What do they mean?" Peiro asked as he let an orb swirl against his palm.

"I'm not sure, but I think they're linked to my emotions. I noticed these before when I felt something intense."

"What are you feeling now?" he whispered as he looked deep into my eyes.

I smiled. "Happiness."

Peiro smiled before leaning in to kiss me again.

CHAPTER 28

I could have stayed in that meadow forever, interlocked with Peiro, until I melted away. But he was ever the gentleman and bid me goodnight before things went further. I've been intimate before, although never in an open field. I don't think I would have minded the idea, until a bug flew into my hair and caused me to yelp, fizzling out our heat. We had walked hand in hand to my room, where Peiro kissed me goodnight and I dreamed of silver eyes and deep kisses.

I was up before the sun rose and headed straight to the new pell Peiro had constructed for us. I still didn't have it in me to practice with my *illicitus* power, let alone talk about it. But I could wrap the pell with a thick vine and pull it close like a lasso, while striking it with my other hand that wielded a sword. Or force a gust of wind to push it toward Peiro for him to strike. Each time I practiced, the better I got.

I tilted my head, inspecting the new notch I had cut into *Vovias*, the name I gave the pell. The notch was deep but I knew I could strike the exact spot again. Before I could step back, a presence swarmed me, instantly charging the air. Soft lips pressed against the exposed crook of my neck, sucking and biting just enough to draw blood up to my skin's surface.

A light moan involuntarily escaped my mouth as my hand clutched the sword's hilt. A large hand wrapped around my waist and pulled me hard against a wall of muscle. I felt the growing evidence of his desire through his trousers as the other hand pressed against my shoulder, pulling it down to further expose my neck. His fingers flexed against my tingling skin as my body grew hot.

I brought my free hand up behind me and threaded my fingers into the strands of both silky and coarse hair. I tugged gently, prompting a low growl from behind. Another moan escaped me when I felt his lips trail up my neck, teeth placing little nibbles along my ear. I'd never experienced this sensation before and it. Was. *Glorious*.

The hands pulled away and spun me in quick motion to face silver eyes. Before I could say anything, Peiro's lips crashed into mine, much firmer than the night before, like he was starving. I relished in the building tension that his tongue created. My hands roamed his back as he pulled me even closer, exploring the swells of my backside. My skin was on fire. I needed something to ease the growing tension between my thighs. I didn't care if our first time together was on a bench. I needed something to quench this thirst.

A loud *bang* of a door closing at the front of the cabin caused me to jolt and pull back. Peiro's skin was flushed and his eyes wild. I brought my hands to my mouth and laughed, thankful no one had walked around the corner and spotted us.

Peiro sheepishly grinned as he said, "Good morning." His voice was low and rough.

"Good morning." I giggled—actually giggled. "Did you sleep well?"

Peiro took a step forward and traced a small strand of hair near my shoulder with his finger. "It could have been better."

"What would have helped?" I asked, as I was sure Fyom could concoct sleeping draughts.

"If you were in the bed with me. Preferably nude."

My eyes widened as I swallowed hard. My words were swept away as Peiro planted a heated kiss on my lips before pulling away once again. He sauntered over to the sword rack, pulling free his usual blade, and twirled it back and forth. I was more than ready for his assault as he launched his training attack.

My blade met his right as he swung downward. My free hand called forth water droplets from the air and misted his face and eyes as I swung my foot down low, striking the backs of his legs and forcing him to the ground. He fell with a *thud* but then sprang back to his feet at a frightening speed before shaking his wild hair back and forth, spraying me with droplets. "Very clever." He laughed and swung again.

I parried each strike, finding my way back to offense. I stalled his next blow with a gust of wind, slowing him a fraction, but just enough for me to dodge and strike in defense. We continued to practice, my footing getting more precise with each round. Peiro occasionally called a move or critiqued my stance, pointing out what would allow me to use more momentum or force.

Between the sweat and the water that I Wielded, Peiro's shirt became drenched. He peeled it off and hung the material over the sword rack to let it dry.

"You're cruel," I said as I drank him in. He had stopped drinking Fyom's Healing tea but was fully back to his muscular form, one that he continued to hone with his ceaseless training of sword and body. Deep lines cut through his arms, chest, and back. I bit my lip as I drank in the deep lines of his abdomen that veed down into the waistband of his trousers.

"Like what you see, *Naa'n le'ya*?" His voice was low and rough. I narrowed my eyes, not dignifying that with a response, then sparred in offense once again.

In an easy move, he twirled and caught the hand I Wielded with, causing me to lose balance from the forward momentum of my sword arm. The move was effortless as he spun me to hit his chest with my back, his arm wrapping around me tightly, while his free hand stilled the arm that still held the sword.

I was pinned hard against him, feeling every point of contact where our bodies touched. His chest grazed harder with each breath he took as his mouth once again found its way to the crook of my neck. His tongue tantalizingly stroked the skin, whisking away the salt from training.

"You're cheating," I heaved in a whisper.

"On the contrary," he whispered. "I think I'm winning."

"This won't happen on a battlefield," I said, closing my eyes, too mesmerized by the teasing strokes.

"Hmm," he continued. "Battles are everywhere. You just have to decipher them." I dug my nails deep into his forearm, not wanting him to stop. He let go of my sword arm and caressed the front of my shirt until his hand grabbed and kneaded the swell of my breast. I arched back, granting him more access.

"Is this a battle?" I whispered, rubbing my backside against his growing arousal. "So anything goes?"

Peiro only growled in response.

I pulled away hard and twirled on my toes to bring the blade of my sword inches away from his neck. Peiro's eyes grew wide and wild as a slow grin etched against his face.

"I guess I win." I smirked.

"Oh, my love, you've won before we even started."

Heat flared against my skin, which was begging to be touched.

His head snapped to his left and my gaze followed. We spotted Ora walking in the distance toward the open meadow. Peiro nudged his head in her direction. "How is she doing?"

"Doing better than I thought. But I've also learned she internalizes more than I had realized." I watched as Ora found a spot in the grass and sat down. "I'm going to go check on her. See how she is today."

"We'll continue our training later." Peiro's eyes sparked as he smiled.

"Training? That's what we're calling it?" I asked as I arched a sarcastic brow.

"Battlefields come in all shapes and forms. The bedroom could just be my most preferred one."

I bit my lip, then handed him my sword and turned to leave. I felt his hand close around mine as he pulled me in for a deep kiss before releasing me. "I'll be here if you need anything," he said, then shooed me away. I narrowed my eyes and walked to where Ora sat.

"Good morning," I said as I folded down beside her. She looked up and smiled. I was taken aback by how her smile seemed to glow. She looked just like the sister I knew before our worlds were completely gutted and turned upside down. My string of hope thickened again.

"Happy morning." She beamed.

"Sleep okay?"

Ora nodded and looked out to the distance, at the black outline of the Shadowcraig Mountains. "Fyom gave me more of his Healing tea and said I would only need one more day of it to completely heal my body."

"That's wonderful!" I exclaimed.

Ora nodded again just as a shadow crossed her face. "If only it would heal the mind, right?"

I knew what she meant and I wished the same. Wished something could take away all our pain. "You don't have to talk about it, you know. Not until you feel fully ready."

"No, no, I need to talk about it." She took a deep breath and began to tell her story. "All I can remember about the first part is the fight in the forest and the Raider that attacked us. I don't know how long I was unconscious, but I remember seeing the camp and fire, then it was all black. Like the life was sucked out of me right then."

She paused and took another cleansing breath. "Occasionally I would wake up and see more trees before we came to the mountains. I saw this large gap that was covered by a thicket of trees that looked freshly carved."

"So they're tunneling through the mountain? That breaks the treaty that was signed by our ancestors." I recalled the details from grueling history lessons. That might also be the entry that Peiro had mentioned.

Ora just nodded. "I fell unconscious again until I smelled the most horrendous stench in the air. Dokvalon is worse than what our mother and father told us. Everything I saw was dead. I don't know how it's even still a kingdom."

I sat very still as I listened to every word.

"It was horrible. The rivers and trees all smelled foul and it looked like life itself was fading. The very ground was brittle and full of dead grass. Rocks and boulders were all split and broken. I never saw the sun. A thick cloud always hung in the air and made the sky look like there was a never-ending fog."

She adjusted herself on the ground before continuing. "I never saw the castle or the King of Dokvalon himself. They took me to what looked like a fortress built inside the mountain. Then they took me to this room beneath the fortress floor, to this chamber..." She stiffened.

I grabbed her hand and squeezed tight in silent comfort.

"One side of the chamber was a room, with a bed that had mildewy sheets. On the other side...there was a...there was a table." Her lip began to quiver. "All day, cloaked figures would put me on that table and force these disgusting vials of liquid down my throat. I could feel everything inside of me, like a fire that I couldn't extinguish. Somehow they paralyzed my magic. Phe, I didn't know such a thing was possible!"

I tightened my grip on her hand and used my sleeve to catch a tear that fell from her eyes.

"I couldn't move my body or stop anything they did. The Wielders that came in seemed like they were trying to take my magic away from me. My very essence! I know there are those who are born without the ability to Wield, but what happens to a Wielder when their very magic is ripped from them? Why do they want my magic?" Ora's grip trembled as a storm clouded her eyes.

"I don't know," I said softly. These revelations frightened me but I held my own shock. "I'm learning that there's a whole truth that's been hidden from us about our Wielding."

"They kept mentioning something about life and death, but I was so confused. I lied and told them I tested and obtained fire.

They weren't convinced, especially when they saw this strange green and gold ribbon of Wielding they pulled from me. The force of it being pulled against my will was a pain I'll never forget…" Ora sobbed.

"Please, take your time…" I tried sending soothing strokes against her back.

"But then they were angry at *me*! They began yelling that I was doing something wrong. That *I* was an issue for them. An inconvenience!" Ora yelled. "That's when they left me alone in the chamber. Sometimes for hours. Sometimes days. I lost all sense of time in the dark."

I threw my arms around Ora and let her weep into my embrace. I heard a faint shuffle over my shoulder and saw Peiro standing at the bend of the cabin with his arms folded, a look of concern on his face. I lightly shook my head at him, a silent message to not intervene.

Ora shook as she continued. "The guards spoke a language that I couldn't piece together. After the cloaked Wielders had gotten angry, it seemed like they and the guards were in a panic. It was like they were waiting for a commander or something, and worried someone would be furious. The Wielders kept saying, 'They got the wrong one.' Someone mentioned your story about the Ancient One missing. It was so strange."

My spine stiffened. I grabbed Ora by the shoulders, peering into her eyes. "What do you mean?"

Ora wiped away the tears that fell. "I thought it was all a story until the guards kept repeating the same phrase over and over—echoing in such a creepy way. That's when I realized it's not a story. Not to mention we saw real-life urthens that night. Nasty creatures that should be terminated. They roamed the halls and sniffed the bars of my cell."

I thought of the rurons and bratrians that had helped me, but decided I would wait until later to explain how there were good urthens.

"They said they needed *her* and the Ancient One." Ora sniffled. "Said I was the wrong one. That *she* would lead them to the missing Ancient One. The one who can Wield it."

CHAPTER 29

A hearty mix of emotions expanded in my chest all at once. Relief. Curiosity. Doubt. I had clung to this theory like my very lifeline and wanted to find anything I could to build the hope of saving Ora.

I exhaled, absorbing the fact that Dokvalon was after the Ancient One as well, or at least the entity it was based off of.

"I'm glad you're back." I planted a swift kiss on her hair. "Soon we can start planning how to attack and regain control."

"After what they've done?" Ora lashed out. "What they tried doing? I want to act now! I can rest later."

"We'll think of something. Vovias and Ariadne won't get away with this." Anger brewed with each word. "Please, sister. Let's take a break for you to rest. We'll talk more later."

I knew this was a mental game of chess and felt Vovias had outmaneuvered us in every way that mattered. I briefly looked over my shoulder to see that Fyom had joined Peiro, both deep in what looked like a heated discussion.

Ora said abruptly, "I might have an idea...from something I overheard from the guards." She let out a sharp exhale as she continued. "The guards kept referring to the Ancient One. I thought it was all a myth. From Mother and Father's stories, and from your book, Phe—but you were right. There is a kernel of truth there. We could use this against them."

Through the countless hours I had poured into Fyom's books for any hint of the source to the story, I began to doubt that this thing, this entity, this weapon had any truth to it. I was even too nervous to admit that I might have wasted time chasing a story. But the fact that Dokvalon was also searching for this being had me curious as a sense of urgency roared in me.

"What did you hear?" I whispered, anticipating her next words.

Ora shook her head and closed her eyes as she tried to recall what she heard. "To them, he's very real. But we could use this against them." Those words alone amplified my relief that I hadn't wasted my time. But this also sparked a very real fear in understanding there was a dark force that Dokvalon was chasing.

"Something about it is real enough, at least. It might not be the same thing we learned about in those stories, but it's apparently magic that's older than we can even dream of. And from what I briefly heard where I was held," a dark shadow crossed over her face, "they want to use that magic against us. Against Gria."

The confirmation made my heart sink.

What were the odds that I sought the very same thing that Dokvalon was searching for?

I worriedly glanced to Fyom and recounted the small findings in his text. If he couldn't find much about it then it must be because no one wanted this information found. Wanted it to remain a child's nightmare.

"We must keep searching Fyom's books for answers," I said to Ora. "If it can be a weapon, then we must figure out *how* to use it, and then use it against them to protect our people. We need to figure out what their plan is," I said, more so to myself. "Come." I pulled Ora to stand. "We must tell Fyom what you know. This might help his research."

We crossed the meadow and walked back to the yard, where the men continued to talk in hushed tones. Fyom looked up as we approached. "Good morning, ladies," he said with a slight bow of his head.

"Ora, tell him what you told me," I said, skipping over the pleasantries.

Ora recounted all she had told me about what she overheard in the guards' whispers. Fyom held a pensive look as he absorbed what Ora said, while Peiro's large frame was practically frozen. A look of apprehension crested over his face. Instinctively, I discreetly brushed my knuckles across his as I watched shadows rise and fall across his face. I looped my pinky around his and tugged tightly, bringing him back to the present and out of his dark thoughts.

"We haven't found anything that states how to control the creature...if it truly exists," Fyom noted.

"I want to return the atrocious favor of what they did to me." Wrath seethed out of Ora like oil seeping from a vial.

"Ora?" I whispered.

"I'm fine," Ora clipped back at me. She looked vacantly in the distance as if her mind had suddenly shut off to the present world.

I placed my hand softly on Ora's back but was instantly shrugged off.

"I said I was fucking fine!" Ora snarled.

Anger swept through me, but not toward Ora. No. The anger was toward the vile people who snuffed out her spark of joy. That bright light that once so easily shone around her.

Ora blinked numerous times, like she had been locked in a mental trance, before speaking again. "Bits and pieces were shared in front of me. Most of the time I was conscious, I would keep my eyes closed. Over time, the guards got sloppy with what they would share near my cell." A cell. I swallowed hard and tried not to let images come to mind of what her confinement looked like.

"But," Ora continued, "there was a chant or a code or something the guards kept saying to one another. Almost like they were repeating it so as to not forget it." She brought her hands to her head as she tried to recount what was spoken. "Maybe it was an incantation? I'm trying to remember. It was an old, odd language."

"You're playing a very dangerous game if you don't know what they were saying," Peiro grumbled. I noticed he had grown more rigid.

"I second that," Fyom said. "Let us pause for now and reconvene after lunch, perhaps? There's a fresh loaf of rosemary and thyme bread. My specialty."

Completely oblivious to their remarks, Ora continued, "It was so strange. Something like *thgil eht...*"

"Stop!" Peiro roared. "You don't know what you're doing! What you could be conjuring here!" Peiro's stance tensed and appeared rooted to the spot, unable to move.

"What is she doing?" I called out frantically, trying to reach for Peiro, who swatted my hand away.

"Words from the giants," Peiro heaved. "Words no one should know, let alone speak."

Ora's eyes fluttered closed, seemingly locking herself in the torment she'd experienced. Her breathing hitched just as a strange green and gold aurora covered her body. Her voice turned trancelike. "*Thgil eht otni...*"

"Stop!" Peiro shouted again. He thrashed against phantom hands. My breath caught as I witnessed pain cascade from his face and into his body as it twisted in unnatural ways, like he fought some invisible storm.

"*Fuck*," Fyom shouted, trying to push Peiro back, but he was met with resistance.

"Ora," I gasped. "Aurora, stop!" I kept my eyes on Peiro as I shook Ora's shoulders. The magic in my veins thrashed wildly against my skin, screaming for release.

"Run!" Fyom yelled over the roar of wind that fought Peiro's twisted form. My heart sank as I watched his body convulse, his eyes rolling to the back of his head.

Ora, still lost in her thoughts, was unaware of the surroundings. "*Thgil eht otni emoc ssenkrad!*"

"*No!*" Peiro roared in agony as his body froze in place.

He clawed his throat as he started to choke. His breathing turned raspy and his eyes fully glossed over into a misty white. His face paled and the veins in his face turned dark. He screamed again and again as black clouds swirled around, encasing him in a dark cyclone.

His shoulders shifted. The sound of bones breaking and tendons snapping filled the air as his shoulders began to widen. His feet grew and tore through his leather boots. The very air around his presence formed into a walking dark cloud. Black. Empty. The feeling of fear was tangible as he let out a guttural scream.

The sun dimmed as darkness crept high above us. The swirling clouds moved faster and rose higher to hover above the magical facade of the cabin before dwindling back down to the ground as fast as they grew.

Without my command, my hands flew high as my Wielding erupted from and formed an iridescent shield around us.

In front of us stood a large black cloud in the shape of a man's body. Tall, misty swirls of blacks and grays continued to rotate, like this being was grounded in the middle of a tornado, and loomed over Fyom, hovering at a height at least twice his size. The air stood still but the grass under the being's large feet lost its vibrant green hue and faded into an ashy gray.

Its eyes were a blinding white, encased in red sockets, and hollow. Just two holes of white light. It stretched its leathery skin into a wicked smile, showcasing sharp, pointed rows of teeth. Its forked tongue flicked past its teeth as it mockingly bowed forward and rose again, the smile still plastered on its face. The air became foul and everything fell silent. It turned its head, observing the surroundings. Each move it made sounded like worn leather being twisted and pulled.

"What have you done?" I gripped Ora's shoulders tightly, demanding an answer.

She fluttered her eyes open. "The stories *are* true," Ora whispered out loud, not breaking her wide stare at the being. A manic smile crept up the sides of her face as she continued to stare at the vile thing.

"But at what price? It's unpredictable! We don't know how to control it!" I gasped as I shook her shoulders.

"*Ah, how I've misssed thisss,*" the Ancient One hissed as it looked around the clearing and into the trees before meeting Fyom's stare. "Ah, thisss isss Fyom? I've heard so many storiesss about you. Peiro seemsss to believe you're helping him with the *voicesss* inside hisss head. But we all know thisss is just a fun game." The thing laughed in a way that mimicked the sound of a fork scraping glass.

It turned its gaze toward me and held a wicked stare, smiling something cruel.

"Ah, now I sssee why hisss heart has ticked with more beatsss of late. You *are* as beautiful as he claimsss you to be. Oh, he has such high hopesss for you, Princessss." The hiss grew softer with each passing word, leaving an eerie chill in the air. "Or I guesss, *Naa'n le'ya*. His moonlight."

I gritted my teeth as I held the shield around us three. My jaw set tight as I pinched my lips together, wanting to spew hateful words, but some instinct told me to keep my mouth shut. I could feel how this thing was a disgrace to nature and balance. An abomination.

This wasn't a weapon. This was a monster.

A feeling of butterflies entered my stomach—the same ones I felt around Peiro. No, not butterflies. It was my magic, clearly warning me about the abuse of magic around me.

It finally turned its gaze to Ora, and its smile wavered a blink before holding steady. "Ah, and thisss is the *queen-to-be*? In my time, the time when magic was raw and in itsss purest form, *queens* were only meant to be on their kneesss before their king. This race of humans has softened," it spat. "You lot are not worthy of the magic that this world hasss to offer. No wonder I can sense that it's been sullied sssince my time has been...*delayed*."

The being took a small step forward toward the cabin and the very air seemed to hold its breath. The trees' leaves outside the meadow's circle slowly changed to a bright yellow before merging to a deep golden brown, then fell off, one by one.

"Now," it continued, "who mussst I thank for releasssing me before I take my leave?"

"You will *not* leave," Ora said sternly. Her eyes narrowed and her chin jutted out confidently. "*I* said the incantation. You are under *my* control, Ancient One. That's what the guards said!"

"Ancient One? That'sss the moronic name he hasss called me? And what do you mean, *control*?" It took a step forward. My Wielding flared bright against my skin and fed into the shield, fortifying its hold. My outstretched fingers trembled slightly. "Oh, you pretty girl. You cannot sssimply control the purest form of dark magic. It might just drive you...*insssane*. Isn't that riiight, Ophelia?"

I said nothing as I continued to assess this entity. The more I looked at it, the angrier I felt. Out of control. The very balance around me and in my mind went askew.

The wicked smile grew wilder as the creature brought its hands together. From the cracks that could be seen between its fingers, a vast orb, dancing with red in various hues, grew as it pulled its hands steadily outward. "I'll ssshow you *control...*" it said, then turned to throw the raw magic at us.

"Get down!" I shouted, quickly throwing up my hands to deflect. A cannon sound exploded into the air and ricocheted against the forces of magic. Fyom flew from where he had stood and onto the remnants of the practice pell, unconscious and surrounded by splinters of wood. Ora had been slung into the cabin's side. She grabbed the back of her head and pulled her hand away to reveal bloodied fingers.

Ringing pierced my ears as I found myself flat on my back on the ground. I opened my eyes rapidly, momentarily forgetting what had happened until I looked at the forest and noticed that the birch trees' bark had turned from white to gray.

As quickly as my pounding head would allow, I rolled over to find the Ancient One had staggered back but remained on its feet, creating another orb of raw magic. Quickly I scrambled to my feet and drew in deep from my belly, pulling what normally felt wrong, but seemed right in this moment.

"*NO!*" I cried defiantly as I released all that I knew and hurled silver-tinged daggers of all sizes, encased in shadows, to the Ancient One, slowing its forward assault. A few found their mark; others were easily deflected. Instinct demanded that I call on the giants and the moon and the stars for their power. I hurled my very essence and demanded even Thuvina's death to greet me so I could Wield it and slice through the vile being before me.

I lost my breath and felt my heartbeat slow to a grave rhythm as the essence of death intertwined with my fingers. Shadows curled around my feet. I didn't need to be taught or guided how to Wield it—the feeling simply came as if I knew all along. *Illicitus.* With all that I had within me, I thrust my hands forward, full of Wielding, full of death, and aimed for the Ancient One's throat.

The creature tensed and its back arched unnaturally as my orbs that now shone more silver than teal wrapped around its neck like a bolas, then yanked the being backward. It howled a screech of pain as it clawed at its neck. Slices of skin peeled back from its body in slow curls that mimicked the burning edges of paper.

My vision clouded gray as the being fell to its knees, urging my magic off its leathery skin. "*You willll pay for thisss,*" it hissed.

I turned my wrist and clutched my fingers together, seeing the shadowy tether of my magic against the creature.

"Looks like now you're under *my* control. Be gone," I spewed with venom as I arced both of my hands up high before throwing down all that I had. My heart sputtered and my muscles coiled as I fed from the well of my magic and poured it into the being in front of me. Sparks of grays, silvers, and blues thrashed against the being.

My arms grew immensely heavy and failed me, but not before witnessing several deep gashes across the being's body, each one mimicking the cut at its throat with the skin curling back. The being kneeled on the ground in submission. The very wind around the creature began to spiral and spin once again, encasing the creature in a curtain of clouds. Dark winds turned white and opaque before revealing the image of a man with torn clothes and wild hair, unconscious on the ground.

Peiro.

The grass beneath him turned back into a vibrant green and the birch trees' bark resumed their staggering white. Ever so slowly, each branch produced the tiniest of green buds before blossoming into bright leaves. The air smelled like a warm spring day, fresh with blossoms and flowers, and *breathable*.

A grunt from Fyom shook me from my shock as I watched the massive man climb to his feet and shake bits of wood out of his dreaded hair. I dashed for Ora, who still looked half-dazed. Thank the giants there were no injuries other than the one on the back of her head. "We need to get you cleaned up and take care of that before it gets infected," I whispered as I helped her rise off the ground.

"Dammit!" Fyom yelled and raced over to see if Peiro was still breathing. "How could you lose control like this?" He tossed his question down to Peiro before scooping him up off the ground.

"You *knew*?" I yelled out, making Ora wince and cover her ears. "You knew Peiro was the Ancient One?"

"It's complicated," Fyom sighed.

"*COMPLICATED?*" I roared with anger. "For weeks I've been sitting in that library, looking for any hint of clues to the Ancient One's source and how to Wield it to save my sister! This kingdom!" I steadied Ora on her feet before I made the large strides to face Fyom. I could feel my fury etched deep on my face. "For weeks you acted clueless, ever searching your tomes. '*I'm getting close! Let me check another book!*'"

And then Peiro, who said my mission was a failure from the start, was the key I needed the whole time. I poked my finger into the swell of Fyom's chest. "You've known about this the whole damn time? You've had me searching for answers, and for what?"

Questions swirled in my head. Lies and deceit filled my heart from the very people I thought were on my side. I felt the same betrayal as when I learned of the court's lies. Wind and dirt swirled around me. My Wielding rose to lash out in anger.

"You made me waste time. You acted clueless." I panted hard from my growing anger. "You deceived me and pointed me in the wrong directions! *Why*? Are you with Dokvalon? What reasons do you have?" My voice rose higher as each word grew more intense. "What did this kingdom ever do to you to earn such disloyalty?"

"There is more here than you can understand!"

"Clearly! Not only did you know who it was that I sought, but even *how* to evoke the weapon I needed with the words from the giants. Who else has this knowledge?" My throat ached against the roaring I let out.

"He learned the words when it happened and shared his story with me. No one else is supposed to know. How this was discovered is even news to me."

"*LIES!*" I roared harder.

"*ENOUGH!*" Fyom yelled back, his green eyes glowing and his mouth in a snarl, showing his white teeth.

"Don't you dare yell at me, the Princess of Gria, when *you're* the one lying!"

"You will be treated as a *princess* the moment you stop acting like a child having a tantrum! It is *his* story to tell. Not mine. I swore an oath and I plan to keep it until he tells me otherwise! Now calm yourself!"

Twigs and leaves and small rocks instantly dropped to the ground as I relaxed my shoulders and forced a steadying breath.

Fyom sighed. "Give him a chance to explain." And he pushed past me, Peiro still in his arms, and disappeared into the cabin. My breath was too quick to be able to think straight. The air around me became too suffocating as my breathing ebbed. Magic bubbled within me, spewing to the surface, needing release. With a guttural scream, I threw my hands toward the remnants of the pell and poured all my fury into the structure, fully encasing it in shadows of silvers and blacks.

My fingers trembled from exhaustion, my chest heaving as I fought for breath. I poured everything I had into the magic, feeling my muscles tense and seize, until there was nothing left. When I finally dropped my hands, the shadows dissipated to reveal the wooden beam—decimated and drained to a lifeless gray.

"What just happened?" Ora whispered behind me.

I turned and gave her a warm hug. "I'll explain what I can after you're cleaned up."

"No, Phe. Your magic. What happened? I've never seen you do that before."

In truth, I had never seen it before either, and I couldn't quite process what I'd just done.

"Looks like I have more explaining to do," I replied.

"Phe!" Ora gasped as she brought her hand to her mouth in shock. "Your eyes. They're silver."

CHAPTER 30

It was hours before my eyes returned to their usual teal, but a faint silver continued to shine along the outside.

"Ophelia? Are you okay?" I didn't realize I had been staring out the window, looking at absolutely nothing. Flashes echoed in my mind of Peiro shifting before my eyes and into the... I couldn't bring myself to believe it. I tucked the scene into a far corner of my mind as I tended to Ora's wounds.

The gash on Ora's head healed more quickly than I anticipated, before I could even try my hand at Wielding the Healing Spiritus. I made sure to avoid Fyom's room full of medical supplies as he tended to whatever state Peiro was in, and I instead searched the kitchen to find something to spare for her head.

"Yes. Yes, of course." I blinked and turned to Ora, who sat on the divan with her feet propped on a small table. She had remained silent for a while after I told her about my Wielding and the lies Ariadne spewed. I even put on a small demonstration for her when she asked. Her face was in wondrous awe as I showed her the tiny moonbeams and stars, but I still couldn't bring myself to touch the *illicitus* again.

The feeling was...indescribable. It was magnificent. It was cruel. It was power. It was horrid. It was the most exhilarating thing I had ever felt and it absolutely terrified me. I could still see the shadows dancing at my fingertips, swirling and swaying like soft billows of smoke in the breeze.

Her white stone necklace glinted in the sunlight, the one I had guarded for her. Its coolness once felt like a dreaded weight around my neck, reminding me it was still there. It was only fitting now that it was returned to her. To its rightful owner.

"This changes nothing," Ora said as she gripped my hands hard. I didn't even notice that she had moved to stand before me, her eyes brighter than ever. I fought against a recoil as soon as her fingertips tightened around mine.

"But doesn't it?" I urged.

"You're still my sister." Ora gripped harder. "You're good. Don't let the stories decide your fate..."

I shook her hands away, not bearing to hold them a second longer. "This is reality, Aurora! Whatever this magic is that I hold is dangerous. Why else would even a whisper of someone holding this kind of Wield be an instant death sentence? Who knows how long it'll take before I go mad? I'm just as unreliable as him!"

My breath caught. I closed my eyes, remembering the soft caresses he'd given and the knowing glances from across the room. I shed a tear as I recalled the betrayals. Why was my heart behaving so erratically?

"This doesn't have to be a bad thing," Ora whispered from behind me.

"What doesn't? Me being walking death or us knowing we practically have a ticking time bomb so close to us?"

"Both."

"How could you say that?" I whirled around and stared at her with fire in my eyes.

"Because, sister." Ora laid a gentle hand on my shoulder. "I feel there's a balance around us and that things will be okay. I felt a serene feeling of balance earlier today. Just trust me, please?"

"You're mad," I scoffed. "You're probably going insane before mine sets in."

"Why does this have to be a bad thing?"

"What world are you living in, Aurora? Wake up!" Anger fueled me as I sputtered. "It's written that it causes imbalance. And who knows how much destruction I'll bring? Please, for once, pretend that you give a damn about order and start acting like a queen!"

Ora looked out the window. "It's possible you're just looking for a way for this to be a problem and are now holding *yourself* back." She took a deep inhale as she said, "I'm going to go check on Sury."

"Ora, wait," I called after her, but it was too late. Tension grew in my head as the guilt swelled in my belly. I didn't mean to sound so cruel—I knew she was only trying to help. And maybe she was right.

I heard muffled arguing between her and someone else in the hall as a door slammed before it was quiet again. I followed the sound to see if she was okay and found Peiro standing in the hall with his back against the wall opposite my bedroom.

He stood still, one foot propped on the wall behind him and arms crossed tightly at his chest. His head was angled down like he was staring intently at the carpet beneath his boot. He could have been a statue with how still his body was.

I felt my heart betray me as it skipped a solid beat, while my brain warred and yelled *fool!* at my chest. The pulse behind his deep brown eyes intensified as he caught me stepping toward him. The lines on his face had faded greatly. His hair looked soft, so different than before, and shone where he had tucked loose strands behind one of his ears.

He looked years younger and less weary, yet something hard still held behind his eyes. Eyes that had seen too much.

You do realize what he is, don't you? An abomination. A curse. A liar. The once-inky voice felt deeper, stronger. I felt it slither across my mind and burrow deeper than it had done before.

I blinked through the burrowing feeling as bergamot and mahogany ensnared my senses and warmed my veins. My brain yelled out once again (*imbecile!*) but I found it quieting with each inhale of his scent, which calmed me. In a smooth motion, Peiro pushed off the wall and stood directly in front of me.

His presence wasn't menacing or threatening but simply there, warming my heart. His soft eyes peered down into mine, a look that said everything and nothing at all. The silence grew. He continued to search my eyes, but his lips failed to move.

A moment passed with neither one of us knowing what to say. What could I say? *Why didn't you tell me? How could you not tell me? Didn't I deserve to know? What even are you?*

My Wielding thrummed to be released and to put a great distance between me and this creature that could destroy everything in a matter of moments. I felt that power it tried to unleash. Raw. Relentless. The kind of power that could decimate villages with a snap of its fingers.

And yet my body craved to lean closer, acting like it knew me better than I knew myself. I felt the deep pull. I was drawn to it.

"Good night, Peiro," I said to finally break the silence. I stepped around him to walk down the hall before I felt my hand being grabbed and pulled tight, forcing my body to stay rooted in its spot.

I whirled to find Peiro looking intently into my eyes as if he were searching for my very soul. "I am the same man," he whispered. Pleaded. His face was inches away, allowing me to notice the tiny green patterns in his eyes that I had never seen before, which interestingly helped deepen the softness. Strands of auburn shined through his deep brown hair and fell to the tops of his shoulders in loose waves. My fingers itched to run through the tresses.

The scruff on his face, which also held an auburn sheen, had grown a bit. It cast a tinted shadow across the lower part of his face and outlined his angular jaw sharply. For the first time, I noticed the tiniest of scars around his upper cheek and lower lip. The lips that looked soft and full. I felt my core tighten and turn warm.

Ever so slightly, his mouth quivered like he was trying to make it move on command. Finally, he gently whispered, "I'm sorry. You needed help and I lied."

"We're strangers to one another, you and I. I don't expect a stranger to tell me everything about—"

"No. We're *not* strangers. I don't feel what I feel, this connection, for *strangers*. I know you feel it, too." Peiro shook his head. "I had a duty, my word, and...and I was a coward."

Scared. Wasn't that understandable, though?

"Why didn't you tell me?"

"How could I?" Peiro threw out his arms in frustration. "Would you have believed me?"

"It must be easy knowing you have that thing you can call on. *Ancient One*," I spat.

"Don't you dare call me that!" Peiro snarled. His face was mere inches from mine but I refused to step back. His eyes narrowed and the lines around his eyes dug in deeper. "It's not what anyone thinks it is." The volume of his voice dwindled to a whisper as he closed his eyes to take a cleansing breath.

I scoffed and turned to leave, the anger roaring inside me, needing release.

"Where are you going?" Peiro called out from behind me.

"Out!" I yelled as I stormed down the hall. I heard his footsteps as he ran to catch up.

"Would you have truly believed me, that the very entity you thought was a fairy tale is the demon that lives inside of me?"

I stopped in my tracks, my hand hovering over the front door's handle, then whirled on my feet. I might have had to crane my neck to look in his eyes, but at that moment, I did my best to look down my nose at him. "You could have tried!" I snarled between my teeth. "You knew I needed to find it to save Ora!"

"It's not the weapon you think it is!" Peiro's eyes grew frantic. "It's not a weapon to simply wield against a foe. It's a curse. A curse I didn't ask for." Peiro released a breath.

Irrational anger took root as my skin grew hot—evidence that my emotions were too close to the surface.

"You could have told me!"

"I COULDN'T!" he roared. The veins along his neck thickened as he strained against some invisible force. "It wouldn't *let* me tell you! It recoils around *you*."

I scoffed as I stormed out the door and across the worn grassy path that led around the cabin and toward the destroyed pell. If I didn't release my Wielding soon, I might explode.

Before I reached the clearing, I felt a strong grip around my elbow, yanking me back toward the cabin. My back hit the wall with a hard *thud*, but not enough to hurt. Peiro planted his arms on either side of me against the wall, caging me in. He leaned in close, his nose a breath's width away from mine as he stared down into my eyes.

"I've been in bed with the devil for far too long." His voice was practically a whisper. "It does what it wants. It makes me witness the vile and atrocious things it craves, and nothing. Will. Satiate. Its. Cravings." I saw the real fear in his eyes. My hand found the warmth of his forearm before I could register what my body was doing.

"It hates being caged and punishes *me* for caging it in here." He pointed to his head. "And here," he said, this time pointing to his body. "And here." His voice whispered again as he pointed to his heart. "In my time chained to it, it's only felt true fear once. And that was a couple of months ago."

"What changed?"

"You. You, *Naa'n le'ya*. You've given me hope. It knows that. And that scares me."

I scoffed. "And how did I give you hope? What did I do that was so special?"

"It knows that *you're* the key to controlling it."

My head rushed as I realized I had been holding my breath. My words were lost as my heart pounded against my chest so loud that I was sure he could hear it. The anger that had boiled inside me became chaotic and ricocheted within my body. I couldn't control it. Each wave grew and crashed into one another. The feeling I've grown to know as my rising Wielding swallowed me, demanding to be released.

I listened to its command and broke through Peiro's loose cage. I aimed my hands toward the already shattered pell and released every bit of my Wielding, barely touching the *illicitus*. An agonizing scream pierced behind me. I looked over my shoulder to see Peiro clutching his temples as his eyes shimmered from deep browns to a hazy gray to a piercing silver.

The realization hit. Those were not Wielder's eyes.

I pulled back the stream of power and turned my body toward him, ready to take a step forward to help him as I've always been so ready to do—but stopped in my tracks when his eyes snapped up. I saw it then. This wasn't fully Peiro that I was looking at. I could sense it now. Feel it.

It must have shown on my face because he said, "My, my, now you get it." His voice was rough like Peiro's with the hint of some hidden elegance and an accent from another language. Another time.

"Let him go," I demanded.

"But we would miss all this fun, wouldn't we?" He cocked his head a little to the side and rose to his full height.

"What do you want?" I found myself asking before I could stop.

He shook his head and wagged his finger at me. "We don't want to give everything away so soon, do we? Why do you think he was so ecstatic when poor little Peiro ran into the teal-eyed princess? So willing to help you escape from Zonnagberg?" It paused. "He felt something I had successfully avoided for so long. Everything was going to plan until you threatened us and forced me to crawl back to this place I hate. Until Peiro regained his wits enough to return here."

"You want me. Don't you?" The thing inside Peiro gave a twisted smile that sent the wrong sort of shivers down my spine. "It wasn't Ora that Dokvalon wanted." I gambled a thought and took steady steps forward until I was right in front of him.

"We could be powerful, you know? Have a partnership. We can rule over Dokvalon and Gria together. He would very much like to be by your side. He can't hide what he wants from me. I know him better than he knows himself." The smile twisted crueler as his eyes flashed to an iridescent hue.

I steadied my hand to rest on the panels of Peiro's tunic, feeling his skin rapidly cooling as this thing dug its claws deeper into him. I let my hand climb up his chest and cup his jaw as tenderly as I could, feeling my body pull in. "I would very much like that," I whispered, bringing myself to the tips of my toes, angling my mouth toward his.

The thing smiled at me. I could see it now, how this smile differed from the genuine one I've come to know from the man beneath. His was warmth and sunshine. Strength. Curiosity. This one was malice and ice. Sneering. Vindictive.

My Wielding thrashed wildly inside me. "There's just one problem," I whispered to his lips. "I never wanted to rule." As soon as the words left, I brought the *illicitus* to the surface, just enough to hum underneath my skin, illuminating my palm in a shadowed silver glow. It was just the amount I needed to earn a reaction from Peiro, but not enough to make him lose consciousness.

"Leave us," I commanded, in a voice not quite my own.

A single tear fell from my eyes and I watched Peiro silently scream as he fell to his knees. I fell with him, cupping both my hands around his face as I let my Wielding hum. His eyes flickered wide, allowing me to watch the glowing silvers dull rapidly back into their deep, warm browns.

Peiro's body slumped forward but he caught himself with one hand. The other gripped mine, which was still on his face. He coughed viciously as he worked to steady his erratic breathing into a moderate rhythm. His head snapped up and he locked his wild eyes onto mine as he blinked, trying to bring himself back to the present.

"Did it hurt you?" he panted, shifting on his knees, cupping his other hand around mine. He didn't wait for my answer as he looked me over, inspecting my skin.

"No. No. It didn't hurt me." My breathing matched his, deep and heavy. "Are you alright?" The question was meant to drive much deeper than the surface. Because I saw it—the amount of control the entity had on this man. That knowledge hurt my very soul.

"You did it." Peiro looked at me in wonder and awe, in joy and relief, right before his lips crashed into mine. My body seized, the feel of his body leaning into mine surprisingly warm. My shoulders and arms relaxed as I leaned in deeper and placed my hands on his chest to steady myself.

Large hands wrapped around my waist and gently pulled me in closer, tighter. One hand let go and found its way to my neck, lightly cupping my jaw. The act tipped my head up more. His fingertips felt featherlight, almost too afraid of what was happening.

I leaned in more.

The invite ignited the man before me and his soft lips parted mine. We shared a breath as our tongues slowly danced together. He tasted smoky with something sweet on the back end. A light moan escaped my throat that would have been embarrassing if it weren't for Peiro pulling me in tighter.

His kiss turned from gentle and comforting into something starving. His tongue coated mine like he was trying to quench a longtime thirst. His fingers curled into my hair while his hand squeezed tighter around my waist. In one quick motion, without losing our connection, Peiro shifted me to my back upon the ground where we had kneeled.

The sensation of his body being pushed against mine was almost overwhelming. I had never kissed anyone like this before. There was that one time with that one advisor, but it was nothing like this. I mentally kicked myself for even thinking of that one time with that one advisor and redirected my thoughts on the man before me.

Another moan escaped me before I could reel it back in. The sound made Peiro release his hold from my hair and slowly cascade his fingertips down my neck and arm, silhouetting the curve of my breast.

Peiro's hips pinned me harder to the ground, his mouth never breaking its hold on my lips. I felt his hard outline along my inner thigh, which only ignited my own excitement further. My body rolled delicately, striving to find friction against him to help relieve the sensitive area that had coiled so tightly. His other hand that was settled on my waist moved forward to where my trousers were tied. Tension swelled deep in my belly.

The air around us became warm. Almost too warm.

I wanted this, didn't I?

My brain and heart battled one another. I wanted this. Wanted him. I couldn't explain it, but something inside me just *knew*. He sparked something deep within me that called to me like nothing else ever had.

Peiro tore his lips from mine and landed his hungry mouth on my neck. The lap and pulls of his tongue and teeth sent fresh waves of heat down my spine. My core tightened as liquid heat pooled. Yes, I wanted this.

He was naturally quiet, yes. Stoic even. And the playful moments and banter with Fyom easily took away years of emotion from his hard features.

The glimpses of happiness and joy I saw on his face were as beautiful as gems and also as rare. I could see the torment. Understand it even. But before I gave my body, I needed answers. Why press on loyalty, then shun saving the queen? Why say the plan was folly only to execute it on his own, while withholding it from me?

How is the Ancient One inside him? And why? Common sense finally overtook me. I shook my head in frustration, knowing this moment was about to come to an end.

"Tomorrow," I finally stammered. "We'll talk tomorrow."

Peiro's touch froze as he heard the underlying command to stop. With a final slow peck in the spot between my neck and shoulder, he slowly lifted his head and stretched his fingers, letting go and shifting back to his knees.

In a soft motion, he grabbed my hand to help me stand and held it firm for a moment before letting go. "Tomorrow," he said as he walked backwards toward the cabin door, never taking his eyes off mine.

Stupid, stupid, stupid, I kept whispering to myself as I mustered the courage to reenter the cabin and got ready for bed.

Thoughts swirled in my head like a rushing waterfall—thoughts of Ora, thoughts of what to do about the kingdom and the Ancient One, thoughts of Peiro and where his lips could travel. What his touch could explore.

Idiot! I hissed to myself again, then had the worst sleep in months.

CHAPTER 31

A soft, distant pecking noise pulled me out of my fitful sleep. I could feel the bags under my heavy eyes as I looked for the source of the relentless pecking. Without a warning, Ora sprang through the bedroom door with a small tray in her hands.

"How long are you going to make me wait?" she said as she twirled through the room, glowing like the sun. She seemed so full of life again. With swiftness, she began opening the curtains, letting the sun's rays shine into the room and right on my face.

I hissed as the beams of sun hit my eyes and threw a pillow in Ora's direction before taking another to smother my own face from the light. "Looks like you slept just as well as I did," she said as she banged and clattered around the room to purposely annoy me, just like she did back when we had adjoining rooms in Grianmore.

"I thought I missed you," I breathed harshly into the pillow. "How did you grow more annoying? Why are you even awake at this hour?"

"It's the afternoon, *Princess*. You have to wake up sooner or later. We have a kingdom to save, after all."

"And why are you always so *cheery*?" I groaned in my pillow.

Ora stopped whatever she was doing and threw the pillow meant for her back to me, hitting her target. "You've already missed breakfast and Fyom's been waiting for you. Peiro and I had a nice little *chat* this morning and he agreed to train us. I mean, I guess *he* of all people would understand how we should be trained."

"You two...talked?" I huffed inside the pillow.

"We did. About many things, really. And we came to an understanding of sorts. In fact, he's on his way here now, wondering why it's taking you so long to come out of your room."

At that mention, I popped my head up to look around the room, then sprang to my feet to change my clothes and fix my hair into a very messy braid.

Ora laughed behind her closed fists. "I knew it! You *are* smitten!"

The sudden realization that Peiro was *not* indeed on his way to my room and that it was only Ora's ruse made my cheeks turn bright pink. "Oh! YOU!" I yelled, and chased Ora out of the room.

The sound of laughter filled the gaps of the cabin and echoed off the walls—a merriment that neither of us had felt since our parents had become ill. It was strange but in this moment I could feel *peace*, despite the chaos around us.

I chased Ora out of the cabin and into the clearing and sunshine. The air was warm but a light breeze was enough to whisk away the heat. Neither of us noticed Fyom standing near the clearing's edge and we nearly ran into him, and one another.

Fyom looked down at us both and simply smiled. "It is good to have such joy back in this cabin. For a time there was too much solitude and silence."

"Thank you again for talking to me this morning. Your help for your kingdom will not go unrewarded. I promise you that," Ora said and placed her hand over her heart.

Fyom slightly bowed his head. "You are still my queen here, Your Majesty."

I could only look at him.

While I was indeed grateful for his help and echoed the sentiments of my sister, I couldn't help but feel misled. Fyom must have sensed the reluctance as he turned toward me. He raised an eyebrow as he looked down and assessed, like he were inspecting a foreign specimen.

A deep sound vibrated within his chest and his shoulders slightly shook, the corners of his mouth turning up. The sound grew deeper and his shoulders bounced faster as a deep chuckle escaped and turned into a booming laugh.

"It looks like you and I are the hardheaded ones of the group," he said with a large white smile. "Please accept my deeply humble apology for what transpired yesterday." He placed his hand over his heart once again and tilted his head forward.

I just stood there.

Can you really trust him? What else could he be hiding? That voice slithered across my mind again.

Fyom lifted back to full height, practically casting a shadow down on us. His smile faded fast and his eyes turned serious. "Please know, I would have said something sooner but I'm bound by my word through the *chinsaya*. I promised him I would never speak of his story and what's involved. And you know anyone bound by *chinsaya* would only welcome extreme consequences if it's broken."

The ire that held a steady flame inside my chest diminished as I heard the urgency and empathy behind his words. It was true that the consequences were extreme. Stories of people losing everything from their limbs to their lives if they broke the bonded promise.

A sharp pain shot through my ribs and as I turned my head to see Ora elbowing me in the side. She tilted her head toward me, quietly nudging some sort of silent message. I only rolled my eyes, silently communicating back the way sisters do.

I cleared my throat. "I guess I can understand." My natural curiosity of course began to peck forward, but I resisted the rising questions in my mind. Instead, I stuck out my hand, offering it to Fyom. The gentle behemoth took my smaller hand in his and shook. A smile etched itself upon my face as I let go and turned to the direction where Fyom had stood before we ran into him.

Wielding bowls were set about on their stands once again. Each bowl held the same pieces I'd used when I retested the will of my Wielding power.

"What would you like me to try next?" I asked Fyom.

"Actually, I was hoping that perhaps your sister would be willing to try another test."

Ora looked at us, confused. "Me? What do you mean *retest?* I thought once we tested that it was complete?"

I shook my head. "Ariadne is not who she says she is. Actually, we don't really know who Ariadne is. Fyom recalls her being at the temple, at the same age she is now, when he went through his testing."

Ora stood there in shock and wonder, trying to decipher this new revelation.

"Do you think if she was lying about me that she could be lying about Ora, too? Even though she tested high?"

"After yesterday, I have strong suspicions that there's even more to our queen's story. If there is some truth to uncover, this could help us begin to understand why you have been magically suppressed and why they were after you, or your sister."

"What do I need to do?" Ora asked.

Fyom pointed his large hand toward the center of the ring. "This will look and feel very much like what you encountered those years ago, but I would like to see it for myself. If you please, Your Majesty."

Ora waved her hand in annoyance. "Call me Ora, for *now*," she said with a wink, and walked toward the circle.

"You and your sister are not much for titles, are you?" Fyom mused as he followed behind her.

I stood outside the ring at a healthy distance, but still close enough to observe and listen.

Very carefully, Fyom explained the meanings of each bowl as a reminder to Ora, but to also share his intention with the retesting. "I'm curious if you and your sister share more traits than what meets the eye. If you can, Your Majesty..." Ora shot him a dirty look. "Ora. If you can, *Ora,* please work through every bowl, including the seventh."

"The seventh? Are you sure? That's dark magic!"

"It doesn't have to be a bad thing." I echoed her words back to her.

"Will it hurt?"

I shook my head.

Ora cocked her eyebrow before breezing through the first five bowls. At the sixth bowl, she was in her element of the sun. At ease, she was able to harness the beams and fling her magic in the air and around her, dancing with familiarity.

The trusted golden ribbons wove between the stands and bowls, fluttering to the trees and fractured light, emitting soft rainbows along the ground. The leaves turned a vibrant shade as the ribbons slightly caressed each one before finding their way between birds' wings and through blades of grass.

As quickly as her smile radiated on her face, it quickly disappeared. The golden ribbons of power vanished as if nothing had been there, leaving everything it had touched in a vibrant state. Ora stared off into the distance, not looking at anything in particular. Her shoulders began to shake as her eyes welled with tears. She dropped to the ground and began to cry.

Without hesitation, I ran to her with a quick embrace. "What's wrong?"

"I thought they were so close to taking it," she stammered. "My magic. I never knew how much I took this for granted."

I wiped away a stray tear with the sleeve of my shirt. "No more. They will never get that close to you again. They will never lie to us again without consequence. They will not strip away this kingdom that our mother and her family have worked so hard to build." My jaw tensed as I felt my teeth clench with each word.

Ora nodded and centered herself, returning to the sixth bowl—the one that held the essence of the celestials. Without another word, Ora dove into her magic to call on the sunstone. The vibrant yellow rock viciously vibrated and lifted into the air, rotating in circles like it was a tiny sun itself. The rays and fractured light glowed against Ora's skin, making her appear as if she herself were sparkling.

Ora beamed before gazing back at the other bowls. "What am I to do now?"

"I believe this is where your sister can come in to teach." Fyom cast his soft gaze in my direction.

"Me? But I only just learned!"

"Exactly!" Fyom said with vigor. "Help guide her in what you experienced and see what she can do. If my suspicions are indeed correct... And I'm hardly ever wrong..."

"Stand here, Aurora," I said as I stepped toward the final bowl. "Focus on your sun magic and dive. If you feel the nudge to dive further, don't stop. Dive deeper than you have ever allowed yourself. There are no blocks. No barricades. No one here to tell you *no.* Swim in the magic and allow it to Wield for you!"

"And where has this part of my sister been my whole life? I like this newfound confidence." Ora winked again before placing her focus on the solitary seed meant to signify the beginnings of life.

I stepped back, allowing Ora as much room as possible, not knowing what to expect.

Ora stood in silence and closed her eyes. Her hands delicately hovered over the bowl and she stretched her fingers. A soft golden essence escaped from her fingertips, clearly showcasing how in tune she was with her Wield from her celestial source. But the seed remained untouched inside the bowl.

She cracked open an eye, seeing that nothing had changed. "What is it supposed to do?" A frown crept down her face. "Maybe you're mistaken?"

I looked at Fyom, who had his large arms folded, scratching his chin with one hand.

"There has to be another block. Another fog," Fyom said.

Stepping closer, I looked at the bowl. "When you tested, do you remember anything Ariadne might have said to you? Or maybe even over the course of your training?"

She looked baffled as she stood there, deep in thought. "The only thing that comes to mind is that she seemed so confident in what my source was going to be before I even stepped up to the bowls."

"What did she say?"

Ora brought her hands to her face and rubbed before letting go of a deep sigh. "She said this was the end for the Endromeon line." I thought that statement was something curious to tell a small child. "She said that at least one person in the royal line *has* to Wield high, Wield strong, in order to continue the reign. And she said she could see in my eyes what I could truly Wield. Matter of fact, we bypassed the Elementis altogether and simply focused on the Spiritus and celestial sources, and that lasted only a handful of moments."

So that's why Aurora had come back to the castle so quickly after her testing, I remembered. The test itself was rigged. But did it really matter if she still tested higher than the average Wielder?

"And that's all we've focused on since. Adding in light lessons on Elementis and such, but she emphasized and repeated only on the celestial."

"As soon as you showed the sun's essence, she simply stopped your testing?"

"Well, yes. I proved I could Wield a high source. What else was there to prove?"

I looked at Fyom over my shoulder, beginning to understand, before turning back to Ora. "Try the seed again."

Ora raised her eyebrow. "And do what with it?"

"Make it come to life, Ora."

A light laugh came out of her throat. "The *illicitus*? Really?" She looked at us both in disbelief. "Oh my giants. You two are serious!"

"Trust me," I said as I clasped my hands into hers. A hum vibrated against the skin where mine met hers. "I don't know why this is happening, but we're trying to figure out the source behind everything. This can help us understand the reasons *why*."

"But I'll go mad. The *illicitus* brings the madness!"

I sighed. "We don't know that either. For all we know it could be a ploy to deter people from even trying." I hoped. "Plus, it doesn't have to be a bad thing, right?" I smirked knowingly.

Ora narrowed her eyes. "Fine."

"Good. Now imagine your well. Imagine the barrier that you delve from. See that essence. Touch it. Dive deeper. Imagine it continuing to inch forward, just beyond reach, until you simply can't anymore. Until you feel like your very chest might burst. Go past what Ariadne has told you for years. You know your own limits."

She nodded in understanding and closed her eyes again. I stepped back next to Fyom.

Ora tilted her head up toward the sky and let the sun's rays shine down on her golden face. The wind around her began to turn, letting her loose strands ripple with each gust. The blondes and browns in her hair began to glow brightly and sparkle like bright gems.

A faint yellow aura enclosed her and rhythmically moved with her heartbeat, growing bolder in color. The sun's light above her intensified like they were feeding the air around her. A faint green sheen could be seen around the outside of the aura before melting back into the golds.

I gasped when I saw the tiny seed begin to vibrate and ascend into the air. Piece by piece, the seed began to unravel its outer hull to reveal tiny green life. In the air, the seed began to sprout and form tiny roots. Ever so slightly, it grew taller and new leaves sprouted from the stem. The plant grew a small bud from its stem and, petal by petal, began to uncurl to display its beautiful white blossom with a bright yellow middle. The solitary flower dipped and bobbed in the wind and began to shake. More tiny seeds appeared from the flower and balanced in the air beside it. Steadily each seed turned into a new flower until a massive bouquet hung in the air.

"New life," Fyom whispered beside me. We were in awe as we watched Ora, whose eyes were still closed and unaware of what was taking place.

Neither Fyom nor I dared to say anything, as we were both equally curious just how much control Ora had on the newfound magic she was diving into. Finally, she fluttered her eyes open and her smile reached the very corner of her eye's creases.

One by one, on instinct, Ora silently whispered to the flowers to arrange themselves in a beautiful bundle, all tied together using one of the stems, and it landed delicately in her hands.

"Phe! Did you see that?" Ora squealed in excitement and ran to me with the flowers on display.

"You were magnificent!" I beamed down at my sister.

"So I have the ability to Wield life?" Her brows furrowed together. "None of this makes sense to me. No one has heard of a Life Wielder in centuries!"

"And no one has dealt with a Death Wielder since that age, too."

"Because history states that if any were found, they would be sent to the gallows," Fyom replied.

Ora gave me an intriguing look. "The sun and the moon. Life and death. We can master them all?"

Fyom gently stroked his chin and chuckled. "It would seem."

"But no one should be able to control life *or* death," I said in a cold defiance. "How this came about in the first place..."

"That's what we need to figure out—what happened to those keys. And if this has something to do with the raid." With that, Fyom turned on his heel and stormed back to his cabin, surely to bury himself in his library once more.

But keys? I'd never heard anything about Wielding and keys, outside of his tale about the giants.

"This is too exciting not to try and figure out, though! Think of all the good we could do. What we could restore! The wars we could win! I'll see if I can help him search," Ora said before skipping off behind him with the bouquet still in hand.

"But you've *barely* read our own kingdom laws! You're going to read *now*?" I called behind her. Ora turned her head and stuck out her tongue.

While having the ability to contain life in one's hand *sounded* like a good thing, what about death? What then could death control? Control. That was the underlying concern though it all and what sparked so many generations to grow their paranoia and fear.

I ruminated on the idea and perhaps began to understand why the first laws revolved around this being illegal and unnatural, and why it was indeed deemed the *illicitus*.

My mind came back to the present when I heard people talking and saw Peiro and Ora in a quiet exchange. Peiro had been continuing his training again, each day appearing stronger and faster than the one before. Every day his muscular frame became more defined. I was happy to see he'd decided to wear a cream-colored tunic today instead of opting to train in just his pants and boots.

I needed to focus and not think about the night before. Not think about the fullness of his mouth and how his hands felt when...

Stop it, I hissed to myself as I watched him and my sister exchange words I couldn't make out. He towered over her and nodded with a soft chuckle. Ora simply smiled and extended her bundle of flowers for Peiro to take. He rustled through them, taking a single stem from the bouquet's middle before turning to walk toward me in the clearing. Ora quickly turned her head to give me a quick wink and a wiggle from her brow, then disappeared inside.

I rolled my eyes and turned my attention back to the bowls in front of me, trying to ignore that Peiro stood so close beside me.

"What was that about?" I asked, refusing to look up.

"Your sister is very fond of you...and protective."

"That she is," I mumbled. "Did you see her a moment ago? She was magnificent. I've seen her Wield many times before but today was the brightest she's ever glowed."

"Hmm. I prefer the glow of the moon. She's beautiful, serene, maybe even a bit mysterious."

"All that in the moon?" I asked, finally looking up and finding him staring back at me.

"No. You." He smirked and held out the single flower for me to take while extending his other hand. "Come. I owe you answers."

He sat on the ground in the same clearing that looked toward the mountains that used to keep Dokvalon at bay, and drew in one knee to rest an arm on top of it.

I sat close beside him with my knees drawn to my chest, waiting for Peiro to find the words.

CHAPTER 32

The clouds overhead provided the perfect amount of shade as we stared off in the distance. I found myself subconsciously smelling the center of the flower, inhaling its delicate scent.

"May I?" Peiro leaned in, taking the flower from my hand and gently placing the stem in my hair above my ear. His fingertips lightly brushed my ear as he tucked loose strands of hair behind it. I leaned into the touch, savoring the feel of his warm skin.

His eyes had faded from their browns to a honey-hued color. I shied away with a smile and nonchalantly played with the blades of grass around us. We sat there for a moment, welcoming one another's company as the clouds rolled by.

"When I was much younger, times were different," he began slowly. "Different kings and rulers of lands."

Different kings? Confusion creased my forehead, because my ancestors had united these lands over a century ago.

Peiro continued. "There was a race to find this *myth* of raw magic. Magic, said to be shaped into anything the Wielder needs it to be, regardless of the source. It was said this magic laid the foundation for Wielders. The origin. Of course this was desired by everyone, Wielder and ruler, since they said it could be shaped into *anything*."

I remained silent, trying to recall the tale Peiro recounted, but nothing came to mind.

"The king's banner I served under was just as curious as anyone and didn't care about any warnings or consequences given by his inner counsel. He sent five of his best men, all Veiks, to search for this *raw* magic and bring it back to him. He was a cruel king, so one can only imagine what he wanted it for. It was guessed he wanted to unite the lands himself and be an emperor of sorts.

"There was a strong theory that those who were born without magical ability could not do anything with this token of raw power, and that we were the safest bet to fetch and retrieve. Like the dogs we were." An emotion flashed across his face just fast enough for me to notice but not catch.

"We searched far and wide until we came across a place where this *thing* was rumored to be true. It was said Graevick touched this relic, but we didn't know what we were looking for. We were only told we would feel the pull of the power. Some of the men thought we were on a pointless mission, that our king was as mad as people claimed, while others suspected we were really sent to bring back gold. Gold for a failing king, whose children and court visited the coffers a little too much. How wrong we all were in our assumptions."

"What king did you serve?" I was determined to break holes in this preposterous-sounding story.

"King Jaris Ailethian." Peiro huffed in annoyance at the name. The tendons in his forearm feathered as he flexed his hand.

"*Ailethian?*" I sat quietly, trying to recount the kingdoms I'd learned about in the history classes I personally found fascinating, while Ora often dozed off or flirted with whatever young guard was present. "But the last Ailethian to rule was centuries ago. That bloodline is the predecessor to the King of Dokvalon. Their line was drawn on the map the same time as Gria. You're honestly saying that you're..."

"Hundreds of years old?" Peiro looked at me with mocking disbelief in his eyes. I saw the color of his eyes muddle further, almost to their gray color.

"This is mad," I said in disbelief. "You're serious?"

"So we've..." He stopped and closed his eyes as he worked through something in his mind. "*I've* been told." Another shudder coursed through Peiro's body. He looked away but the tension in his body gave away the pain he endured.

"How old were you when this happened?" Fascination coursed through me.

"Thirty-six." He smirked. "Do we... Do *I* look good for my age?" He chuckled, actually chuckled, as he playfully nudged my shoulder with his own.

My mind couldn't wrap itself around this piece of knowledge and how he seemed frozen in time.

"You're speaking in *we* again?" My heart dropped, knowing the entity inside him was drawing strength once more.

Peiro nodded as he placed his hand on top of mine. "Sometimes it'll stay in the far corners of my mind. Other times it roars back, fighting harder."

I squeezed his hand tighter, trying to bring a sense of comfort to his pain. He produced a small vial of liquid from his pocket, similar to the one I saw Fyom give to him the day of our arrival, and emptied the contents into his mouth. The tension noticeably rolled off of him in waves.

"Does that help?" I nodded to the now-empty vial.

"That has been my saving grace. I had never been so thankful as I was when I found Fyom."

"What does it do?" I couldn't stop the overflow of questions pouring through me, begging to know this man more.

"It keeps the headaches at bay so I don't have to *use,* as Sury was so quick to point out."

"Then why did you?"

A moment passed. I didn't think Peiro was going to answer. His large shoulders rose as he inhaled deeply before answering. "It had been a long time since I'd been able to visit Fyom. I'd hurt many around me and didn't want to risk hurting him or his family. So, I sought to soothe the aches myself. Thought I could find control. I was very wrong."

A pang of sorrow dove through my chest. This entity I once sought to help my sister was indeed a curse, and anyone with a heart could see how much pain it brought upon this man. The courage it must take for him to open up so willingly made my heart grow. He could have told me any lie to simply save himself from his story, but he seemingly chose to share everything.

"You said King Ailethian sent Veiks. But your eyes...?"

Peiro simply nodded his head before continuing. "The Ancient One. We found what the king wanted but the myths and legends were wrong. It can be Wielded by *anyone*, even by those who are unwilling." He turned his head a little toward me, just as a silver glow flickered across his eyes.

"What happened?" I whispered.

"It was in a cave, where my men wanted to rest, of all places. It had to be an ugly fate that led us there." A mix between a chuckle and growl came from his throat. "I think we were called to that cave. As we all tried to sleep, we kept hearing whispers and voices that lured us further in. We had one torch left to guide us. I'm not really sure how far back we'd gone when we found this *thing*. It looked like a simple dark stone. Just sitting there on a boulder."

My eyebrows rose. I scooted closer until the sides of our bodies touched.

"The whispers grew stronger in some of the men's hearts and minds. They started fighting amongst one another. The others and I tried pulling them apart, but each seemed to grow desperate to fight the man beside him. Before I knew it," he paused, "that thing, that rock, had been pushed over and cracked. A bright white light burst from those cracks and startled us with how quickly the cave became illuminated. Then it happened."

A soft breeze tickled my face as Peiro stared at the mountains and I at him.

"That thing that you saw the other day came from that light. We tried running away but it was too quick. Broken bodies and sounds of screams filled the cavern. Before I knew it, that thing had grabbed me and then, it was in my head, whispering these awful things in my ear. But I listened. It was like I had no control over what I was anymore. My eyes saw my hands taking my men's lives, the men that trusted me. It felt like a terrible nightmare."

"Why did it choose you?"

Peiro shrugged. "In all our years together, I've never been able to piece together that riddle. I just know this thing that you seek is nothing good." He spat. "This isn't raw magic to be Wielded at will, like people thought. This isn't something that can be morphed. Something to be tamed. Something to be used at one's will. This is something else."

"What did the king do once you returned?"

"I didn't. From what I had heard, the king became so irate that he fabricated that the story of this raw power was just that—a story. He convinced everyone that it was a child's tale sent from another land. But I knew that *he knew* it was still out there. I knew he still hunted."

A moment passed as I processed what he had shared. It felt like my entire world had been stripped and turned over, again. For my whole life, I was told I would amount to nothing. Was told stories of how urthens weren't real, that they were simply scary fictional beasts that roamed the roads to keep children in their beds.

Made-up tales about how the Ancient One would roam and discipline naughty boys and girls.

All had been a lie. But why?

Did my mother and father know of these lies? Were they part of the fabrications? Surely the queen of Gria had to know what was out there. Her court had to have known.

Did Sury's father know and refuse to tell me? How far did these lies go?

"You said it's nothing good, but I can tell that *you* are good. Your actions speak it. You helped me and Sury get here. You rescued Ora. There has to be something there, right?"

He remained silent for a heartbeat before drawing in a deep breath. "It's made me do great and terrible things. Things I cannot be redeemed from, no matter how many good things I do."

"I don't believe that." Without thinking, I curled my arm around his, pulling in closer. "Everyone can have redemption. A new page in their story."

A light huff escaped his chest. "Does it count if it made me kill my own family?"

The confession struck me hard. I quickly realized I'd been holding my breath when I witnessed a single tear escape Peiro's eyes. Tension radiated off his shoulders, his knuckles turning white as he gripped at the ground. I could feel the light trembles of his body as he tried to remain stoic.

Instinct made me curl my hand tighter around his, giving him encouragement for his story. The strength to let him know wasn't alone. A sense of forgiveness even if he couldn't forgive himself.

"Every day I miss them. It took me months to get back to them after it happened. I thought during my time alone I could control this *thing* inside me. I sang the songs my wife loved the most to keep the whispers at bay, and I thought I was winning. It fooled me into thinking I could control it."

More tears ran down his face as his breath became more ragged.

"My wife immediately noticed something was wrong, even as I reassured her I was okay. You would have liked her—Talia was her name. It wasn't uncommon for Wielders and Veiks to marry back then. She was a spark. Her skin reminded me of the richest earth and her dark blue eyes matched. I tried every day to act normal, but the whispers grew. I tried finding solace in my children's eyes, my two daughters and my son—who was barely running steady on his own feet and showed the early signs of Wielding fire."

He paused his story as his mind's eyes traveled to a faraway place. A wide smile grew on his face, almost reaching his eyes. I could only imagine that he must have mentally gone back to that life, seeing his wife. His children. I barely breathed for fear I would disrupt the rare happiness I saw etched on his rugged features.

I started to wonder what his children looked like. Did his daughters have full lips like his? Did his son have the bold brow and sharp jaw that he did? Or perhaps his smaller eyes and sharp nose? Did they have rich brown skin like their mother or something in between?

More moments passed before Peiro's distant smile dropped. His eyes saw something of horror and terror as he looked out at nothing in the distance.

"Then something clicked."

I felt a wall of tears form and fall from my eyes. The shimmer matched the glint of the silver hoops along his ear. Without understanding why, I gave him another reassuring squeeze and held.

"Like in the cave, I saw my hands and my sword, but something was driving my body. Brehm, my oldest daughter, was the closest to me and I saw the life behind her dark blue eyes, her mother's eyes, fade. I heard my wife screaming as she ran toward me. I found my son, Calum, hiding. His older sister, Thea, attacked me, trying to make me stop."

The walls around his stoic nature cracked. I held his hand steady as his body began to shake. The tears rolled quickly now. I could only guess how long he had held this side of him in. Could only guess how few people knew of his story. Now I understood the meaning behind the tattooed bands on his arm.

"I remember seeing my family's eyes before I blacked out." His voice had grown to a hoarse whisper. "When I came to, I saw what I had done to Talia and Brehm. Through the destruction by my hand, I couldn't find Thea or Calum. I didn't want to." He paused, trying to find the next words. "So I ran like a coward. Ran and ran, fighting this thing inside me.

"For years I wandered and waited until Ailethian was dead. I filled my cup, unable to quench my thirst. Abused every substance known to man but nothing blocked out what I saw in my mind. I ran through body after body, desperate for warmth. Desperate to satisfy my flesh. But all I could see was Talia. Decades passed and I was sure the notion to find this *thing* was lost, but I was wrong."

I finally found my voice, carefully speaking up. "What do you mean?"

"Ailethian's successors kept the knowledge alive and kept searching as that kingdom expanded. I had stayed far away. Something lured me back to my home. When I came back to revisit where I lived, somehow they just knew what I was and captured me in shackles.

"I remained their slave for a very long time while the kingdom you know as Dokvalon grew. For years, I was in their experiment rooms, until they figured out how to unleash the Ancient One. I don't know how they did it but they did. Made it...made me...do the king's bidding. Assassinations, theft, manipulation, torture were just a few of my skills I was called upon to use.

"All until one day about thirty years ago"—a small spark lit behind his eyes—"I broke free. The old door loosened, and I've been running ever since. So you see, Phe, I'm not afraid of any wars you might wage against my sins. I've been battling myself for a very long time."

We let the silence take over as we stared off to the mountains, watching the sun set. I wasn't sure what to say. What could words really do for this kind of revelation? He was in pain. A pain I couldn't begin to fathom or understand. Your family ripped away from you, yes. But by your own hands?

And it was so clear how much of a fight he put up to find control. I had assumed he could simply control this entity and wanted to keep the knowledge for himself.

Oh, how I was a fool.

"Where does Fyom come into the picture? How do you know him so well?" I looked at Peiro and traced the lines around his temples and jaw with my eyes. A side smile crept up, enhancing the lines I was growing to admire. A small chuckle escaped from his breath before he replied.

"For years I wandered, consorted with Wielders of all kinds, to find anything to stop the voice in my head and to keep that *thing* at bay without divulging too much about what I really was. Nothing ever helped, not even the gilliflower. For so long I sought Healers, shamans who claimed they walked with the giants, anyone to rid me of this. They all proved what I already knew—it's impossible. It's now a part of me, like a disease. Like a curse with no cure. I was going mad. Until one day...I bumped into this young man, about your age at the time, who had the same bright green eyes as my daughter Thea.

"He was in Zonnagberg working in a Healer's shop when I saw him conversing with another man about a trade. He didn't look familiar to me at all, but his eyes...his eyes spoke to me. For years I came to him, explaining my intense headaches and body pains, and for years he created something to help.

"I always picked and prodded about who his family was and never recognized any names he spoke. He started catching on that he was aging and I was not, so I decided to break away and hide. I wandered aimlessly, using the last vial of tonic he had given me before I fell back into old habits. Anything to take away that pestering voice inside my head. *Anything.*"

I squeezed his arm tighter, reaffirming that I was listening. Fully, with no judgments.

"Drugs. Alcohol. Women..." Peiro said cautiously. "Nothing. Nothing helped and I knew it didn't. I was desperate for anything to stop it. I tried my own hand at stopping it and failed every time. I didn't know night from day as I wandered through fields and forests. It lets me starve but it won't let me die.

"So, fast forward a few more years. Fyom finds me half conscious in the woods, not too far from where we are now, and brings me into his home. His late wife helped nurse me back to health, while his sons fetched whatever they needed."

"He has a family?"

Peiro nodded. "Yes. His wife was lovely. She passed from a fever about ten years ago. His sons left soon after to start their own lives. They visit every now and again."

"Do they know about you like he does?"

He shook his head. "That, I'm afraid, has been only his and my secret. I can tell when one of them is on their way to visit and I make my exit for a while. It has given me abilities not many men or Wielders possess."

"Is that how you were able to reach Ora the way you did?" Peiro slowly nodded, letting out a deep exhale as I continued to press. "How did Fyom find out about *the* Ancient One? Did you tell him?"

"Unfortunately, he's seen it before. At my absolute weakest it can overpower me and take over. Fyom was able to contain it somehow, and since then has been experimenting with his Healing to help keep it and the headaches at bay. To a degree."

"Why has he always kept your secret? Knowing what he knows, anyone would have sold that knowledge back to Dokvalon."

"Well, I forced him to make the *chinsaya*. But it also turns out, he's my distant grandson."

I was stunned into silence. "Wait. What? But he..."

"He doesn't *look* like me? He favors Talia's lineage."

My curiosity bubbled to its threshold, the energy forcing me to move and shift to my knees directly in front of him. I was eager to learn more. "How did you find out?"

"In his study."

I huffed at the snippets of detail and was exploding inside to know the full story. I bit my tongue to stop from asking the plethora of questions that swirled in my mind.

"You're quite adorable when your heart rate starts fluttering. It brings up the simplest shade of pink to your cheeks and brings out more of the teal hues in your eyes."

I rolled my eyes and smacked Peiro on the shoulder. "You're doing this on purpose!"

Peiro gave a hefty laugh before continuing. "Seeing just how impatient you get is rather...*cute*."

"Do not call me *cute* and hurry up with your damn story! How did you find out you two were related?"

With a smirk, he replied, "Have you seen his library? Fyom has a vast gift of knowledge and research. He said from the moment I started inquiring about his lineage that he was also curious, and he began to learn more about his family. He went back as far as land records and deeds and had them spread across a table. I couldn't keep my prodding eyes away. I found an old deed to this land registered to my daughter Thea."

"Thea!" My heart was elated to know she survived that nightmare. "So Fyom's green eyes are a trait from her? She was a Wielder?"

Peiro slowly nodded as his mind's eye wandered back to a previous memory. "She Wielded the earth beautifully. Her grandmother, Talia's mother, was a Wielder and Thea inherited her traits. She also became a noblewoman it would seem." The pride on his face spoke volumes about the love he still carried for his daughter.

I was afraid to ask my next question but he was willing to share. "What happened to Calum?"

A shadow crossed his features as he took another deep inhale. "That is still a mystery to me, but when I saw Fyom, I just knew in my heart that he was familiar to me. My heart swelled knowing Thea at least had turned out okay. I never found her after...the event. But that's when I first began to feel it."

"Feel what?"

"Redemption." A small smile flashed across Peiro's face before hiding once again. The sun's descending rays cast brightly across his features, illuminating a youthful glow that had been betrayed by the blades of time. His growing silver eyes looked like small stars that were peeking behind the rays of dusk.

"What does it whisper to you?" I asked cautiously, curious to know more.

"Wretched things. Its favorite thing is to show images of all the sins I've committed. Enough sins to cover a thousand men's lifetimes and more. It tricks me thinking it's *me* thinking these thoughts. Until you came along and disproved it."

I tilted my head, taking it all in. "What do you mean?"

"It can sense that you can control it somehow. And it doesn't like it."

I reclasped my fingers over his. "I want to help. Tell me how to help."

Peiro licked his bottom lip and locked his fingers around mine. I don't think he *intended* for that to cause my body to shiver, but lately it had a mind of its own. He kept his gaze locked on our intertwined fingers, losing himself to a distant thought.

"Don't give up on me, *Naa'n le'ya*. When the world grows black and the souls have turned, know this." He dropped one of my hands and cupped my cheek. "You can throw away my hand. Disregard my soul. But I have found my moonlight in you. The essence of the night that caresses my secrets and sees my darkness. I am yours until Thuvina calls me home. If I live another thousand years, it would still be too soon to forget you."

I swallowed hard, feeling my chest bloom with feelings I didn't have names for. For years I wouldn't be able to tell you why I did what I did next, but I gently touched the hand that caressed my cheek and called the *illicitus* to rise.

Ora's words, *this doesn't have to be a bad thing*, echoed inside my mind. I measured Peiro's reaction as I slowly and gently Wielded the shadows to come forward, ever present but on my command. His pupils dilated against the grays and silvers now in his eyes and his breathing became ragged. Ever so slowly and delicately, I told the *illicitus* to hover to my hand but not break the surface. It was still low enough that my palm barely illuminated against the waning sun.

Peiro's breathing picked up harder. His other hand clenched tight on my shoulder as his eyes widened with a controlled fear. A fear where you're scared of the outcome but trust the one you're with. I didn't want to hurt him and would stop the instant I saw his agony. Peiro clenched his jaw tight as he kept his eyes locked on mine, growing more wild.

"I can stop," I whispered.

"Keep going," he said between bated breaths.

It hummed. My eyes drew closed as I lost myself to the steady feeling that caressed me. Nothing could be seen to the wandering eye, but I could sense the cold shadows that whispered over my skin like a tender lover. Something caught my attention, bringing me back to the now. Then I saw it. Peiro's eyes had turned from that silver to honey to brown.

He sagged against me, his breathing still at a hard pace. His gaze snapped to mine again, immediately seeing the sense of relief, that freedom I knew was indescribable for him.

"Come." Peiro stood in a swift motion and held out a hand. "Night is coming and I don't want you to catch a chill."

I had more burning questions and my thirst to know more was not even close to being quenched, but I took Peiro's cue and let him help me up from the ground. My body froze in shock when he pulled me in close. The heat of his body soaked into me as his lips found mine, coaxing them open with his tongue. I leaned in and melted into his embrace. This dance, I realized, was much slower than before as each stroke lapped against my tongue, like he was trying to memorize every detail of this moment.

My body radiated with fire and the heat settled deep between my thighs. He clasped both of my hands within his and pulled them tightly between our bodies, then pulled back just enough so I could see his deep browns searching my mine. They asked—no, they pleaded—for an answer only I could give.

I nodded. "Yes," I whispered. Before the word fully dissipated into the air, my lips collided with his, being desired and worshipped.

I suddenly felt something hard and cold against my back. A shockwave of sensations against my heated flesh. It was only then that I realized that Peiro had me held up against a door as he worked the handle open. I wasn't sure how we got back to the cabin, let alone unseen, because I don't remember pulling away from his embrace or walking inside.

I felt reckless but it was so freeing.

I noticed that he had brought us to my room, and in just a few steps, Peiro walked us over to my bed and gently set me down. He pulled back again, causing me to immediately miss his warmth, and placed his hands on both sides of my hips while looking into my eyes. His smile forced tiny creases between his eyes that framed them beautifully.

"What are you looking at?" I asked. His fierce gaze made me blush.

"Something like a miracle," he replied and leaned in again, taking my lips into his. The kiss was like one he had given before. Hungry, yet more patient. He teased and stroked my tongue with his, pulling me in closer as he held the back of my head in his palm.

A liquid heat crept inside of me as I wrapped my arms tightly around his shoulders and kissed deeply, pulling lightly on his hair. A growl escaped his throat as he planted his hands on my waist, his arousal prominent where I was most sensitive.

I tilted my head, seeing those beautiful, brown eyes smile back at me, and tugged on his lips with my teeth. This caused his hips to tilt forward, rubbing deeper against my sensitive skin. My breath hitched a moment as his tongue clashed with mine. That slowness had my patience wearing thin.

"I've wanted you for a long time," Peiro said in between our ragged breaths, "but I wanted to be *me* before I tasted you. Thank you for this gift."

I didn't have time to think as his hands roamed across my body, kneading every bit of flesh he could touch. Peiro pulled off the tunic that covered my body and delicately kissed my bare shoulders. My breasts ached for his touch, and as if on command, he pulled away the fabric that bound them, cupping one with a delicious pressure as his mouth claimed the other. The warmth of his breath on my skin sent tingles as he nipped the peak.

My hands roamed through his silken hair, enjoying every strand that wrapped around my fingers.

"I didn't know when," he said as he took his mouth to my other breast, "but *giants*, I wanted you to have me whole. Even if it's temporary. I wanted to have you as the man I once was."

The fire crept hotter deep within my belly. "Then have me," I panted as I rocked my hips forward, grinding against his length.

My legs instinctively wrapped around his waist, pushing his arousal center to my own.

I planted a kiss at the crook of his neck and nibbled delicately on his collarbone.

"Fuck. If you keep doing that then I might have to waste what I wanted to do for our first."

I stopped and smiled as I planted another kiss on his neck, enjoying how his grip grew firm as his fingers kneaded the flesh of my legs and backside.

"Are you sure?" I heard what he was asking and looked up to nod, unable to catch my words. "No." Peiro shook his head. "I need to hear you say it."

"Yes," I whispered, my voice stuck in my throat. "All the yeses."

Peiro chuckled as he took in the sight before him. Ever so softly, he ran his fingers along my bare skin next to my heart. Gooseflesh skittered across my body just as he cupped another full breast in his hand, kneading the flesh into submission, forcing me to moan at the sensation when he pinched and rolled my nipple between deft fingers.

His other hand worked the laces of my trousers and tugged them down and off with my boots, fully exposing me. I felt the urge to hide myself but gave in as he traced the lines of my body with his finger, traveling up and down my sides, across my naval before dipping into my center.

I gasped as I felt his finger slide back and forth across my liquid heat, letting the tip of his finger enter ever so gracefully. Peiro's lips closed around the flesh of my neck once again. Another shockwave of sensations ricocheted against my nerves as his teeth and tongue lashed against my skin. All the while he continued kneading my breast. His finger plunged deeper inside me, hitting that tender spot within, causing my hips to rock forward against his hand.

"Fuck," Peiro growled against my neck. "You're ready for me."

I took in the steady strokes, slowly losing myself to the relentless rhythm.

My body grew cold once again as he pulled back. I looked up. In any other moment I might have felt the need to cover my body, as those dark brown eyes never strayed away. But I stayed still, watching as he pulled his shirt up and over his head. His trousers hung low on his waist and encased the tightly packed muscles of his abdomen.

I struggled to swallow as I took him in.

The thick muscle had returned and was honed and defined. My mouth watered as I drank in the man before me and my breath caught when I saw more of his body on display. My eyes traced the four bands tattooed across his forearm that stood out against his sunkissed skin. Scars of different shapes and sizes covered him, but somehow made him more beautiful. And I planned to touch and kiss each and every one of them.

Peiro looped his thumbs into his waistband, adding his clothes and boots to the pile on the floor. I took in the full sight of him in wonder. Lines of ink traced his upper thighs and down his legs. More ink covered the entirety of his left shoulder that almost looked like a plate of armor, forever etched and part of him.

Ever so slowly he walked back to the bed and towered over me where I had propped myself up on my elbows. He leaned in and held my jaw with both hands, tilting my neck to bring my lips to his. The warmth of his body radiated against my peaked breasts and abdomen while I glided my tongue across his lips and pulled him closer. As we matched the strokes of our kiss, I felt him settling us further into the bed, positioning himself to my center while leaving a trail of kisses along my skin. His hands roamed my body, this time not wasting a moment before finding my center again.

My eyes fluttered back as I felt the rhythmic strokes again, intensifying my fire. My hands found his girth, teasing him with light strokes of my own. He growled as he rocked his hips forward. My pace began to match his rhythmic circles, my breathing quickened as I felt the intensity build inside my very bones.

"You'll make me finish quicker than I'd like with smooth hands like that, and I plan to go much longer with you." Excitement coursed through me while instinct told me to bend my knees a bit as I adjusted my hips, taking in the delicious pressure of his body on mine.

I felt him at my entrance, begging to be let in. With another tilt of my hips, Peiro inched in slowly, allowing my body to grow accustomed to him. Heat flared as I felt each and every delicious inch push deeper. His intense gaze never faltered as he began to rock his hips forward and back, pushing and pulling.

My body matched his, rising and falling with each thrust. Slow, undulated movements carried on. Each move became hungrier. More desperate. Patience to see it through waned. I wrapped my arms tightly around his neck as he buried his face into the crook of my shoulder.

I closed my eyes as I felt the waves build, climbing higher and higher. It all almost became too much until I felt a crest of sensation. The intense pressure peaked and suddenly I was falling. Falling into an abyss of pleasure. I didn't know which way was up or down. I couldn't find it, even if I tried.

I cried out, panting Peiro's name over and over. My body tightened with each crashing wave while Peiro's ragged breaths came to a halt as he moaned in my ear, finding his own release after mine.

We laid there, neither one of us willing to move after a few precious moments. Dozens of bright blue orbs slowly spun on their axis high above, almost touching the ceiling, while I lazily stroked my fingers across Peiro's back, coaxing him to find his own calming breath with each movement. After a few more heartbeats he climbed to rest on his elbows, overlooking me, and smiled.

He then planted a tender kiss on my lips as he moved to his side and pulled me into the bend of his arm, giving me his shoulder to rest on. I didn't know when I had fallen asleep, but I later opened my eyes to find the night was still present. Gentle fingers ran through the loose strands of my hair, lulling me back to sleep.

"Sleep, *Naa'n le'ya*. I have you," he whispered into my hair. My eyes fluttered closed and I dreamed.

When I finally came to, my eyes opened to a sleeping Peiro next to me with the sun shining in.

His leg was nudged between my thighs and his arm was draped over my waist, pulling me in close. The lines around his face were smoothed out, sans the smile lines around his lips. Those lines were my favorite and I drank them in as the morning sun crept through the window.

Peace. He looked at complete and utter peace.

It was then that I knew I would do anything in my power to make those that hurt him pay. Make the very thing that cursed him pay. I never again wanted to see the pained look in his eyes as his mind drifted to somewhere unknown.

If I could paint, I would capture this image to keep forever.

Reluctantly, I removed myself from his grip to relieve myself. When I came back to bed he had shifted to his back, eyes wide open as he watched every step I took. I didn't cover myself in front of him. Never felt the need to hide my soft curves as I climbed back into the bed and nestled beside him under the soft sheets.

"Hi," I whispered, drinking him in.

A small smile crept up his face and almost reached the corners of his brown eyes. "Hi," he whispered back. He tilted his head down and planted a tender kiss on my temple. "Did you sleep well?"

"Wonderfully."

"Hmm. And what do you think helped you sleep so wonderfully?" he mused.

I smiled. "Not sure. Maybe just feeling relaxed for once."

"Oh." He turned as he growled, "I think I know what must've helped." Then he was on top of me, pressing his lips to mine. His hips tilted forward to where I could not mistake his arousal.

Fire built inside me once again. A liquid heat pooled as I wrapped my arms around him. My tongue danced with his, taking him in, as I was fully awakened by his tender touch.

CHAPTER 33

The cabin was eerily quiet when we finally dressed. Peiro had helped me see the stars twice more before my stomach growled, begging for nourishment. He reluctantly helped me dress but then commanded me to the kitchen with him where we helped ourselves to the usual spread.

It was odd that neither Fyom nor Ora were at breakfast, and that the cabin was still silent. We eyed one another in a silent cue and walked back to the front of the halls.

Ever so slowly Peiro removed a dagger from a sheath wrapped around his leg. "Fyom?" He spoke loudly yet cautiously to test out the room.

A loud grumble came from above, followed by a high pitched, "We're up here!"

Peiro's large frame was able to take two steps at a time up the stairs to the study while I did my best to catch up. We found

Ora sprawled on the floor with a litter of trays of food and cups around her, hidden behind massive towers of books. Fyom was buried under a mountain of old scrolls that looked similar to the ones I had once seen at the High Seven Temple. I could only guess how he got his hands on something like them.

Fyom made a loud triumphant noise, signaling for Ora to jump up from her spot and immediately run over to Fyom, whose expression turned from excited to ominous. She flipped through various pages of the book she had in her hand, pointing to random figures and runes on the scrolls and speaking too fast to Fyom for me to understand.

"I have never, literally never, seen her open a book before," I whispered to Peiro, who chuckled. "Let alone *read*."

"From this translation, that image looks like it's the letter 'P.'" Ora had pointed to some figure on the page and then to a rune sitting on Fyom's desk.

My mouth dropped. In all of our years of training and classes, I had wagered that Ora never paid attention. "Nor did I even know she was capable of translating runes?" I added through the corner of my mouth.

"HEY! I heard that!" Ora looked up from her text and gave me a pointed look.

I rolled my eyes. "Oh, it's the truth and you know it."

Ora rolled *her* eyes, turning her attention back to what Fyom held as they silently read simultaneously from the text before them. Fyom scanned the other tomes on his desk, one falling off and making a loud *thud* on the dusty carpet beneath them, and abruptly shifted his attention to another bookcase with dark-colored cylindrical containers that housed *more* scrolls.

"Well, this doesn't look good, does it?" Peiro said slowly as he walked to where Ora stood and read through a scroll she had laid on top of a pile.

How anyone could stay organized with such a large disarray of books and papers was beyond understanding. But Fyom seemed to have a process and I was not going to risk his train of thinking by pointing out the mess.

I walked in step behind Peiro and positioned myself on the other side to read what laid before me. Runes and ancient text were scribbled across pages. Wax seals on parchments with faded writing littered the desk and floor around them.

"What are we looking at, Ora?" I asked pointedly.

"None of it makes sense." Ora shook her head and held a finger to her temple, slowly massaging a headache away.

"What did you two find?" I asked more sternly, getting annoyed at the vagueness and the unanswered sense of urgency between her and Fyom.

"There's a prophecy about the keys," Fyom said flatly as he rounded a hidden cabinet with more scrolls in his hands. Where were these scrolls coming from? "You and your sister are a part of something much greater, I'm afraid."

"But what this prophecy has to do with *us* is what I don't understand," Ora said as she shifted to a nearby chair and sat down. "Maybe we're misinterpreting it."

"These runes look to be Feodean. I haven't seen this language since...well, in a long time," Peiro replied as he laid down an old parchment. "This looks like it was all set from the moment the Ancient One was released." He turned and gave me a knowing look.

"Or even before. These are secondhand *and* thirdhand accounts. But it appears that, well before the laws of magic we know today were written by our dear priests and priestesses, things were already in motion that only a select few knew of." Fyom huffed as he dropped the scrolls to the floor and kneeled down to skim through them. "From a text your sister had found deep in my, uhm, *collection*, there is an account of a Wielder, recorded from someone inside *the original Council*, that tried to split magic into light and dark components. As for why, there's no clear reason.

"Apparently in this Wielder's endeavor, they were successful in creating what we know as *the keys* to life and death. The very power it seems you and your sister possess." Fyom didn't even look up from the page he had turned to and simply pointed to me and Ora as if he had just given us a chore to do around his home.

"But haven't there been other Wielders who sourced from the *illicitus*?" I started. "What does this have to do with me and Aurora? Perhaps you *have* misinterpreted it."

The accounts of anyone Wielding from these sources were very few and far between, with most written accounts having been lost or disappeared. With evidence being so rare, rumors vastly circulated that anyone who was found with such power would be put to death without question.

"It's a prophecy, Ophelia! It doesn't have to make sense or have rules!" Ora roared.

My nose scrunched as my lips pulled in tight. Before I could yell a rebuttal, Fyom gently held his hand up to silence us both. "Ladies. Please," he said before continuing. Ora stuck out her pink tongue while I flipped her off.

"What does this have to do with *it*?" Peiro directed his question to Fyom.

"From what I've gathered, the Ancient One was created when the Death Key was created. My Feodean is rusty when reading these runes, but it seems to say that *it* is the Keeper of Death and can lead the undead. But whoever can Wield death can wield the Ancient One."

"That's why it thrives on killing." Peiro scratched the fine hairs on his face.

"It roughly translates to say that it's the commander, but the Wielder is the general."

The words haunted me.

"That's what Dokvalon is wanting." Peiro turned from the desk and walked over to the large windows that took up the length of one of the walls. I wanted to go to him, to ask him what he was thinking. I could see his eyes staring off into the distance and wanted to know where he was mentally going, but my feet stayed planted.

"You mentioned *keys*, as in more than one..." I glanced at my sister, nibbling my thumb, trying to digest everything. "So where does the Life Key come in?"

"Ah. Yes." Fyom looked up from the text in his hand and at me. Lines and dark circles were etched on his skin. He looked like he was on the borderline of exhaustion.

"When was the last time you slept, Fyom?" My heart ached knowing this man was doing more for us than I could have ever asked for. But if he neglected his health for the sake of answers, I would have to put a hard stop to it until he recovered. We were already watching Sury slowly recover—we didn't need to go through that with another.

"Sleep is for the dead, my girl!" Fyom's large frame shook with mirth. "Besides. It's been far too long since I've gotten to dive into my books again! But yes, the Life Key. One moment—I think I left the 345th edition of the Feodean-to-Nuvati translation on that other shelf." The man practically galloped across the wide span of the room.

My eyebrow raised at seeing such a large man being filled with so much excitement. "Trust me. He gets like this with his research. He's been this way for a long time," Peiro stated matter-of-factly over his shoulder.

Ora turned to him with both eyebrows raised and then to me as she mouthed, *a long time?*

I shook my head and replied in silence, *later.*

My golden sister shrugged her shoulders and turned just in time to step aside, away from Fyom's path as he barreled back to the desk with the book in hand.

"My Nuvati is a little more rusty than my Feodean but it looks like it translates into something about the Life Key being able to balance death. That one cannot exist without the other."

Tension grew in the air between the four of us. We stood still, taking in and absorbing all that we'd learned and comprehending what we could. Peiro remained silent, still staring aimlessly out of the window and beyond the trees.

He crossed his arms, causing his shirt to pull a little tighter across his back and shoulders. He stared intently at nothing in particular, but I could sense the tension that radiated off of him.

"The prophecy. What does it have to do with *us*?"

Ora lifted her head from her hands and stared at the ceiling of vines and branches. "Apparently, if the translation is correct, we not only have this ability, but we can demolish this magic once we reunite these keys. But that's a strong *if*. We don't even know what these keys look like."

I looked to Peiro frantically, wondering what that meant for him and the thing inside of him. Wondering if the thing he had seen in the cave that day was one of the *keys*.

"So you're saying it can bring back the balance? Potentially restore the Ancient One back to its place?" Peiro didn't look over his shoulder as he asked his questions. The thought sounded more rhetorical than aimed at anyone in particular. I couldn't understand why—perhaps it was instinct, or the sense that his mind was racing with questions about the very thing he had been wrestling with for so long.

"And whoever has a key can Wield its power while the keys are separated," interjected Fyom. "Once the keys are reunited, however, no one will be able to manipulate this way of magic. Anything created from the split will return to its natural order and not exist."

Peiro whipped his head to our direction, unfolding his arms and turning to face us. He slowly clenched and released his hands.

"That means the balance of Wielding will be restored?" I started. "What would that look like? All of our history books speak of nothing prior to the seven circles of power."

Fyom continued. "But the laws abolished the testing for the *illicitus* since it was deemed unnatural for anyone to control these elements, right? Said it was *light and dark magic.* My guess is that the original council of lawmakers encountered the person who created these keys and wanted to stop anyone from learning more about this magic, not realizing a prophecy had been tied to it."

Silence roared again as everyone slipped into their own mind, trying to uncover the meaning of what we were learning.

"She's looking for something." Peiro's rough voice broke through our thoughts and all eyes were on him. The sun's rays danced brightly around him. "If the testing for the magic was deemed unlawful but she's been able to infiltrate an entire learning establishment at the High Seven Temple, then she's been looking for something or *someone*."

No one made any moves or sounds as we took in Peiro's words. We all began to wonder what Ariadne's true intentions were and what power plays she was making against the kingdom she swore to serve.

Peiro adjusted his stance to face everyone. He glanced at Ora before landing a long stare at me. Lazily, he stole his eyes away to face Fyom. "She knows. She's looking for me."

Immediately Fyom's strong stance shuddered and his shoulders rolled forward. He rubbed his beard as he tried to formulate his next thought. "But why?"

"Well, it seems obvious, doesn't it?" Peiro adjusted his arms to rest his hands on his hips and tilted his head to the ceiling. He closed his eyes and took a deep breath. "She must have figured out another way to control it, or she wants to use the person who *can* control it. She knows more about you than what she led on," he said as his graying eyes pinned mine. "You control the Wielder, you control it. You control *it*, you control the undead. What better army than soldiers that have already died? Dokvalon is going to war."

CHAPTER 34

W e stared at one another and fumbled to find the words to say. Panic was written all over Ora's face, as this was her first test to save her kingdom, and her test would be more difficult and consequential than what those before her had to endure. Before our own mother's rule.

"This prophecy," I started with a shaky breath, "what does it say exactly?"

Fyom slowly rose from where he had propped himself on the floor. "As I've said, my translation needs some work." He went on, reading from a scroll that looked to be on the verge of disintegrating. "But it's essentially saying something about life and death. Something in accordance? No, abundance! This rune looks like it says death will be...a cow? No, that's not right."

"That was probably the shittiest attempt in translating that I've seen you do in a long time." Peiro laughed from his corner.

Fyom flipped him a vulgar finger before turning back to me. "I'm obviously rusty. And can keep working to decipher it."

"We clearly have the upper hand as we wait." Ora smirked as she pointed in Peiro's direction.

"We need to start looking for these keys before Dokvalon finds them," I said. "Have you uncovered any possible location where we can start looking?"

Both Ora and Fyom shook their heads right as an idea struck me.

"What about the Rising Rock?" I gasped. "What if it's been hiding in plain sight?"

"Nothing guards that temple. It would be too easy to steal from." Fyom disputed.

"But why else would they attack it? Especially right when Ora was there?" I urged. "We have to have missed something about it. Some telling or folklore or some information our parents told us." I could see the cogs turning in Ora's head as she pondered the idea. "So we go back," I stated. "To the Rising Rock."

Ora clenched her necklace tight. "But what about Sury? He's been asleep for so long." She took a small step to stand in front of me, meeting me with large golden eyes. They shone so brightly against the clouds in the window behind her. "We're not going to leave him here."

"Of course not," I said reassuringly as I grabbed her fists. "Of course not. But..." I couldn't bring myself to say it. What his fate might end up looking like.

"Don't you dare start." Ora's eyes began to glisten. A wall began to crack as her bottom lip quivered. "We have to find a way. We *have* to."

Before I could say another word, before I could make a move, the wall Ora held in place around her resolve cracked. Her eyes welled with tears and one by one they fell, landing along the collar of her shirt. "*We have to,*" Ora whispered, then pushed past me and raced to the steps.

In this moment, despite what I had felt before with Ora's whereabouts unknown, I felt completely incapable. Sorrow crept over my heart, not knowing when Sury, my friend and my sister's lover, would ever come to.

Desperation took over my thoughts. Finding the answers to these runes was a priority. Figuring out how they fit into a prophecy, of all things, and how the survival of their kingdom hung in the balance.

But...but so was Sury. We had already been here for weeks, and Fyom was a more gifted Healer than all the Healers at the palace combined. If he wasn't able to heal Sury, then could he be healed? If so, how long would that take? How long would we be able to wait for him to wake up? He had been in an induced sleep for so long, his body growing weaker by the day. He would need time to recoup. Time for his muscles to relearn how to function.

We have to rang again inside my mind. "I don't know what to do," I whispered to myself, but felt a large presence stand before me.

"Go to her," he said. I looked up, seeing the silver behind Peiro's eyes had grown sharp, the browns barely visible around his pupil. He searched my eyes as he lightly tucked a wild strand of hair behind my ear. His hands delicately grabbed the tops of my shoulders, slowly caressing them. "Your sister needs you now more than ever." He finished with a delicately placed small kiss on my temple. My body leaned in more.

I could only nod. My heart jerked with where I might find my sister, and I ran down the stairs and into the hall to the room where Sury had been resting.

Ora was halfway spread across the bed with her head resting on Sury's chest, crying. She didn't hear me enter the room and continued to sob over Sury's shirt and gently caressed his lower jaw. Incoherent words were repeated as her body shook from the force of tears.

I sat down at the edge of the bed, laid a hand over her shoulder, and gently squeezed. Ora's head shot up. She gave me a longing and pained look before continuing her sobbing. Without any words, I pulled my sister into my arms and wept with her.

Everything we'd been holding was released.

The pain from our mother and father's passing. The sadness of seeing our friend lying there on the bed, with no resolution in sight to help him. The misery that my golden sister had endured in her captivity and me, the silver sister, not knowing how to move from here. Ache for a kingdom that will soon face a terror that hasn't been seen in generations. A deep sorrow for the unknown and the darkness that rides it like a cloud.

"I'm sorry," I whispered as I continued to let Ora cry out all her hurt. My own tears released in a steady rhythm down my cheeks, and I wondered how many more tears my body could produce.

"I'm sorry, too." Ora sniffled as she wiped away the tears from her eyes and the snot from her nose. "It's just been so much since they died. Mother never prepared me. Prepared us. We just thought it would be a simple succession, in the distant future, when their *fading* was supposed to happen. Not before seeing either one of us find love or have children."

She pulled herself out of my hold and turned to face Sury in his peaceful slumber. "I really wanted Father to see how much of a man Sury has become. How much he truly loves this kingdom because he also loves me." Ora looked into my swollen red eyes. "I wanted you to see how much he truly admired you as a friend. How strong his desire was to create a new regime so Veiks would never feel like they were *less than* ever again. Feel a sense of shame. He truly wanted to take down Ariadne before we knew who Ariadne really was."

I found myself taking Ora and Sury's hands and squeezing them both, another tear escaping my eyes. "Aurora, he's *not* dead. You two will find your happy ending. We just need to figure out how to stop what's inside of him. He's not dead, he's just..." I stopped mid-sentence and began to think. "He isn't *dead*! He's only been shot with a *death arrow*!" I sprung with excitement and turned to Sury, pulling down the collar of his tunic to reveal the black webbing underneath his skin.

The sickly pallor of his body made the webbing look darker. His once-muscled chest now sat sunken and almost concave. The tunic that had once fitted him just right was now too large for his shrinking frame. Even the skin around his eyes had sunken, and his cheekbones were much sharper than before. I hated to admit to myself that he looked like a living corpse.

"Phe, what are you doing?" Ora shifted frantically. "You're scaring me."

"He's not dead, but *that's* death inside him." I pointed to his chest. "The death arrow. I didn't think about it at first, but before you were found, for whatever reason, I came in here to see if I could heal him on my own—the webbing only grew. Now I understand. I didn't know about our Wielding then and I thought when I had tried that I could only manifest this death in him—but maybe I've had it wrong all along."

I leaned down and studied the webbing and the black markings that inked deep across his chest, and the remnants that crept higher across his jawline and down his torso.

"Do you trust me?" I looked into Ora's swollen golden eyes that sparkled with intrigue.

"What are you thinking?"

"I think...I think when I tried, I might have called it to stretch further and not to recede."

"But it's been inside him for so long. Who's to say that when you remove it that the damage will be irreversible?" Worry creased over Ora's brow as she began to observe how deep the black webbing had crept, even in the time she had been at Fyom's.

"Sister, *you* bring life. *You* can restore."

Ora gave me a blank stare as she tried to understand what I was telling her. She shook her head, stood to her feet, and folded her arms across her chest. "I can't do that." She continued, shaking her head more. "I don't know anything about this new power yet. There's no way I can restore him. I just...I just can't." Ora's pace began to grow frantic as she moved across the floor.

I caught her by the wrist and stared deep into her eyes. "I believe in you. I know *he* believes in you. We've tried every other effort we know of and Fyom is brilliant. We *can* do this." Hope filled my chest as my excitement grew.

Reluctantly, Ora shifted herself away from my grasp and positioned herself next to Sury. With one hand she combed through the strands of his long, dark hair, while the other clasped his folded hands that laid on his chest. "I never said *thank you* for taking good care of him. He looks like he's only sleeping, despite the poison that's sweeping through his body." Ora looked up at me with fresh tears and smiled. "Thank you."

Another tear escaped me, but I quickly swiped it away with the cuff of my sleeve. "I love him just as much as you. I mean, not in the *way* you do by any means, but I've always adored him like a brother. An annoying brother. Almost as annoying as you are. But a brother nonetheless."

Ora huffed a small chuckle as she began wiping the tears from her eyes. She nodded that she was ready, giving me time to position myself on the other side of the bed. Ever so gently, Ora removed a few laces from the front of his tunic and shifted her arm beneath his shoulders so she could pull it completely away from his body. She leaned in and brushed a soft kiss over his heart.

The webbing was worse than I could have anticipated and I released an involuntary gasp. The muscle around his abdomen had completely vanished, leaving concave skin around his ribcage. His hip bones jutted up above the waistline of his pants and his stomach looked like it had not seen food in weeks, despite Fyom's every effort to prepare bone broth or other magical remedies to keep his body nourished.

Ora's lip quivered but I could tell she tried her hardest to rebuild her emotional wall so she wouldn't break down again. "So. What do we do?" Ora kept her eyes on the small rise and fall of Sury's breathing.

Instinct drove me again. "Dive deep inside your well and follow my lead. When I pull the webbing back, jump in and let your magic do what it's called to do."

Ora lightly laughed as she reached her hands out and positioned them over Sury. "You know what's funny?" I raised an eyebrow in answer. "I remember when *I* used to have to boost *your* confidence when it came to magic. And now the tables have turned."

I gave her a small smile and then began.

I did what I'd grown comfortable doing and dove deep within my newfound magic, my new Wielding power. New source. In my mind's eye, I found it dancing with my own energy and the shadows and small orbs it created. With each breath I took, I felt the pull call me down further and further until I took in all I could.

My hands began to ache as I called the *illicitus* to the surface and directed it toward Sury's chest. The blackness in his veins began pulsing and moving like waves in water underneath his skin. A sickly feeling curdled inside my gut when I felt the Wielding begin to connect with the very energy underneath Sury's skin.

It felt foul and tasted as such. A thick coating covered my tongue and settled at the back of my throat, striving to choke me. I needed to work fast. The webbing underneath Sury's skin rippled faster as I hovered my hands over the markings in his neck. "Follow behind me," I called to my sister and began to siphon the death away from him and absorb it with my fingertips.

Dark tendrils shifted from Sury's body in a serpentine manner. The dark matter was thick as smoke as it rolled and coiled, resisting the pull I had called to it. Still I tried, feeling a cramp form within my fingers as I curled them in, pulling the tendrils in tighter. I concentrated on the matter more, feeling a steady formation of sweat bead along my brow. The tendrils coiled around my fingers like snakes and pulled in tight to cut off the circulation. I cried out in pain from the sensation.

"Phe!" Ora yelled frantically.

"It's okay," I gasped. "I've got it. I know I do." And with that, I felt my Wielding nudge against the tendrils and cause them to shudder. The orbs manifested around my fingertips and shot across the room and back, each one dividing into a smaller version of itself until they penetrated both sides of the dark matter, lighting it up to match their blue-tinted silver. The tendrils responded with a shudder and released the tightening coil around my fingers.

Wisps of the black matter began to dissipate and continued to be absorbed into my fingertips once again, without resisting. A sweet taste now coated my tongue and warmed my veins.

As if on cue, I felt Ora's magic closely behind, a foreign and warming feeling compared to the comforting and cooling sensation within my own hands. Together we moved slowly, me calling the sickness to leave and Ora calling for restoration to follow. Her own movements brought ribbons of sparkling gold to travel deep under Sury's skin.

As we moved in tandem, blood flowed faster within Sury and brought color back to his cheeks and hands. Silver scars from where the webbings resided had marred his copper skin, leaving a trail of markings in their wake.

Together we were able to recede the webbing from his jaw and torso, but found our challenge at the heart of the infection where Sury was initially hit. Sweat grew on our brows as we steadily guided our energy deep within. I unraveled every string of darkness tied inside as Ora reattached new life in each fiber.

The sun had begun to set, casting a deep pink and gold hue on the horizon, when we finally finished and cleared the last dark spot from the arrow's wound. Our clothes were soaked in our own tears and perspiration as we laid back in exhaustion.

Ora caught her breath and repositioned herself to look over at Sury, waiting for any sign that our Wielding had worked. Her eyes grew frantic when Sury didn't move, and she started tapping his face and pushing on his shoulder, urging him to wake up.

"It didn't work? It didn't work!" Ora screamed.

"Give it time! He's been unconscious for so long," I called out. "We don't know how long this will take." I also didn't want to admit that I too wondered if we'd done it right.

"This is hopeless! What good is any of this, this *illicitus*, if it doesn't work? Why did I listen to you?" Ora screamed louder. "We probably just put him in his damn grave! I can't handle another death, Ophelia!" She paced back and forth next to the bed as her breath grew ragged and frantic.

I sprang up and in two steps made it to her. "Ora! Give it a chance, please!" I felt the volume in my own voice start to rise but stamped it down. I forced my calm to the surface in hopes of soothing her. "Please," I pleaded.

"I can't believe..." Ora grabbed at her chest as she tried to find her breath. "Phe? Your eyes! They're starting to turn silver again!"

Instinctively, I brought my hands to my eyes and turned to look in the mirror, and then...

"Why are you two screaming?" A hoarse voice called out to us. "Did Phe take the last piece of pie again?"

Both of us gasped and whipped our heads to find Sury trying his best to sit up in the bed. We both rushed over to help prop him up with a few too many pillows as I grabbed a ewer of water and quickly filled a glass for him to drink. Ora sat closely beside him, brushing his now-longer hair out of his eyes, inspecting every inch of him that she could.

"Sury! How are you feeling?" Ora asked, seemingly restraining all the overwhelming questions racing through her head.

"A splitting headache, to be honest." He took the glass of water from me and emptied the contents down his throat. The tendons of his hands and fingers flexed against the sunken skin. "Did I drink too much wine again? I've had the oddest of dreams." He looked around the room and down the bed. He looked over at the window and beyond it. "Are we at the Inn? Is this another room?" He looked at Ora, confused. "Wait. We were looking for you!" He dropped the glass. I quickly caught it as he threw his arms tightly over Ora and held her like he would lose her the moment he let go. His sobs were muffled inside her shoulder where he rested his head. "Aurora, you're here."

"It's okay," Ora whispered and set to run her fingers over his brown locks.

Reluctantly, he pulled back to inspect her, both of his hands clasping her face, and then pulled her close again for a passionate kiss. My heart swelled as I watched the pure happiness between Ora and Sury—a love finally reunited. Sury looked around the room and gave me a shining smile before worry crept across his face.

"What happened?" he demanded.

"You're safe. She's safe. All in good time. I promise," I replied with a nod of reassurance. "What do you remember?"

Before Sury could speak, a light but forceful knock echoed through the room. I turned to slightly open the door and Peiro stepped through.

Sury tensed and brought Ora closer within his grip. He scanned the nearby tables for anything he could use as a weapon. "You," he said, just short of a growl.

I stepped in front of Peiro, my back to him defending any move, and calmly raised my hands. "*He* saved you, Sury. We owe him a great debt in getting you here."

Ora began to chuckle and gripped Sury's wrist, pulling his eyes toward hers. "Plus, they're kind of smitten so there might be a need for a clean slate now." She finished her words with a wink.

"*What?*" Sury turned to face me and Peiro with a confused and bewildered look. "How long have I been out of it? What the hell is going on?"

"He also saved *her*, Sury. If it weren't for him, we would all be worse off," I added softly.

Sury turned back to Ora and scanned her with awe in his eyes. He pulled her in a tight embrace again and sat there with her in his arms. Another small sob escaped his mouth and a tear trailed down his face.

Peiro stepped around me and toward the bed. He looked down to Sury and extended his hand. "Clean slate?" Sury looked into his eyes. He shifted slowly on the bed, struggling to find the strength to reposition himself. "Please. Remain where you are. You've been through hell, and I'm sure these sisters will tell you about it soon enough." A small smile etched across Peiro's features.

Sury's eyebrows pinched together, remaining still as he studied the hand in front of him and its owner. He turned his gaze to Ora, who smiled softly at him and nodded her head. Sury shifted his eyes to me, reading something I couldn't see before landing his intense gaze back on Peiro.

He nodded. "Sir. For what you did for Aurora, I owe you my life." He then took Peiro's hand in a firm, gripping handshake. The two men stared at one another as if silently communicating, the male hubris palpable, before Peiro let go. While making his exit from the room, he looked at me in wonder. The corners of his mouth tilted upwards briefly before falling back to its usual scowl.

I followed his footsteps in eagerness but to also leave Ora and Sury time to themselves. I could only imagine the relief they felt at finally being reunited. "I'm sure they have much to discuss from their time apart," I said casually.

Peiro lowly chuckled. "*Discuss.* I'm sure that's exactly what they're going to do."

I rolled my eyes. "If they have any sense they'll wait until he's recovered to do more than *discuss.*"

"It's a man's nature to be in the arms of his woman."

Something about the way he looked, with his eyebrow raised and the small curl of a smile reappearing, made me feel a sudden heat down low in my belly. I quickly turned my attention forward, anything to stop from my face turning a sudden shade of red.

"So...smitten, eh?" he said with a laugh as we continued down the hall and through the front door. The stars shone bright and the air was cool enough to relieve the heat that radiated off my skin. A quick coolness coursed through me as I slowly peeled away some of the tunic that was plastered to my skin.

Despite the air cooling parts of my body, I felt the tops of my cheeks flush hard.

Peiro guided us to our favorite spot in the meadow, saying nothing. His lips twitched to reveal a small smile once more. He was strikingly handsome in that rugged way when he smiled.

"Come," he said as he took my hand. The rough calluses on his hands and fingertips were ever so gentle as they wrapped around mine, like I was a delicate flower and he wouldn't dare crush the petals.

Once I was settled on the soft ground, I found myself riddled with exhaustion and laid my head against his shoulders. He adjusted us slightly to wrap one of his arms around me, pulling me in close. The heat from his body seeped deep into mine, warming more than my flesh.

I hadn't realized just how soaked my tunic had become, nor how much time had passed in Sury's room. "I smell..."

"Like moonlight and jasmine," Peiro cut in, handing me a waterskin he had brought. My throat clenched against the coolness as I chugged the waterskin dry. I wiped the remnants from my mouth with the back of my hand. So very ladylike.

I handed the skin back to Peiro, taking in his profile and the steep angles of the outline. The moonlight kissed his tanned skin so perfectly. "Are you okay? Did my magic hurt you earlier?"

"Do you always try to take care of everyone around you? Are *you* okay?"

"Stop deflecting."

"I'm not deflecting," Peiro huffed. "Now answer the question. Are you okay?"

I paused for a moment to reflect on the revelations—what I'd found through the course of several hours and what Ora and I had just accomplished. "Numb. I feel numb."

"Go on," Peiro urged.

It took a moment to find the words. To make sure they were the right ones.

"My life has turned upside down. I used to be simply a *princess in the high tower*, a princess with no power in magic or rule. Now I seem to be someone with more power than anyone has seen in centuries and it doesn't feel real.

"My mother was the most powerful woman I knew, aside from her magic. She could walk into any room and demand the attention of everyone without having to say a single word. Ora is a lot like her. I've always been like my father, content with the shadows."

"Shadows have more power than you realize. Do you truly believe that your father was not as powerful as he let on?"

The question sparked something in me that I didn't realize was there. "With everything that's happened lately, I'm not sure. But I don't see why he would lie to us. But anything's possible now..."

"When my life changed," Peiro started, "I felt a great numbness. I let my thoughts swirl into despair thinking of all that I have lost. I let the darkness win for so long. Don't let it win over you. You are much stronger than I am, even without your newfound Wielding source."

Crickets and all other sorts of nighttime creatures spoke into the night, echoing around us. My mind felt foggy and muddled. I blamed the increased exhaustion for my words that tumbled out.

"I'm scared," I whispered. The confession felt both like a weight being lifted and a weight being thrown. Was the confession too heavy for Peiro to bear? "I don't know what this Wielding can do. Yes, Sury is better, but we only have stories to base our knowledge on. I don't want to lose myself to the shadows. To the madness."

Peiro's arm clenched harder around my shoulders, drawing me in tighter. "If you could see the way I see you, you would never wonder just how truly magnificent you are. But I'm right beside you in those moments you might become scared of the dark. If the shadows lie to your heart, saying that you're weak, I will do everything in my power to light up your path. No matter what you feel, come to me. Let it go and carry on."

I picked my head up off his shoulder to look him in the eyes. He gave me a small smile—one I knew was only a fraction of the sight. I turned just enough to brush my lips against the corner of his mouth, but he shifted, capturing my lips with his and holding the kiss. No hinted notion for anything further. No movements that said this would lead to something else. Just pure bliss. Just two bodies needing the other's presence. Our breathing synced, and my heart just knew our heartbeats grew in sync, too.

I pulled back before nuzzling in closer within his hold and rested my head on his shoulder once again. No other words were said as we simply looked up at the night sky. It was so light that I could have imagined the small kiss Peiro placed on my temple before he rested his jaw against the top of my head. The soft act warmed my heart and evoked a feeling of care I had never received outside of my family.

Our breathing fell in tune with one another, deep inhales and slow exhales creating a shared rhythm. Footsteps thrashing through grass and weeds shattered the silence. We looked back to find Ora and Sury approaching along the path we'd carved to our meadow retreat. My heart sank as I spotted Sury leaning heavily on a wooden cane as he walked.

"Well, that was fast," I said, mumbling under my breath.

"Don't tell him that and hurt a man's pride." Peiro laughed with wild eyes.

I smiled and smacked him as hard as I could in the arm. "I didn't mean *that!* I just figured they wanted more time together before talking with anyone else."

Peiro laughed again and it sounded like liquid honey to my heart. He jumped to his feet and extended a hand to help me rise from our shared spot. Ora held onto Sury steadily as he worked hard to find his balance within the mounds of grass and scattered rocks, letting his arm interlace through hers.

"Beautiful night. We thought Sury needed some fresh air and saw you two sitting here," Ora called out. "Fyom had a tonic ready to give him some strength and it's working wonders already. Isn't it, Sury?"

He didn't immediately reply. Concentration laced every sunken line on his face as he took cautious steps forward. A sense of grief wrapped around my heart as I watched him move forward. Once he moved with the fluidity and grace of a hunter, steps ever so delicate to never spook his prey. Now, the small shuffles he made with his ill-fitted boots echoed against the trees in the forest.

His dangerously narrow frame was swallowed by a fresh linen shirt and baggy trousers that I was sure were given by the cabin with the intent for Ora to wear. His knuckles were white as they gripped the notch of the staff. I saw how he put in every effort toward not looking weak. Aside from his physical form, Fyom's tonic must have been working, since anyone would notice how much color was returning to Sury's skin. What was once an ashen gray, inches from death, now bloomed into a dull copper.

Peiro and I quickly closed the gap between them for the sake of Sury not needing to walk much farther.

"How are you feeling?" I asked, desperate to grab his hand to make sure I wasn't dreaming and that my friend was indeed standing before me.

"Like I might have been run over by a few caravans from that traveling circus from the north." Sury gave a half-hearted chuckle, one that seemed to require extraordinary effort. "But Fyom seems like a miracle worker. One moment I could hardly wiggle my toes and the next, well, here we are."

"The tonic tastes like shit, doesn't it?" Peiro lightly clasped his large hand on top of Sury's shoulder. I could have guessed that if he wanted to, he could snap Sury's shoulder with how frail he had gotten.

"I swear I taste hints of horse manure." Sury shook his head in disgust.

Peiro replied, "The damn mountain of a man won't tell me what he puts in it but swears by its contents."

A wave of relief met Sury's features once he adjusted himself to stand against the staff, but they quickly flashed into neutrality.

"Speaking of the giant," Ora started, "Fyom said Sury will need a few more days to recover, and once he's well enough to travel, we can make way for the Rising Rock...if that's what we choose?" She looked to me, reading my face for the answer.

"Are you sure? It would be extremely dangerous, given how close we are to home. Close to Vovias and Ariadne."

"I'm more than sure." Ora nodded.

I turned to Peiro, who reciprocated a soft look and nodded. I turned back to Ora, with Sury in her grasp. "To the Rising Rock, then."

Sury grumbled something under his breath before the pair shuffled back to the cabin for him to rest.

We watched the two walk away then returned to where we were sitting before. I wasn't sure when it happened, but I must have dozed off. I found myself flickering my eyes open and seeing dark clouds overhead. The moon waned and cast a dull glow against the night sky. The bright stars twinkled in sync with one another.

I was on my back, still encased in Peiro's arms. He had fallen asleep beside me. I gently raised myself to my elbows and stared into the lines of his face, taking in all I had learned of his past, him at the present, and what his future might look like with the Ancient One and the kingdom.

"I must have dozed off, myself," Peiro huffed with his eyes still closed. "Like what you see?" he teased with a small smirk creeping up the side of his face.

"How did you know I was looking at you?" Curiosity coursed through my veins like an unquenchable thirst.

"I can...sense things," he opened and looked at me, the silvers shining brightly. "*It* has a heightened sense of awareness. Pushes the body and mind. There are things it's allowed me to do that

I know my mortal body could not endure...aside from being as old as your fifth or sixth great-grandfather."

I shook my head and stuck my tongue out with disgust. "Let's not mention that ever again." I rose to sit and stare at the mountains once again. "We won't let Ariadne win, with you or with Gria. We'll figure this out. Together."

CHAPTER 35

"**T**HIS IS INSANE!"

"That's why it *will* work! Think of the impact this could have!"

Peiro and I had heard shouting inside the living room and walked in to find Sury and Ora in a heated debate. All the while Fyom sat calmly, watching from a nearby lounge.

Sury caught sight of us entering the room and frantically pointed in Ora's direction. "Phe! Talk sense into your sister. This is a suicide mission!" He had begun to fill out in the days of his recovery and started to look like the Sury I knew, but I could see the fatigue still etched deep in his features.

Ora huffed and rolled her eyes before sitting down angrily in a large wingback chair. "You're not listening to me! We can improve the logistics, but we could send the biggest message possible."

"We have no army, Aurora!" He was definitely angry. "There's no safe way to get you in and out undetected, especially if Ariadne and Vovias are teaming up with Dokvalon. Think of your safety and your kingdom's future, for giants' sake!"

"What is going on?" I stepped in front of Sury, who was trying hard not to throw something.

Ora brought her fingers to her lips to think. "I told him our plan. For the other reason to go to the Rising Rock." She took a deep breath before continuing to Sury, "We have the advantage of surprise. They don't know if I'm still alive and they sure as hell don't realize the Wielding we are capable of. Especially her." She nonchalantly pointed toward me. "We hold more cards than they realize. So it would show tremendous strength if I completed the ritual at Rising Rock."

I couldn't deny Sury's fear of her being so close to where she was attacked, but we knew this was a good plan.

"You're not thinking!" Sury tapped his head with force and gritted through his teeth. The exhaustion finally won when he caved into a chair facing hers. "We don't know if Dokvalon is still at the temple! We don't know if they retreated or how much further they've marched. They attacked you and massacred your court, for giants' sake, Aurora!"

Ora swatted her hand like a gnat had flown in front of her. "Technicalities."

"She might be onto something. Could it be worth hearing out her plan before shutting her down?" Peiro leaned against the wall with his arms folded. Ever stoic.

I was beginning to dislike just how much I enjoyed the site of him leaning up against a wall with folded arms. I fumbled over my bottom lip, my mind wandering in the wrong direction as I took in Peiro with his soaked tunic from our training wrapped tightly around his arms.

"Heartbeat, *Naa'n le'ya*," Peiro said softly as he winked. *Later*, he mouthed.

I blinked, then the heat rose to my cheeks as I lightly smirked.

"*Ophelia!*" Sury bellowed, calling my attention again.

Before I could speak, Ora cut in, "Our ancestors claimed the land through this ancient magic, but it's the Rising Rock that symbolizes our heritage's connection to the land and signals peace and prosperity. For protecting the people.

"Without our claim, Dokvalon can cross our borders unchecked with our magic not intertwined in the land. People will *want* to step up and fight for their kingdom." She shot Sury an intense glance. "They will want to form an army to stop their lands from being taken and their families from being wiped before their very eyes. We can round our armies on our way to the Rising Rock. We can stop at other regions. Once we arrive, we complete the ritual and restore the land, eliminating any further threat Dokvalon might pose."

"While searching to see if a key is indeed there," I added. Sury's look could throw daggers.

Swift thoughts of variables and controls swirled through my mind, trying to find validity to the plan. It was worth rechecking every angle and poking every hole we could.

"There's a flaw in your plan." Fyom spoke up from his recliner.

Ora rolled her eyes and sighed. "Naturally, you would find one."

"It is a solid plan, but the flaw is in your surprise."

Ora straightened her back and Sury tightened his grip on the wooden bauble he looked ready to fling. "What do you suggest?"

"He's right. Ariadne and Dokvalon will smell an army rising the moment you begin to collect one. They will be onto your game and set a boundary at the Rising Rock. Dokvalon's armies have been known to be impenetrable in the past and would immediately set up a defense there," Peiro said, still standing against the wall.

"Their Raiders are already within Gria. In the time we've been here they've probably sent more soldiers toward the castle," I added, furrowing my brow.

"Precisely my point. They will formulate a defense well before you gather enough men to march on them." Fyom sat up and swung his feet to the floor to stand. "You need to stop the overflow of soldiers entering the kingdom unchecked by completing the ritual to know you are indeed alive. *And* to have more of an advantage is to finish the ritual without an army. You do this with *no* army behind you, then...then run like hell."

"*No!* This risk is too much to take. You need defenses!" Sury shot up from his seat and almost toppled over.

I closed my eyes and released a long exhale. I folded my arms to bring myself comfort and caught Peiro's stare, like he was calming me from a distance.

Ora slowly rose from her chair, looking more regal than she intended with her head held high. "I will do this for my kingdom. Phe and I can practice our Wielding, to see if that can help us more with the surprise element. Get us there safely and get out before we're detected."

She looked at me with a knowing gaze before she continued. "We'll take the time we need to train. But then we will decide when to leave and make our way to the temple."

The finality in her words was impressive, but also very Ora-like.

"Phe, talk sense to her! This is madness—she can't put herself at such risk. Please!" Sury's voice was frantic. His eyes grew wild as he tried to plead his case to deaf ears.

I slowly turned to face her and took my sister's hands in my own. "Are you sure?"

Ora's response came as a tight squeeze before she withdrew her hands and placed them down by her side. "A queen must make necessary sacrifices for her kingdom and people."

"We won't have a Blood Moon." I reminded her. We searched all we could about the ritual but failed to uncover how important this aspect was.

"We still have to try." She said sternly.

I saw it then. The image of our mother. The bold and courageous queen our mother was and would always be in our hearts.

The image was uncanny. I could almost see a faint glowing aura around her.

Peiro stepped forward and kneeled to the ground, head bowed. "You have my service. I will defend you until any end."

Fyom walked toward Peiro and repeated the same motions and words.

I cast my eyes upon Ora. "You know I will always support you," I said as I too kneeled and bowed my head. "Until the end."

With a small nod, Ora clasped her hands together and exited the room.

"We can't let her do this," Sury gritted through his teeth as he stumbled behind Ora, trying to catch her. "I just got her back!"

My heart ached at that truth.

Muffled shouting could be heard in the distance but no one said a word. I knew in my heart how much Ora and Sury deeply cared for one another and for their kingdom. The sacrifices we'd all have to make would be greater than anyone could imagine.

CHAPTER 36

As we patiently waited for Sury to gather his strength, Ora and I took the time to train against one another in both sword and Wield. I never dared to touch the *illicitus* or test its power while in proximity to Peiro for fear of what it might do to him. The pain etched across his face was too much to bear.

In the moments where my *illicitus* was called forward, I noticed the aftermath caused Peiro to sleep deeper and longer. The years that had been wiped away from his face were too stark not to notice. But the deep browns of his eyes, curtained by thick dark lashes, were too beautiful to resist.

Under Peiro's instruction, we parried and dodged one another's methodical attacks and countered one Wield by enabling another. The call to my Wield grew easier each time I practiced. The tether that was once tied so deeply to my emotions now felt free to Wield as I desired.

The doubt etched away.

On demand, I could Wield my bright blue orbs to take the form of what I needed, to defend against Ora, or when Peiro decided to jump into the training, never letting up his strength for the sake of emotions or thoughts. He told us both that we needed to be ready, regardless of who crossed our paths.

I was thankful that he taught what he knew and never came at me at half-speed. While most of the time he would parry my sword in quick and methodical moves, I was greatly rewarded for my advancements during our nights alone in my room. Sweet kisses placed here. Mockingly revengeful ones placed there. I didn't mind any *punishments* for missing a strike because they were still very much a reward.

I laughed when I finally bested him (though it was only the one time). I stole his sword while tripping him to the ground, resting his blade close to his heart for a mocked death blow.

"Job well done," he called from the ground, holding his hand up for me to help him off the ground.

I cast our two swords aside and grasped his hand, my calluses pressing against his, and pulled him to his feet. In one quick motion, he jumped from the ground and pulled, pinning me hard against his body while his other arm wrapped around my shoulders.

He bent his head and crashed his lips to mine. I craned my neck up and pulled in his bottom lip with my teeth, the act releasing a husky growl from his throat.

These small acts ignited something within me—the small games I knew I played to entice Peiro further. The teasing kept the darker things that loomed over me out of my mind, even for a moment. When we weren't practicing our footwork, Ora and I were tasked with finding anything helpful in Fyom's library, including magical remedies we could prepare prior to our time on the road.

In the small spare moments, I would sneak a kiss to Peiro, finding the courage to pull him in by the nape of his neck and nibble his bottom lip. It garnered a rough growl from him every time. Once, when that happened, I found myself pinned against a wall in the drawing room. Peiro's leg wedged between my own and caused the heat to pool right where the top of his thigh met my desire. His hardening body matched my tempo. I curled my arms around his neck and greedily ran my fingers along his hair.

He nipped and pulled at my bottom lip, his tongue coaxing mine. Instinct led me to match each stroke as I brought my hips forward, seeking anything to alleviate the pressure that was building. The friction sent shockwaves along my nerves and it didn't help when Peiro started touching the delicate skin under my tunic, wrapping his hands around my breasts and squeezing.

Fire erupted under my skin as I arched into his touch.

At that moment, I felt brazen. I fumbled for his belt, urging him to be set free before me, wanting him to take me right here, in the downstairs drawing room of all places. My desire bloomed and I wanted to feel him as my world turned ethereal.

But my wrists were caught and forced above me, my hands pinned together by one of his own to a bookshelf. I was unable to move. That little slice of pain, my wrists forced into the hard angles of the shelf, fueled my desire and forced a small moan to escape my lips.

His hips pinned mine while his free hand dipped beneath the waistband of my trousers and skirted his fingers along my flesh, stoking the fire to burn brighter. Heat scorched inside my veins as his fingers danced along that tight bundle of nerves in rhythmic strides that caused my hips to involuntarily rock forward against his hand. My body demanded the friction.

"Eyes on me." I heard the command and obeyed.

His silver eyes looked at me as his fingers moved expertly. I needed something to ground me and wrapped my leg tightly around his waist. The build was too much. The sensation was overwhelming.

His fingers dipped into that sensitive place and curled in, setting fireworks ablaze with each and every stroke.

"Hush now," he said, never letting up the pace. I couldn't help my panted breath the higher I climbed. Hard lips consumed mine to muffle my light moans. I was losing myself to the rhythm of his fingers, on the precipice, about to fall.

"Come for me," he growled as his lips overtook mine again, stifling the sounds of my pleasure. Peiro applied more pressure against my wrists, still held above me, as light and sound escaped me and bliss overtook my body in wakes.

I whimpered as his fingers coaxed me back to the present and I rode one blissful wave after another. My senses were enhanced once again, reminding me where I was.

"There she is," Peiro whispered roughly, planting kisses along the column of my neck.

A soft chime of laughter was heard down the hallway. I immediately realized where I was and what I was doing and pushed Peiro away.

The force of the empty space was so great that I felt myself tumble sideways on the side of a chair and toppled into its seat just as Ora rounded the corner and entered the room, completely unaware of what was transpiring just moments before.

"What in the world are you doing?" Ora looked down at me, still stuck half-upside-down in the chair.

I fumbled quickly to right myself onto my feet. "Stretching my lower back. All that training has made my body tight."

Ora arched a questionable brow and turned her head to see Peiro standing too casually in the corner, holding a broken trinket, inspecting it too closely.

"Uh-huh," Ora said as she glanced between the two of us and smiled brightly. "Well. I hope you feel very stretched. And that all your tight places have been attended to. Thoroughly."

My eyes bulged out of my head. *Giants*, how I wished I could die right here on the spot. "Did you want anything, my sweet...darling...adorably hilarious sister?" If looks could kill, I would be throwing daggers.

Another chime of laughter filled the space between us as Ora smiled even bigger. "Oh, stop with the compliments. You know they only make my head grow bigger."

I rolled my eyes.

"But yes. Matter of fact, I came looking for you two." She looked over at Peiro, who had sat the broken trinket down with such care it was almost comical.

"Go on," Peiro said hoarsely, his words seeming to catch in his throat. It was then I realized he stood directly behind a large wingback sofa to hide himself.

"Sury is on his last draught that Fyom made, and he told me he feels ready to start on the road. Fyom will prepare some additional draughts for him to take every few days to steady his progress once we set out."

"That's wonderful!" I said, realizing I was still catching my breath.

Ora looked back and forth between us once again and continued. "Yes, so with that said, Fyom has prepared a feast in the dining room. I came to let you two know...if you're hungry?" She quickly covered her smile with her hand.

I played along with the charade and perked my voice. "Yes! Of course! I'm hungry. Are you hungry?" I turned and asked the lighthearted question to Peiro as I clasped my hands before me.

He locked his stare onto me, heat still in his eyes. "I'm starving."

I felt myself swallow hard. The cooling heat rose once again in my lower belly.

"Good! Because we were waiting for you to join us." With a clap of her hands, Ora pivoted to exit the room.

Peiro cleared his way from behind the chair and wrapped one arm tightly around my shoulder as he clasped his hand to the back of my neck, pulling me in for another greedy kiss. My excitement flared once again as I felt his rigid length against my hipline.

"This feast better be damn worth it," Peiro growled as he rested his forehead against mine. We took a moment to steady our breath, both flickering our eyes open. Both seeing the fire behind them.

Every nerve screamed in protest when I finally spoke up to say, "We need to start heading that way or they'll wonder."

"Let them wonder," Peiro said as he greedily wrapped his lips around mine.

Reluctantly, I pulled away. "But we must."

"Says who?" Peiro buried his face into the crook of my neck, sucking and biting the spot that had grown to love his attention.

"Says me," I said with more reluctance and swatted at Peiro's shoulder.

"*Giants*, so help me," he said as he pulled away, taking a few steps back to distance himself. After a few cleansing breaths, we steadied ourselves and made our way to the hall.

"Wait," he called.

"We really need to..." I started, but then stopped when Peiro grabbed me by the hand and pulled me to a halt.

His eyes practically glowed in delight as the corners of his mouth tilted upward. Ever so delicately he tucked a wild hair behind my ear and planted a soft kiss to my cheek. "Perfect."

Butterflies swarmed my insides as I clasped my hand around his. We walked hand and hand down the long hallway and into the dining room.

A feast was putting it lightly. How the table held the amount of trays and cups was beyond my understanding, let alone the thought of how we could eat it all. Pies of every kind. Meats that were smoked, grilled, and baked, all still sizzling in their rich aroma. Platters of vegetables that were both grilled and fried, oils slowly dripping off the battered coating. Desserts that could make anyone's heart swoon (though the array of fruit tarts certainly were meant for my own heart).

Fyom, Ora, and Sury all sat at the table with large cups of something brown in their hands. Fyom took a deep swig from his, almost emptying its contents, before he realized that Peiro and I had joined them.

"There they are! Our final puzzle pieces!" His voice boomed higher than it typically did. I suspected something quite merry was inside his cup.

A small twinkle sparked in Sury's eyes as he took his own swig. His complexion had finally come back to its rich copper brown and his bright brown eyes were full of life. He had slowly regained his stature, not looking near as deathly as he did before.

"Come, sister! Let us feast before our new adventure!" I felt my arm being pulled in the direction of the table and plopped down at the opposite end where Fyom sat. A large cup of brown liquid was thrust into my hands, and some of the contents jumped over the sides and sloshed onto my fingers. A hint of cinnamon and nutmeg itched my senses.

I took a cautionary sip, immediately feeling my taste buds come alive. Each cell and nerve ending blossomed with warmth and joy. It wasn't ale, nor was it whiskey, but something in between.

"My own creation!" Fyom boomed from down the table, taking another large swig, emptying the contents in his mouth. Of course it was.

"Fyom. Ever creative," Peiro said as he took a seat to my right, next to Sury. He took a healthy drink from his contents and sighed. "And ever delicious." He raised his cup in the air, a toast. "To good fortune. To new friends." He turned his eyes to me and winked. "To new adventures."

"*Pli'vat!*" Fyom boomed. The Olden Language phrase that meant *may one be blessed in the good times and during trials.*

All of us chimed in unison before taking a healthy gulp from our cups. Fyom's refilled almost instantly from the magic of the cabin.

Ora and I celebrated the memory of our parents. Our sisterly reunion. We toasted to the promise of a new kingdom. A new age. A time where Wielding would no longer rule in a hierarchy, but would simply be celebrated in all ways.

Day turned into night as the platters refilled themselves. I knew I couldn't take another bite without feeling sick. At one point, I noticed Fyom had left the table and returned with a dusty case, dropping it in front of Peiro.

He almost jumped, distracted from a deep conversation with Sury, and looked at what fell before him. His eyes widened at the case. With shaky fingers he sat his cup on the table and traced the edges with his fingertips.

He looked up to Fyom, who boasted a proud grin. "Is it...truly?" Emotion swelled in Peiro's eyes. I watched the exchange closely, seeing some inside story unfold between the two.

"The one and the same," Fyom boomed.

I eyed the case as Peiro fumbled with the worn leather buckles. The once-rich brown material had turned to an off-shade of tan. Once they were free, Peiro quickly flipped open the brass latches and opened the case to reveal a honey-colored gittern.

The wood was delicately rich and looked new. The soft silk that held the gittern was a bright red that held its shape once Peiro picked up the instrument from its case. Upon further observation, I noticed it was made of two sets of wood. The front of the body was the rich honey brown while its back and neck matched a deep mahogany.

The sound hole was encased in a floral design that matched the front body's color. The pick guard matched the deep mahogany, and the simple design of a bird flying onto oak branches was painted beneath its shiny strings. A bright leaflet-like design was etched along its neck and base.

Peiro smiled broadly. I felt my face flush, but not because of the drink in my hand.

"Well, go on then. Play us a tune, you bastard," Fyom called from down the table.

"You play?" Excitement filled me as I watched Peiro observe the instrument, becoming reacquainted with a memory.

"It's been a very long time. Especially with Margeaux."

"Margeaux?" Ora eyed him suspiciously.

Peiro chuckled. "Yes. Every instrument needs a name before it can be played."

Sury chuckled from behind his cup, his eyes glazing over. "Hmph. Sounds like something the travelers from the north would say."

The lines in Peiro's face tightened as the smile reached the edges of his eyes. "Yes. Yes, they do." And with that, he brought the gittern up toward his ear and plucked a string. The sound was melodic. "She's still in tune?" He looked at Fyom, who only shrugged.

"She sounds lovely," I found myself saying, immediately hiding behind my cup and drinking deeply from its contents.

After a few picks to practice, Peiro found a rhythm with his fingers and the strings, and a sorrowful tune emitted into the air.

"No, no! This is a celebration! Joyful tunes only!" Fyom called once again.

On cue, Peiro's fingers danced easily along the strings, steadying the rhythm to one more fast-paced. I watched as his fingers dipped and slid along the gittern. Each move was methodical and careful. My imagination wondered what else his fingers could do, but I abruptly stopped when I felt my cheeks raise to an alarming red.

The night went on with merry music filling the air. I don't remember when it happened but at some point, I found myself dancing on top of the empty dining room table with Ora. Fyom smoked a large pipe, his laugh booming against the walls.

Sury's face held a seemingly permanent smile as his gaze continued to follow Ora wherever she went. Catching her breath, Ora doubled over, bracing her hands on her knees in front of Peiro. "Do you know any tavern songs? Brewery tunes? Drinking melodies?"

Peiro never once stopped plucking the strings. "Depends. What tale are you looking for?"

Ora looked over to Sury before looking back to Peiro. "We heard it once a while back, with a traveling circus."

"Oh, the one with the beautiful brunette? With curly hair?" Sury piped up, hiccuping from his drink in the process.

Ora cut him a hateful look. "Yes, the *beautiful* brunette. The one who performed with the oh-so-*gorgeous* blonde boy who also played a gittern."

Sury cut back a glance. "Yeah... I remember. What of it?"

"The one where they did that one jig and everyone clicked their heels in the air at the end."

Sury hiccupped again. "I don't recall. Something to do with a story of war coming. That's all I remember."

"Of course you would..." Ora glanced away and looked back to Peiro. "But yes, a readying for war. A war song, I suppose."

"Well," Peiro started cooly, "there are many songs about war, but if they were merry at the end, it sounds like it could be this one..." Immediately, the tune changed into something that started solemn but then picked up immensely.

"Yes! This is the one!" Ora screeched, immediately bellowing out the lyrics she could remember. They were simple enough that I caught on and bellowed and danced on the table as Peiro continued to play through the night.

In unison Ora and I, broad in smiles, sang the ending as loud as we could:

This is the day we stand up! This is the day we bring our might! This is the time we plan to fight.

Our hearts are not waiting for a war, so let's bring the war to them.

***

I knew my head should be feeling dizzy. That all of us should be feeling lightheaded, if it weren't for the warm cup now in my hands. After the eighth song we'd danced to, we found our cups refilled and sang to tragic melodies as we all reclined in chairs.

Even Peiro hummed along with one of them.

After he retired the gittern, Fyom produced a tray of steaming mugs that frothed with a green foam on top. The smell alone made us gag but he swore it would prevent anyone from feeling ill from all we had consumed.

I knew I had enjoyed myself far too much to embark on the road in the morning without at least a few sips. Ora and Sury were the first to retire from the table after finishing their own cups of the frothy recovery.

Their eyes sobered but a heat replaced it quickly. While their intent was obvious, it was nice to see that Sury was able to move around easier. He quickly grabbed Ora's hand and led her away from the table and down to the hall, before a loud *bang* of a closing door echoed through the rooms.

"Love. It's a beautiful thing." Fyom chuckled as he gathered his own frothy cup. He saluted, "To tomorrow's adventures."

"I guess we need to sort out some details," Peiro muffled as he took a deep drink from his own cup, but not without making a face in disgust. "*Fuck*, this is awful."

"Ah, but it gets the job done." Fyom swatted him on the back and tightly grabbed Peiro's shoulders to rock in jest.

I downed my own cup, eager to lay down on a feathered pillow one last time, not knowing when I'd have the chance again. I knew our traveling party would be more prepared this time around versus when Sury and I traveled together.

If I had to eat one more damn rosehip, I might scream.

The drink *did* taste like what one would imagine shit to taste like. But instantly, the haziness and fog that had crept into my senses lightened and my creeping headache receded.

I bade Fyom and Peiro good night, but not before catching Peiro's gaze and the hint of a smile that held in the corner of his mouth.

***

"Does everyone have what they need?" Fyom asked the next day. Five packs were laid neatly next to the cabin's door as everyone checked and rechecked to make sure we were all set.

My body ached in delicious ways, remembering how my hips had tilted high to allow Peiro to dive in deeper. I wasn't sure when we would have another moment to ourselves and welcomed the sweet kisses that woke me from my slumber when Peiro had returned to my room for the night.

Fyom's dreads were tied back with a piece of leather, and he looked menacing as he towered over everyone. I suspected his pack was filled with books and herbs he couldn't leave behind.

Peiro and Sury both had daggers strapped to their leather holsters. Peiro had two broadswords interlocking on his back while Sury carried a new quiver and bow. Sury had cut his hair short once again, while Peiro tied his back into a half-braid.

Ora and I donned dark tunics, brown leather pants, and riding boots for easier trekking. We braided our hair similarly to stay out of the way and cause little fuss while in the wilderness.

"Did you sleep well?" I asked her as I rechecked the laces of my boots for the second time.

"Like a dream." Small bits of pinks rose to Ora's cheeks as she turned to pick up her pack.

A small chuckle escaped from Sury, who was adjusting his belt to be one notch tighter than he normally did. He was slowly regaining size, but his frame was still smaller than before. He stopped what he was doing and stared between Ora and me in awe. Blinking hard and shaking his head.

Ora shot him a look.

"Sorry, but you two look almost identical. I've never seen it before, but you look the same...only—"

"Night and Day." Peiro finished his sentence and gave me a knowing look before he turned on his heel and exited the cabin.

Each of us filed after, with Fyom being the last one to leave and close the door. He took a few steps off the porch and into the clearing before stopping and turning back to face the cabin.

Peiro, Sury, and Ora didn't see he had stopped, but I had turned around in time to see a small glint run down Fyom's dark cheek. I stood beside him, looking at the small-appearing cabin that held a great secret within.

"I have not left my home in almost ten years," Fyom said quietly.

"Is that when she passed? Your wife?" I asked.

Fyom nodded and stood in deep thought. "Something like that."

"Peiro told me a little about her. I would have loved to have met her."

Fyom turned his gaze from the house to me and laughed. "She would have enjoyed every moment of the company if she were here. She would have also loved to team up against Peiro with you. She always loved to jest with him."

"I would love to learn more about her, if you'd like to talk about her?"

"I have enough stories that might embarrass her, but that also might make this trip a little more bearable. I know she would use *my* embarrassment to help others, so fair is fair," Fyom said with a wink and laughed. He held his arm out for me to loop through his and together we walked into the wilderness, following behind everyone else.

CHAPTER 37

For days we made our way south, staying off the main roads. Sury and Peiro hunted for what we needed and Fyom visited townships to listen for any news that was worth investigating.

The forest and fields around us faded and lost vibrancy the closer we walked toward Grianmore Castle. Flowers that once shone brightly in the sun were now dull and shrunken in size. A sickly feeling filled the air with each step forward. Even an encounter with the gentle urthens I had discovered on the trails north were very few and far between. But the moment we spotted a bratrian grazing in the distance, Ora's eyes widened in glee. She immediately began devising a plan to build coops and keep some at the castle.

"In a day's time we will be at the *rock*," Sury said as he hunched over a map that sat on a table inside Fyom's tent. I could hardly believe there was a full-sized dining table inside, let alone a full-sized bed that could fit three grown Fyoms, a chaise lounge, a full wardrobe—oh, and not to mention, four tall bookshelves *filled* with books and scrolls.

Somehow he'd done it again. During our first night on the road, Fyom had set up his seemingly *small* tent, while I noticed no one else had a tent in their own packs. I had assumed the open sky would be our blankets, just as it was when Sury and I trekked for Zonnagberg.

But I was so gladly wrong. All of us could easily move around in the tent and sleep comfortably. Peiro opted to stay outside to keep watch for any of Vovias's or Dokvalon's men, while I learned then that it seemed he hardly slept at all.

I suspected Fyom's concoctions might have been losing their potency with the herbs he had to supplement on our travels. So I watched the battles that Peiro tried to hide as his brown eyes dulled and offered my hand of comfort when he needed it.

"Would it be best if you and Peiro scoped out the township closest to the Rising Rock and sent word before we followed?" Ora asked Sury.

"I could go," I stated.

Ora gave me a look. "They know who you are, *Ophelia*."

"But they know Sury too, *Aurora*," I countered. "Plus, since he's known to be *close* with you, that might not be wise."

"I can handle myself," Sury stated as he crossed his arms. Sury had finally regained his full strength. His arms once again held tight and toned muscle, and his waist settled back into a healthy state. Even the muscles around his jawline had filled out once more.

"But..." I started to protest but was interrupted as Fyom opened the flap of the tent, allowing bright rays from the sun to shine through.

"We need to leave. Quickly gather your things."

A steady hum filled the air. A loud shrill pierced the space around us, forcing us to cover our ears with our hands.

"What's going on?" I questioned as I saw Fyom putting small things into his canvas sack. We didn't need to wait for an answer, because right on cue, we heard the pounding sound of hooves meeting the earth.

Ora's face paled. "It can't be."

"How did they find us?" Sury demanded as he took two steps toward where he had laid his bow and daggers.

Peiro ran through the tent flaps as if he had been sprinting but not a drop of sweat covered his body. He looked to Sury with a sense of understanding as he gathered his own swords. "Fyom. I need you to get ready."

Fyom turned on his heel to face Peiro as he stuffed a jar into his overflowing sack. "And do what? All giants above, I'm a *Healer*! I *treat* injuries, not cause them!"

I could almost smell the fear that radiated off of Fyom. Large as he was, he was even more gentle.

"And you're about to become a Death Dealer if you don't at least pretend to hold your ground," Peiro growled between his teeth.

Fyom huffed in annoyance and grabbed an herb-cutting dagger off the table, sticking it into the loop of his belt.

"Sury, stay by the door but stay hidden. You two—" he looked to both me and Ora, with his gaze focusing on me. His hair had grown more brittle and the lines on his face had grown deeper the last few days, but I could tell he was still in control, even as his eyes steadily turned gray.

"Stay here. A merchant at the last trading post told me that these men check every traveler to make sure they're not harboring any fugitives from your court. And I would say you two are definitely fugitives." He took one lasting look at me before he finished with, "If you have to, call on your power. Use it. You are strong and capable. Do not worry about the consequences."

I knew what he meant. *Don't worry about his pain*. But before I could reply, Fyom and Peiro were out of the tent. Sury posted himself near the flap, keeping his eye on the flowing gap to listen for the sound of hooves growing nearer. Ever so delicately, as he had practiced hundreds of times before, he picked an arrow from his quiver and nocked it inside his bow, ready to aim and fire at the ready.

Ora flexed her fingers, emitting a tiny glow from her fingertips, ready to Wield the sun.

My own fingers flexed over the hilt of a sword. It was similar in size to the one I had trained with at Fyom's and I felt the familiarity in its weight. The palm of my free hand lightly glowed as small lights of blue danced between my fingertips.

The sound of the hooves grew closer and came to a halt mere feet outside the tent. A low muffling sound could be heard, words being exchanged between Fyom and whoever was on horseback. I couldn't make out where Peiro was and assumed he might have hidden somewhere.

Sury's spine straightened to a point, his shoulders stiffening. The act didn't go unnoticed by Ora as she motioned to catch his attention.

As if he could sense her, Sury turned his head just enough for us to see him mouth *Black Raiders*.

Dokvalon.

I didn't realize I had been holding my breath the entire time.

"My good sirs, you don't need to go in there. Inside are just my private things. I'm a Healer by trade and 'tis only my tinctures and herbal books."

A gravelly voice, one that sounded like it was chorded against death, spoke. "A Healer, you say?"

"Just a humble Healer."

"I thought Gria's Healers were stationed amongst the royal families and governing court's manors? Why would a *humble Healer* be out in the woods? So far from the nearest estate?"

I could hear Fyom mumble through his words. His nerves were catching up with him. "You see, I...ah. I needed to collect some specimens...for my..." Someone else that stood close to the gravelly-sounding man said something I couldn't understand.

But what I could hear next was clear as day—someone yelling, "Oh, shit!"

And with that, the sound of metal against metal clanged high in the air. A roar of thunder beat against the earth as it sounded like horse hooves and feet clamored across the ground.

"Fuck," Sury hissed as he let one of his arrows loose. A high-pitched screech pierced over the clanging metal.

My heart stalled when I heard it.

Before I could gather more of my thoughts, a large individual, fully covered in black armor with silver insignia, bombarded through the flaps and knocked Sury off his feet.

I was led through instinct and training as I guarded myself with my sword, blocking the Raider's sword as it swept downward. I used both hands to stop the attack and didn't have the strength to continue my guard one-handed to work my Wielding with the other.

Bright, gold light erupted from behind me and knocked the Raider back into the air, causing it to twist and land with a loud *thud* against the ground. In one swift move, Sury had jumped to his feet and held a dagger in his hand, pushing the blade into the Raider's neck.

A jet of red liquid erupted and covered Sury's pants and boots while another pool of it collected under the Raider's armor. "Weak spot. Always look for the weak spot," Sury said as he twisted the dagger, causing a sickening sound.

"But why is that so *hot*?" Ora said from across the room.

Sury looked up with heat in his eyes and was about to speak before I interrupted. "Oh, you two. We have more pressing things to focus on right now." And with that, I ran out of the tent.

There was a flurry and flash of metal that glinted against the midday sun. Fyom removed the end of a sword from one of the Raiders as I noticed three more on the ground.

Urthen beasts, just like the ones I saw at the temple, lay dead. Black horses had scattered and ran in the opposite direction.

Out in a small field, Peiro was in combat with the two remaining Raiders. With a sword in each hand, he commanded his opponents in such a way that screamed decades of execution. He remained quick on his feet as he pivoted and pulled, countering each attack from the Raiders on both sides.

The ire across his face was like acid. I could feel the loathing from where I stood and watched in awe as years of Peiro's emotions played at the surface. The rage radiated and rolled off in waves as he continued his attacks and counterattacks, screaming a war cry with each blow of his sword.

And I hated to admit just how in tune I was as I watched him, in his full form, and a dull ache grew at the base of my stomach. I bit the inside of my lip as I watched his body twist and move in the artful way that shadows danced in the night. He was a predator and they were the prey. He was the night sky and they were a mere blade of grass.

He cut one of the Raiders in the back of the leg and the Raider pivoted and fell to its knees. Red spray was cast into the air, followed by a hollow scream. In two quick moves, Peiro's sword cut another vital tendon in the same Raider's leg, rendering them utterly immobile.

As he counterattacked the standing Raider, Peiro twisted and brought the momentum and force behind his blades, swiping both swords in opposite directions and relieving the immoble Raider of its head.

The one that was standing immediately pivoted and ran. Peiro looked in the direction of the tent just as Ora and Sury made their exit. Slowly, Peiro lifted one of the bloody swords and pointed to Sury. The silvers in his eyes shone almost iridescently.

He smiled a sickly smile. "Happy hunting," he said in a twisted manner, and turned to chase after the fleeing Raider.

"Oh, the fuck he's *not* going to claim more than me," Sury said as he pushed between me and Ora to chase after Peiro in hopes to claim another Raider for himself.

"Men," Ora huffed under her breath as she turned to see the bodies before us.

Fyom had already begun to remove a helmet from one of the fallen Raiders and immediately jumped back from where he had knelt. He gasped as he ran into the tent and back out while clutching a canvas bag.

"What is it?" I asked as I knelt beside Fyom while he removed a pair of tweezers and some other sort of medical-looking instrument.

But I didn't have to wait long to understand what had caught his attention. The face that was underneath the helmet was no longer that—a face. Instead, it was a rotten skull with slabs of decayed skin clinging to its host. The nose was missing entirely and the eyelids were ripped, revealing large, clouded eyes. The whites were almost completely gone, replaced by a multitude of small veins that fueled the clouded irises.

"What in the giant's name?" Ora whispered behind us, holding a hand to her mouth and clutching the stone of her necklace with the other.

"Check the other one," Fyom called.

I didn't need further direction and steadily took off the helmet of the Raider next to me, afraid of what grotesque image I would find. As I pulled, bits of long blonde hair escaped from a braid that had spilled out of the helmet's base. The skin around the neck was smooth and whole and a beautiful shade of cream. With one final tug, the helmet revealed a particularly beautiful woman underneath.

I thanked the giants that this Raider's eyes were closed, but she looked so *normal*. Her rosy cheeks were still flush and whole, and her bright blonde hair—much more yellow than Ora's—was thick and pulled into a war braid.

I went to the next fallen Raider and as I removed the helmet, I found that this Raider looked a lot like the one Fyom had inspected. I jumped to the next, revealing a dark-complected man with tightly coiled dark hair. His eyes were open but void of light, and pained in a way that reflected the last moments he endured.

Ora had found the courage to check the others, all resembling the first one we saw. Two humans among this squad of the *dead*? Moments later, Peiro and Sury returned and the two men debated loudly about who relieved the fleeing Raider of which limbs and who executed the final death blow. Sury caught Ora's broken demeanor first and began to run, with Peiro not far behind.

"What happened?" Sury wrapped his arms tightly around her, trying to calm her shaking. "What in the giant's name is this?"

Peiro scooped my hand into his and held onto it gingerly. "Are you okay?" He softly caressed the tops of my knuckles in soothing circles. Such a stark contrast to the wrath and death he had dealt just moments ago.

My adrenaline was subsiding. I didn't realize how shaken I was, seeing flashbacks of the attack at the temple. An intruder in our tent. Seeing Ora fight. Seeing her being ripped away. "I'm okay," I lied.

Peiro looked at me as if sensing my lie, but didn't press further. He looked down to the soldiers at our feet. I felt him tense. "Burn them," he commanded out loud and to no one in particular. "Burn them all. Now." His voice dropped into deeper octaves, death snaking along his tongue.

Instinctively I reached for his arm, hoping to provide him calm.

"What is it? Have you seen this before?"

"It shouldn't even be on this side of the mountains," he seethed.

"What do you mean by that?" Ora stomped over to him, her head barely reaching his chest. "What are you not telling us?"

Peiro released himself from my grasp and squared with Ora. The move alone forced Sury to react and stand especially close behind her, looking over the top of her head to match his glare to Peiro's. Just then, I saw something flash across Peiro's stare right as I felt the tension building, an antithesis forming between the two that hadn't existed moments ago.

Peiro laughed and bent forward just enough to even his level with Ora. "You're on your way to be queen and I do not think anyone has prepared you for what you're facing. These are Dokvalon's creations. Take a look. Unless you can control them, this is what your Grian army will be against should you claim back your throne and fight." He did a large sweep of his arms to point to all the dead and undead soldiers around us.

"She's more than capable of reclaiming her throne *and* taking on Dokvalon." Sury practically foamed at the mouth with the sensed threat between the two. A steady green sheen illuminated Ora's features. Peiro coiled back.

I reached out to touch his arm with delicate fingers, trying to grab his attention away from Ora and Sury. "Peiro. Peiro, look at me," I whispered. Immediately, I was met with dangerous silvers. He tried pulling his arm away but I grabbed harder—showing I wasn't going to give up so easily. Something told me to *push*. "You told us to burn them. Why?"

"It's the only way those will *stay* dead," he said as he pointed to the strange corpse at our feet. "And it will prevent those poor human souls from turning into one of *them.*"

"How do you know?" I was almost too afraid to ask. "How are they doing it?"

Peiro flinched. "*We've* seen too many horrors within Dokvalon's borders. Some that would make your nightmares scream."

My heart dropped a beat before I glanced at Sury and Ora. Fyom finished inspecting the dead soldiers before Peiro retrieved the fallen Raider who had fled earlier. Then, together with Sury, they quickly gathered all the bodies and dead urthens into a pile. I gagged at the rotten smell they emitted into the air.

Ora and I took turns casting our Wielding to ignite the pile and send a wind to disperse the smoke methodically, hoping the pillar wouldn't alert other soldiers to our presence.

"Are you okay?" I found Peiro standing fifty paces away, looking off in the distance. I rested my fingers along the stubble on his jaw to pull his attention to me.

Peiro remained silent for a few heartbeats before he flickered his eyes open. I could see his pain increasing. "It senses when you're close."

My breath hitched. "What does it do?"

"It gets angry and thrashes. Orders me to flee from you. Sometimes it hides, granting me a momentary peace I have not felt in a long, long time. It fears being controlled."

An image of a caged animal came to mind. I didn't know what to say. His inadvertent confession made my heart soar, knowing he was experiencing peace, but it quickly crashed knowing that I was causing him more pain.

"Can I help?" I asked, delicately touching his jaw.

"No." His grip was firm against my waist. "Save your strength. We...I can see what your power does to you and how it can drain you."

"I'll be fine. Please let me help."

"You've done more for me than you know." He planted a kiss on my forehead and lingered for a bit, taking in steady breaths. "Thank you," he whispered. "I should apologize to them for my outburst." He turned back toward the others, intertwining his fingers in mine for me to follow along.

Soon we were traveling again. Fyom led the charge while Ora and I quietly followed behind. Sury and Peiro guarded the back, still bickering about who hunted what and how many Raiders they'd claimed just hours prior.

Before our journey, Ora had shared what she knew about Peiro. Sury was understandably shocked and seemed to be keeping a close watch on Ora, as if Peiro would outright attack her. But I could also tell he tried granting Peiro more grace where he could.

A quiet hum continued to hang in the air the further we traveled. A vibration that caused the hairs on my arms to stand on end. I stopped listening to Ora prattle away about something and took in the electricity around me, sensing *something*.

"What is it?" I felt his presence before he had even spoken. A quiet comfort I didn't realize I needed. It steadied me. I came up to his shoulders but still felt the need to crane my head up to look into his face.

"I don't know."

"What are you feeling?"

"How do you know I'm feeling anything?"

"I can hear your heartbeat. It was calm—well, as calm as it can be when you're around your sister. But then it started palpating in an odd rhythm. Almost like it was fighting to beat."

The thought spooked me a bit. "Could you hear my heartbeat when we first met?"

Peiro nodded and answered with a sly smile. "Yes."

"Can you hear everyone's?"

"I can."

I felt embarrassment rise as I recalled all the times I tried to keep my heartbeat under control when he was around in those initial moments. What good that did.

Peiro huffed a small laugh, sensing what I had to be feeling. "It helped build my own courage around you," he whispered as he planted a swift kiss on my cheek. I leaned into the tender touch. "Now, what were you feeling?"

I looked around the rolling fields and the thick tree line. Nothing in the hills or in the air seemed out of sorts, but something wasn't right. Fyom had continued walking, not sensing we had stopped. Ora and Sury continued their hushed conversation as they held hands behind Fyom, but she must have sensed our absence and looked over her shoulder, because she stopped at once.

I held my hands out in front of me, fingers splayed, and felt the vibrations again. Something stirring. Something dying. Without calling on it, my Wielding flared underneath my fingertips, pulsing a light gray underneath my skin.

Peiro gasped, almost in pain, but was cut off by a shout in the distance.

Fyom.

Two blades were pulled out of their sheaths with lightning speed as Peiro pivoted and ran in Fyom's direction, passing Ora and Sury with fast intensity. Sury followed suit with his own blade and sprinted behind Peiro as fast as he could.

I grabbed Ora's hand and ran wildly after them. Around a bend in the tree line, we saw Fyom standing there. No injuries, no blood. Peiro and Sury caught up to him and looked around, waiting for the unseen foe to attack, before relaxing their stance and turning in the direction Fyom was facing.

We gasped in unison at what we saw. The township nestled on the north side of the Rising Rock Temple was covered in billows of smoke. Skeletons of buildings stood, telling the tale of destruction, of a fire that swept through and claimed the town.

Our feet stampeded toward the fire-charred remnants of the village. We called out as we looked for any survivors. Thick ash covered our clothes as we searched, finding no one. Not even a stray dog.

Fyom had given us small vials of a peach-colored concoction, instructing us to pour three drops down any survivors' bodies before he attended to their Healing. He said it would numb their pain, even if it meant they crossed over to Cisoi's doorstep. Ora immediately called onto Ythos, the giantess said to grant life, to help those who could be brought back. Peiro snarled beside me and stepped away from her.

Street after street was empty; only small fires throughout the buildings remained. My senses felt overloaded and over-whelmed. At one point, Peiro pulled me away just in time as a large structure collapsed to the ground. Just as he steadied me on my feet, we heard a cry of anguish to our west.

We didn't hesitate as our feet pivoted and ran. Peiro was ahead, moving inhumanly fast and carving a safe path for me to follow. I found him at the end of a scorched stone alley with his back toward me. The cry turned into a desperate wail.

I pushed forward, sprinting with all my might. Peiro was now ten paces ahead but quickly turned around, his eyes a new kind of wild and filled with panic. He reached out to try and stop me in my tracks but I still pushed forward. He wrapped his arms tightly around me to stall my run, but it was too late.

He couldn't stop me from seeing the horrid sight.

I don't remember him holding me steady, nor the quiet shushes he whispered into my ear as he stroked my hair. I don't even remember falling to my knees, and only heard my own scream that matched the one I'd heard before.

How did we miss the large pillar of smoke? A blazing fire roared and consumed the largest pile of remains I had ever witnessed. The licks of the flames climbed higher than the tallest of the buildings with no ceasing in sight.

Images intertwined with my memories of the night Ora was taken. The fires that erupted around us. Through the tears that ran down my ash-ridden face, I saw something I hadn't recognized at first. This was an unnatural fire. This fire defied the laws of nature and the impending end for flames.

No. This fire was set by a Wielder, and I only knew of one Wielder strong enough with fire to do this.

Vovias.

I heard the scream again and this time saw that it was Ora screaming in Sury's arms. I pushed through Peiro's hold and tore through Sury's to get to my sister. I held her tightly as she gripped my tunic with all her strength.

"That bastard!" Ora screamed into my shoulder. She'd figured it out too.

"He'll fucking pay," I vowed. A wave of anger built inside me just as something pushed my Wielding. Death. I was surrounded by so much of it that my Wielding was forced to respond. "He'll fucking pay!" I shouted again into the air.

I shifted my body to place Ora back in Sury's arms before I stood. I felt strong, familiar hands loosely grab my arm, but I shook them off. I was consumed by my rage.

How could someone do this to innocents? What role did this town play in his game? Was it for bloodsport or for his ecstasy?

I would never get the answers I sought. Never would they tell me the *whys* to all these questions. My own parents would never tell me why they decided to leave me and Ora alone. Leaving us caught off guard by the threats that lurked in the unsuspecting corners of our world.

A scream pierced through me. I didn't even realize it was my own as I brought my hands up in front of me and into the sky. My Wielding forced me to shake as my mind saw each unknown face being needlessly slaughtered. My body coiled and my shoulders tensed as I dove deep into my well and pulled up *everything*.

The once-beautiful, delicate blue orbs that resembled the stars in the distance were now dark shadows and billows of smoke that rivaled the never-ending smoke in front of me. With a hard swing, I threw my arms down and focused my fingers toward the fire and poured and poured and *poured*. I didn't need to call upon death, nor Thuvina's strength, because death was here.

In crashing waves, my shadows overtook the town and snuffed out fires, looping the smoke into my own. The shadows that were drawn to abandoned buildings curled tightly into mine and built my wave even more.

I saw them then. Translucent figures standing before me. Each one sad and solemn. My heart panicked as I took in the sight of a small figure, a child no more than seven, walking forward in a bloodstained dress and pointing to the fire. I knew then that these figures, hundreds of them, were the victims of the fire.

Beads of sweat crested my brow just as I felt drops slide down my back. I was nearing burnout, yet I raged. Just then, a whisper in my ear that sounded like my father's told me to release my hold. To let go of everything within me.

And I did.

The shadows I had built, the height marveling to that of the townhomes in Grianmore, the power that amplified against what I threw at the Ancient One, came crashing down over the fire, ceasing the flames altogether. My surroundings went black.

I thought for a moment I had passed out but the shadows dissipated and returned to me, absorbing back into my hands. It felt cold, like a winter breeze cutting through me down to my bones but an intoxicating sweetness returned in my mouth. A shiver tore through me just as my knees crashed to the ground. I caught myself with my hands, feeling the ash through my fingers.

Soft hands caressed my cheeks but I didn't hear what was said as I tumbled forward, falling into black.

CHAPTER 38

I dreamed.

The man's face was stark compared to the forest that we stood in. I knew I was dreaming by the ethereal glow that edged the bright green canopy overhead. The man was just feet away from me. He would have been handsome, I thought, but something about his appearance was off.

The lines were too sharp. Too severe. His hair was too dark, as if it had consumed the light of the sun itself. His skin was too pale. But the glow in his upturned eyes made it clear that he was a Wielder.

I stood there, watching him saying something but unable to hear. No sound escaped him, not even a whisper, as he seemingly started to yell. He took two steps forward, fully in front of me. But I wasn't scared. I knew this man couldn't hurt me.

He was slightly taller, so it was easy to look into those eyes.

His silver eyes.

***

The heat consumed me when my eyes flickered open. Blankets on top of blankets were piled onto me. The pressure of them felt suffocating. Slowly I peeled them back and planted my feet upon the ground, next to my dusty boots. Fyom's tent was empty and eerily quiet, but I heard muffled voices on the other side of the canvas.

I stepped outside into the cool night air, welcoming the sensation against my warm skin, and found Ora and Sury nibbling on a catch while Fyom lay on a bedroll next to a small fire.

"Hey, you," Ora said as she climbed to her feet. "How are you feeling?"

"What happened?" I asked, instantly feeling a sharp slice against the inner walls of my mind. A canteen was placed in my hands, full of cold water that I sloppily consumed. The bits of water that escaped the sides of my mouth cooled my skin further.

"You almost burned out," Ora whispered. "But you stopped in time. Before you passed out."

"For how long?"

"About three hours."

I squeezed my eyes shut, letting the pain in my head edge away.

Before I had time to register, Ora asked, "Do you remember what happened?"

Small pictures of memories played in my mind. Smoke. Fires. Those *people*.

"That was by far the most badass thing I think I've ever seen you do, Phe. Even your eyes turned this eerie silver color." Sury chuckled. "Remind me to never piss you off *again*."

"Yeah, like that'll happen," Ora snipped.

"My eyes?" I looked at Ora, touching my cheekbone. I shut my eyes tightly as another wave of pain seared through my body. What did this mean?

"They're normal. Well, except that silver ring is a little thicker now." Ora tilted her head and looked at me with burning questions in her eyes. "Phe, who's Sedgwic?"

I looked at her, confused, ransacking my memory. "I've never heard the name before. Why?"

Ora scrunched her face, hesitating a bit. "Well, you called out that name while you were recovering. To be honest, I thought maybe it was someone you *knew* but forgot to mention to me," she said with a sheepish smile.

"No. I don't know anyone by that name," I confirmed, but there was one name that belonged to someone I needed to see. I looked around the dark campsite. "Where's Peiro?"

A realization sank into my heart. I had not only touched the *illicitus* but Wielded it in such a degree and intensity, who knows what it would have done to him. "Where is Peiro?" I repeated, more sternly.

Ora nodded to a tree line in the distance. "He's over there. But he's not himself."

"What do you mean?" I heard the warning, suspecting her meaning.

"He's fighting," Fyom said out loud, looking at no one in particular. "The vials aren't working anymore."

"I can help! I can..." I knew what this meant.

"No, Ophelia. You were too close to burnout. With being on the road, who knows how long you need to recover before you..."

I heard the strain in my sister's voice and could see the battle she fought on my behalf. It was the same fight I'd had when easing her into seeing Sury when he was on death's doorstep.

Before she could stop me, I ran on weak legs in the direction that she had pointed, into the trees. It didn't take me long to find him sitting on the forest floor next to a tree. My body and being were pulled in his direction. His gaze snapped up to mine just as I crashed on my knees before him, cupping my hands around his face, inspecting him.

"We're not hurt." There was an edge to his voice I couldn't quite understand.

"What do you mean?" I asked, taking in the planes of his face. The fullness of the moon radiated against his eyes. Steadily, the silver intensified closer to the pupils, clearly winning an unseen battle.

The deep lines of his face had returned, and his hair frayed at its end. He sat still as if he were finding control in his center, but barely. I needed him back to me and in the present.

He turned and looked into my eyes. "Your power has grown. Intensified. You're the most marvelous thing I've ever witnessed."

I sat there, deeply confused. Why weren't his eyes brown if he felt my power?

"It made me run," he said, reading the emotion on my face. "In the moment you needed me, it tore me away from you. Punished me for being so close to you. And we..." He swallowed hard as he squeezed his eyes shut before he slowly reopened them. "I am so sorry." His hands lightly cupped mine as I still held his face.

I shook my head. "It's not your fault."

"But I saw you. In the distance. And you were beautiful."

I kneeled there, staring at him. "We'll fight this. We'll figure this out together." I took his hand in mine, the coolness granting me release from my own heat.

"I saw them," he said out loud, withdrawing. My heart stammered, thinking of all those innocents. "I saw Talia. And Brehm. Just like the day I remember. Right before I lost my grip on control." His silver gaze flickered to mine. "A reminder that it will always win. I was a fool to think otherwise."

"You don't mean that," I stammered, reaching for his touch again. He pulled back, wincing in pain.

"Let me help you," I whispered, slowly calling on the slow dredge of power beneath my hands. Peiro's hand squeezed mine to stop.

"No. You almost burned out and we will not let you risk yourself further for me, more than what you've already done."

"But..." I started.

Peiro moved unnaturally fast to his feet, towering over me. "We almost lost you, Ophelia. You were too close to your edge, and I cannot risk losing you over my momentary relief. No more. Promise me." Panic sat deep in his eyes. But how could he ask me this?

"I can help," I said softly as I climbed to my feet.

"Promise me!" he urged, gripping my shoulders. The swirls of silver in his eyes thrashed violently, illuminating against the sky. I couldn't. Seeing the battle he was fighting, the invisible grip tightening his hold, caused my heart to ache in new ways. Memories swarmed of our first encounters in Zonnagberg, and in the woods on our way to Fyom's, and the internal battles that seeped to physical ones.

How he opted for the poison of the valley gilliflower to grant him just a moment of peace.

"No." I shook my head.

"Don't be a fool!" Peiro snarled in my face but I saw what it really was behind those eyes. "You're a fool if you think you can win against this! You think you can control me? Girl, I have a tighter grip on him now because I know his greatest weakness. And you've given it to me!" he hissed in my face.

Peiro rapidly blinked and took large, staggering steps backwards, shaking his head. "I'm sorry. I'm sorry," he sputtered as he backed away, fighting. He roared into the night, slamming his fist into a nearby tree, sending shockwaves through its branches and tremors into the ground.

I hoped to the giants no one heard that. I couldn't imagine them seeing Peiro in this state or what Sury would do to try and protect us.

Peiro continued to thrash against himself as he gripped his hair tightly at his temples, screaming and begging for the voice to stop. My heart couldn't take it, seeing the violent exchange with his invisible foe. Tears cascaded down my cheeks as I pushed with all my effort toward him.

I reached out my hand to pull on his wrist, hoping I could lighten his grip and prevent him from pulling his hair out. A deep growl released from his throat just as his hand swung mine away, landing its force across my face. My body hit the ground just as my vision blurred.

He stood over me, those eyes glowing wildly as he cocked his head to the side. A face I didn't recognize stared down at me. The features were too sharp; the kind eyes I had grown to know over the last few months were intense. The deep lines around those full lips were pulled tightly into a snarl. I didn't wait for what came next. I wasn't going to be another victim of this entity to unabashedly mark the innocent man's soul.

I dove and pulled whatever scraps I had left, instantly feeling an internal heat flare inside my body and scorch me from within. Burnout was so, so close. My body hadn't healed enough to pull this kind of power again.

But I brought my Wielding to the surface anyway. My palm littered with serpentine black shadows. It looked just like the smoke from the village. *Illicitus.*

Peiro hissed and stumbled back as if being pushed by an unseen opponent. I stood on shaky legs, keeping my hand held out in front of me. The resistance felt like the opposite pole of a magnet—an initial pull forward met by an invisible barricade—as I stood before Peiro's body, now bound to a tree by wisps of dark shadow.

I pushed again, taking steady steps forward to not lose my hold on the entity before me. I was so thirsty. So hot. My vision dimmed, but still I pushed until I was mere inches in front of him. He craned his neck away, desperately trying not to look in my direction.

"Look at me," I commanded, my voice not entirely my own.

Silver eyes stared into mine as fresh tears fell down my face.

"*You cannot have hiiiiim,*" the thing hissed.

"Peiro, come back to me," I commanded in a whisper as I rested my hand, full of power, onto his skin. Something flared as I fell to my knees in pure exhaustion.

Callused hands caught me right before my head hit the ground and rolled me onto my back. A body pressed over mine on the forest floor, and delicate lips placed a soft kiss upon my own. The touch was so tender, like someone was afraid to taste what was already theirs.

"I'm here," Peiro whispered softly against my clavicle. "I'm here," he repeated again and again as his lips worshipped my skin.

I leaned in, furthering the connection. A light moan escaped from him as I wrapped my arms around his broad shoulders. His skin was cool next to mine but I deepened my hold, coaxing his lips open. My tongue waltzed with his, taking each stroke carefully. I looked up and saw a dull gray. Still not the usual deep browns, but he was back in control for now. I felt his growing arousal along my waistline and smiled. He needed this just as much as I needed to know he was here with me.

Hands roamed. Kisses turned feverish.

And the stars witnessed our growing devotion.

CHAPTER 39

I agreed to rest for a day before we continued. Peiro never left my side.

The area was eerily similar to when we arrived for the ritual all those months ago. All except for the destruction that took place. Stone structures stood on their own, in pieces and scattered across the forest floor. Parts were either burnt or held heavy scorch marks.

The Rising Temple still stood in the middle of the clearing, its stones no longer covered in the rich vines as when I last saw it, but black shadows from the fire marred every inch of it.

With her necklace clutched in her hand, Ora stepped in front of Peiro's leading position, taking in the area where she was abducted by Black Raiders. I could sense that she saw the images from that night flashing through her mind's eye as she turned and turned, looking around her.

Because I saw them too.

Peiro lightly grabbed Ora by the elbow and brought her closer as we all formed a circle around her, as planned, checking for any signs of soldiers in the area.

Caws of birds broke the silence. Without a word, Peiro held two large broadswords and gave the signal we had practiced to move toward the inner part of the temple. Sury had an arrow nocked in his bow while Fyom held a large dagger in one hand and an iridescent green Wielded shield in the other.

Ora and I had small ribbons and orbs, respectively, floating in our hands, ready to strike at a moment's notice. Together, we inspected the temple and were in awe at how much the fire had engulfed and left its mark, what felt like so long ago.

Light pierced the treetops and through the cracks of the temple. Through a tiny gap in the ceiling, I caught a glimpse of something that made me gasp. The moon had turned into an ominous shade of red. A Blood Moon.

The giants must be on our side.

Ridges and divots in the floor forced us to pace slowly to avoid tripping or setting off any loud noises. The temple would have been a marvel, if not for the scorch marks. My curiosity to study the reliefs and sculptures called to me, but we had to keep moving. Chamber by chamber, we made our way through until we entered a great hall that held a jutting stone tower in its middle.

The hall itself looked remarkable with not a single touch by fire nor smoke. Its walls and floor were smooth sandstone, with beautiful vines creeping up through cracks in the floor and twirling around six stone pillars in the center. Candles burned brightly along the walls, highlighting the monument the pillars encased.

To anyone else, it might look like a simple jagged rock that rose out of the ground, but the meaning behind this monolith was everything to Wielders and those who ruled in Gria. It represented a promise, and the rulers who promised to protect it.

Imbuing magic wasn't a halfhearted promise, no. It meant that the ruler would rather die than see something horrid happen to their people. Imbuing their magic was the lock and key that promised protection and prosperity.

The chain of power had never been broken until the attack.

Only the upcoming ruler could step into the inner circle to promise themselves to the land and imbue. We studied the room, waited, and listened. Everything was in place for us to proceed.

The fire in the sconces burned brighter, highlighting the swirls and runes etched deeply in the stone, some language lost to time and only shared during the ritual. The ritual that only the High Priestess of the High Seven could commence. Giants only knew if Ariadne would have recited what these lines truly said, and not something with hidden malice.

I wiped my hand across my forehead. This room held so much heat compared to the hallway and forest outside. Peiro stood close to my left, facing the outer wall and one of the doorways that led to a smaller, adjacent chamber that Sury had left through just moments ago to ensure no one was in the temple.

Fyom continued to face the doorway we had just entered through, keeping an eye out for any movement we might have missed. The sconces burned noticeably brighter, imitating true sunlight within the hall.

A realization shook me.

Ora was just a hair's breadth away from the pillars, hovering over the threshold to where the Rising Rock stood. I looked over my shoulder and toward Fyom, and then quickly turned to face Ora.

"Ora," I hissed. "Did you light the sconces with your fire?"

Ora's hand rested on the pillar she stood beside and she turned half her body, clutching her necklace. "No? I thought you did when we walked in. Fyom?" The gentle man only shook his head.

My heart sank, trying not to let the worry set in. "*Phe*," Ora started, her eyebrows furrowing, "what is it?"

There was no time to answer. I turned to Peiro, who quickly scanned the room before turning his attention back to the doorway where Sury had yet to return. It should have taken only a couple of minutes to make a sweep.

The silence was deafening. And then—

"Yes, Ophelia, tell your sister what you must have been figuring out."

I hated the voice that called out from the interestingly-placed shadow. Everything was lit other than the smaller chamber beside us. My heart sank as I saw Vovias holding a knife close to Sury's throat as they reentered the hall. A thin trickle of blood slid down Sury's neck and pooled into a growing stain at the collar of his leathers.

Vovias's other hand was stretched out wide as a tiny ember of fire flickered back and forth in a phantom wind.

"Son of a bitch," Ora hissed as she stepped away from the circle of pillars and toward Sury. Vovias instantly whipped his hand in Ora's direction. A flash of fire caused her to stop in her tracks and shield her eyes.

The bastard *tsked* at her. "Nuh-uh-uh, Aurora," Vovias said as he moved farther into the room but kept a wall to his back. He forced Sury to lean further back as he dug the blade higher into his throat. Sury hissed at the pain. "Stay where you are, Princess. No need for Sury to get hurt." A dismissive tone was heard as he said *Princess*. It was clear as day, what he truly thought of her. The look on the man's face sickened me. I already hated the sight of him but the smile on his face that grew wasn't natural.

"I've heard a lot about you, Fyom," he continued as he turned his head. "A Healer, right? But aren't you also a coward? Addis sends her regards."

Who was Addis?

A sound short of a roar escaped from Peiro as he took a step to stand in front of Fyom, while lightly pushing me to stand behind him.

The act made Vovias cock his head. The move was too jagged to be natural. "Ah. Yes. The star of the show."

"How did you know we would be here?" I demanded.

"I have eyes everywhere, my girl!" Vovias laughed. The up-and-down movement made the blade to deepen more, causing Sury to cry out in pain again.

"Fucking *destroy* him!" Sury yelled out as he looked at Ora. "Just fucking end this!"

Ora shook her head. "What do you want?"

Vovias whipped his head back toward her and smiled that sickly smile again. "He wants you both. I promised, and I *will* deliver."

"*Who* wants us?" I called out as I inched slightly out from behind Peiro's guard.

"Oh, my girl." I really wished he would stop calling me that and looking at me as if I were a prize-winning mare. "You could hold all the cards if you truly wanted to. He knows this. But Ariadne did a number on you. Some would say *too good* of a number. She got too prideful. Too sloppy. She fucked up and now she will have to pay for that."

"So she *is* working with you?" Ora called out.

"Of course, you foolish girl! Are you a harebrained tart? This part was her idea! Oh, the potential she and I create together." At that, the sconces flared high into the ceiling. "Her stronghold on dark magic was too intoxicating to give up, even after all my years of searching. The power she promised me that I now receive." At the end of his sentence, he narrowed his eyes on Peiro.

"A puppet. How perfect," Peiro growled.

Vovias took in the man who stood in between him and me. That sickly smile was etched on his face once more. He barked a sarcastic laugh before he said, "Isn't that rich? Coming from *you*? The very thing people have been chasing and desiring, yet I see you for what you have been for so long—a monster. Do you not recognize who I am?" His hubris knew no bounds, even in the moment. The fire in his hand flared once more.

"Why are you doing this? What did my family ever do to you? What did *we* do to you?" I spread my arms wide in anger.

Vovias said nothing as he looked at us briefly, his eyes lingering on Peiro before directing his hateful glare toward me. "I'm tired of this. Give me the key."

"What key?" I seethed between my teeth. My mind raced to sift through any hints around the keys Fyom had mentioned. I drew a blank. This only seemed to anger Vovias more.

He let out an annoyed sigh as he said, "Fine. You girls come with me. The men will die. There's no alternative. You'll accomplish his wishes either way." Before I could formulate a thought, a low screech echoed across the halls. It was distant but definitely inside the temple.

I heard the scraping of claws trotting down the hallways just as I saw the fingers that held the dagger to Sury's throat twist and dance, as if signaling a silent command.

Urthens.

I turned my head just in time to see the creature crawling down the hallway that led to where we stood. It moved too fast on its five spider-like legs. The head swiveled from side to side, stopping occasionally as it appeared to sniff before crawling forward.

Its leathery skin glowed black against the sconce light, and it rose up to its full height once it detected the higher ceiling. I couldn't decide what sickened me the most—the fact that the five legs rose higher to tower over us all, or the fact that its eyes and nose were nothing but slits on its shapeless head.

Or maybe it was the human-shaped smile, which opened to reveal rows of jagged teeth guarding a sickly green tongue that dripped some sort of ichor as it flicked into the air, tasting what it sensed in the room.

Or perhaps it was the fact it could draw onto the three of its hind legs and raise up the front two, which ended in sickle-shaped claws.

"Your choice. You can go with me peacefully or my sweet pets will have their fun."

"I always envisioned you would be into something like fluffy bunnies, but now it makes sense that you're into sadistic, freaky things," Sury spat, trying not to lean into the dagger's edge.

"The fact the late queen's father allowed you, a disgusting Veik, at the table was the greatest insult to Wielders. The very people that your kind are so ungrateful for. The people that protect you from beasts like these."

The spider-like urthen clashed its two claws together, mimicking a command from its invisible puppeteer.

"You mean the ones that sit in their high towers and spit on those who aren't born to Wield? Or is that just *you*?" Ora hissed.

I watched, feeling the hum in my hand grow to the point of aching. It was the giant's luck that the moon was visible at this hour, helping the draw be stronger. I knew I had this element of surprise to my advantage. He might have found out about our movements somehow, but I had this. I kept my eyes locked on Vovias as I worked hard to keep my hand from bouncing.

"Sury," I called out. Both Sury's and Vovias's eyes turned to me. "Remember that time, when we were all kids, and it was weeks before the Spring Harvest? And Ora made us learn that stupid dance routine?"

"It was not *stupid*," Ora hissed.

I ignored her. "And you joked about the moves and how they mimicked the birds we used to watch in the pond of the Royal Gardens."

"What does this have to do with anything?" Sury rasped.

"I agree with the peasant. What does this have to do with anything?" Vovias huffed.

"What was the name of that bird?" I urged.

Realization crossed over Sury's face.

"Duck!" I yelled. In one blink, he was being held at the throat by a dagger; in the next blink, he had positioned his body to shift away from the man behind him and bent forward just enough to give me the space I needed to find my target.

I thrust my hand forward, finding relief as I forced a myriad of blue daggers toward Vovias. Each one found its mark and blasted into his chest. The force was so great that it knocked him back into the wall, drawing cracks. He slid down, leaving a trail of blood in his wake.

"Fu—" Sury grabbed his chest just as Ora called out his name and ran to him.

I didn't have time to ask if he was hurt and barely registered Ora's screams just as the urthen behind us screeched in three blasts. Beyond the walls, I could hear an echo of screeches that replied in unison.

My face paled as I finally decided on the most sickening feature on this creature. Its exoskeleton rippled and cracked in a sickly succession as it opened down its middle like hard-shell wings. Two sets of spindly legs crawled out and landed abruptly onto the temple's floor. Two urthens, identical to their host, only smaller, now stood beside it. They came up to my waist in height but were much faster than the one that towered over them.

"*MOVE!*" Peiro bellowed as he stepped toward the taller one, aiming for its legs with a sweep of his swords. The two smaller ones scattered out of the way as the edge of his sword found its mark on the taller one's leg, slicing it in half.

Black ichor sprayed out, coating the front of his tunic. He bellowed in pain as he turned, revealing holes in his shirt where the ichor had sprayed and burned his chest.

So, kill the creatures without letting their blood splatter. Piece of cake.

Peiro barked some sort of order that I didn't comprehend as I took in the sight of three other, identical urthens that crawled in our direction. Nine, actually, if they all unfurled their disgusting bodies to release the smaller ones.

I saw Ora curling over Sury, protecting him from the smaller one, as Peiro continued to hack away at the larger one. Fyom held back the remaining small one with his shield, forcing it back toward a corner of the temple.

None of them saw the others barreling down the hallway toward us. I took off in a sprint, hearing my name called out behind me as I ran toward the hallway, already pulling up my Wielding and forcing it at the creatures.

The force pushed them back, flipping them off their legs. They each held out a sickle-shaped talon to stop themselves from skidding backward and turned upright again. The one in the front screeched and skittered along the wall, heading straight for me again.

The call was instant. I Wielded my power again and again, each force pushing back the creature. The second-to-last blow took out a large chunk of its shell and sprayed black all over the walls, melting into the stone.

Orbs continued to escape from my clutches, each time sizzling into the urthen's skin. I had figured out that directing my Wielding to the urthen's face was a sure way for it to die, and made one crumble a few feet in front of me.

A sort of high crept along my senses the more I dove. The feeling of power. The feeling of freedom. Again and again I Wielded, until only the last urthen stood.

It was too fast for me. Before I could block the smaller urthen that had hatched from its host in the hall, it sprang on top of me. The force knocked me back hard and pounded my head to the floor. I saw its human smile grow wide and its jaws unhinge, ready to bear its rows of teeth on me. The ichor that dripped from its mouth landed on my arm, causing me to scream as I felt the liquid fire burn my skin.

In one moment I was trying to shield the urthen's mouth with my other arm, and the next, it disappeared. I whipped my head around to find that Peiro had pushed the creature away and driven his sword into its skull, twisting the blade for good measure. A sickening crunch followed.

He turned and was on me in a moment. I could see that he was peppered with burn marks and part of his hair was burned at the bottom. "Ophelia! Are you alright?" His silver eyes pierced through me as he assessed me for wounds.

"I think it just dazed me," I replied as he pulled me to my feet. The act made me wince in pain.

"You were wonderful. Your practice is paying off," Peiro said with pride in his voice, taking in the dead creatures in the hall. "You may be increasing your body count to surpass Sury at this point. Might not want to tell him that though. Hurt a man's pride and all," he said with a smirk.

I rested my head on his chest, trying to avoid the burn marks that remained there. "I guess I had a decent trainer."

Peiro was just about to say something when we heard a shriek in the main chamber.

We turned and ran to discover a risen Vovias holding Ora, his blade hovering over her heart, while Sury still lay at her feet, unmoving. Fyom adjusted his green glowing shield, watching Vovias intently as he let his Wielding enclose Sury's body in a protective shroud.

I took three steps forward, breaking out of Peiro's guard, and watched Vovias sputter and speak too fast. I saw the fear in Ora's eyes as I looked at the dagger so close to ending her. My vision grayed.

I no longer saw the dead urthens we had killed. I didn't see anything but Vovias's glowing eyes as I continued walking forward. Then I saw *it*.

A dark shadow only I could see floated inside of Vovias's chest. It was plain as day and I wondered how I had never seen it before. I just knew that I had to take it. My hand didn't sputter or vibrate this time. No. And I didn't even want to hold it back. My fingers splayed out as I continued marching toward the man holding my sister against her will.

A hiss of pain was heard behind me, but I didn't turn to see who was hurt. No, I focused on the site before me. That black shadow grew more defined as I honed my sight on it. Something must have been written on my face because Vovias's eyes grew wide. He sputtered something, spewing moisture into the air as he turned the dagger in my direction, bringing his flicker of fire to life in the other hand.

Silence engulfed me as my eyes saw that shadow flicker then disappear when I closed my hand tight, ensnaring the life force from his body and plucking it from him with ease, like it was a wildflower. Holding something so precious in my hand felt so...powerful. I could taste the magic that continued to glow in my hands before absorbing into my palms. It. Felt. Euphoric. I wanted more.

Vovias's face crumbled in a silent scream as the flame in his hand snuffed out forever, dropping to the ground, his heart no longer beating.

My eyes fluttered as my senses reopened. Sound returned to my ears. The taste of something sweetly metallic coated my tongue but nothing was there. Slowly I uncurled my hand, the tendons and muscle already in protest.

A soft gray-colored ash floated out of my hand and landed onto the temple's floor.

"Phe?" I heard my name being called by a frightened voice.

I turned my eyes to the source and found Ora staring at me, awestruck. "What did you do?"

"He was hurting you," I whispered as I felt my body tremble. An understanding took place as I stared at my fingertips. I just took a life. I Wielded the *illicitus* for its purpose.

What is going to happen to me now?

An array of movements blurred beside me. I was brought back to the present by another scream and watched Ora crumble around Sury's body. I saw it in him, too, his life force, but instead of it appearing solid like it did in Vovias, it was flickering in and out. He was dying and there was nothing I could do, but the call to take it tasted so tempting. I took a step back, distancing myself.

"PHE! *DO SOMETHING!*" Ora screamed. Sury's blood—from a stab wound to the chest that Vovias had some-how managed—was seeping into the ground and all over Ora's clothes. "You Wield death. Command it to leave!" she cried at me in exasperation, tears welling in her eyes.

I shook my head, whispering as I said, "I don't think it works like that." My hands shook.

"Don't let him die, Phe!" Ora whimpered into Sury's neck as she held him close. "I can't bear it! Not after losing Mother and Father. *Please.*"

Another realization coursed through me, instantly delivering me out of my hold. "Ora, look at Sury. Really *look* at him." I ran to her and crashed onto my knees in front of her. "Do you see it? The gray force around him? It's pulsing."

Ora tilted her head and looked down into his paling face. A dawning appeared across her face. "I see it. But it's gold...?"

We could hash out that meaning later.

"Good! You Wield *life*! Demand it to come back to you! *You* have the power to save him!"

"But how?" she asked as she wiped a rogue tear off her cheek.

"I'll guide you and will amplify your magic with my own when you're ready," I replied with a small smile.

Ora nodded as I steered her hand over to Sury. We watched her trembling fingers hover over the seeping wound in his chest just as a bright light radiated from her palm. I felt the call to my power from hers with its pull just as I felt a simultaneous push against it. The call for balance. The bright side to the dark new moon.

I dove in deep, emitting silvers and blues from my hand that seeped into hers. The light in her hand immediately flared and held so much intensity that I had to cover my eyes with my hands. It left as quickly as it came, but the seconds we waited felt like years before what came next. Sury's chest sharply rose as he deeply inhaled new life into him, causing Ora and I to both jump where we sat.

Relief flooded my body at seeing his wound close, inch by inch, and his eyes flicker open. Ora gasped his name in relief and buried him tighter within her embrace. I quickly got to my feet to grant them space as they shed lovers' kisses and held one another.

I felt cold as I stared into the nothing around me; the gray in my vision steadily receded as the vibrancy around me came back to life. The fire a little brighter. The vines more green. My thoughts battled to find the here and the now.

I sensed his presence before I heard him speak. "Look at me." Peiro walked in front of me and placed both of his hands to my head to tilt my gaze to his. "You are the bravest soul I have ever met. My soldiers were not half as courageous as you showed yourself to be today. Take the victory now. Tomorrow we can work through the wounds."

His lips crashed into mine, soft yet demanding. I leaned in, taking in his scent of bergamot with faint swirls of musk and fire, and felt his safety. I knew he didn't mean just the physical wounds of this day. No. This was only the beginning, and the harsh reality of what was to come.

Thankful for the distraction, my body melted into his and I kissed him back.

CHAPTER 40

O ra stepped forward and inspected the impressively large stone and ancient writings etched on it. "I remember asking you before, Phe, if this was going to hurt. Now I don't think I care," she said matter-of-factly over her shoulder. "Is everyone ready?"

Even after Fyom had checked his books, we could only guess how the ceremony was to take place. Before I could say anything, I watched Sury move toward her.

"Aurora," he called as he stepped inside the circle of pillars. "Are you sure?" He scooped her hand into his and gave a firm kiss to her knuckles. "They'll know you're alive, and won't stop until they get what they want. I can't let anything happen to you."

"Yes. I am," she said with a smile and let go of Sury's hand. "Be prepared to fight like you love me, Sury Anmathios," she added before grabbing him by his tunic and kissing him deeply. "It's time," she said as she pulled back with a knowing look on her face. Sury took a few steps backwards, out of the circle, and leaned on the outside of a pillar.

Ora took a deep breath and dove into her magic and revealed a bright light within her palms that made us all stare in awe. The ribbons transformed into a blinding white with flares of golds and yellows, encasing her and radiating so much like the sun she was called to be. The energy from her hands sent wisps of air around us, disrupting the dirt and dust on the old floor. I marveled at the force I felt—the equal push and pull, calling to my own deep within me.

Ever so slowly she outstretched her hand, inching closer to the stone before her. The runes etched deep within glowed like burning embers, shining brighter with each passing moment. I watched as her lips parted into a gasp and her hand suddenly shook, just a hair's breadth away from imbuing her power into the stone.

"No," she said as she dropped her hand. "You're right. I'm not ready yet." And she immediately turned her head over her shoulder and extended her reach toward me.

I looked at her in confusion.

"What better way to surprise our *guests* than with a great show of force?"

"But the claim can only be taken by the most powerful *and* successor to the throne!"

Ora rolled her eyes and gave me a grin. "You and your rigid lines. Who said? There's no written rule about this, is there? We've proven we have *equal* power, and the last part is just a technicality." She winked. "What better way to show force than with not one, but *two*, opposing forces?"

"This has never been done before." I called out.

"There's a lot about this that hasn't been done before. And so what? You know I'm not the best at following rules anyways. I'm going to be queen—so really, I make the rules."

I hesitated a moment and paused to think. This was madness. But was there a reason why only one knelt before the Rising Rock? What would happen if we both imbued? Would we disrupt everything we've ever known?

With Dokvalon at our heels, rules be damned.

I returned her grin and grasped her hand as I stepped through the inner circle. My body pulsed against the hum of the stone. How could I not feel this before? Centuries of power imbued into this very thing before us, and the rulers who promised themselves to the land.

Now it was our turn to promise that this land would not be taken or left for greedy hands to conquer. I turned my eyes upon the Rising Rock and watched the runes grow brighter. Faint whispers of old and new languages swirled around me, instructing me on what to do. I looked at Ora, assuming she could hear it too.

Together we stood by the pillar and dove into our magic, reaching for each Circle of Wielding. I smelled the dirt from the earth and felt the wind in my hair. A coolness from water was met with the brief warmth of fire. The spirit of Healing swirled around and through us right before touching our celestial magic of the sun and moon.

Beautiful hues of golds and blues glowed around us in a soft vortex, lifting the strands of hair that had loosened from our braids.

I looked at Ora just as she turned to me and nodded.

We dove deeper to touch the Seventh Circle of Wielding, the *illicitus* of life and death, and brought a small piece of that power to the surface. Grays and greens wrapped around us, respectively. The rock now illuminated with a bright glow and hummed more. The pillars and floor began to vibrate steadily as our surroundings whirred louder.

A faint glow at Ora's chest caught my attention as she tightened her grip on my hand, a signal for our next move, and we placed our other hands on the Rising Rock to connect to our kingdom.

I immediately felt the rock close in around my hand, pushing and pulling against my magic. Pain and pleasure radiated up my arm and into my spine. Lights flashed and glowed around, blinding us in a white light. I wanted to shield my eyes with the hand that held Ora's but couldn't move my body.

Light bounced all around and *within* me. Time and space felt like a mystery as I was being pulled in so many directions and nowhere at the same time. The light faded just enough that I saw something that looked like a mirror floating toward me. It wasn't my reflection, but my sister's—covered in a bright light, she radiated with life and energy in greens and golds.

The cycle known as death was just the beginning as my energy force held a floating sensation. I looked around and saw the spirit of the moon and universe, and felt my body speeding past unknown objects and masses. A tiny outline of the continent of Wieldera stood out, vast and green to the east and north but a sickly dark color to the west.

Everything slammed to a halt like a punch to the stomach. I gasped, finding myself back at the pillar as if I'd never left—but now it was dark and silent, the whispers gone. Ora's hand was still in mine, and she looked as disoriented as I felt, both of us struggling to catch our breath.

I let go of her hand and turned to face my sister, each of us studying the other in stunned silence.

"You felt it, too." Ora wrapped her arms tightly around me. "We can do this," she whispered into my hair. We stood in silence for a few seconds before letting go.

I felt different. I couldn't explain it, but I suspected she might share the feeling. My feet were a little more planted, my back straighter, my shoulders holding a little more assurance. A mental binding I didn't realize had been placed on me had now disintegrated into metaphorical ash, and the one who put it there? She would pay.

We turned and faced Sury, Fyom, and Peiro, who were all bent to their knees with their heads bowed and a fist over their hearts.

A faint glow filled the room around us all before Peiro jumped to his feet with the others close behind.

Deep vibrations and groans from the earth released to signify the ritual had been completed, roughly shaking our feet before trembling out into the forest and beyond.

There was no chance that the signal went unnoticed to whoever might be near us.

"Time to run," Fyom said sternly as he shifted his things to take flight.

"And go to war," I muttered under my breath.

We sprinted to the exit of the temple and set off on our quest.

To rally our kingdom.

And prepare for war.

The End.

For now...

Acknowledgements

Writing an acknowledgments section is both incredibly fun and nerve-wracking—so I will try my best!

First and foremost, I wouldn't be anywhere without my Lord and Savior, Jesus Christ. Thank you for blessing me with the gift of imagination and the ability to put words to paper.

To my husband, thank you for picking up extra hours of kiddo duty and entertaining our munchkins whenever inspiration struck! And thank you for encouraging me during those moments when I wanted to give up. I love you.

To my E's—everything I do is for you two. You are my light and my world, bringing me incredible joy each and every day! Mommy loves you so, so much! I can't wait to see how your imaginations grow as you get older. Actually, on second thought... Don't grow up. It's a trap!

To those who have been behind me from day one and never stopped believing in me—saying thank you doesn't do it justice. Amber, my soul-sister who's too far away: Even though you're my friend and you claim you "don't read" (which makes me sick, but I guess I forgive you), thank you for always showing interest in my writing, asking thoughtful questions, and being my go-to person to share excitement in all its forms. You're the rockstar and the sister I always needed!

To my beta readers: I truly don't know what I would do without each and every one of you. You each provided something my soul needed as I worked to turn my dream into reality, and saying "thank you" just doesn't feel like enough. K. Flem, you've been with me since the first rough draft, and rough it was! Your input and feedback are and always will be the gold that I need. Above all, you didn't give up on me and my vision, and that shows just how special you are. Hollie, I'm incredibly grateful that not only did our paths cross and you tackled this monster with me, but that you saw the potential and hyped me up at just the right times when I needed it most! Your feedback fostered growth, and for that, I'm forever grateful. Jessica, you're the cousin I always wanted. Your thoughtfulness and questions brought new life and excitement to this story, and I'm so excited you were willing to take this on and that we got to connect in new, fun ways!

To Megan at Clarity Copy Co., your kindness and flexibility with my craziness restored my faith in so many aspects of this journey, and without your editorial direction, I would be a mess!

To every author I've had the pleasure of meeting, thank you for giving me beautiful words of encouragement and wisdom to push me through. It's not forgotten!

To you, the reader—thank you. Whether you enjoyed the story and its characters or decided to DNF it, thank you for taking a chance on me. Your willingness to give my work a try means the absolute world to me, and I wish I could share more gratitude than just words on a page.

About the author

L.P. Brooks is a dreamer who has always lived inside of her head with make believe and fantasy. When she's not curled up with a book in one hand and hot tea in the other, she's playing with her kiddos or having nonsensical conversations with her husband. She resides in Tennessee and enjoys making new friends wherever she goes.